For Tony Heather, Ciel
With his career and mar
unexpected end, a new start in the Spanish holiday resort couldn't have come along at a better time. After all, who better to deal with the drunks and badly behaved British holiday-makers that blight the town than a former member of Her Majesty's Constabulary? Tony soon finds, however, that his experience is put to a far greater use…

For Leanne Piggott, Cieloventura is a place of adventure. If only she could shake off her parents and irritating younger brother, that is. Traipsing around foreign markets and cathedrals is hardly a teenage girl's idea of a good time, not when the beach and the nightclubs along the Avenida Del Puente held such a magnetic appeal. Still, her parents were deep sleepers, and what they didn't know wouldn't hurt them… would it?

For Inspector Jefe Roman Chavarría Lopez of the Policia Nacional, Cieloventura is an ideal place to commit murder. And the worst place to try and solve one…

IN THE DARK
SHADOW
OF THE SUN

DANIEL WARD

To Carla & Joe,

Hope you enjoy the book!

IN THE DARK SHADOW OF THE SUN

DANIEL WARD

First Edition © 2013
Gallows Publishing

The right of Daniel Ward to be identified as the author of this work has been asserted by him in accordance with the Copyright, Designs and Patents Act 1988.

All rights reserved.
No part of this publication may be reproduced in any material form, including photocopying, without the permission of the author, except in accordance with the provisions of the Copyright, Designs and Patents Act 1988 or under the terms of a licence issued by the Copyright Licensing Agency.

This book is sold subject to the condition that it shall not, by way of trade or otherwise, be lent, resold, hired out, or otherwise circulated without the prior consent of the publisher in any form other than in which it is published.

This is a work of fiction and any similarity to real events or people, living or dead, is purely coincidental.

A CIP catalogue record for this book is available from the British Library

Typeset in 13pt Perpetua
Gallows Publishing, USA

ISBN-10   1492238333
ISBN-13   978-1492238331

ALSO AVAILABLE AS AN E-BOOK

gallowspublishing@outlook.com

To Mum and Dad

Thanks for all the love and support

IN THE DARK
SHADOW
OF THE SUN

CHAPTER ONE

THE weather was mild enough even at three in the morning for Tony just to slip on a short-sleeved shirt for the five minute amble to the town square. The phone call, when it came, had been short and to the point, and Tony was out of bed and dressed within seconds. He knew the drill by now. With the tourist season in full swing, he knew to expect such calls at any time, even at night, and he hadn't been disappointed. Only once, Tuesday the week before, had he been allowed a whole night's uninterrupted sleep, and he had been so surprised to wake to the glorious morning sunshine streaming in through the window that his first instinct had been to reach for the phone to check it was still working.

Tony stole quietly down the stairs and let himself out of the back door. He didn't know why he bothered to take such precautions. Pat and Dave, who ran the bar on the ground floor, lived out of town, and the current inhabitants of the dwellings either side of him had not cared a jot at disturbing the peace of others at whatever hour they saw fit to stumble back to their pits. Tony knew there was little point complaining. He had visited the office of the letting agency twice already to voice his discontent at the antics of previous guests and, though the attractive lady behind the counter had nodded sympathetically as he listed his grievances, nothing had been done, and Tony didn't yet feel 'in' enough with Consuela or Rafá to ask them to have a quiet word with the agents on his behalf.

Tony broke into a brisk walk as he made his way along the narrow alley at the rear of the block. There was something about darkness that still made him feel uneasy, something that brought sweat to the surface of his skin with alarming speed. The memories were fresh. Too fresh. It had been almost two years now, but it seemed a fraction of that. The darkness felt unreal to Tony, illusory almost. The way the slightest sound could be amplified five times over, the way shadows formed by innocuous objects seemed to morph into something perversely different.

Despite an uninterrupted four hours sleep, itself a luxury, and a mere twenty yards to the road, the brief burst of exertion was still enough for Tony to need to take a moment to catch his breath before heading out into the main thoroughfare. Making a mental note to ask Sergio about that free trial gym membership he had once mentioned to him, Tony began the casual stroll to the town square. He felt no real sense of urgency. Whoever it was who required his services certainly wasn't going anywhere in a hurry.

Natalie was well aware she had drunk too much, but actually felt a sense of pride that she was still able to walk home under her own steam. Her colleagues had once again proven themselves to be total and utter lightweights, and Natalie knew such ammunition against them would be priceless in the days to come. With one hand against the side of a telephone booth, she stopped briefly to remove her shoes. If anything was going to send her arse over head, she thought, it was more likely to be those than the drink. Still, they'd done their job. The high heels and the micro miniskirt had proved a deadly combination. Natalie knew the drink never affected her head for business, and from the feel of the small sheets of paper tucked inside her bra, she knew it had been a successful night.

Holding both shoes by their straps, Natalie flung them over her shoulder and slowly withdrew her hand from the side of the phone box. After a few moments, all that was needed for her to be confident enough that she wasn't in immediate danger of falling flat on her face, she set off along the pavement. Natalie knew only about five hours sleep awaited her before the first flight of the day arrived, less when you added in the need for a shower and a layer of slap, both of which would be mandatory after a session like this. If there was anything better at concealing the sins of a heavy night before than a liberal application of Boots No. 7 (Instant Concealer), she was yet to discover that particular wonder. Looking after her skin was the one thing she had promised herself she would do, especially after seeing the alarming photographs about sunburn and skin cancers she had been instructed to dish out religiously to each new set of arrivals, but her long-established routine of cleansing and moisturising hadn't lasted long out here.

A couple of locals passed on their mopeds, sounding

their horns and shouting out remarks Natalie had heard many times before. Though she wasn't sure of the exact translation, it not being the kind of thing you could easily look up in a phrase book, she knew enough by now to hazard a fair guess. Whilst hardly flattering, it wasn't exactly unwarranted. Natalie knew what she must look like, tottering along the street in such a state, and her sober self had no doubt used many a similar expression to describe many of the like-dressed girls she saw around the town.

The cool breeze that blew in from the sea was keenly felt, a little too keenly for her liking, and Natalie tried to pull her skirt a little further down. She couldn't remember which guy had been lucky enough to receive such a souvenir, but knew it must have been richly deserved. Chances were she'd been seeing them again. The last pair she dispensed with in similar circumstances had been worn around that particular recipient's neck like an Olympic medal for the rest of the week. And why shouldn't they be worn with such pride? Were they not a trophy after all? With ten pairs only costing €6 from the indoor market, Natalie laughed at the idea they could be so highly prized, even to the extent of once provoking a mass brawl, the simple spark that was all that was needed when thrown into the incendiary mixture of testosterone and alcohol, but hers was not to reason why.

Natalie stopped abruptly and instinctively brought a hand up to her mouth. There was no way of avoiding it this time, she thought, and looked around for somewhere suitable. The sound of another vehicle could be heard approaching, this time from behind, and Natalie decided to hold it back until whoever it was had passed. It was hardly the kind of thing she wanted people to see. The resolve didn't last long. The first wave took her almost by surprise, and it hit the inside of her closed mouth with a bitter sensation. The tree would have to do. Planted in a raised bed at the side of the pavement, the base of the trunk was surrounded by red gravel. Natalie gripped the side of the wooden surround, momentarily surrendering her shoes to the ground, and let nature take its course. Never again, she repeated to herself. Never again. But she knew, even as she said it, that she didn't mean it. At least the gentle purring of the engine at the side of the road was calming, reassuring even, and Natalie was more than a little disappointed when it was switched off.

The stench of vomit struck the back of Tony's throat as soon as the small grill was pulled back. Holding his breath, he dared to peer through the opening into the room beyond. The shape under the blanket seemed to shift slightly, but he wouldn't have sworn to it.

'Alright. You'd better fetch a mop and bucket.'

The door was unlocked and Tony waited until he was alone in the corridor before opening it. For a man in his line of work, the smell wasn't something he was unfamiliar with, but he still took a second or two to get accustomed to it before stepping across the threshold.

'Excuse me, sir? Are you awake?'

The shape twitched again, and Tony waited patiently for a face to appear. This one, when it came, was topped with spiky bleached blonde hair. A lightning bolt had been shaved over each ear.

'Who the 'ell are you?'

'My name is Tony Heather. I believe you were told about me.'

'Yeah, an' you can fuck off an' all!'

'The sooner this can be sorted out, the sooner you can leave,' Tony replied, the abuse another thing he had got use to over the years. 'It's your holiday you're wasting, not mine.'

The young man kicked the blanket to one side and sat up in the bunk.

'Cunts won't even make me a cuppa. They treat you like a dog over 'ere.'

'I'll see what I can do. But you really need to start co-operating. It's for your own good, believe me.'

'Ain't tellin' 'em nuffin'. Look at the state of this!' He pulled at his Manchester United shirt. Tony thought it funny how he always expected the young men who wore such tops to speak with a Manchester accent, even though he'd yet to meet one who actually did. This one was so pure Thames estuary that the subconscious aroma of winkle stalls on Southend sea front that wafted across Tony's nostrils helped to drive away the smell of vomit. The shirt was stained and some of the stitching had been pulled apart at the side. 'Gonna pay for this, are they?'

'Well, that's something I can chat to them about,' Tony lied, 'but first I'll see if I can rustle you up a cup of tea. But I do need your name. Believe me, we can sort this out a lot quicker if I know it.'

'Luke Bigley.'

'And where are you staying, Luke?'

'Paradiso.'

'With family?'

'Mates.'

'And how old are you?'

'Eigh'een.'

Tony nodded and, noting the large pool of greasy-looking vomit in the corner, stepped back out of the cell. He pushed the door closed and headed along the corridor to find Felipe.

'And does our guest now have a name?'

The young officer appeared from a darkened storeroom, pushing a metal mop-bucket on wheels out in front of him.

'Luke Bigley, eighteen years old. Staying at the Paradiso. Are charges going to be pressed?'

'Not if he pays for the damage he caused. Owner wants two hundred Euros.'

'And how much will the damage cost to repair?'

'Two hundred Euros.'

Felipe's look of innocence may have convinced his own mother, but Tony doubted anyone else would be taken in so easily. Not that he was bothered. He thought it only right the bar owner should have something extra for his trouble, and the less yobs like Luke Bigley had to spend on drink for the rest of their stay the better.

'I'll have a chat with him. Do me a favour, Felipe, and make him a cup of tea, will you?'

The officer nodded, albeit with reluctance, and

headed off towards the small staff kitchen. Tony looked down at the water that was already in the bucket. Hardly clean, but it would suffice. He wheeled the bucket back along the corridor, leaving it at the side of the cell door.

'Why didn't you use the toilet to be sick in?'

'Why d'you fink? Let the bastards clean it up 'emselves.'

Tony sat down on the corner of the bunk. 'So do you want to tell me what happened?'

'Nuffin' to tell,' Luke shrugged. 'Bastards wouldn't serve us anymore, that's all. We weren't bein' too lairy or nuffin', jus' 'aving a good time.'

'So how have you ended up here?'

'Look, we would've walked away, no problem. Plenty of other places to get a drink, we didn't 'ave to stay in that shit'ole. It was the fuckin' gorillas on the door, weren't it? Started gettin' 'eavy, didn't they?'

Tony thought there was probably an element of truth in what Luke was saying. Some of the doormen in the town used muscle first and asked questions later, but not, it had to be said, without some provocation. Tony knew from home that trying to calm down drunken young men who were spoiling for a fight was an almost impossible job, but when both language and cultural differences were thrown into the mix, the difficulty must be multiplied.

'Well, paying for the damage you caused is the best, and the quickest, way of sorting this out. If not, you'll be in court in the morning.'

'I'll take me chances.'

Luke Bigley was probably no stranger to standing in a court, Tony thought, but this wasn't Britain, and things were very different here. If facing a local magistrate held no fear for the young man, Tony had no choice but to change tack.

'How much is left of your holiday?'

'Five days.'

'Well, all day tomorrow will be wasted. You'll be kept in the cells until the fine is paid. How long do you think it would take your friends to raise two hundred and fifty, maybe three hundred Euros?'

'You what?!'

'Maybe your parents will need to pay it from home. That'll take another day or two to organise, maybe more with the weekend coming. Chances are you won't be let out until Monday. When's your flight home?'

'Wednesday mornin'.'

'Well, at least you'll have all of Tuesday to enjoy yourself, so that's something.' Tony got to his feet. 'I'll go and see what's happening to that tea.'

Five minutes alone with his thoughts would be enough, Tony hoped, for the lad to come to his senses. €200 was a lot of money, but if it meant getting him out of the system and relieving the pressure on the local courthouse, then all well and good. After all, that's why Tony was here. Chances were the court fine wouldn't be much bigger, if at all, that the deal offered to Luke Bigley by the unfortunate bar owner, but he was more than happy to keep that particular nugget of information to himself.

The gentle snores that tickled Tony's ears as he walked along the corridor mostly belonged, he guessed, to drunken fellow countrymen. They were either resigned to their fate, being held until the banks had opened and they could pay the on-the-spot fines they'd received from the police for whatever public order offence they had committed, or sleeping off their over-indulgences until they were in a more appropriate state to be processed. Either way, they were none of Tony's concern. It was only Luke Bigley's uncooperation that had dragged him out of bed.

'One cup of tea.'

Tony was glad Felipe provided him with a description as he handed the cup over, as he wasn't sure he would've recognised it otherwise. He nodded his appreciation and returned to the cell. The vomit would still need cleaning up, of course, but Tony was buggered if he was actually going to do that. No, no, that privilege he would gladly leave to the fine specimen of British youth who had put it there.

The beach at night held no particular allure for her. During the day, it was a fabulous place. She loved the dizzying array of noise that battered her from all sides; the laughter, the chatter, the shouts of chastisement from parents who had seen their little brats stray too close to the water's edge, the endless music pumping out from the DJ station. She loved the smells from the beachfront cafés and restaurants. She loved the attention and the admiring glances. She loved the sun beating down with such ferocity that she could almost feel the blood bubbling under the surface of her skin. It seemed a different place now. A faint rumbling could be heard from the direction of *Platinum* and, with her eyes closed, she tried to pick out the tune from the succession of dull thuds that travelled through the night air. A distant splashing, and the peel of drunken laughter that accompanied it, disturbed her concentration. The signs warning of the dangers of swimming at night, especially after the consumption of alcohol, had been freshly painted – she had seen the workman herself only the day before – but they weren't having much of an effect. It was getting chilly too. A beach had no right to be cold, and the arm around her shoulder was far too little to be of any real use. Maybe the shared body heat to come would be better. The sensation of flesh against flesh. The feeling of another's breath gently dancing across her skin. If he didn't initiate something soon, she would need to do it herself, and the thought of that made her feel cheap. The fingers slowly began to caress the back of her shoulder. Progress. The fingers then traced a line up to the nape of her neck, where they lingered, gently stroking the skin. She was starting to enjoy this. She hadn't been sure she would, but there was something about it she liked. She even liked it when the fingers began to press deeper and deeper into her flesh. It was only when it started to hurt that she first said no.

The Paradiso Hotel was beginning to look its age. Built more than thirty years ago during the first wave of the town's expansion, it had seen several facelifts but was now in sore need of a complete renovation. That or razing it to the ground and starting again. The succession of corridors that Luke Bigley led Tony and Agente Valdés down to Room 334 were all the same; poorly lit with vaguely yellowing walls. Whatever charges the owners made to the travel agents who sent their undiscerning clients here, Tony considered it too much. Still, it was acceptable fare for the likes of Luke and his two friends, who were both in such a drunken state of comatose that they offered no resistance when Luke rifled through their pockets in search of any spare cash.

'This is gonna ruin our fuckin' 'oliday, this is! Six fuckin' months it took us to save up!'

The small room reeked of alcohol and body odour, and Tony was perfectly happy sitting out on the small balcony. There wasn't much of a view in the dark, but in such a built-up area, dominated by high-rise hotels and apartment blocks, he doubted whether that in the daytime would be any more pleasing to the eye. The notes on the table in front of him amounted to €135, and Tony waited patiently for Luke to collect the rest from his friends, with or without their knowledge or approval.

'Right, now you can both sod off! Go on, sling yer 'ooks, you got what you came for!' Luke collapsed into the sole chair in the room and began to remove his trainers. 'Go an' do somefin' more useful. Find a street corner to stand on, you'd make a fuckin' good traffic light lookin' like that!'

Tony refused to rise to the bait. He counted the

money three times, going deliberately slower on each occasion, before handing it over to Agente Valdés, who had remained less than two yards from the young man's side throughout. The officer placed the notes into his shirt pocket and wrote out a receipt, which Luke Bigley snatched from him brusquely.

'Another satisfied customer,' said Tony as, having successfully re-negotiated the warren of corridors and stairwells to find their way out of the building, he and Valdés walked out together in the open air.

'You want a ride back, Tony?'

Tony stood on the steps of the Paradiso and looked up towards the sky. It was getting lighter and dawn, his favourite time of the day, wasn't far off.

'No, no, I'll take a walk. It looks like it's going to be another beautiful day.'

Tony bade farewell to the officer and set off on the long walk back. It would take a good half an hour, but he didn't mind that. There was little chance of him getting back to sleep even if he'd accepted the offer of a lift, which would've had him back in his bed within minutes, and he would have to be up at eight anyway. Though the first session of the day didn't start until nine-thirty, Tony needed to be at the courthouse early to have a brief chat with those who were due up.

When the sun finally appeared over the horizon, the town was slowly bathed in a golden orange glow that never failed to take Tony's breath away. He sat on one of the wooden benches that lined the beachfront, not looking out across the stretch of sand to the sea, for which they were designed, but towards the town instead. Tony watched in wonder as the sunlight gradually crept its way across the rooftops, breathing life and colour into the buildings, and trees. He waited until the sun had fully revealed itself, and he could truly appreciate the majesty of the mountains, cast against a cloudless titian sky, before continuing on his way back. This was why he came here. Nothing else.

'Move yourself, woman, for crying out loud!'

Barry Barrett stood in the doorway of the apartment, rolled-up towel under one arm, three-day-old Daily Express under the other. On the opposite side of the room, perched on the corner of the bed, Linda was completing her final toenail. Why such an operation needed to be done with such delicacy Barry would never understand. It irritated him they way there was a little ball of cotton wool between each of the toes, and the way she wriggled them like slugs in bleach. It made his skin crawl. The first few hours of the day were an ideal time to visit the beach, and every precious moment was being eaten into with each precise stroke of that little brush. By mid-morning, there would hardly be a grain of sand to be seen, and the constant screaming of the thousand kids who treated it as their own private playground got on Barry's nerves. The sun was far too hot in the middle of the day to just lie there, getting slowly frazzled, and he had plans to take a trip into the mountains, where the leaflet had promised a beautiful lunch gazing out across the most spectacular views in the entire region.

The brush being placed back into the bottle was like

a starting pistol going off in Barry's head. He saw no reason to wait any longer, and strode off along the corridor, ignoring the cries of his wife to wait that echoed after him. Barry kept the pace up unremittingly until he was able to kick off his sandals and step onto the soft sand. There he waited for Linda to appear at his side before, choosing this moment to relieve her of one of her bags, setting off together for their favoured spot. Barry cursed her thoughtlessness as he realised, upon approaching the rocky outcrop that would protect them from the cool breeze blowing in off the water, that it was already occupied. Damn the woman! Who cares about painted toenails anyway? Did they think they made her look more attractive? Men didn't look that far down for goodness sake! Mind you, if her tits continued on their steady journey south, it wouldn't be too long before they'd be noticed, albeit unintentionally. Barry stood in the sand and looked at the young female lying in their spot. Perhaps she was planning on a full day's sun worshipping. She could certainly do with it. He could spot the paleness of her skin from here.

Barry wondered whether he could ask her to move over a bit. There would be plenty of space on the small area of sand for all three of them if only she didn't take up so much room. And having her young and firm body to look at through the side of his wraparound sunglasses appealed to him. He made up his mind to go and ask her. What's the worst that could happen?

CHAPTER TWO

THERE was something incongruous about Roy Butt. Of course, he stood out sitting among the row of young men on the long bench at the side of the room. But it was more than that. While those to either side of him uniformly stared at their feet, the retired train driver from Didcot held his chin high in a gesture of pride and defiance. Tony had tried to impress upon him how such antics was not tolerated by the local magistrates, even more so since the Mayor's re-election, which had been largely fought on a ticket of increased efforts to control the behaviour of drunken tourists, and how expressing his deep shame and regret for the incident was the preferred way to go. That and blaming the twin devils of a strong sun and strong alcohol, both of which were strangers to him in his leafy Oxfordshire enclave. The gentleman, however, dismissed such notions.

'I've not lied to an official of the law before, and I don't intend to now,' was Butt's response. 'I'll take whatever punishment they deem fit.'

Most public order offences were punishable by a fine and, if no actual damage, either to person or property, had been caused, Tony knew this didn't typically go about €150. Usually less. The fines had been increased since the start of the new holiday season, that was true, but so far there was little evidence this was having its intended deterrent effect. Standing on the edge of the fountain in the town square, shorts around his ankles, mimicking the pose of the little stone boy in the centre and sporting the most impressive erection Roy claimed he'd had since 1986, was by no means, however, a typical public order offence. Tony feared the magistrates would come down hard on him. If it was a twenty-something lout who had exposed himself in such a manner, making obscene hip movements to each passing female, Tony would be keeping his fingers crossed that they would throw the book at him, but he hoped there would be some leniency towards Roy Butt.

Roy was old school, the type who believed in taking responsibility for their actions, even those committed under the influence, and Tony admired this stance enormously. Oh, how very different from the likes of Luke Bigley. There were a dozen young men sitting on the bench in the courtroom with Roy, aged from late-teens to early-thirties. Tony hadn't had a chance to talk to all of them, but the order sheet indicated they were all up for public order offences ranging from drunkenness to brawling. The court-appointed lawyer was ferrying back and forth between them, explaining to each the likely consequences of their actions and how, should they so desire, to best address the magistrates in pleading mitigation and sorrow.

As the clerk read out the arresting officer's statement to the magistrates, Tony swore he saw a slight smile appear, albeit briefly, on their faces. Even magistrates were human, and the thought of this distinguished-looking elderly gentleman, sitting in the middle of a row of football tops and T-shirts in a smart collar and tie, exposing himself by the town fountain, no doubt tickled them, even if they tried their utmost not to let it show. Roy Butt stood up when his name was called and made his way to the table where the lawyer sat. He confirmed his name and age, answered briefly and honestly the few questions that were put to him, and was out in the street within twenty minutes.

'They know the difference between a young hooligan trying to squirm his way out of trouble, and a responsible man like me,' Roy said, replacing his credit card back into his wallet without a hint of resentment or regret.

'Even so, one hundred and seventy-five Euros is a lot of money,' Tony replied. 'The least I can do is treat you to a cup of tea if you fancy it?'

'Why not?'

Tony led Roy on a brief two-minute walk to The Green Dragon, a café owned and ran by an ex-pat from the Rhondda Valley. The tea was served in a proper china pot, with individuals cups and saucers, and it was Tetley. Tony had only discovered this place by accident while attempting to find his way back to his rented apartment in his first week, most of which was spent – map and guide book in hand – trying to get his bearings in the complex maze of streets. Since then, it had almost become his second home. It was far enough from the beach, the main shopping streets and the motorway to be able to enjoy sitting outside without having to put up with any noise or traffic fumes, and the cakes, many made on the premises by Karen herself, and biscuits on offer were second to none. Although it was too early in the day for Tony, and it wouldn't help in his grand plans to get fitter, he happily bought Roy a jam doughnut.

'So how have you ended up here?'

It was a question Tony was expecting – it always came at one point when he was in conversation with someone from home – and he was prepared to fend it off. Not that Roy Butt wasn't a friendly chap, but he didn't feel ready to talk so openly just yet. Best keep his answer short, he thought. 'Oh, that's a long story. Basically, I was offered retirement from the force on medical grounds, and was looking for something else to do. I ended up here quite by accident, but it's suiting me.'

'The sun isn't.'

Tony chuckled as he poured them both a second cup. While glib comments coming from the likes of Luke Bigley stung him slightly, he didn't mind seeing the humour of his situation when talking to people like Roy.

'I just need to keep covered up for a while, that's all. Plenty of cream.'

'You look like a beetroot.'

Tony laughed. Was a beetroot better than a traffic light? And was either preferable to the nickname he'd been given, all in good spirits, by the officers at the station? 'So what on earth possessed you to behave like that in the first place? I know you were paralytic, the officers told me you feel asleep in the back of their car and they had to carry you to the cells.'

'This is the first holiday I've had without the wife since I went on a bowls trip to Weston-Super-Mare in 1973. Can't be blamed for letting my hair down.'

'And your wife...?'

'Passed away last year.'

'Right.'

The obligatory awkward silence followed, which Tony sought to cut off at the right time, leaving enough to show due respect but not allowing it to linger too long and cloud the rest of the conversation. 'Still, parading yourself like that in front of passers-by...'

'Use it or lose it, I thought.'

'Well, perhaps you'll know better in future.'

'Indeed I will. Are there any brothels in the town?'

Tony baulked at the question, almost choking on a mouthful of tea. There would undoubtedly be a few such establishments, like any other large town or city, particularly a holiday resort, but he'd not personally come across them yet. The police had driven off the few girls who plied their trade on the streets, Consuela had once mentioned to Tony, and unless you had a car and could prowl the slip-roads off the N-332 where he'd heard such activity might still be going on, there wasn't much you could do. Maybe a hint in the right ear, a barman or a hotel doorman maybe, but Tony certainly wasn't going to suggest that to Roy Butt. While he looked generally fit enough for a man of his years, the thought of some sultry señorita bouncing up and down on top of him might very well prove fatal, and Tony hardly wanted that on his conscience.

'I don't really know.'

'I thought a man in your line of work would've known that. So what are you, then? A policeman?'

'My official title, for what it's worth, roughly translates as British Liaison and Communications Officer,' Tony replied. 'I'm employed by the town hall to work with the municipal police in their dealings with UK tourists. Act as a middle man, so to speak. Try to bridge the gap between the two cultures.'

'And you spend most of your time dealing with herberts like those in court this morning?'

'More often than not. Things are done very differently out here. Most people don't appreciate you can be in the court the next morning, given a stiff fine and, unless you can pay it immediately, you're banged up until you can.'

'Should do that back home,' frowned Roy. 'My niece's boy, Dylan, has been in trouble all his life. Just gets a slap on the wrist and told not to do it again. Does it work? Does it hell! Gets away with blue murder, he does!'

'Of course, they think they can just plead ignorance of the local laws and that's enough. It's not quite that simple.'

'You can say that again! There's coppers in blue uniforms, coppers in bleedin' black. I even passed some in green the other day on the road from the airport.'

'Welcome to the complex and confusing world of

Spanish law-enforcement!'

'Hence why you're here...'

'Precisely. I'm putting together an information sheet at the moment that I'm hoping the Mayor's Office will get behind,' Tony said. 'Something that can be displayed in hotels and apartment blocks. It'll explain the roles of the different types of police, and point out a few of the main differences between the way things are done at home and the way they're done here.'

Roy nodded. Tony knew the plan made sense, but the Mayor's Office had other, more elaborate, ideas. They had asked him to deliver a series of talks in the major hotels, but Tony was not keen. He knew the majority of holiday-makers were loathe to even attend the welcome meetings by their reps, in spite of the free sangria and promised discounts on excursions, so why would they attend a speech, however short and informative, given by an ex-policeman about the Spanish police and justice system. There was a problem with a small minority of tourists behaving badly, he knew that, but that wasn't unique to Cieloventura — there wasn't a single resort along the Costa Blanca that didn't have the same problem — but the type of people who might be interested in such a talk — the worldly travellers who enjoyed learning about other customs and approaches to life; those who sought out the restaurants patroned by locals and tried national dishes and wines — were not the type to cause trouble. It was something he would need to think about but, as the town hall paid his wages, Tony didn't really know if he was able to avoid doing it. Maybe if he arranged one, and the Mayor's Office got to hear what a shambles it was, then he wouldn't be required to do anymore. That might work. Tony knew the real difference could only be made by meeting the people likely to be caught up in any trouble on their own terms; visiting the bars and clubs in the evenings, before too much drink had been downed and their inhibitions shed, and just chatting, not lecturing, to them. He'd started doing this the week before, and most of those he'd spoken to had listened politely and assured him that they'd bear in mind all that he'd said. The message had been kept short, of course – he knew the average attention span of a British eighteen to twenty-one year old was comparable to that of a goldfish – but it was accurate nonetheless. Behave or face a hefty fine or the premature end of your holiday.

It wasn't just drunks and louts. There had been a substantial increase in the number of foreign tourists stopped for traffic violations on the major roads leading out of the town and this was something Tony felt a need to address. How many tourists actually went to the trouble of reading up on Spanish road signs and regulations before coming here and hiring a vehicle? Very, very few. He hadn't even done so himself, so knew he couldn't get too angry about it. A different police force was responsible for patrolling the highways – the *Guardia Civil*, those in the green uniforms Roy had mentioned seeing – unlike in town, where the local force took charge of such matters. Tony wondered whether some members of the Guardia Civil could be deliberately targeting tourist hire cars, which could usually be spotted a mile off, and waiting for some minor transgression to occur. Traffic cops could be the same the whole world over, he thought, especially those who were able to impose, and collect, on-the-spot fines, but his only dealing with the Guardia Civil personally had been nothing but courteous.

The officer who stopped him on the main Alicante road for failing to give way to another vehicle was polite and friendly, giving him only a verbal warning and a photocopied sheet of Spanish road signs with English translations underneath. This had impressed Tony, and he saw something of a similar role for himself – education and the prevention of offences being committed – and was due for a meeting with Maria Ocasio Cruz, his contact at the town hall, in the next week to discuss some ideas.

Roy made entertaining company in the half an hour they spent together. He had been retired for nearly ten years, and was absolutely buggered if the money he and wife had diligently saved up over almost their entire working lives was going to be passed down to his children and grandchildren, especially as he didn't see hide or hair of them for months on end. No, he was going to enjoy that money if it killed him, and Tony thought it most probably would. A fortnight on the Spanish coast was going to be followed by a week in Portugal and one in Italy. The money wasn't able to be enjoyed while Roy's wife was still alive, as they'd planned, as she sadly developed ill health. Roy was even considering moving abroad, and asked Tony how he had found the experience.

The two men parted with a warm handshake and a promise to have a pint together one evening later in the week. If only all those who Tony dealt with were like him. He decided to head back to the courthouse to see whether there was anybody else who needed his help. Typically, the morning session would last until around eleven 'o' clock at the latest, and there may be some, perhaps those who were unable to pay their fines and wanted someone, aside from the lawyer, to discuss their options with.

As he approached the courthouse, Tony saw Consuela Rocha Cában de Cordo heading out and waved to attract her attention.

'I am sorry, Tony, but I cannot stay and talk. You have heard the news?'

'I don't think so. What news is this?'

'A body has been found on the beach.'

Even for an officer with over ten years experience, Consuela was clearly disturbed by the news.

'My god. Washed up, you mean?'

'I do not think so.'

'A tourist?'

'It is possible. Do not worry, if they are British, I'm sure you will get to hear about it.'

Consuela smiled politely and hurried off. She and Rafáel Arguello Péna were Tony's principal points of contact in the local force, the *Policia Municipal*. They both spoke very good English, as well as a smattering of German and, in Consuela's case, French, and had made Tony feel very welcome since his arrival. He had already dined twice at Consuela's house with her family, and was due to visit Rafá's apartment this coming week.

Tony headed on into the courthouse. There was only one British tourist left in the building, a nineteen year-old called Garth Endicott, who had sworn at the magistrates and threw his glass of water at them. He had been summarily slung in the holding cell in the basement, where he was awaiting further charges and a van to transfer him to the local jail. Tony spoke briefly to the public lawyer and told him he'd be happy to go with him if and when he planned to visit Endicott at the jail. There was no British Consulate in the town, the nearest was in Alicante, and Tony knew it would save one of the officials a journey.

Tony decided to spend the rest of the morning in and around the square. This was the centre of his world – the courthouse, the town hall, the offices of the Policia Municipal and, of course, The Green Dragon - and if there were any developments regarding the body on the beach, he would hear about it here first. Tony had half-a-mind to head down to the beach and see for himself what was going on. Although it stretched for over two and a half miles, he doubted it would be difficult to find where the body had been discovered as it would clearly have attracted a crowd of curious onlookers and frustrated sunbathers. However, Tony soon dismissed the notion. It would be pointless. He had no official status anymore and would just be one of those curious onlookers himself. That was taking some getting used to.

Roy Butt was incongruous in another way. Not many people came on holiday on their own, a few admittedly but not many, so chances are there would be friends or family members out there somewhere. Tony decided to be proactive and wandered over to the offices of the Policia Municipal, housed in a small building attached to the town hall.

'Buenos días, Tony.'

Sergeant Jóse Hernández Escobar sat behind the front desk, the welcoming smile that Tony thought was probably the main reason he had been given the job was still stretched broadly across his chubby face, where it had been ever since he had first met him.

'Buenos días, Jóse. Have you received any reports of missing British tourists this morning?'

'Three times already I am asked this question,' replied the officer, 'and you get the same answer as I gave the others. No. And no missing Germans or Belgians either.'

'Locals?'

Jóse shook his head. Tony thanked him and headed back outside. Well, it had been an idea, and little short of visiting all the hotels, apartments and villas in the town, an impossible task, there was nothing more he could so. Still, time and tide waits for no man and that poster about local policing wasn't going to design itself. Maybe just one doughnut wouldn't hurt.

Emily was stressed. She had been on the phone all morning trying to arrange emergency flights home for the Green family after a family bereavement and now, sitting down to have her first coffee of the day, she could see Mr. and Mrs. Piggott sitting down at her desk. Well, they could wait, she decided. Friday was a very busy day. There was the Fiesta of Fun for the under-twelves from one 'til four, and the karaoke and flamenco show from eight 'til midnight. That could either be a damp squib or the highlight of the week, depending how many people were prepared to relax a little and get up and have some fun. Emily knew she would need to spend a good hour at least around the pool, drumming up interest for the evening's festivities. She only had a few 20% discount vouchers left from the weekly allowance given to her by the hotel, so knew she had to be frugal with those. This was going to take all her powers of charm and persuasion. Emily rested her head against the back of the armchair and closed her eyes. She breathed in the fumes from the hot coffee and felt herself relaxing. The Piggotts could wait a few more minutes.

Inspector Jefe Roman Lopéz Chavarría knelt down in the sand and placed the back of his fingers gently against the girl's cheek. She was cold. With death already certified by the police doctor, his actions were not done to confirm in his mind that she was dead, but rather to remind himself she had once been alive. Looking at the body from a distance made her seem unreal somehow, doll-like, but the feel of her icy flesh against his own warm skim brought him back to reality.

'Do we know who she is?'

'No, Inspector Jefe,' replied one of the few police

officers standing inside the inner cordon, which had been set back twenty yards from the body, 'and there are no reports of any missing females.'

'It is early yet.' Chavarría glanced at his watch. It was approaching eleven 'o' clock, and he knew that for many holiday-makers, those who frequented the clubs, bars and cabarets of an evening, this was about the time they would only just be rising for the day. 'Her skin is pale. And not just due to death.' Chavarría stood and brushed the sand from his knees. 'She has not been in our country long.'

The paleness of the victim's skin also made the marks on her neck stand out even more. The Inspector Jefe took one last look at the body before nodding at the two men from the coroner's office, who had been waiting patiently for some time to remove the body, to proceed. Chavarría had left instructions for nothing to be moved until he had had a chance to observe the body *in situ* himself, to see exactly what the killer had left. He had been halfway to a conference in Murcia when the call had come.

As the body was carried from the beach, the crowd of silent onlookers parting like the Red Sea, Chavarría strolled to the water's edge. This wasn't going to be easy. If you wanted to choose an ideal place to commit murder, Cieloventura would be high on your list. If you wanted an ideal place to solve one, it wouldn't be. The population during the main tourist season could reach over eighty thousand, nearly three times the town's permanent number, and there would be a regular weekly turnover of at least five thousand.

Five thousand people – who at this moment were walking the streets of the town, eating in the restaurants, sleeping in the beds, swimming in the sea – who wouldn't even be here in a few days time.

Chavarría reached into his jacket pocket and brought out his case of cheroots. He lit one and slowly savoured the initial wave of strong flavour before turning to the uniformed officer that stood just behind him. 'We need to work quickly on this one. She needs to be identified as soon as possible.'

Chavarría was glad the argument he'd had with his wife the night before had led to her storming out and spending the night at a friend's. It meant he had had his most relaxing evening in weeks; feet up on the sofa, glass of whisky in hand, *Lole y Manuel* on the stereo. Bliss. He was also glad of such a good night's sleep too, as heaven only knew when he was likely to see his bed again.

Emily checked her hair and make-up in the mirror before leaving the staff room and making her way across the foyer to where the Piggotts were waiting. She wondered what the problem could possibly be? John and Shelley Piggott had made a few complaints already since their arrival three days before, mainly to do with their room, and Emily's patience was starting to be tested. They were unhappy facing the pool, as it was too noisy during the day, and were equally unhappy facing the road, as the fumes and traffic noise were disturbing their sleep. Emily had persuaded the manager of the hotel to let them have a suite overlooking the gardens. They were premium rooms, she realised that, but the manager would be more than appeased if the evening went well, and the bar takings up, so Emily had every reason to make sure it was a success.

It wasn't just complaints *from* the Piggotts, there had also been a few about them from other guests. They had two children; a fourteen year-old girl and an eleven year-old boy, both of whom seemed to have left their manners back in the UK before flying out. The girl was a typical surly teenager, who walked everywhere with her long fringe practically covering her face and never saying a word to anyone, and the boy was noisy and obstinate. Emily thanked her lucky stars he wasn't going to be at the Fiesta of Fun. Since she'd sorted out a better room for them, though, the family had seemed happy, and Shelley had mentioned to her only yesterday how this was the nicest resort they'd been to in many years.

'Mr. and Mrs. Piggott? Sorry to keep you waiting, but it's been something of a morning. What can I do for you?'

The middle-aged couple glanced at each other anxiously. 'It's most probably nothing, and we're not sure we should be bothering you with it, but…'

'Well, if I can help in any way, I would be delighted. Please.'

'It's our daughter,' said Mrs. Piggott. 'Leanne.'

'Oh?'

'The thing is…we don't know where she is.'

'Right.'

'When we got up this morning, she wasn't in her room. We just assumed she'd gone for an early morning swim, or maybe for a walk around the complex. We thought she'd soon be back, though, as we were all booked for the ten-thirty trip to the Santa María.'

'That's right, I remember. I arranged it for you myself.'

'Well, we thought she'd be back for that, but there's no sign of her anywhere.'

An astray fourteen year-old girl. This was not something Emily wanted to deal with. A toddler or a young child was one thing – there were strict procedures in place for that – but this hardly merited the same response. She remembered what she'd been like at fourteen. The idea of going on holiday with her parents, and being dragged on excursions to markets, churches and museums, filled her with dread, and any opportunity to get away from them for a while would have been frantically seized upon. Still, she would have to do something. Emily smiled reassuringly, told Mr. and Mrs. Piggott she was sure there was nothing to worry about, but asked if she could borrow Leanne's passport. There would be no harm in taking an enlarged copy of the girl's photo with her while she was going around the pool. Maybe someone had seen her. Emily wasn't going to waste her time doing anything more than that, though. Leanne had probably spent the morning flat on her back on the beach, she thought, completely oblivious of the fuss people were starting to make over her.

CHAPTER THREE

CIELOVENTURA was a town making up for lost time. As a tourist resort, it had long been in the shadow of its more famous coastal cousins of Benidorm and Alicante, but two major periods of development – the first in the late seventies and another in the mid nineties – had seen both its size and fortunes swell. A third wave of expansion was also beginning, though the extent of this was contentious and a hot topic of debate among local politicians and permanent residents.

The town had been established as a small fishing community by the Ancient Greeks, and had remained that way until the Moor invasion in the mid 8th century. With high cliffs at either end of a long stretch of coastline, complete with several natural inlets and coves, the town was ideal for fortification and several defensive structures had been built across its face. The main castle – left in ruins after the *reconquista* by forces of Alfonso X and subsequently rebuilt by the new Christian settlers – still dominated to this day from its position high in the hills to the north-west of the town.

The first period of development had seen the main stretch of stony beach replaced by sand and it was this, together with the ideal year-round climate, that saw the town throw its hat into the ring as a major destination for holiday-makers. Cieloventura, however, still retained much of its traditional Spanish charm, which many felt would be under threat if the further period of expansion was not kept in check. Indeed, there was still some places in the town that had remained virtually untouched by over thirty years of progress, as Tony had discovered to his immense joy during those first few days, when his time was filled with casual strolls through the streets, developing a growing admiration for the traditional Spanish and Arabic architecture that could be found nestling among the high-rise hotels, apartment blocks and shopping plazas, and drinking wine in delightful bars.

The vibration of the mobile phone in Tony's pocket woke him from his slumber. Maybe he should've grabbed that extra hour or two of sleep this morning after all. The message that flashed up on the display was from the lawyer, informing him that if he wished to visit Garth Endicott in jail, he would need to make his own arrangements as his services had been dispensed with. Tony shook his head in despair. He didn't know whether this was something that fell into his remit, but certainly knew he couldn't leave him there. The authorities would no doubt be contacting the British Consulate, but Tony decided to head over to the court and collect Endicott's details. He could pay a visit to whoever he was holidaying with, friends most likely just like Luke Bigley, or perhaps, if requested, make a call or two home on his behalf.

'I'm sorry, but nobody seems to have seen her.'

Emily stood in the doorway of the Piggott's family

suite. Her hour around the pool had been rewarded with twenty-seven tickets sold for the karaoke and flamenco evening, with at least half-a-dozen who promised they would get up and sing, and three more children pencilled in for the Fiesta of Fun. However, no-one had reported seeing Leanne Piggott that morning.

'So what do you think we should do? Call the police?'

'Well, perhaps it would be best, yes. They'll be able to drive around the town and cover a far greater area than we possibly could.'

John and Shelley glanced at each other before nodding.

'Just leave that to me,' Emily told them. 'I'll give them a call straight away.'

Leaving Mr. and Mrs. Piggott to their thoughts, Emily headed down to the hotel reception. The Fiesta was due to start any minute and, while Casey and Ben were okay holding the fort for a while, as head rep, the event was her responsibility. She didn't want to be gone for long, and with over forty kids there, it would be a case of all hands to the pumps. Emily headed into the small room at the side of the foyer that acted as the office for the *SunTravel Premier* staff. She wasn't going to ring the emergency number, and so flicked through the rolo-deck on the desk for details of the local station. Making the most of the opportunity to use her Spanish — something she wished she did more often, but this was Cieloventura after all — Emily introduced herself, mentioned where she was phoning from, and was little more than halfway through explaining her reason for calling when the barked shouts down the line almost made her drop the receiver. She was told to wait outside the front of the hotel, and that officers would be with her as soon as possible. Emily hung up the phone. Casey and Ben would need to manage without her for a bit longer, as her rudimentary Spanish translation of the phrase 'missing teenage girl' was clearly capable of provoking a far stronger response than she would have ever thought possible.

Tony typed a quick e-mail to the British Consulate in Alicante, explaining the circumstances of Endicott's arrest and incarceration, and offering his services should they be required. Fontcalent Prison was also located in Alicante and, as far as he was aware, he had no opposite number, so to speak, in that city. The position of British Liaison and Communications Officer was new, created by the Mayor's Office as part of their new initiative to reduce the number of British visitors either committing or becoming victims of crime. A survey of tourists the previous summer had discovered both a sense of distrust and a general ignorance towards Spanish police and policing, and while almost all officers in the Policia Municipal spoke English, there was still cultural barriers to be overcome. The town council in Cieloventura was considering setting up a dedicated foreign tourist police – with separate British, French, German and Belgian divisions – to assist the large number of visitors to the area from those nations. A similar scheme was already in operation in Madrid and a pilot programme was being planned for Benidorm. The idea was considered by many to be too ambitious for Cieloventura, though, and the appointment of a Liaison Officer for both the British and German visitors, who made up the largest proportion of holiday-makers, was the first step by the town council to address the issue. Tony's German counterpart, a former officer with the Hamburg police, was due to arrive sometime this week to take up his position and Tony planned to meet up with him at some point. There had been a few minor problems between British and German tourists, mainly verbal handbags in nightclubs and bars, nothing serious, but it would be a good idea for the two to build a working relationship.

Tony knew he needed his own computer, and soon. As an employee of the town hall, he was informed he was entitled to a discounted laptop, but still needed at least €300. His first pay-cheque had gone mainly on things for his small apartment in an attempt to make it feel less like a holiday let and more like a home, and his next wasn't due for another three weeks. A laptop and his own broadband connection would make life so much easier, he thought, especially in keeping in touch with those back home. The e-mail and photo from Lucy had cheered him up enormously. He missed her so much. Once the laptop had been bought, every spare cent he earned would be put aside so she could come out for a week just before the school holidays were over. If he could persuade Helen to let her come, that is, and that remained far from a foregone conclusion. Tony pressed the icon marked *Enviar* and waited patiently for the green flashing envelope in the bottom right of the screen to turn a solid blue. Having done so, he logged out and made his way out of the office. Until he had his own computer, Sergeant Hernandéz allowed him to use one in the small room at the side of the reception area at the station. Tony decided not to spend any more time on Garth Endicott until he heard back from the Consulate. He was hardly surprised to learn that the young man was staying with friends at the Paradiso, and certainly didn't fancy another trek back there quite so soon.

Shelley Piggott collapsed into her husband's arms, and it needed both him and the uniformed officer who had accompanied Inspector Jefe Chavarría to Room 421 of the Solanis Resort to carry her to the sofa.

'It is impossible for us to say whether the young lady found on the beach this morning is your daughter,' Chavarría explained, 'and the photograph given to us by Miss Johnson is not conclusive. Do you have any others I could perhaps take a look at?'

Almost on autopilot, John walked slowly to the coffee table and picked up his new 12.5 megapixel digital camera, bought solely for the purpose of this holiday and his pride and joy. He began to flick through the photos he'd taken since their arrival and, coming across one of Leanne, sitting on the bench in the ornamental gardens beneath their balcony, showed it to the Inspector.

'There are similarities, the female found on the

beach had long brown hair, but this is too small to be of any real use,' said Chavarría. Shelley began to sob bitterly, her face buried in the cushioned back of the sofa. 'Will one of you please come with me to make an identification?'

John glanced at his wife. 'Well, I guess I'd better come, if someone will stay with Shelley. And there's our son down by the pool. He doesn't know anything about this.'

'Agente Narváez will remain with your wife,' Chavarría said, motioning to the officer, 'and I will send your holiday rep in also. Please, this will not take long.'

Anxiously pacing the corridor, Emily Johnson jumped slightly when the door to the suite opened. Chavarría gently took her by the arm and led her to one side. 'Please stay with the woman until we return. Until then, there's no need to say or do anything that will alarm your guests. I will return presently.'

'Of course.'

Emily watched as Chavarría and John Piggott walked off towards the lift. She could hear Shelley's cries of anguish and dreaded going into the room. What on earth was she supposed to say to her? She had already told her twice today that she was sure there was nothing to worry about, and the pangs of guilt were beginning to rack their way through her body. Was there anything she could say now that would actually help the situation? Emily prayed the body on the beach wasn't that of Leanne, and that the girl would walk in at any moment, laden with shopping bags and complaining she was old enough to make up her own mind about what she did with her time and there was no way she was going to traipse around some bloody cathedral all day. But Emily knew that wasn't going to happen. She had seen the Inspector Jefe's face when he first caught sight of the enlarged copy of the photo from the girl's passport. She knew Leanne Piggott was dead.

'She was British, Tony. A guest at the Solanis Resort.'

'Oh no! How did it happen?'

Sergeant Rafá Arguello searched his mind for the correct word in English. He made to move his hands towards his own throat, as if it were a cue to aid his recollection. 'Strangled, they think, but we will need to wait until the autopsy.'

'My god!'

Tony and Rafá were sitting together in the *cantina*, a refreshment area for staff at the rear of the police station. The officer had brought in a Belgian tourist for crashing his hired moped into a tree and, while he was being processed, had taken the moment to have a quick coffee. After the discovery of the body on the beach, Rafá explained how he and Consuela had been assigned to traffic control along the Paseo de la Solana, the main beachfront road, which had been affected by the crowds of people waiting to get onto the beach.

'Is there anything I can do?'

'I do not think so. This is a matter for the Policia Nacional, not us.'

'Perhaps her family...?'

'Perhaps. I will let the investigation team know you are available to assist them.' Rafá downed the remainder of his coffee and got to his feet. 'Are we still on for Wednesday?'

'Dinner? Absolutely, yes, if the invitation is still open?'

'I am looking forward to it. My cooking is, how you British say, the dogs' bollocks!'

Tony chuckled. He had picked up a few pieces of Spanish slang already, and it hadn't occurred to him that, surrounded by Britons all day, the same would apply to Rafá. The officer casually saluted and walked off towards the exit.

Tony needed another coffee. A dead British tourist. A young girl. Murdered. He had not considered the possibility that such a crime could ever happen here. Serious crime seemed alien, to him, in an environment like this. Unnatural. People came to Cieloventura to enjoy themselves, to escape from the real world. Worries, debt, misery, pain – they seemed foreign concepts against a backdrop of sun and sand. Tony knew, of course, he was being fanciful. Such things were no respecters of environment, they existed absolutely everywhere. But murder was different. The beach had seemed such a perfect place. An idyll. It would forever be tainted for him now.

In his first week in Cieloventura, one month ago, a married middle-aged woman, on holiday with two friends, had arrived at the station in the early hours, claiming she'd been raped by a waiter. Tony had been allowed a brief moment with her before she was taken to the *comisaría de policía* – the headquarters of the Policia Nacional – for an interview and medical examination. He planned to talk to her further the next day, to help guide and assist her through the investigation, only to discover, when calling at her hotel, that she'd taken the first available flight home. Tony was at a loss to know why things had gone so wrong that the woman's first thought was to flee. Did she not think she would get justice in a foreign country? Was she ashamed about what had happened to her? Maybe nothing had happened at all, and the new day had brought with it the cold realisation that a drunken shag couldn't be kept hidden behind a false accusation of rape. Whatever the truth, Tony realised at that point that his new job was not the token gesture he'd heard some refer to it as, but that he could actually make a difference. But what could he do in this latest case? Tony knew where the Solanis Resort was, but he could hardly just turn up on the grieving family's doorstep, especially in the middle of a murder investigation.

The Policia Nacional was a separate organisation from the Policia Municipal and Tony perfectly understood the confusion a lot of visitors to the country must experience. The national force, whose officers wore black and white, were responsible for investigating serious crime – from theft and assault to rape and murder – while their blue uniformed counterparts of the local force took charge of traffic control, public disturbances and low-level crime. Consuela and Rafá were officers of the municipal police, which came under the jurisdiction of the town hall, and it was this force that Tony spent his time working alongside as it was they who tended to deal with the excesses of British tourists. His dealings with the Policia Nacional had been confined only to a small handful of incidents so far; still, if Rafá was able to have a word with those investigating the poor girl's death, maybe he would be able to play a part after all. He wanted to. He felt a responsibility to help.

'She ain't here, Marie.'

'Well, at least let me have a look in her room.'

Ross stepped aside from the door and allowed Marie into the apartment. He knew that Natalie wasn't in, but if Marie wanted to see for herself, then that was fine by him. He was too hungover to argue, anyway.

'She was supposed to be at the airport to meet the nine-thirty from East Midlands. I had to double up, it was a bloody nightmare.'

Ross headed into the kitchen and flicked the switch on the kettle.

'Fancy a cuppa?'

'I've no time for that,' Marie's voice came from the empty bedroom, 'and nor have you. You'll have to cover for her.'

'What?'

'Look, there's no choice in the matter, Ross. Everyone else is busy.' Marie appeared from the bedroom. 'There's the twelve 'o' clock from Gatwick to meet.'

'For fuck's sake, Marie, I ain't had a day off all

week!'

'Don't blame me, blame Natalie. Wherever the hell she is!'

Marie left the apartment, slamming the door behind her. Ross cursed and, heading for the bathroom, glanced up at the clock on the wall. If he hurried, he just had time to take a quick shower and have a shave. Perhaps he would be able to grab a coffee and pastry at the airport. Damn her! This wasn't how today was supposed to be. He stepped into the shower and took a sharp intake a breath as the spray of cold water hit his skin.

There was a cruel torment to death. As the white sheet was pulled back from his daughter's face, the first thing John Piggott did was to look carefully at her in case she was still breathing. Surely this wasn't true? Someone was playing a trick on him! This cannot be his daughter! Not his baby! He slowly sunk to his knees and let out a howl of pain that even brought a tear to the eyes of Inspector Jefe Chavarría. The detective reached down and placed a hand on John's shoulder.

'Please accept our most profound apologies for your loss, señor,' he said, 'and I give you my word. I will do everything in my power to find whoever is responsible.'

Official Luís Molina Banda – Chavarría's right-hand man – slipped quietly out of the room and reached for his mobile phone. The identification had been made. He had only had a few moments alone with the

Inspector Jefe when he and the girl's father had arrived at the hospital, but it was enough.

'I want to know everything Leanne Piggott has done since she arrived in Cieloventura,' Chavarría had told him. 'I want places, times, names, everything. I want her face on the evening news. I want every car coming in and going out of the town stopped and her photo shown to every driver. And I want a statement from everyone staying at the Solanis.'

'Do we have the man-power for all this, Jefe?'

'Get it. Get onto the Ministry if you have to. We cannot spare a single moment. If the killer of this girl was another tourist, we will have our work cut out. For all we know, a few days from now, the person responsible might no longer be in Cieloventura.'

'What will you do?'

'I will be talking to the parents.'

The reply from the British Consulate was music to Tony's ears. They were going to send someone to see Garth Endicott in Fontcalent and so his offer, whilst appreciated, would not be necessary on this occasion. He was glad. He could not get the thought of the murdered British girl out of his head. There must be something he could do, and he decided there was no real reason why he should wait to be asked. He did have an official position, after all, and a remit from the Mayor to act with and on behalf of British tourists in the town. How best should he approach the situation? Consuela and Rafá would not be able to help him much, and he had no actual contact in the Policia

Nacional, except for the direct phone number of an administrator in the *extranjeros* – foreigners – department.

Tony decided to take a stroll to the Solanis Resort. While not planning to talk directly to the parents, he could at least start by getting a feel for the place, check out the security arrangements, things like that. No doubt there would be a police presence at the hotel complex, but he would be able to mingle among the guests. That way, he may learn something that could be of use to the investigation.

'We didn't know she was missing until we woke up,' Shelley Piggott said, 'and then we just thought she'd gone for a swim. She'd done it yesterday.'

'You do not know when she left the suite?' asked Chavarría.

'Well, we assumed it must've been just before we woke up, but I don't really know.'

'She was discovered quite early, and it appears she had been there for some time, possibly several hours.'

Shelley and John, sitting on the sofa and holding each other's hand tightly, exchanged a bewildered glance. The Piggott's hotel suite consisted of a small lounge area, with two sofas arranged in an L-shape, two bedrooms and a bathroom. There was no kitchen – it was not designed for self-catering – but there was a tray with drink-making facilities on a unit just inside the door. Agente Narváez was busying himself making three coffees.

'She shared a room with your son?'

'Yes,' nodded John.

'I will need to speak to him.'

'He's downstairs. The rep took him along to the Fiesta. We haven't had the heart to break this to him. He adored his sister.'

'If it's any easier for you, we have trained officers who…'

'Heavens, no. We'll do it.'

'But I do need to speak with him as soon as possible.'

'Yes, of course. But let us have some time alone with him first. Please…'

Chavarría nodded and walked over to Agente Narváez. 'Go down to where the children's party is taking place. Find the rep who was here earlier and tell her to bring the boy up here.'

'Yes, sir.'

Chavarría picked up the tray of coffees and carried it back to where John and Shelley sat, placing it down on the small glass-topped table in front of the sofas. 'Tell me about your daughter. What did she like to do?'

Shelley shrugged slightly. Chavarría wondered at that moment what answer he would give if the roles were reversed. And he struggled to find one. He really needed to take more of an interest in what Téresa did, who she saw, where she went. But that was for another time.

'She's into her music, fashions. She likes films, shopping…'

'Boys?'

'She's too young for that!' snapped John. 'She's just

a kid for Christ's sake!'

'Please, do not misunderstand me. I do not mean to cause you any offence.' Chavarría paused. He decided to change his approach. 'Has she made any friends since your arrival?'

'No, I don't think so,' said Shelley. 'She's always been a quiet girl. Doesn't mix very easily.'

Chavarría nodded. He didn't think he was going to get much from the parents, and felt their current state of composure was hanging by a thread, but it was important these questions were asked. John and Shelley Piggott clearly thought their daughter was tucked up safely in her bed, and were stunned to learn, and at a loss to explain why, she was at the beach at such an hour. The Inspector Jefe continued to gently probe, eliciting as much information as he could about their time in Cieloventura, until a discreet tap was heard on the door. Chavarría excused himself and went to answer it. Emily stood outside with Todd Piggott. The young boy, clearly aware something was wrong, rushed past him and over to his parents. Chavarría stepped out of the room, closing the door behind him.

'Did you have to allow him to have his face painted?'

'He had it done himself. What could I do? I could hardly stop him.'

Chavarría led Emily away from the door. 'Tell me about Leanne.'

'There's not much I can say, I don't think,' said Emily. 'She seemed a normal teenage girl. A bit moody.'

'Moody?'

'Didn't talk to anyone. Maybe she was just shy.'

'Have you ever seen her out without her parents?'

'No. Mind you, she's usually traipsing five yards behind them with her hands in her pockets.'

'What about late at night?'

'No, never.'

'Have you ever seen her speak to any other guests, or any of them trying to speak to her?'

'No.'

'Her parents said she came down to swim in the pool early yesterday. Before breakfast.'

'Well, I wouldn't know anything about that. I didn't come on 'til ten.'

'And would the pool be busy at that time?'

'Before breakfast? Not really. A few of the more serious swimmers might try and make the most of it before those who just want to muck about take over. It's usually packed by mid-morning.'

Chavarría rested his forearms against the wooden rail and looked down across the gardens. There was something nagging at him, and Emily was maybe the one to ask. 'How old did you think she was?'

'Fourteen. Said so on her passport.'

'But how old did you *think* she was?'

'Can't say I took much notice of her. Maybe she could've passed for older if she made the effort.'

Chavarría told Emily he would need to speak to her again but, for the moment, she could return to the Fiesta. There was no doubt word would be spreading through the complex of Leanne Piggott's death, especially as the police presence on the site was increasing, and Emily's place was with her guests, especially young children who may be traumatised by such news. The Inspector Jefe knocked on the door of Room 421 and waited patiently for someone to answer. It was eventually opened by a distraught-looking John. The sound of uncontrollable crying could be heard coming from one of the bedrooms. The man stood aside, allowing Chavarría to enter.

'Shelley's in with him.'

'I am so very sorry for all of this, Mr. Piggott.'

'Can you give them some time?'

'A few minutes, then I must speak with him. It is important I should do so.'

'I understand.'

'In the meantime, would you allow me to have a look around?'

John returned to the sofa, giving the slightest of shrugs to indicate he had no objection. Chavarría went into the small bathroom. There was a bar of soap and a flannel on the back of the sink, both dry to the touch, and bottles of shower-gel and shampoo on a small shelf inside the shower. He turned his attention to the mirror-doored cabinet above the sink. It contained a tube of toothpaste and four toothbrushes, a packet of plasters, some tablets that Chavarría didn't recognise but which, to him, looked like a remedy for diarrhoea, a can of shaving gel, and two razors; one black and one a turquoise blue. There was nothing he wouldn't have expected.

Chavarría walked back into the living area just as Shelley and John were heading out of the bedroom the two children shared. Tears streaming down the young boy's face, which caused the colourful paint on his face to streak, he was holding tightly onto his mother's arm. The Inspector Jefe looked at John and gestured to the room his wife and son had just vacated. John nodded. Chavarría entered the room and, pushing the door to, glanced around. There were two single beds, with a small cabinet in between, a chest of drawers, and a wardrobe. He took the wardrobe first. It had been divided into halves – the left side for Todd's clothes and the right for Leanne's – and all seemed normal under a cursory glance. A more detailed search of the suite would take place later, this was just for his own curiosity. Chavarría moved to the chest, again equally divided between the two children, and ran a hand under the clothing in each of the four drawers. Nothing. The single drawer in the cabinet also yielded nothing of interest, so the Inspector Jefe dropped to his knees and glanced under the beds. Apart from several items of footwear, there was a holdall under each one. Chavarría pulled out the pink holdall – he couldn't see Todd electing for a colour like that – and looked inside. There was a MP3 player with earphones, a paperback novel, some fashion and celebrity gossip magazines, a box of tampons, and a small vanity bag. He took out the bag and, unzipping it, emptied the contents onto the bed.

Tony walked into the foyer of the Solanis Resort, an

all-inclusive hotel and leisure complex popular with British holiday-makers. This was one of the hotels that had been provisionally selected as a venue for his 'talk', but as he had discovered on his one and only previous visit to the Solanis, there were plenty of other, and more preferable, attractions on offer; a gymnasium, a games room, adventure playground, and a tennis and basketball court to name but a few. Tony knew that many of those who went 'all-inclusive' never left the four walls of the complex for the entire duration of their stay, and he could never quite grasp the reasons why. Sure, the Solanis was equipped with everything a holidaying family could wish for, but there was a whole different world out there to explore.

There were officers of the Policia Nacional at the desk, and Tony could observe several more talking to some guests in the lounge, which was obviously being used an interview room. He walked through the foyer and out into the central hub of the complex. The centrepiece was a large swimming pool, with a fountain in the middle and a couple of diving boards at one end. There seemed few children around, but from the sound of music and laughter nearby, an event was clearly taking place. The atmosphere around the pool seemed muted. The news was out. Many people were engaged in quiet, almost hushed conversations and, as Tony walked around the pool, he was able to pick out a few broken sentences.

'Who ever would've thought somethin' like that could happen here?'

'I 'eard it wa' that family from Warrington.'

'Oh, what a terrible thing!'

Tony discovered there were only two ways in and out of the Solanis Resort; the main entrance on Calle De San Antonio, from where he had come, and a gate by the tennis court which led out onto a cobbled pathway that, within five minutes, would take guests to the centre of Cieloventura. A sign on the gate said – in five different languages – that it was closed between the hours of 2000 and 0700. During those times, the only way into the complex was through reception.

Tony doubled-back on himself and returned to the main building. The only CCTV cameras he had seen on his travels had been in the car park at the front. There weren't any covering the pool or leisure areas, nor the back entrance by the tennis court. Tony took one of his cards from the back pocket of his shorts and penned a short message on the back. He headed to the desk and, after introducing himself, passed it over to the receptionist.

'Could you make sure the family of the young girl get this?'

Tony didn't know the poor victim's name, but the saddened nod from the receptionist meant she knew who it was intended for. Tony thanked her and made his way out of the hotel.

'I just need to ask you some questions, Todd,' said Inspector Jefe Chavarría. 'I will not take long, I promise. Is that okay with you?' The young boy, gripping tightly onto his mother's dress, stared at him. He didn't respond. 'Now, I need to ask you about your sister. It seems Leanne left your room either late last night or very early this morning. Did you hear her leave?'

The boy remained silent.

'If we are going to find out what happened to Leanne, we need to know. What time was it, Todd?'

'If he doesn't know, he doesn't know!' barked Shelley, throwing a protective arm around her son. Todd burst into tears once more and buried his face in his mother's chest. Chavarría didn't allow himself to be sidetracked, refusing to take his eyes from the boy.

'I need to know, Todd.'

Slowly, the boy turned his head back towards Chavarría. 'She told me not to say anything,' he said, his voice barely above a whisper.

'You do not have anything to worry about,' said the Inspector Jefe reassuringly. 'You are not in any kind of trouble. What time did she leave?'

'Dunno. Midnight?'

'Was this the only time?'

'No, she did it the night before as well.'

A quick glance at John and Shelley's faces told Chavarría this was obviously news to them.

'And do you know where she was going?'

'Just clubbing,' Todd cried. 'She told me if I kept quiet about it, she'd take me to the Splash Park.'

That would be enough for now, Chavarría thought. The grieving family needed some time alone. The make-up in the girl's holdall and Emily and Todd's statements confirmed what he had suspected. Leanne Piggott was a bored teenage girl on holiday with her family, forced to share a room with her kid brother, and, apart from the odd hour at the beach, only ever left the confines of the hotel to go on yet another coach trip. So she had decided to seek some adventure. Chavarría thought it was the kind of thing he might have done at that age. But Leanne Piggott had paid the ultimate price for her teenage spirit. She had met a murderer.

CHAPTER FOUR

MARIE couldn't wait any longer. She had to do something. Another quick glance at her watch told her it was approaching eight 'o' clock, and she knew Phil would only be accepting calls from that time. She knew it may lead to disciplinary action, but couldn't let that affect her decision. Natalie couldn't just drop her colleagues in it like this and expect nothing to happen. The Cieloventura Carnival was due to begin at nine, and at least five of them would be needed for that. Craig, Baz, Mel and Simon were already pencilled in, but Ross had let her know in no uncertain terms that he wouldn't be attending the evening's festivities or else, as he had said when Marie brought the subject up, he'd be making a few complaints himself. Phil, the regional rep, was based in Benidorm, and it was him that Marie would have to call. He didn't come on duty until eight and Marie watched as the second hand of her watch slowly ticked around. She picked up the phone and began dialling. She and Natalie were good friends, and had shared many fun times together. This was Marie's third season in Cieloventura, and Natalie's second, and the friendship had even seemed to overcome, minus the odd awkward moment, Marie's promotion to senior rep. Still, she had no choice. No choice at all. None. Marie cursed loudly and slammed the phone down. She stormed over to her wardrobe and rummaged through the pile of clothes at the bottom for the skirt and top that looked the cleanest. Natalie owed her big time for this. Whoever's bed she had spent the day in, Marie hoped he was bloody well worth it, that's all!

Tony was having a restless night. It was hot and clammy, more so than any other night since his arrival, but he knew it wasn't just that that was stopping him sleeping. The television news a couple of hours before had put a name and a face to the poor girl on the beach. She was just fourteen years old. He had seen for himself the efforts that were going on in the town to find out what exactly had happened. The Guardia Civil were mounting road checks on the major routes in and out of Cieloventura, while the Policia Nacional were conducting door-to-door inquiries within the town, and talking to holiday-makers on the beach and in the cafés and restaurants. Officers of the Policia Municipal were not directly involved in the investigation, though each had been given a photograph of the girl and her details. Tony had called Consuela for an update, but she could tell him little more than he already knew. Apparently, the focus of the enquiry was the bars and nightclubs along Avenida Del Puente, the centre of Cieloventura's nightlife. Tony shuddered at the prospect of a fourteen year-old going to a place like that.

He hoped he would be in for a quiet night tonight. If the police presence along the Avenue — as it was known simply – was increased, then the clubbers may well feel inclined to rein in any excessive behaviour. Tony had hoped to receive a call from the detectives leading the investigation, or perhaps Leanne Piggott's family, but that call never came. The one that did – and which had raised his hopes for a few moments – was from his contact in the extranjeros department. A tourist had had her handbag snatched by a young man on a motorcycle, pulling her to the ground in the process. She was carrying some medicines for a heart condition, and the officers at the comisaría were so worried about her state of hysteria over the incident that they called for an ambulance. With their manpower stretched in the Leanne Piggott enquiry, they had requested for one of their colleagues at the Policia Municipal to accompany her to hospital. They, in turn, had asked Tony. He did so gladly and, while she was being checked over and her scratches dressed, had spent the time chasing up authorisation for her to be issued with replacement medication. Bag snatches and pick-pockets, while not a serious problem, were not uncommon in the town, as in any tourist area, as thieves knew most visitors would be carrying a large amount of cash on them.

'It's impossible to know what to do for the best,' the victim of the robbery, a Mrs. Bennett, had told Tony as they shared a taxi back to her apartment block. 'We're told not to leave any valuables in our rooms, and we're told we shouldn't carry too much of value on our person! It's all a ruse to make us pay to use those little safes in our wardrobes! Anything to get us to part with more of our money!'

Tony turned and fidgeted in an attempt to get more comfortable. He had arranged to pay Mrs. Bennett a visit the next morning, after the morning court session, to check she was okay after her ordeal. After that, his day would be free to do what he wished. It was a Saturday after all, and though his contract of employment didn't specify the hours and days he worked, he knew he would only be called in an emergency.

Tony sat up in bed and switched on the lamp. He reached for the glass of water on the bedside cabinet and downed it in two large gulps. It was warm to the taste and not very refreshing. But Tony knew it wasn't his physical thirst that needed quenching.

'So you're none the worse for the experience, then?'

'Take more than a hooligan to ruin my holiday, love.' Mrs. Bennett said, reclining on a lounger by the pool with a fruit juice in hand. 'A bit bruised but, other than that, I'm fine. And I must say how nice it is to deal with someone from home. Not that I mind the locals, of course, they're lovely people, but it was comforting to have you with me.'

Tony smiled. He was glad the woman had recovered so well, and was always grateful for praise, even if he had actually done very little. She had seemed so shaken up yesterday that he feared it would be another case of someone disappearing on the first flight home. 'So what are your plans for today?'

'Just lounging by the pool, my love. I've had

enough excitement for a while.'

'Well, you've got my card so don't hesitate to give me a ring if you need to,' said Tony. 'And I'll be in touch with the police sometime today. I'll let you know straightaway if they recover your possessions.'

Mrs. Bennett scoffed. That was a long shot and they both knew it. The two said their goodbyes and Tony made his way out of the apartment complex. His day was now done, and he could afford to take some time for himself. He fancied a walk along the coast to the village of El Marquesa, some four miles away. He'd been there only once, when he had enjoyed a charming red wine in a waterfront bar. The village had the largest fishing fleet for many miles, and Tony could sit and watch the boats for hours. It reminded him of his childhood. Four miles would be quite a walk, especially in the heat, but he knew he could always get a bus or a boat back and some time out of Cieloventura would be good.

'Excuse me?'

Tony stopped and looked around to see a young woman — a holiday rep, he thought, by her uniform and the obligatory clipboard under her arm — climbing out of a battered Fiat Uno. She walked over to him.

'Hello. I don't know if you remember me, but we've met before.'

Tony struggled for a moment to place the face, then it came to him. He had met her in his second week in Cieloventura. A hotel manager has charged three young Lancashire women €150 for damage to the balcony doors in their room, and was refusing to hand over their passports until the bill had been settled. While it wasn't standard policy in the town, Tony was aware that some hotels and apartment complexes required guests to hand in their passports upon checking in, which were then given back to them at the end of their stay. The guests in question were among a party of ten and, with the coach threatening to leave for the airport with or without them, the atmosphere was getting very tense. After some intimidation and verbal abuse had been aimed at the manager by one of the party, he had called the police, and Tony, who was with Consuela and Rafá when the call came in, had accompanied them. Marie Reynolds was the rep who was desperately trying to keep the peace when they had arrived. In the end, she and Tony, between them, had managed to persuade the party to pay for the damages and have their passports released. Either that or miss their flight home, which, as Tony had emphasised, would end up proving far more costly in terms of replacement tickets.

'I don't suppose you've got a few moments. There's something I'd like to talk to you about.'

Marie opened the door slowly and poked a head into the room beyond. Satisfied there was no-one home, she pushed the door the rest of the way and stepped inside. Tony followed her in.

'Ross'll kill me if he knew we were sneaking around in here.'

'Is it just the two of them who live here?'

'Yes, him and Nat. I share with Mel. I've got keys

to all the apartments because I'm senior rep.'

Tony glanced around the small lounge and kitchen. It couldn't have been much more obvious that it belonged to a couple of youngsters, with empty pizza boxes and beer bottles bulging from the bin, and film and music posters adorning the walls.

'Where is he now?'

'Ross? Probably sailing. It's how he spends almost all his time off. He should've been off yesterday but I had him cover for her.'

'Which is her room?'

'Over here.' The young woman led Tony into Natalie's bedroom. It was as Marie herself had left it the morning before. The bed remained unmade and there was little floor space visible among the discarded clothes. 'Nothing's missing as far as I know. Only the clothes she was wearing on Thursday night, and her handbag.'

'So she's definitely not been back here since then?'

'No.'

'What was happening on Thursday?'

'Nothing special. We were going around the bars and clubs trying to sell tickets for our boat-trips.'

'And that was the last time you saw her?'

Marie nodded. 'Do you think I should notify the police? Look, I'll admit we sometimes skip some of our duties and stuff, but we know never to miss incoming flights.'

Tony opened the top drawer of Natalie's dresser. It contained a number of items of underwear and he only gave them a passing glance, not comfortable with the idea of rummaging through them. 'You'd better. She's been gone for nearly thirty-six hours.'

'Do you think you could make a few enquiries? Without us making this official, I mean? She could get the sack for this. Phil at head office is on some big disciplinary kick at the moment. Wants to get rid of the image us Holiday18 reps have of only being interested in drinking and shagging and having a good time'.

Tony grinned. *Holiday18* specialised in cheap and cheerful package deals for the over eighteens'; a week of organised hedonism, bar crawls and children's party games with an adult 'twist'. Though there was no official upper age limit – age discrimination laws probably prevented that – he knew anyone with an ounce of maturity would steer well clear.

'Well, it's a bit irregular but I'll see what I can do. Give me an hour, and if I can turn nothing up, then you really need to make a missing person's report.'

The second drawer of the dresser contained mainly T-shirts, flimsy summer tops and swimwear, and the third was full of paperwork, including a *Holiday18* staff handbook, various lost property and insurance claim forms, some advertising bumf for a new holiday villa development, and old guest lists dating back to the beginning of the summer. The corner of a British passport could be seen poking out from under a Cieloventura street map. Tony pulled it out and looked at the holders' details on the inside back cover. Natalie Alison Brooks. Ripley, Derbyshire. The small photograph showed a pretty, auburn-haired young woman.

'Thanks so much,' said Marie. 'Look, I might be panicking over nothing, but after what happened to that poor girl...'

Tony replaced the passport, at least they knew Natalie had not left the country, and closed the drawer. 'Yes, it's very tragic.'

'What's happening with that, by the way? Do they have any idea who did it?'

'Well, enquiries are continuing,' Tony replied. 'I'm sure the national police know what they're doing.' He moved to the small unit beside the bed and opened the door at the front. Inside stood an iPod speaker hub, a hair-dryer, curling tongs, a Ladyshave, and a small wicker basket containing some condoms and a couple of sachets of exotically-flavoured lubricant.

Marie sat down on the edge of the bed. 'So you were a copper back home?'

'Fifteen years.'

'So how come you've ended up in Spain? I thought that was more for the crooks?'

Tony grinned. 'It usually is. Tell me, does Natalie have the use of a car?'

'A scooter. But it's locked up downstairs. I'm the only one with a car. Ross keeps the spare keys but he would never lend them to Natalie, she can't drive.'

Tony closed the door to the bedside unit and took one further glance around the room. 'You mentioned on the way here that you thought she'd be back for last night at least?'

'Well, I didn't think she'd miss the Cieloventura

Carnival. She's usually well up for that.'

'And what is that exactly?'

'It's the Friday night bar crawl along the Avenue. Twelve venues in four hours.'

'And what did you think when she didn't show up yesterday?'

Marie shrugged her shoulder. 'That she'd gone off with some guy she'd met.'

Tony realised his expression must have betrayed his sentiments on that matter as he saw the rep roll her eyes.

'Look, I won't pretend we're angels, Mr. Heather. Natalie was no worse than any of the rest of us when it came to putting it about.'

Tony was both surprised and thankful for Marie's candidness. 'Well, there's not much I can do here. I'll make a few enquiries and give you a call in a short while. If I can't find anything, you'll need to come down to the comisaría. I'll meet you there.'

Marie nodded and stood up. The two made their way out of the small apartment.

'The police must be really busy at the moment, what with that poor girl...'

'Not so busy that they wouldn't take this seriously,' Tony reassured her. He said his goodbyes, after first making sure he'd taken Marie's mobile number, and started the ten-minute trek back to the town square. So much for his walk to El Marquesa. Still, this could be serious. While Natalie Brooks hadn't been gone that long, and, as Marie had all but admitted, skipping work was something the *Holiday18* reps were prone to doing, especially the morning after a particularly heavy night before, a missing person was still a missing person. And she hadn't just missed work, she hadn't even returned to her home.

Tony's first port of call were the offices of the Policia Municipal on the northern side of the square.

'José, I'm looking for a British holiday rep that seems to have gone missing. Her name is Natalie Brooks. Has anything come in?'

'The name is not familiar to me. I will look.' José made his way into the small office at the side of the reception area. 'And how are you today, *langosta*?'

Tony winced slightly at the use of the nickname he'd been given. While the redness of his face wasn't as stark as it had been after his first week in Cieloventura, he had thought the inevitable comparison to a lobster would have fallen away by now. 'Not too bad, thank you, José. You?'

'Good, good.'

'Any news on the Leanne Piggott investigation?'

'Nothing this morning as far as I know. Describe your missing rep to me, por fávor?'

'White, nineteen years old, auburn hair.'

'All-bern?' The word was not one José, despite his very good grasp of English, recognised. Tony reached for an English-Spanish dictionary from a pile of books at the side of the front desk. It was a well-thumbed volume, used countless times by visitors to the offices of the Policia Municipal.

'Er...*morena*?'

'Ah! Si, si.'

Tony waited patiently while José searched the computer database for any incident reports or recent arrest records to suggest that Natalie Brooks had come into contact with the police. The database pooled information from the Policia Municipal, the Policia Nacional and the Guardia Civil, though different passwords were required to access each one.

'There is nothing, Tony.'

'No?'

José left the office and, shaking his head, returned to the front desk. 'I am sorry, my friend.'

'I'll need to try the hospitals. Thanks anyway, José.'

'Always a pleasure.'

Tony left the station and flicked through the numbers on his mobile phone. The nearest hospital, which he had visited yesterday afternoon in the company of Mrs. Bennett, was in Villajoyosa, some five miles north along the coast. There were also a number of other hospitals in the Alicante region, however, and Tony wondered how wide he should cast his net. He made for The Green Dragon and, over a pot of tea and some buttered toast, called as many as he thought likely. None had a patient by the name of Natalie Brooks, and only one — the Hospital de Torrevieja — had an unidentified patient that could possibly be her. A female, aged between eighteen and twenty-five, had been involved in a hit-and-run early on Friday morning and was currently in intensive care. Tony doubted Natalie could have been in Torrevieja, which was a good fifty miles away, at such a time but gave as detailed a description as he could and waited anxiously for his call to be returned. When it came, within fifteen minutes, it was clear the unidentified patient could not be Natalie Brooks. She was blonde.

Tony's next call was to Marie Reynolds. She was disappointed to hear there was no news of her friend, though also relieved as well, and agreed to meet Tony outside the HQ of the Policia Nacional. Marie was certainly right about one thing. The force would no doubt be stretched on the Leanne Piggott murder investigation. There were many officers out on the town's streets conducting enquiries. The case had also attracted considerable media interest, and Tony had noted at least four or five Spanish television news crews in the town square and along the Paseo de la Solana. Karen had told him there were also crews from the BBC, ITV and SKY in the town, and several visitors to the café had remarked how they had been stopped and asked for their thoughts on the matter.

'God knows how they knew I was British,' one customer had said to her, describing his encounter with a pushy young reporter. Karen chose just to shake her head in response, professing equal bafflement, rather than point out his pasty skin and the unmissable combination of shorts and socks.

The visit to the comisaría in Calle de Santa Ana was brief. Tony knew that the initial report of Natalie's disappearance was best made by telephone. Visiting the comisaría in person may involve the use of an interpreter, as there was no guarantee an English-speaking officer would be available, and that could involve a long wait, especially if there was a queue. There was, however, a bank of telephone operators who, between them, spoke a number of languages, and a report could be made and translated into Spanish over the phone. This would then be passed onto the correct department. When Tony and Marie called at the comisaría an hour later, an officer and interpreter were waiting for them. They confirmed the information Tony had given over the phone, answered a number of other questions the officer had, and handed over a photo Tony had asked Marie to bring with her. The officer was very professional and assured them the force would do all they could. He was also happy for Tony to continue making enquiries, as long as any new information he discovered was passed onto the Policia Nacional without delay.

'I've called head office in Benidorm,' Marie said, as she and Tony walked out of the comisaría. 'They're going to send one of their team down to cover for Nat if we don't hear anything by Monday. Do you think I should call her parents?'

'Yes, you should. They may have heard from her. Would you like me to do it?'

The worry etched onto Marie's face suddenly vanished. 'Would you? That'd be brilliant. I don't think I'd be any good telling someone something like that.'

'Of course. Tell me, how are your wages paid?'

'We've all got Spanish bank accounts. It's paid direct into there and we get it out when we need it.'

'And is the money good?'

'No, not really,' chuckled Marie. 'But the company pays the rent on our apartments, so anything we get is ours. Plus we earn commission on the trips that we sell.'

Tony and Marie parted once more, with a promise he would continue to do all that was possible to find Natalie. Although he had hoped to play a part in the Leanne Piggott case, it was obvious to him there was little more he could do there, especially as neither the detectives leading the enquiry nor Leanne's parents had tried to contact him. This case, however, gave the opportunity to dust down his years of experience as a police officer and put his skills to good use. He always knew hanging up his uniform, handing in his warrant card, and posing for the obligatory photograph with the Chief Superintendent, gold carriage clock in hand, would not sever all ties with that part of his life. Tony would always possess the inquisitive nature, a passion for justice, and a real interest in people that had made the police force seem an attractive career in the first place. In truth, his time in the force had been largely one disappointment after another. He was in his mid-thirties by the time he received his Sergeant's stripes, and the hoped transfer to CID or Serious Crime never came.

Tony had taken a copy of Natalie's photo for himself before he and Marie had reported to the comisaría. It had been taken in a bar and she was smiling broadly at the camera, holding a cocktail in one hand while the other hung from the shoulder of a handsome young man. She was certainly a looker, Tony thought. He decided his first port of call would be *Breeze*, a small nightclub located a few minutes' walk from the western end of the Avenue. This was where Natalie had told Marie she was heading when they last saw each other on Thursday night. Tony had felt mentally drained when he woke up this morning, not that he'd had much sleep in the first place, but, as he walked off in the direction of the Avenue, he suddenly felt reinvigorated.

The man stared at the photo. It all seemed so unreal. His index finger slowly traced a line along her lips before moving down and swiftly over a series of buttons. *Are you sure to want to delete the image?* He pressed the green button and watched as the revolving egg-timer icon appeared in the middle of the small display. Then Leanne was gone. Gone forever.

Inspector Jefe Chavarría left the pathology building and sucked in enough fresh air to make his lungs feel they could almost burst. Strangely enough, it didn't seem to be the smell of the lab that affected him, more the general aura of death and decay that played games with his mind. He needed some time to take everything in, and so decided to take the coast road back to Cieloventura, rather than the highway.

Suffocation, the pathologist had told him. Leanne Piggott had been pushed face down into the sand and held there, a hand pressed hard against the back of her head. There was also bruising to the base of her spine and the back of her legs where, the pathologist surmised, the perpetrator had placed his knees to prevent the victim from struggling. There was some alcohol in Leanne's system, the blood results and analysis of her stomach contents indicated she had drunk two vodka oranges and a margarita , and tests for drug use had come back positive for cannabis. There were no signs of sexual assault, no bruising or marks of trauma around her genitals, but the pathologist had said she didn't appear to be a virgin. Chavarría climbed behind the wheel of his car and shook his head in dismay. It hardly bared thinking about that she was the same age as Terésa. His little Terésa. He reached into the inside pocket of his jacket for his phone. She would be embarrassed if he called to check up on her, but right now he couldn't care less. He needed to make the call.

'Papa!'

'Easy, princess. I'm just calling to see how you are.'

'I'm fine. What did you expect?'

'Are you having a nice time?'

'Yes. We went to Port Aventura yesterday.'

Chavarría knew his daughter was at the age where she wanted more independence. And they had always been willing to give it to her. They'd had a few minor problems with her in the past couple of months, mainly her lack of application to her school work and staying out too late, but nothing more serious. They hoped that treating Terésa more like an adult would be reciprocated by her adopting a more responsible attitude. She was spending three weeks in Catalonia at the holiday home of her best friend's family. She had never been away for such a long time before, and Chavarría was feeling guilty. One of the reasons they had allowed her to go was so he and Isabel could spend some 'quality time' together and attempt and sort out their issues. Had they been too quick to let her go? Were they being selfish at the thought of having some time alone? He didn't know.

'That sounds good. And what are your plans for the rest of today?'

'We're cooking for everyone.'

'Ooh, I hope you've the antidote ready!'

'Papa!'

Seeing Leanne Piggott, post-autopsy, in the pathology lab had shocked him. The back of her head had been shaved so photos could be taken of the pattern of bruising, and the Y-shaped incision that had opened up her chest was savagery against her young, flawless skin. Without the small amount of make-up she'd been wearing when he first saw her, Leanne looked every day the child she was. He found it hard to reconcile the image of this young girl with the facts the pathologist had furnished him with. Chavarría knew the young Britons that flocked to the various resorts on the Spanish Costas had a reputation for behaving badly but Leanne was still a child. A child.

Three weeks was too long, he decided at that moment. Maybe they could think of a way of getting her to come home early. He would need to talk things over with his wife, assuming she would be there when he returned home. Whenever that would be. The Inspector Jefe had spent the previous night on the sofa in the office so he could be ready to react to any fresh developments. The family had moved to their new villa in the hills, five miles north of the village of Relleu, the previous summer and, though it provided a perfect escape from the hectic pace of life in town, the forty minute drive was too much, especially in the early days of an investigation like this where every second was invaluable.

'Papa, please! Just text me if you have to.'

Chavarría laughed. 'Okay, I'll text. I just wanted to hear your voice, that's all. Have a nice time this evening, won't you? And give my regards to Connie.'

'I will.'

'I love you, Terésa.'

If she wasn't embarrassed he'd called Conchita's parents to check up on her in the first place, she certainly would be now, Chavarría thought, especially as her best friend and family were in the next room. He waited and hoped it would come. It did.

'Love you too, Papa.'

Chavarría smiled. He said goodbye and put the phone back into his pocket. The pathologist's report had given him a good few things to mull over but, as he turned the key in the ignition, his thoughts was disturbed by the phone ringing.

'Chavarría.'

'Jefe, it's Luís.'

'Anything?'

'Yes, we think so. When will you be back?'

'I'm heading off now. Twenty minutes?'

'See you then.'

Chavarría pulled the car out of its space and accelerated towards the open gates. He knew Luís Banda would not call him unless it was important. He would need to take the highway after all.

CHAPTER FIVE

TONY was almost compelled to pinch his nose together as he walked across the floor of the nightclub towards the main bar. Several cleaners were busy slopping their mops in and out of every nook and crevice they could find, and the smell of stale beer, vomit and disinfectant combined to make him feel queasy. Although this was his first visit to *Breeze*, Tony doubted whether any of the other clubs in the town would look any different in the cold light of day. Stripped of their colourful lighting, loud music, and fun-loving young crowds, they were just empty shells with tired, cheap décor.

One of the cleaners had pointed Tony in the direction of a middle-aged man restocking the small fridges behind the bar from a plastic crate. He looked British, Tony thought, but was clearly no recent arrival. His tan was deep-set, almost leathered by the sun, and his hair, which almost reached down to his collar, had been bleached a shade or two lighter than its natural straw colour.

'Are you the manager?'

The man looked around at Tony and eyed him carefully.

'Depends who wants to know.'

Tony took the copy of Natalie's photo from his shirt

pocket and held it up so the man could see it.

'I'm trying to find someone. A holiday rep.'

'Yeah, yeah, that's Nat,' the man nodded. 'She's with Holiday18.'

'That's right. When did you last see her?'

'Not sure. Anyway, why you lookin' for her? What's she done?'

'Done?'

'Come off it, mate. We may be in a different country, but I can still sniff a plod a mile off.'

'I'm not a policeman,' Tony said, which was a perfectly true statement. 'My name is Tony Heather. I work for the Mayor's Office, liaising with British visitors to the town.'

He produced a card from his wallet and handed it across the bar to the manager, who gave it the briefest of glances before placing it in his own shirt pocket.

'Donnie Lane. Sorry, no card.'

'So when was the last time you saw Natalie Brooks, Mr. Lane?'

Donnie shrugged. 'Couldn't say for sure. Weren't last night, I know that. Some of the others were in, but I didn't see Nat.'

'Others?'

'The Holiday18 lot. Last night was their Carnival night, weren't it? We're the last stop on their route.'

'How many punters did they bring with them?'

''Bout thirty or so. Few less than they started out with, I reckon.' Donnie laughed as he put the empty plastic crate down on the ground behind the bar and, with some effort, picked up a full one. 'First holiday away from their mummies an' daddies an' they reckon they can drink wi' the best of 'em. Muppets!'

'Any trouble last night?'

'Nah, not at all. Mind you, there were loads of your lot right along the Avenue. Must be 'cos of that young girl that was killed.'

'I told you, Mr. Lane, I'm not a police officer.'

Donnie smirked and turned his attention back to filling the fridges with bottles of San Miguel. Was it that obvious, Tony thought? Maybe his questioning was too obvious, too off pat to be just that of a civilian worker? His methods had served him well in the past but, still, it was something he would need to bear in mind. It wouldn't do to put people on their guard so quickly, which he knew from experience was most people's initial reaction when questioned by a police officer.

'It must be good for business. Being the last stop of the Carnival, I mean? I doubt the crowd would want to go on anywhere else after all that. They'd probably all carry on drinking here for the rest of the night. Those that were still able to, of course.'

'Yeah, I guess so.'

'Is there any particular reason why the Carnival finishes here?'

'How'd you mean?'

'I mean do you have an arrangement with the holiday company?'

'Oh, I get you. Nah, nah, it's more wi' the reps. They get free drinks, an' I put some prizes up for the competitions they run. Bottle of wine, T-shirts, that kind of thing.'

'The reps get free drinks all the time?'

Donnie roared with laughter. 'Carnival nights only! They'd drink me into fuckin' bankruptcy otherwise, mate. Especially our Nat.'

'So what can you tell me about her?'

'Look, what's all this about anyway? She in trouble?'

'Not that I'm aware of, but nobody has seen her since Thursday night. She told Marie Reynolds, the head rep, that she was going to come here before heading home.'

Donnie screwed up his face in thought. 'Nah, can't say I saw her Thursday.'

'Are you sure about that?'

'As I can be. She usually comes and says hello whenever she's in.'

'So you're friends then?'

'Well, *friendly* more than friends. She even does a bit of work for me now an' then.'

'Oh? What kind of work?'

'Handin' out leaflets along the beach and the Paseo de la Solana. Maybe around the hotels she worked at if Marie didn't catch her at it.'

'Leaflets advertising the club?'

'Yeah.'

Donnie reached under the bar and produced a small colourful pamphlet. He handed it over to Tony to look at. It offered the bearer discounted entry to *Breeze* and a BOGOF drink offer. Tony knew there were many youngsters handing out similar leaflets on the beach and the town's main tourist streets. Competition for custom was no doubt fierce among Cieloventura's many bars and clubs. He had seen them himself many times, though they tended to ignore him as he walked past.

'How much do you pay her?'

'Depends how many punters she brought in,' replied Donnie, closing the final fridge and picking up the pile of empty crates at his feet. 'On a good night, maybe we'd get about twenty or thirty turnin' up with a leaflet. I give her a euro for each one.'

'So it's a nice extra little earner for her?'

'Yeah, as I said, on a good night.'

'And on a bad one?'

'Just a couple, so it was hardly worth her givin' up her free time. She's always moanin' about the hours the company makes her work for such shit money, and how little she has to herself.'

'So she was unhappy working for Holiday18?'

'Dunno if I'd go that far.'

Donnie walked out from behind the bar and carried the empty crates towards a nearby door. He headed out into the corridor beyond, which Tony could see was lined with boxes of spirits and bar-snacks. At the end of the corridor, an open door led out into a back yard.

'D'you think she could've been after another job?'

'Well, I doubt she would've got another reppin' job. Most of the proper holiday companies are lookin' for people who speak the lingo, qualifications in travel an' tourism, stuff like that.'

Tony smiled at Donnie's use of the phrase 'proper holiday companies' to describe those other than *Holiday18*. He knew what he meant, though.

'This is Natalie's second season, isn't it?'

'As far as I know.' Donnie reappeared in the open doorway, carrying a box of Royal Swan, which Tony knew to be a Spanish-produced Vodka. 'Now, if there's nothin' else, I've got a lot to do…'

'Who was working the door on Thursday night?'

'Couldn't tell you off hand. I'd have to check the rota.'

'Well, if you didn't mind…'

Donnie frowned and turned back into the corridor. Tony watched him enter a room halfway along the narrow passage on the right-hand side. He returned within seconds, minus the box, flicking through some documents on a clipboard.

'Er, looks like it was Jimi and Max.'

'I'd like to know if they remember Natalie coming here on Thursday night,' said Tony. 'Could you ask them when you see them next and give me a call?'

'Course, yeah. Anythin' to help.'

'I appreciate it. And, in the meantime, if there's anything you remember that may help me, or if you see Natalie about, you can phone me at anytime.'

'Sure.'

'Thanks very much for your time, Mr. Lane.'

Tony shook hands with Donnie and made his way back across the dance floor towards the club's main doors. The floor was a little slippery with the disinfectant and he took each step gingerly. Donnie

Lane had seemed forthcoming enough, Tony thought, even on questions about how much he paid Natalie to hand out promotional leaflets on the beach, which some might have been reluctant to answer. It was interesting that she was occasionally willing to give up her free time to do such a menial job, though, especially if it was as scarce as she had indicated. Marie herself had said the money from *Holiday18* wasn't that good. Could Natalie have money worries? It would be something he could mention to the Policia Nacional. He didn't have the authority to look into her finances, such as checking her bank account, but, if they considered it an important lead, the police would.

Tony walked out into the bright early afternoon sun and took a moment to get his bearings. The apartment block where the *Holiday18* reps lived was in a residential area in the south-west of the town; a good fifteen minute walk, he estimated. Tony folded up the *Breeze* leaflet and, placing it in his pocket, set off on what he thought would have been Natalie's route home.

'That's her, isn't it?'

Chavarría pulled his chair closer to the desk and craned his neck forward to get a better look at the flickering image.

'Yes, I think it is'.

'We've got her on three cameras so far,' said Luís Banda. 'This one is on the corner of Avenida Del Puente and Calle Veijo.'

The small figure of Leanne Piggott could be seen

towards the right side of the screen, pacing up and down around a single spot on the corner of the busy thoroughfare. The numbers in the bottom left corner told the time: 00:14.

'It looks like she's waiting for someone.'

'That's right. And here he is.'

A young man, casually dressed in ripped jeans and a football shirt, appeared in the frame and approached Leanne. They spoke for a few moments before heading together out of the view of the camera.

'We pick them up a minute later further along Avenida Del Puente,' said Banda, tapping away at the keyboard and bringing up an image of the two walking side by side along the pedestrianised street. 'And then again here outside Platinum.'

The next picture that appeared on the screen showed Leanne and the young man waiting patiently in line outside the entrance to a nightclub. The doorman ushered them forward and, after the briefest of conversations, stood aside and waved them in.

'Is that Platinum's own camera?'

'Yes,' replied Banda. 'We now move forward two and a half hours...'

Further taps on the keyboard followed, and the recording shifted forward in time. 02:49. Leanne appeared on the screen, heading out of the club.

'Leaving alone?'

'Wait. Give it a moment...'

Chavarría watched the screen closely. Nearly a minute ticked by before the young man appeared briefly in the frame.

'Going after her?'

'Possibly.'

'Are they on camera again?'

'No. Leanne must have gone the other way along Avenida Del Puente, towards the Paseo de la Solana.'

'What about the cameras along the Paseo?'

'They're used to monitor traffic rather than people. At night, the view isn't good enough to pick out individuals. You can see people heading along the pavement but it's impossible to tell who's who.'

Chavarría cursed at the provision of surveillance cameras in the area. There were only four along the Avenida Del Puente in total, all in fixed positions. If the Mayor was serious about reducing disorder along that particular stretch, the system needed a serious overhaul. It wasn't so much the cost of new cameras, he had been told, but that they would need manning twenty-four hours a day by trained staff, and the town hall and the Policia Nacional could not agree on the division of their respective investment and labour.

'Do we have a clear image of the male?'

Luís Banda tapped a few keys and brought up a close-up freeze frame of the young man leaving the club. 'This is the best I can do. Maybe it can be cleaned up a bit.'

Chavarría tapped on the screen with his pen. 'Is that a football shirt?'

'Yes. I've been looking on the internet.'

Banda shuffled along the desk on his wheeled chair to a second computer terminal. A jiggle of the mouse and the animated aquarium on the screen was replaced by a photo of a footballer.

'What do you think?'

Chavarría's eyes moved back and forth between the two images. 'It looks like it. The width of the stripes, the logo in the middle... What team is it?'

'Sunderland. English.'

'Never heard of them. Let me watch Leanne leave the club again.'

Banda moved back to the first computer and brought up the previous piece of footage. He played it several times.

'It's impossible to tell if she's upset or angry.'

'Can you give me a close-up of her before she went into the club, and put it side-by-side with this one?'

'Yes, I think I can.'

Banda's fingers worked quickly and skilfully over the keyboard and the requested images were soon on the screen. The Inspector Jefe's eyes flicked back and forth between them; the first showing Leanne's left side as she entered *Platinum* with the young man, and the second showing her right as she walked out alone.

'See something, Jefe?'

'I'm not sure. Can you get these printed off? And the one of the male?'

'Sure.'

'I'll talk to the staff at Platinum. Maybe somebody remembers seeing them together.' Chavarría got to his feet. At least they now knew where Leanne had been in the hours before her death. *Platinum* was the largest and most popular club in Cieloventura, and often attracted 'name' DJ's from across Europe. It occasionally came onto the police radar, usually for drug offences, but the CCTV and the qualified door staff and stewards the club employed generally kept the exuberance of its clientele from spilling over into trouble. It was unlikely two young clubbers among the two thousand that the club held would have stood out, but if there had been an argument between Leanne and the male, someone may remember them. The girl leaving *Platinum* alone was not evidence of anything, but it was suggestive.

The printer in the middle of the communal office whirled into life and the photos soon appeared. Chavarría took them from the tray and looked at them. The male was blonde and certainly didn't appear local. Not that he wanted the killer to be a native, but it meant the clock was ticking faster than he would have liked. There was always pressure in a homicide investigation but the victim being a tourist meant it was magnified. Orders had already come down from above that he was to give a press conference at five 'o' clock that afternoon in front of both the Spanish and British media. He wasn't relishing that. He had also been told the Mayor's Office wanted regular updates, but had delegated that task to Official Elisa Valle Huerta, the latest addition to his department. She was an ambitious officer, intelligent, and more than a little pleasing to the eye. Chavarría saw the annoyance in her eyes when he passed the duty to her, but he thought she would be an ideal buffer between the investigating team and local politicians. The Inspector Jefe had already decided to have her sitting with him at the press conference. It concerned him a little that he had chosen her solely because she was more photogenic than any of his other officers, but he knew the conference was more for PR than anything else and felt he may as well play the game. Chavarría also knew something else about Official Valle that troubled him. He knew he wanted her.

There had only been one murder in Cieloventura in the past year. A barman was attacked with a bottle and a shred of glass had pierced his carotid artery. The perpetrator, a Norwegian tourist, was soon identified but had fled the country within hours of the incident. He was eventually arrested in his homeland and extradited back to Spain to face trial, which was due to begin shortly. The investigation wasn't difficult, merely a text-book exercise in gathering witness statements and tying in the physical evidence. It was an open and shut case. This was different. What sort of person could have killed Leanne Piggott? She was slight in build, hardly likely to cause anyone a physical threat, and the method of her death showed a particularly vicious streak. To hold someone's face down in the sand until they stopped breathing, to be able to feel their body shaking and convulsing under their own as the poor victim fought to stay alive; that took a different breed of killer.

'I need to talk to Leanne's parents first,' Chavarría said to Banda. 'I'll go on to Platinum from there. In the meantime, get copies of these images distributed. And see if someone can clean that tape up.'

'Yes, Jefe.'

'And I want the camera footage from the previous night looked at. Todd Piggott said Leanne went out then also, don't forget. I want to know if she met with this man on that occasion. We may get a clearer shot of him.'

Chavarría walked out of the office. He had never got used to delivering bad news. Did anybody? The first time he had done so still rankled with him. As a probationary officer with the Policia Nacional, he was working under an experienced Agente in his home province of Almeria. The victim of a gas explosion in a factory had been identified and they were duly dispatched to the family home. Chavarría had expected his more senior and experienced colleague to deliver the news, only to find it left to him. 'To get him blooded,' he overheard the Agente say later. Telling Mr. and Mrs. Piggott that a body matching their daughter's description had been found on the beach was hard. Explaining the circumstances of her death would be harder. It would need to be a sanitised version. At least for the moment. They didn't need to know about the alcohol and cannabis, not just yet, and certainly not about her apparent sexual experience. Chavarría doubted the man captured on camera outside *Platinum* was a fellow resident at the Solanis Resort. If he had been, why would they meet at Avenida Del Puente? However, he would take the photo with him and ask the Piggott's if they had seen him around. He would show the staff and the holiday reps too. The football shirt could be important, Chavarría considered. What was it Banda had said? Sun-derland? He would ask Emily Johnson about that if she was on duty. Football wasn't his sport anyway. He liked the Spanish teams to do well in club or international competitions but, other than that, he took no particular interest. At the *colegio de policia*, Chavarría had been introduced to rugby and he had remained an avid fan ever since. The Policia Nacional in Cieloventura had their own team, but he had recently lost his place to a younger officer and hadn't been to training once since then.

Chavarría headed out of the comisaría and took a cheroot from his pocket. He decided to walk to the Solanis Resort. It would give him the opportunity to go over in his mind how he should best convey the pathologist's initial findings to John and Shelley Piggott. The British Consulate had sent an officer to be with the family and he spoke excellent Spanish. That would help the situation. Although Chavarría considered his English to be quite good, he had to concentrate very hard in case he missed something, especially if they had a strong accent like the Piggott's.

The Inspector Jefe smoked two of the small cigars in the time it took to walk to the Solanis Resort. There was a heavy media presence outside the main entrance, but until the press conference later that day, the gathered journalists and camera crews didn't know who he was and they paid him little heed as he walked through the crowd. It wasn't until the police officer standing in front of the doors stood aside to allow Chavarría to enter the building that a few questions were shouted after him, but by then it was too late.

Although retracing Natalie's steps proved fruitless, Tony considered it far from a waste of time. Apart from a few small shops and bars, her route from *Breeze* to the apartment block where she lived was mainly through residential streets. Two of the shops were closed – it was siesta time – but the bars were open and Tony could find no-one who recalled seeing Natalie on Thursday night, or at any time since. If Natalie didn't reappear soon, Tony thought the next step would be 'door stepping' the houses and maybe putting up some posters. That would need to be down to the police, however, as his extremely limited Spanish, courtesy of a six-week evening course at his local adult education centre, didn't equip him for questioning local residents.

Tony called in at the apartments rented by *Holiday18*, a slightly shabby block overlooking the main road out of town. There was no reply at the first two, but a sleepy young man with a week's beard growth opened the door of the third. He introduced himself as Baz from Leicester, and that it was his day off. He had only just woken up, he explained, as, in Natalie's absence, Marie had put him in charge of the Cieloventura Carnival the night before.

'Didn't get in 'til four. I had to make sure everyone got back safely first. Do you want a cup of tea or coffee or something?'

'No, that's alright, but thanks for the offer. I take it Marie mentioned she'd asked me to try and find Natalie?'

'Yeah, she said she'd got the law involved. It's a strange one, that's all I can say. God knows where she could've got to.'

'You've no ideas?'

'No, none. I suppose if it was just the one night, she could've been with some bloke. I don't spend more than a few nights a week in my own bed myself!'

Tony wasn't impressed by Baz's boast, and the wink that accompanied it, if that was indeed the aim. 'Did you know Natalie worked occasionally for Breeze?' he asked. 'Handing out adverts along the beach?'

'Can't say I did, no,' replied Baz, looking genuinely surprised. 'It's not how I'd choose to spend my free time.'

'Does she have any money worries that you know of?'

Baz shook his head. 'No, but she wouldn't be any different from the rest of us if she did. I don't have much left at the end of the week myself. Mind you, Nat earns more than me.'

'Oh? How come?'

'Well, the girls always do better at selling excursions, don't they?' Baz frowned. 'And she could charm the bees from the trees could Nat. Quick flutter of the eyelashes and boom! It's unfair, but what can you do? Don't bother me so much but you wanna hear Ross on the subject!'

'And you earn commission on each one you sell?'

'Ten per cent off the top.'

Tony glanced around the small lounge as Baz prepared himself a coffee. It was identical to the apartment next door, home to Natalie and Ross, in layout and furnishings, and just as unkempt.

'So how long have you been a holiday rep?'

'This is my first season. Well, only season really. I'm on my gap year.'

'Where are you off to?'

'Manchester. I'm studying English Lit.'

'How was the Carnival in the end? Everything go off alright?'

'Not bad,' said Baz, carrying his coffee mug to the sofa and sitting down. 'Could've been better. There were loads of coppers along the Avenue so I suppose that killed the atmosphere a bit.'

Tony made a mental note to inform the Policia Nacional that their investigation into the murder of Leanne Piggott was impacting on the enjoyment of British bar-crawlers. Or rather not. He asked Baz a few more questions but learned nothing more than Marie had already told him. The only thing left to do was to head back to his own apartment and make the phone call to Natalie's parents back home in England. Tony had hoped to have something more positive to report to them but, equally, no news could be good news.

Natalie's mother was not, as Tony had feared, hysterical, but instead greeted the news of her daughter's apparent disappearance with indifference.

'She's done this before,' Geena Brooks explained. 'Whenever the fancy takes her, she's off. She must've ran away more than a dozen times when she was younger. In the end, I didn't even bother notifying the police. She always came home after a few days.'

Well, that was a development of sorts, Tony thought. And he would need to mention it to the officer he'd spoken to at the comisaría. Geena went on to tell Tony that she hadn't heard from Natalie in about two weeks, and, no, there wasn't a Mr. Brooks. Not that she cared about, anyway. Promising to keep her informed, Tony ended the call with Geena and considered his next step. If Natalie had form for this kind of behaviour, perhaps there was nothing sinister or disturbing in her disappearance after all. It was strange that she would choose to go when she did, dressed for a night on the town, especially as she had work duties the next day, but, from what Geena had said, Natalie and responsibility were not words you'd often use in the same sentence.

Tony left his apartment and made his way down to the bar. He found the heat draining and, though he hadn't yet been fully converted to the Spanish way of life in taking an afternoon nap, a cool drink would certainly be in order. Tony asked for a beer and, picking up an English newspaper from the counter, settled himself at a table in the corner.

'Busy day?'

'Very. I'm looking for a missing holiday rep.'

Dave poured Tony his drink and brought it over to the table with a bowl of crisps. He and Pat had been in Cieloventura for five years, and had run *Bar Loco* for nearly four. Tony had arranged his accommodation from England prior to leaving for Spain and, although he'd been concerned at the prospect of renting an apartment above a bar, and didn't anticipate staying there for long, he couldn't have been more wrong. It was more of a social club than a bar, a place where people could enjoy a chat over a drink instead of fighting to be heard over the tub-thumping music that seemed to emanate from the many other bars and clubs in town. Dave and Pat had proved very useful to Tony in his first week in Cieloventura, and had helped him sort out many of the problems he encountered; such as filling in the application for his *numero de identification de extrajeros* — an identification number for foreign residents. Dave was a former soldier with the Royal Anglican Regiment — a photograph of him in dress uniform hung proudly behind the bar — and had emigrated to the Costa Blanca after leaving the army. Tony didn't meet Pat until his second day in Cieloventura and had naturally assumed she was Dave's wife. That was something else he was wrong about.

'Any news on that poor lass?'

'Not that I know of.'

'I thought we'd left that kind of thing back in Britain.'

Dave gave the table a quick wipe around the glass and bowl and headed back to the bar. As Tony enjoyed the refreshing drink, he mulled over his next step. He still wanted to call Consuela and ask for her advice and, of course, he needed to phone Marie and let her know what was going on. In spite of what Geena had told him, however, Tony knew he wasn't going to let the matter lie. Natalie was still missing and, form or no form, he wouldn't be able to rest easily until he had found her, or at least knew she was safe and well. It was prophetic that his mobile phone would choose to ring at that moment.

'Mr. Heather? It's me, Marie.'

Tony stiffened slightly in his chair, clearly able to hear the urgency in the young woman's voice and the raised, angry voices in the background. 'What's happened? Are you okay?'

'Can you come over?'

'Of course. I'll be with you as soon as I can.'

Tony hung up and took one final drink from the glass. He said goodbye to Dave and started back at a brisk pace towards the apartments from where he had just came. It was at times like this he wished he had his own vehicle. Although leasing a car didn't appeal to him, especially as most of the places he needed to visit in the course of his job were within walking distance, he thought a moped or small motorcycle could be the answer. They were popular in the town and, though Tony didn't know whether he could trust himself on two wheels, he decided to look into it when he got a moment.

Struggling for breath and feeling the effects of the lactic acid building up in his calf muscles, Tony arrived at the *Holiday18* apartments within fifteen minutes, and could only manage to slowly walk, rather than run, up the stairs to the third floor. There he found Marie, Baz, and a second young man standing in the corridor.

'Here he is,' Baz remarked to the others.

'What's happened?'

Marie opened the door to Natalie and Ross's

apartment and led Tony inside. Despite the general state of untidiness, he could see at once that the lounge had been ransacked. Cupboard doors lay open, containers and boxes had been emptied, and the cushions on the sofa were upturned.

'Wait 'til I get my hands on the shits that did it!' shouted the second young man, who Tony assumed to be Ross. He made straight for Natalie's room. The dresser drawers were all open to varying degrees, some of their contents scattered around the floor, and the door to the bedside unit was ajar.

'Has anything been taken?'

'Ross's laptop is gone, and his PSP. And I think Natalie had some jewellery somewhere but I didn't want to start looking around for it.'

'You did the right thing. Look, why don't you all go next door? I'll phone the police and wait for them here.'

Marie nodded and, wiping a tear from the corner of her eye, went out to join her colleagues. Tony took out his phone and found Consuela's number on speed dial. She answered on the third ring and he quickly explained what had happened, including Natalie's disappearance and his investigations so far. Consuela told him that she and Rafá would get there as soon as they could — they were just finishing dealing with a minor incident along the Paseo de la Solana — and to make sure nothing was disturbed.

Tony took a long and careful look around the bedroom from his position just inside the door, trying to take everything in. Like any copper worth his salt, he held little stock in coincidence. Natalie Brooks was missing, and now her apartment had been burgled. The officer at the comisaría would also need to be informed but, for the moment, he was happy with the Policia Municipal being first on the scene. Tony had been to many burglaries in the course of his career and, while he didn't want to start jumping to conclusions, things just didn't seem right. And that gave him a horrible feeling in the pit of his stomach.

CHAPTER SIX

IGNORING the barrage of flash-bulbs and questions being fired at them, Inspector Jefe Chavarría guided John and Shelley Piggott out of the press conference to the relative sanctuary of the corridor. He hoped this hadn't been a waste of time, time he could precious afford to waste. The footage would be shown on the television news, but Chavarría doubted whether it would be seen by those who mattered; the tourists who were out clubbing on Thursday night. The morning papers would also carry the story, but he thought it unlikely that foreign holiday-makers would buy Spanish newspapers, and the British newspapers found in various shops throughout the town could be days old. It might be nearly a week or more before a copy filtered its way down into the hands of someone who may have seen something. Still, wheeling out the grief-stricken relatives and exposing them to the media frenzy seemed part of the job these days. Chavarría had explained to the assembled journalists and television news crews of the circumstances of Leanne's death, what they knew of her movements in her final hours, and asked if anyone able to assist in their enquiries could come forward as soon as possible. He then listened as John Piggott told the gathering what a beautiful daughter Leanne was, and how their hearts had been torn out by what had happened. Chavarría wasn't looking forward to broaching the subject of her drink and drug use the night of her death. How much suffering must they be forced to endure?

Shelley was too distraught to talk at the press conference, and the hesitation in her manner and the slowness of her movements convinced the Inspector Jefe she had been put on medication. Chavarría and Official Valle accompanied the Piggotts out to the car park, where they were driven off by the officer from the British Consulate. The family had moved out of the Solanis Resort to a private villa on the outskirts of the town, which had been offered to them for as long as they needed it by a local property developer. John had told Chavarría they would only be staying in the country for as long as necessary, as long as it took for Leanne's body to be released so they could take her home. The two police detectives waited until the car had driven away before breaking their silence.

'What would you like me to do now?' Valle asked. 'Another phone call to the town hall?'

'The Mayor will get his next update from the television news,' replied Chavarría. 'Right now, I want you to concentrate on finding the man Leanne was with.'

There had been over twenty officers from the Policia Nacional along the Avenida Del Puente the night before, assisted by a similar number drafted in from the Policia Municipal and the Guardia Civil, stopping people and showing them Leanne's photo. Apart from a few who said they may have seen her but couldn't be sure, all of which were being followed up, the results had been disappointing. They would all be out in force again tonight, and Chavarría was more confident. This time, the officers would be armed with an image from the CCTV footage of Leanne, rather than the photo taken by her father in the garden of the Solanis Resort, a photo that had been enlarged and hung on the wall behind the Piggotts throughout the duration of the press conference, as well as one of the young male in the football shirt.

Chavarría's visit to *Platinum* didn't throw up any new leads. No-one at the club had reported seeing Leanne, and there were no reports from the stewards or security staff on duty of any arguments or fights that may have involved her. There had been a number of incidents that night, as per any other night, all of which were recorded in a log. A fight between some Belgian and German tourists had been broken up just before midnight, two Scottish men had been thrown out at around two 'o' clock for 'inappropriate behaviour' towards a dancer, and a local man had been ejected into the hands of police officers for trying to sell pills, which he attempted to pass off to gullible clubbers as Ecstasy but, as he admitted under questioning, were actually only headache tablets. No-one had been thrown out of the club for either selling, buying, or smoking cannabis.

The doorman seen in the CCTV footage talking to Leanne and her companion was called into the club by the manager – he lived less than fifteen minutes away – but, even when shown the grainy images from the camera outside the entrance to the club, couldn't remember the couple from among the hundreds and hundreds of others he'd seen that night.

'If the male wore a Sunderland football shirt, it is likely he comes from that area. It is a city in the north-east of England.'

'That isn't necessarily so,' replied Valle. 'My nephews all wear Real Madrid shirts.'

Then your nephews are little glory-hunters, Chavarría thought but didn't dare say out loud. He often saw people, usually youngsters, wearing Madrid or Barcelona shirts and wondered whether how many of them had been to those cities, let alone watched a match. Chavarría realised there was actually nothing about football that he disliked, just footballers and football supporters. If it wasn't for either of those, he might find it quite enjoyable. 'According to Emily Johnson, and she knows her football, Sunderland is not a very fashionable or successful club. Not likely to attract many supporters from outside of the city. Not like Manchester United.'

'Yes, my nephews have those too.'

Chavarría was again forced to bite his lip. 'Now, there are only two or three flights a day to Alicante from Newcastle, which Emily says is the nearest airport to Sunderland. It's about twenty miles away. I want all the flight lists checked, go back at least a week at first, for men aged between eighteen and twenty-five who are staying in Cieloventura. Check their home addresses with their travel companies and prepare a list of all those with a Sunderland address. If we need to, we can cast the net wider.'

'As far as Newcastle?'

'According to Emily, men from Newcastle would not be seen dead in a Sunderland shirt,' Chavarría replied. 'Local rivalry.'

'I'll get onto it right away.'

With Valle and several other officers busily chasing up and cross-matching flight and accommodation records from airlines and holiday companies, and Banda painstakingly watching the surveillance camera footage from Wednesday night, Chavarría turned his attention to the belongings Leanne had with her when she died. They had recently been returned from the police lab, each item in its own individually labelled clear plastic bag. There was a small handbag covered in silver sequins, a gold neck-chain, gold stud earrings, a bangle, and three rings. The contents of the handbag were also in separate plastic bags; a tube of mints, a packet of tissues, a purse containing a €10 note and €3.55 in coins, a mobile phone, and a plastic key card with the logo of the Solanis Resort on it. The phone had been checked but no calls were made either to or from it since the Piggotts arrived in Cieloventura. According to John, Leanne would never be parted from her phone, even if she couldn't use it in another country, as she relied on it to tell the time. Chavarría picked up the bag containing the bangle and looked at it closely. It was made of blue coral and had gold hand-painted edging. He guessed it was a recent acquisition. There were several stalls in the indoor market that sold such items. Chavarría remarked to himself how small the bangle was, and how slight Leanne was to have placed it on one of her wrists, but she was just a child after all. *One of her wrists*. He hurried across the room.

'Get those images up again,' he said to Banda. 'The ones of Leanne Piggott entering and leaving Platinum.'

Luís Banda quickly restored the two pieces of footage to the computer screen. Chavarría leaned across the desk and looked at them closely.

'Her wrists, you see…'

'What is that? A bracelet?'

The Inspector Jefe showed the plastic bag to Banda. 'A coral bangle.'

'Did she have two of them?'

'Just the one. Where are the crime scene photos?'

Banda left his chair and collected a cardboard folder from a nearby table. Chavarría took the folder from him and quickly flicked through the large photos until he found one that fitted his purpose. It showed a section of Leanne's midriff and her arms lying by her side. The bangle could be seen on her lower right forearm. Both men looked at the photo, and then at the computer screen.

'It's on her right wrist when she goes into Platinum,' said Banda, 'on her left when she leaves, and then back on her right when she was killed. Why did she keep moving it?'

'I don't think she did.'

With just a slight detour to scoop up his car keys from the corner of his desk, Chavarría made for the door.

'You don't think it was a burglary?'

'Oh, it was a burglary, and I think whoever did it knew what they were looking for.'

Tony and Consuela stood by the side of the police patrol car, a two year old blue-and-white Renault Megane, outside the entrance to the shabby apartment block. Nearby, Rafá was talking to a ground-floor resident of the building through an open window. Although their conversation had started politely enough, a general enquiry as to whether anyone suspicious had been in the area, the officer was now in the process of being berated about changes in local traffic regulations.

'Then why was the place so messed up? He, or she, must have searched everywhere?'

'I've been to many burglaries, and there's always a *pattern* to the mess,' said Tony. 'You see, most people's idea of the scene of a burglary is one of general disarray, so if someone wants to make a place look like it had been burgled, they empty cupboards and drawers, throw things across the room, turn the place upside down. But, in my experience, it's not often like that. Professional burglars move quickly, they target specific areas. Every second wasted is a second closer to being caught. How many burglaries have you been to where the chairs have been turned over? Magazines and newspapers thrown across the room?'

With such crimes being more in the remit of the Policia Nacional, Consuela had only been to a small number of house-breakings, but she could see the sense in what Tony was saying. She could recall several occasions where people had arrived home and not been aware they had been burgled until they had cause to go into the bedroom or wherever their valuables had been kept.

'But we may not be dealing with professionals, Tony.'

'Oh, if the place had been broken into, I don't know, by teenagers doing it for kicks, or a drug addict looking to steal anything he could sell, then maybe it would end up looking like that, but this wasn't an opportunistic crime. The lock's been forced and there's no damage to any of the others in the building, even on the ground-floor.'

'So you think the apartment was targeted for a specific reason, and Ross's possessions were taken to make it look like a normal burglary?'

Tony nodded. 'It's my guess they've been dumped nearby. Is there any chance of an organised search?'

Consuela blew out her cheeks. They both knew the resources of the Policia Nacional were stretched, and it was unlikely that the Superintendent of the Policia Municipal would allocate a number of his officers to take on the task.

Upon arriving at the apartment, Consuela and Rafá had taken immediate steps to secure the scene and begin the investigation. While Rafá took a statement from Ross, who had discovered the burglary when he and Marie returned from a *Holiday18* boat trip along the coast, Consuela made a brief examination of the apartment. Concerned by the possible connection to a missing person enquiry, she referred the matter to the Policia Nacional and called in a photographer and forensic team. She also left a message for the officer at the comisaría who had dealt with Tony and Marie's initial report about Natalie Brooks.

It took less than a quarter of an hour for a uniformed Agente of the Policia Nacional to arrive and take charge of the investigation. Under his supervision, Ross and Marie had gone through the apartment carefully to compile a list of what had been stolen. Ross added about €60 in cash and a waterproof diving watch to the items he had already mentioned, and Natalie's jewellery, which, according to Marie, was mainly the cheap and cheerful variety, could not be located anywhere. There was nothing else that, to Ross or Marie's eyes, appeared to be missing.

'If the Policia Nacional feel this is linked to Natalie's disappearance, they may wish to organise a search of the area,' Consuela said, 'but I cannot see many officers being diverted from the Leanne Piggott investigation.'

Although Tony understood the reality of the situation, it didn't prevent him from feeling frustrated. Natalie and Ross's apartment had been deliberately targeted, there was simply no doubt about that. There were far easier pickings for an opportunist thief than a third-floor apartment.

'I'm really worried about this girl, Consuela. She's been gone for nearly two days. There must be a connection.'

A voice suddenly came through on Consuela's radio

and she moved away from the car to respond to it. She and Rafá had already received orders to leave the matter to the Policia Nacional and to return to their patrol along the Paseo de la Solana, and Consuela had only delayed doing so to listen to Tony's thoughts regarding the burglary.

'I'm sorry, but we really need to go,' she said, waving to attract Rafá's attention. The officer apologised to the ground floor resident for having to cut their conversation short and, smiling gratefully at Consuela, headed back to the car. 'If you like, I will follow up on the forensic report and let you know what they find.'

'I'd be very grateful, Consuela. Thank you.'

'Can we give you a ride anywhere?'

'Could you drop me close to the town square? That would be great.'

During the short ride back into the centre of Cieloventura, several questions ran through Tony's mind. What could the thief, or thieves, have been looking for? He cursed his inability to remember many details about Natalie's bedroom from his previous visit earlier that morning, and wished he had more diligent in his search. Tony told himself, however, that there was little that gave him rise for such concern at that point, and he had been reluctant to rummage through her personal possessions. Natalie's passport had been located by the Agente in her bedroom, so that at least was not what the thief was after. And when could the burglary have taken place? Ross left the apartment at nine 'o' clock that morning to attend to his duties for the day, and returned at three to discover the burglary. Baz, the only rep who had the day off, reported hearing no noises at all from next door, and the walls, he said, were so thin they could even all hear when their neighbour visited the bathroom. Baz had actually expressed it in slightly more colourful terms, which Consuela had been too embarrassed to translate verbatim for benefit of the Agente, who only spoke Spanish. The rep did admit to being asleep until at least one 'o' clock, so the apartment must have been visited sometime between half eleven in the morning, when Tony and Marie had left, and one in the afternoon.

There was one potentially important lead that Tony wanted to follow up. A number of the guests on the boat trip that day were not travelling with *Holiday18*, and many of them, according to Marie, had purchased their tickets from Natalie some time on Thursday evening. It was company policy, Tony was told, that any tickets for excursions and day trips that remained unsold forty-eight hours before the event could be sold by the reps to other holiday-makers. There were nearly thirty spaces available on the boat come Thursday afternoon, so Natalie, Simon, Marie and Mel had divided the spare tickets between them before heading out that evening. Marie and Mel sold around half their allocation, whereas Simon failed to sell any. Going by the number of extra trippers who arrived at the quayside for the eleven 'o' clock departure, Marie told Tony that Natalie must have sold all of hers. What was it Baz had said to him earlier? Natalie could charm the bees from the trees. If she was indeed short of money, he thought Natalie would do all she could to sell every ticket and earn maximum commission.

Marie had shown Tony a list of all the people on the boat trip, and indicated which ones she believed had been sold their tickets by Natalie. All guests on the boat who weren't travelling with *Holiday18* had to bring their passport with them for identification, something that was clearly stated on the reverse of the ticket. There had been an incident two summers before, which had made headline news in several British tabloids, where a number of guests on a *Holiday18* boat trip had had drunken sex while others looked on and took photos. It later turned out that several of those present were under eighteen and, since then, the company insisted that proof of age must be provided. The *Holiday18* boat trips still had a reputation for drunkenness and nudity but, Marie had stressed, no sexual activity of any kind took place.

At the side of the list of names were the hotels or apartments in Cieloventura where they were staying. Tony made a note of all those he wanted to talk to. He wanted to find out exactly where and when they had bought their tickets. Ideally, there would be one or two who had purchased them after the last reported sighting of Natalie on Thursday night by Marie, which would help to pinpoint where she had gone after she was last seen.

After being dropped off a short walk from the town square, Tony made for the offices of the Policia Municipal to check whether any new incidents, apart from the burglary, had been reported that may have involved Natalie Brooks. As he expected, there was nothing and so, feeling hungry, made for The Green Dragon. While Tony preferred to cook his own evening meal, there was little food in the apartment and he didn't want to waste any time in tracking down those on the *Holiday18* boat trip that had bought their tickets from Natalie. Tony thought they would probably all be heading out for a night on the town and, although it was only half past five, he wanted to try and catch as many as he could that evening, or else he would be forced to leave it until tomorrow.

Tony wolfed down his salad and burger with such haste than Karen recommended his next port of call ought to be the *farmacia* for some indigestion tablets, and then set off for the first hotel on the list. Showing his card to the receptionist, Tony was given the room number he wanted. There, he found two young men who had been on the boat trip. Jamie Bend and Grant Smith were twenty year old friends from Portsmouth who, having recovered from the excesses of the trip with a two hour nap and a shower, were starting the process of preening themselves for their evening out. They recognised Natalie as soon as Tony showed them her photograph.

'Yeah, she's the one we bought the tickets off,' said Jamie. 'It's not the kind of thing we'd normally do, but she caught us when we were a bit non compos mentis.'

'Yeah, an' cos you fancied 'er!' laughed Grant.

'Maybe, yeah. She said she was gonna be on the

trip, but she weren't. Pity, I was gonna try my luck.'

'Could you tell me where you bought the tickets?' asked Tony.

'Er, it was along the Avenue somewhere. We had a few jars in that British bar on the corner, the one with Elvis Presley singing in it, and then went on to Platinum.'

Tony smiled. Tribute acts, of varying quality, were a common sight in the bars and cabaret clubs through the town. He had seen only one himself, and the experience of a chubby, middle-aged Freddie Mercury squeezed into a spandex body-suit would take some getting over.

'And what time would this have been?'

''Bout elevenish, I'd say.'

'Did you see her at any other time that night?'

Both of the young men shook their heads. Marie had last seen Natalie at just before one 'o' clock in the morning, so this information didn't help. Tony wished the men a pleasant night and, hoping he would have better luck elsewhere, headed to the next hotel on his list.

On his previous visit to the Solanis Resort, little more than three hours before, Inspector Jefe Chavarría had been met with a request from John Piggott for the family to be allowed to move to different accommodation. Staying in the suite was proving difficult for them and, though the atmosphere around the complex had been muted since news of Leanne's death, the sound of children playing around the pool and in the gardens beneath their balcony was torture to their ears. They just needed some peace, John had said, some time alone to start to come to terms as a family with what had happened. Chavarría thought it was a good idea, but had insisted that, with the exception of their clothing, the rooms remained as they were. Although he didn't feel the suite was connected to the girl's death, Leanne's personal possessions were his only tangible link to her life.

Chavarría entered the suite and made straight for the bedroom Leanne shared with her younger brother. He searched the drawers of the chest thoroughly before moving onto the wardrobe and the bedside cabinet. Nothing. He reached under the bed for the pink holdall and tipped the contents out onto the bed. Chavarría knew it couldn't be there from his previous search, but needed to satisfy his own curiosity. It wasn't there.

The Inspector Jefe moved back out into the lounge and rummaged through the various drawers and cupboards. Although officers had already made a full search of the suite, they hadn't known what they were looking for. Chavarría didn't know what relevance it had to Leanne's death, but there was an inconsistency between the surveillance cameras outside the entrance to *Platinum* and the crime scene photos, and he didn't like inconsistencies.

Chavarría left the suite empty-handed and made his way out of the complex. A uniformed police presence remained in the reception area, and interviews with guests were still being conducted. Only one had so far reported anything of note. An elderly man called Sidney Mack had awoken early on Thursday morning, just after five, and, troubled by cramp, had decided to take a short walk. As he left the resort, he passed Leanne, who was on her way in. At the time, Mr. Mack said he didn't think anything of it. 'Young people come in at all hours these days', he had said to the officer who took his statement, and he hadn't realised Leanne was only fourteen years old until he'd heard someone mention it by the pool sometime on Friday afternoon. Mr. Mack's description of the girl's clothing matched what she wore the next night and, while the information provided no new leads, it at least completed another small piece of the jigsaw. They knew from Todd Piggott that Leanne had gone out late on Wednesday night, but hadn't known what she time she returned. The night receptionist had been reading a book in the small office behind the desk, and the CCTV cameras covered only the small car park and not the entrance to the building. Mr. Mack said Leanne was alone, and he saw no-one either outside the Solanis or on his brief walk that attracted his attention.

News of the Piggotts' move had soon reached the assembled media outside and the car park and gardens at the front of the building now looked like a car park and gardens once more, and not home to a swarm of journalists and a collection of television broadcast vans. No doubt they would soon find out the family's new address and decamp there, but the British Consulate official said the property had a walled perimeter and the villa itself couldn't be seen from the road.

Chavarría hoped soon to be in a position to tell the Piggotts' that Leanne's body could be released and they could make arrangements to take her home, but that wouldn't be his decision. With officers out in force this evening along the Avenida del Puente and the Paseo de la Solana, and Valle and several others busy compiling a list of possible names for the young man seen on the CCTV footage with Leanne, Chavarría was hopeful there would soon be a breakthrough. He wondered whether he should head home for the evening. Perhaps Isabel had returned. He wasn't in the mood for another argument, that was for sure, but he wanted to talk to her about Terésa. Chavarría climbed into the car and took out his phone. He scrolled down the list of numbers on the display and, selecting *Casa*, raised the phone to his ear. Chavarría listened to the ringing signal for a short time before cancelling the call. She wasn't there. And he didn't want to return to an empty house. It was only at that moment that Chavarría realised he didn't know which friend Isabel had run too, and her own mobile phone had been left behind when she stormed out. He had seen it on the breakfast bar when he left for his conference on Friday morning.

How could they have let things reach such a point? With Terésa at an age where she increasingly wanted to do her own thing, they were all leading virtually separate lives. The Piggotts, in comparison, seemed such a close family, and did practically everything together. But had that really been any better? Leanne, rightly or wrongly, felt she was being suffocated, and he wondered, for all their apparent closeness, just how well John and Shelley had known their daughter.

Chavarría turned the key in the ignition and set off back to the comisaría. The sofa in the office would continue to suffice. While he didn't like the extra pressures placed on him by the town hall and the media, that coming from Juez Sandoval – the examining magistrate in overall charge of the investigation - was enough, things were progressing as well as could be expected. Valle had told him the Mayor was demanding a result as soon as possible, and was even due to appear on a live satellite link-up with SKY News in the UK later that night to assure the British people that all was being done to catch Leanne's killer, and that the crime rate in the Costa Blanca, and particularly Cieloventura, was relatively low and remained a safe tourist destination.

Another important line of enquiry Chavarría had initiated was to talk to some of Leanne's friends back home. He wouldn't be doing that job himself, that was currently being undertaken by officers of the Cheshire Constabulary. He'd had one version of Leanne from her parents, now he wanted the other version.

As Chavarría pulled the car out into the traffic on Calle De San Antonio, he glanced at his watch. It was nearly half past six but, for a town like Cieloventura, the day was just getting started,

'We're just on our way out, mate.'

'This won't take long. I just need a minute of your time.'

The young man stood aside and gestured for Tony to enter the small hotel room. This was the final address on his list, and he hadn't had much fortune elsewhere. Two hotels had no record of people staying there with the names he'd provided, which he was puzzled by, there was no answer at a third, and the three guests on the boat trip he had managed to trace had all bought their tickets from Natalie between ten-thirty and midnight. As Tony entered the room, he saw a young woman sitting on the edge of the bed. To his initial surprise, she appeared to be miming playing the piano, her long and dexterous fingers moving up and down with speed. He then realised she was trying to dry her nails.

'I understand you both went on a Holiday18 boat trip this afternoon?'

'Yeah, that's right,' said Stuart Miller. 'Had a blindin' time an' all. We were gonna come wi' them in the first place, but it worked out a bit cheaper to book the flights an' accommodation on the internet ourselves.'

'When did you buy the tickets?'

'For the boat trip? Thursday night.'

'What time would this have been?'

'Oh, it must've been quite late. We were just leavin' to come back. I'd say about half one-ish, I reckon.'

Although Tony felt the tingle of excitement run up his spine, he made sure his expression remained unchanged. The years he had spent in the force had taught him not to visibly react to any information he was given, whether good or bad. Often, people were happy to talk to the police about things of no consequence, but as soon as they thought what they were saying could be valuable, they tended to either clam up or make the interviewer work even harder for it. Tony had learned that eye contact, a polite nod, and what was referred to in one of his handbooks as 'facilitated grunting' was all that was necessary to encourage a person to continue talking.

'We got back just after two. So, yeah, it must've been about half one, I'd say. Can't be any more precise than that.'

Tony produced the photograph of Natalie and showed it to the man. 'Is this the girl you bought the tickets from?'

'Yeah, that's her. Gave us a good deal an' all. We got 'em both for, what, twenty-five quid?'

Stuart looked around at his girlfriend for confirmation. Blowing gently on her freshly-painted nails, she nodded.

'Where did you buy them?'

'Just some club.'

'You recall its name?'

The man slowly shook his head. 'No, don't think so. We went with some mates we made, a couple from Liverpool. They'd been there before. Reckoned they played some bangin' stuff.'

'And where are these friends of yours staying?'

'Oh, they've gone home, mate. Went this morning.'

'Can you describe the club to me?'

'There was a logo outside,' Stuart said after a moment's thought. 'You know, one of those neon ones. It was white. Some sort of . . .'

The man twirled his index finger in the air. Tony reached into his back pocket and produced the promotional leaflet he had been given by Donnie Lane. He held it up and pointed to the graphic in the centre. It was a column of twisting wind, like a small tornado, with its tail-end forming a distinct letter 'B'.

'Like this?'

'Yeah, that's the one.'

'You've been a great help,' said Tony. 'Have a very good evening now.'

Tony left the hotel room and, after a moment to gather his thoughts, made his way back to the stairs. Though he had succeeded in finding a confirmed sighting of Natalie after the time she had last been seen by Marie, he hadn't been expecting that. Donnie Lane had lied. Natalie Brooks had been to *Breeze* after all.

CHAPTER SEVEN

CARRER DE TRATO had always been a hive of activity in Cieloventura. In the days when the town was a thriving fishing community, the street was where the fishermen and merchants met to barter their goods and make their living. Now, in the evenings, with tourism long having overcome fishing as the main industry, the pedestrianised area joining the town square to the Paseo de la Solana was bustling with a variety of street entertainers, such as jugglers and fire-eaters, competing for pavement space with vendors selling hot crêpes and waffles. Tony had become seriously addicted to waffles with lashings of thick chocolate sauce and sliced strawberries, and knew they would need to be the first thing to go when his new fitness regime kicked in. There were also stalls selling curios carved from driftwood, people braiding hair or doing henna tattoos, and artists creating classical cameos or caricatures of tourists, the latter of which would normally induce roars of laughter from those able to see the picture as it was being drawn, much to the embarrassment of the subject who was forced to sit motionless on the other side of the easel when the artist went about his craft.

The restaurants along the Paseo de la Solana were also buzzing with life. Families chatted and laughed, and couples gazed across the candle-light into each others' eyes, as waiters and waitresses ferried trays of food between kitchens and tables with remarkable balance and fleetness of foot. Tony had only eaten once in a restaurant along the promenade since his arrival in Cieloventura, and had vowed not to do so again. Not on his own, at least. Eating alone in a restaurant was an awkward experience. In a café or bar, he could banter with others, listen to the music or television that was usually playing in the background, even read a book. In a restaurant, you were never just eating alone. You were lonely.

Tony often felt the pangs of loneliness. The end of a marriage brought so much more with it than just the end of a relationship between two people. He felt it right that Lucy should stay with Helen, and that they should remain in the family home. Even though it was Helen who had initiated the break-up, and subsequent divorce proceedings, Tony thought he should be the one to leave. The split would have enough of an effect on their daughter without the added stresses and upheaval of moving house, and possibly even school. Friends they had made as a couple had also largely burned their bridges with him. Invitations to dinner parties or birthday and anniversary celebrations, which he and Helen would have attended together, no longer came. Tony knew there was no malice in it, he was just a victim of circumstances. 'Sorry, but it's just really awkward,' one of his friends had said to him. 'It's not that we want to take sides or anything.'

By ten 'o' clock, the families were largely absent

from the centre of town, and the nightclub crowd had taken over. Tony had spoken to several of the Policia Municipal officers he recognised as he made his way along the Avenue, and had been shown the images from the surveillance cameras of Leanne Piggott and her male companion. Strange how she looked older in the photos, Tony thought. There was little wonder that the girl hadn't stood out, and that so few people could recall seeing her, as the officers had indicated to him. Tony thought Leanne looked no different than the hundreds of other young women along the Avenue, queuing up outside clubs, drinking in bars, and generally making the most of every precious minute away from work and home.

On his previous visit to *Breeze* earlier in the day, Tony had noticed a small Irish bar opposite. Now settled there at a table by the window, he looked out towards the entrance to the club. There was no queue outside, unlike some of the more popular venues in the town, such as *Platinum* and *La Vida Grande*, but, in the hour he'd been sitting there, there had been a steady trickle of young clubbers go inside.

Tony had not yet received a call from Donnie Lane regarding his doormen, and whether they remembered seeing Natalie Brooks on Thursday night, as he had promised. Tony wasn't surprised about that and, even if the call came, he could hazard a fair guess as to what the answer would be. He wondered why Donnie Lane had lied to him. Natalie had been in *Breeze* on Thursday night — or rather the early hours of Friday morning — selling tickets for the *Holiday18* boat trip. What did he have to hide? Tony was tempted by the idea of heading on over to the club and challenging Donnie with his new information, but thought better of it. He had decided to go to the comisaría first thing in the morning and talk to the officers there. Being a Sunday, however, he wasn't sure what response he would receive. Tony knew from experience that investigations on a Sunday, particularly those involving commercial premises, could be hindered, but in a holiday resort like Cieloventura, where most businesses were open every single day, he didn't think there would be a problem. With the targeted burglary of Natalie's apartment, and now evidence that someone hadn't told the truth about where and when she had last been seen, Tony was confident the Policia Nacional would launch a full investigation. However, he also had an alternative plan in mind should he not get the response he felt the matter merited. It would mean being a touch devious, but that didn't trouble Tony. He was determined to get to the bottom of it.

Tony drained his glass and signalled to the barman for another, his third of the night. He had never been much of a drinker, not beer anyway, but in the friendly atmosphere of the Irish bar, Tony found himself relaxing. It had been a long day, perhaps the busiest since his arrival, and it had come at the end of a long week. With the Policia Nacional taking a far greater role in the search for Natalie – and he knew they could do more than he, as an individual, ever could – Tony thought he would be able to take some time tomorrow for himself. Come Monday morning, he would be busy with his official duties and didn't know how much time he would be able to devote to the search for Natalie. Until that point, however, Tony resolved to do everything he could.

Whatever developments tomorrow brought, Tony knew he would need to keep out of the direct sun. Precautions to protect himself properly had been neglected again today and, stretching his facial muscles in a number of different directions, he could feel the soreness of his skin. Tony's face was still bright red and there were signs that the skin, especially around his nose, was beginning to peel. Not leaving the apartment unless he wore a generous layer of sun cream would need to become habitual. He always knew it would take time to adapt into a different way of life, and the changes to his daily routine it would bring.

Tony was in his early thirties before he and the family had had their first holiday abroad, a week in Tenerife at an apartment part-owned by a work colleague of Helen's, and it was on that occasion that he first thought he'd like to retire somewhere sunny. He hadn't realised then that his career would be over within a decade, as would his marriage. The decision to leave the force had been a tough one to make. Tony could have stayed, or even moved sideways into a civilian post, but felt a clean break would be for the best. It may have been an unexpected turn of events that caused him to pack his bags and head for the Spanish coast, but it was a welcome one.

Life had certainly panned out very differently. Plans

and ambitions had been laid by the wayside, dreams crushed, and constants broken. Helen ending their marriage was perhaps the least surprising. She had nursed him through his recuperation but, as time passed, it was clear to both of them that love and affection was gradually replaced by duty and resentment. There wasn't anyone else. Well, not in the strictest sense. The question had to be asked, of course, but Tony wasn't surprised at the answer.

'There is someone I need to start paying more attention to,' Helen had told him. 'Someone whose life has been on hold for more than a year. Me.'

It wasn't a selfish attitude, Tony knew. Just the truth. Helen could always be relied on to tell him that. The relationship was fractured long before the incident and, if anything, it had probably kept the marriage together for longer than it may have lasted otherwise.

As Tony began his third and, he decided, last drink of the night, his attention was caught by a car pulling up outside the entrance to *Breeze*. From where he was sitting, Tony could see two men in the back of the vehicle, though the tinted windows made identification impossible. The men spoke together for a few moments before the far-side door opened and Donnie Lane stepped out onto the pavement. He was dressed a lot smarter than when Tony saw him before, in a light-coloured cotton suit and a white shirt opened midway down his chest, and looked much more the manager of a nightclub than previously, when he could easily have passed for the potman.

A chuckling Donnie waved goodbye to his

companion and, after one brief final exchange, closed the car door. The silver saloon then pulled away from the kerb and made off along the narrow street. As it passed the window of the Irish bar, Tony hoped to get a clearer look at the man sitting in the back but was without success. The driver, however, could more easily be seen through the untinted front windscreen. He was in his fifties, Tony guessed, with a thick neck and closely-cropped greying hair. He wasn't dressed like a typical chauffeur, and his shirt sleeves were rolled up to his elbows to reveal two forearms covered in extensive tattooing. As the car passed from his range of vision, Tony turned his attention back to *Breeze* just in time to see Donnie disappear into the club. The doorman, a heavily-built man of North African descent, re-attached the small length of rope across the entrance and took his position, hands crossed in front of him, back at the side of the door.

There weren't any security cameras outside the entrance to *Breeze*, not overtly anyway, and Tony couldn't recall seeing any inside the small reception area when he was there earlier in the day. The nearest street camera was on the corner of Calle Veijo, where the club was located, and the Avenue, some fifty yards away. It seemed to be a fixed camera, from what he could tell, and was pointing along the Avenue rather than along Calle Veijo, so the footage wouldn't be of any use.

Tony went over his conversation with Donnie in his mind. If the interview had been conducted when he was a police officer, Tony would have been able to refresh his recollection from his notes, which he would take profusely and accurately. Now he would have to rely on memory alone, and that had never been quite the same since his injuries. Tony realised that Donnie hadn't actually *said* that Natalie wasn't at the club on Thursday night, just that he hadn't *seen* her there. It was a typical non-committal answer that Tony had been given many times in his career, neither one thing nor the other, the response of someone who was used to dealing with, or rather fending off, enquiries from the police.

Tony finished his beer and began a slow walk back to his apartment, the cool night air helping to ward off any adverse effects of the alcohol. He hadn't known what he hoped to achieve by spending part of the evening in the Irish bar but, for some reason, had felt drawn to *Breeze* since speaking to Stuart Miller and his girlfriend earlier in the evening.

The journey to Calle Neuva took little over twenty minutes. Stopping only to chat briefly to Dave and Pat, Tony headed through *Bar Loco* and made his way up the rear stairs to his apartment. He didn't know how much sleep he was likely to get, especially if his neighbours were spending their Saturday night out on the town, so he took a quick shower and headed straight for bed. The apartment consisted of two identical sized rooms, one overlooking the street at the front of the building and the other the alley at the rear, separated by a narrow hall, from which a small bathroom and kitchen, as well as the stairs, led off. The front room had originally been the bedroom, but after several nights disturbed by occasional traffic noise and tourists laughing and singing as they made their way to and from the town's nightlife, Tony had spent a busy evening exchanging the furniture between the two rooms. Although the room at the rear received most of the natural sunlight during the day, hence its original choice as the lounge, Tony preferred the shade of the front room. Besides which, he rarely found himself in his apartment during the daytime, and remembered with some amusement the concerns he had had about renting it in the first place. Tony thought he might find the apartment a little cramped compared to the family home back in Aylesbury only to discover, if anything, that it was more than enough for him. Still, it would be worth it if he was able to persuade Helen to let Lucy come out for a week. The sofa in the lounge unfolded into a double bed, which he would take, so Lucy could have the bedroom. Tony decided to send an e-mail to Helen some time tomorrow. Talking to Lucy about it first would no doubt cause a row and he wanted to avoid that. In spite of her wanting to end the marriage and move on with her life, Helen had not exactly been overjoyed when Tony told her of his plans to take a job in Spain. She had accused him of failing in his duties as a father, something which cut him deeply, and though she had later apologised, their communications since had been short and a little brusque. Maybe even Helen herself could come out. Tony reined in his thoughts before they took a life of their own and, kicking off the single sheet that covered his body, tossed and turned in the bed to try and get more comfortable.

He thought being an air steward would be a really interesting job, and had even considered trying for it himself once, but his mates had soon put the kibosh on that. 'It's a job for poofs, you muppet!' Not just that, but the steward standing just in front of him, performing the safety instructions for the benefit of the passengers, looked bored out of his head. Although it was only his second time on an aeroplane, the young man frowned in frustration at the monotonic voice of the chief stewardess coming over the PA system.

'In the event of an emergency on board, we ask all passengers...'

He wondered what was taking so long. Inefficient bloody Spanish airports, he cursed. They hadn't stayed this long at the gate back home. The young man turned his attention out of the small window and gazed across the runway. The sun beating down from above and the hot tarmac combined to produce a shimmering effect in the distance that held his concentration. It was another scorching day, and he wondered where else he would be right now. The beach maybe. Or around a pool. The one at Hotel Mar Azul wasn't anything to write home about, but the pool at the Solanis was fantastic. Not that he would ever have gone back there. Not after what had happened.

The young man flinched slightly as someone sat down in the seat next to him. He cursed his luck, having hoped it would remain empty for the duration of the flight home. Then he could've spread out a bit and been more comfortable. How they expected people to relax and enjoy the flight when they were cramped in like sardines, he would never know.

'In the unlikely event of loss of cabin pressure, the …'

The person sitting next to him was looking at him. He could sense it. He continued staring out of the window, determined not to give in and glance around. Eventually, though, he could stand it no longer and turned to meet the person's gaze. The man looked Spanish, he thought, and was maybe as old as his Dad. Going grey as well. That was like his Dad too, but this bloke, whoever he was, hadn't yet turned to the dye bottle to conceal it.

The man smiled and reached into his jacket pocket for his wallet. He opened it out in front of him to reveal a badge and an identification card.

'Good morning,' said the man. 'I am Inspector Jefe Roman Lopez Chavarría from the Policia Nacional.'

'Thank you for your attention, and we hope you have a pleasant journey with us today.'

'And I am arresting you for the murder of Leanne Piggott.'

Tony drummed his fingers on the arm-rest of the chair and glanced for the fifth time at his wrist-watch. Unlike his last visit to the comisaría, with Marie Reynolds, he had not telephoned in advance and was now waiting in line for an appropriate officer and interpreter to be available. Being a Sunday morning made things worse. The whole town seemed to be on a go-slow, Tony had remarked to himself, as he walked from Calle Neuva to the comisaría. Most of the tourists were no doubt recovering from the night before, while the few locals he saw were either heading to church or enjoying the few restful hours where the town was their own again. The only people who seemed busy were the street cleaners efficiently cleansing the town of the detritus of a Saturday night; the discarded cans, broken bottles, junk food wrappers and a disturbing number of small pools of dried vomit. The ringing of the bells of Iglesia de Santa Matilde that accompanied Tony on his journey reminded him of his plans to attend a service one Sunday, which he had still yet to do. He had never been the religious type, but there was something about churches – particularly old churches – that he liked.

Eventually, an interpreter appeared in reception and asked Tony to come through. Shown into an interview room, he found a young Agente of the Policia Nacional waiting for him. The officer was different to the one Tony and Marie has spoke to on his previous visit, and so Tony found himself going over the original facts of Natalie's disappearance before moving onto the subsequent developments. He told him of the burglary of Natalie's apartment, the officer having details of the incident in front of him, and his opinion that it had been targeted and not an opportunist theft. Tony also told him of his visit to *Breeze* and his conversation with Donnie Lane, and his interview with Stuart Miller and his girlfriend. He felt the Agente was getting more interested as the meeting went on and, as it came to an end, he felt reassured that the Policia Nacional would now take important steps forward. Tony knew what measures he would take next if he was in charge of the investigation; a full search of the immediate vicinity of Natalie's apartment for the missing items, a check of Natalie's bank account and current financial status, and an official interview with Donnie Lane. But, of course, he wasn't.

Tony shook hands with the Agente and the interpreter and made his way out of the comisaría. He knew he needed to call Marie and let her know what was happening, but that would need to be left a while. If Saturday night for the *Holiday18* reps was as hectic as he thought it would be, she would certainly appreciate as long a lie-in as she could get. Tony glanced at his watch. Buses to El Marquesa on a Sunday were few and far between, but according to the timetable he looked at before leaving home, one was due to leave from the main station shortly. The idea of lunch and a glass of wine in the picturesque surroundings of the small village appealed to him, there was certainly nothing more to keep him in Cieloventura, and he could then take a leisurely stroll back along the coast. Some me time, he thought. At last.

Ryan Dinsdale looked down at the photograph placed in front of him and realised there was little point in denying it. It was so obvious it was him that such a blatant lie now wouldn't help to serve any real purpose. On the contrary, it would probably mean the lies, when they did start, would be even less likely to be believed. And he needed to be believed.

'Yeah,' he nodded. 'It's me.'

'We have searched your suitcase for these clothes, the ones you were wearing on Thursday night, and cannot locate them,' said Inspector Jefe Chavarría, tapping the centre of the photograph with the end of his pen. 'Can you tell us why this is the case?'

'They got ruined.'

'How?'

'Sick on 'em.'

'And so you…?'

'Chucked 'em.'

'You discarded them?' asked Official Valle, speaking for the first time since the interview began. She could sense how nervous the young man was, despite the passive expression on his face, and varying who asked the questions was important to keep him from relaxing too much. 'Where?'

'Dunno,' Ryan shrugged. 'Some skip somewhere.'

Chavarría reached into the folder in front of him and took out a second photograph, which he placed on top of the first. Ryan looked down at the grainy black and white image of him standing on the corner of Avenida Del Puente. He wasn't alone, but couldn't bring himself to look at the girl standing next to him. He just didn't want to see her.

'Tell me about your relationship with Leanne Piggott.'

'There weren't a relationship!' Ryan responded, a little startled by how loud his voice seemed in the small interview room. He took a moment to calm himself before continuing. 'I only took her out clubbin', that's all.'

'How did you met her?'

'I saw her along the Avenue on Wednesday night. She looked a bit lost, like, so I just got chattin' to her. We had a drink an' I asked her if she fancied comin' out wi' me.'

Chavarría nodded slightly, offering no sign that he was struggling to understand the young man's accent. No doubt it would be easier in Spanish, but conducting an interview via a third person would rob him of his most crucial information. A word here or an inconsistency there that may not survive translation intact, the flicker in a suspect's eyes, there one moment and gone the very next, when a question struck a nerve. No, he would persevere in English. And there was always Valle to step in if he was thrown, as she had done once already. Chucked 'em? What kind of English was that anyway? A more detailed interview would take place later, in Spanish, but Chavarría wanted to strike while the iron was hot. The British Consulate had already been informed of Ryan Dinsdale's arrest, and an official was said to be on his way. It would have been inappropriate for the Consular officer who had been with the Piggott family to attend, and there was no knowing how long it would take for someone to arrive. A glance out of his office window while Dinsdale was being booked in told the Inspector Jefe that word had already got out. The small number of reporters gathered outside the comisaría would soon swell, increasing the demands on him from all quarters. Chavarría had left a message for Juez Sandoval, informing him of the arrest, and then promptly switched the ringer off his phone. He would conduct the interview in his own way, without the guiding hand of the examining magistrate. And with Luís Banda and a search team dispatched to the Hotel Mar Azul, where Ryan Dinsdale had been staying, Chavarría was confident another important piece of the jigsaw would soon be in place. He told them what they were looking for, and just hoped they would be able to find it.

'Leanne was a little young to be going to a nightclub, was she not?'

'I never asked her age, did I?' Ryan shrugged. 'I just assumed she was over eigh'een, like.'

'Did you take drugs together?'

'No!'

'She had drugs in her system.'

'Well, it was nowt to do wi' me!'

'Had she made friends with anyone else in Cieloventura?'

'How would I know? Look, I don't know anythin' about the girl!'

Ryan closed his eyes momentarily and rebuked himself. Stop! Stop! Stop! He wasn't going to say anything more. Nothing. Fuck 'em. He'd already said far too much, and the so-called lawyer sat at his side seemed a complete waste of space. Foreigners! They're all the sodding same!

'But you do know she is dead,' said Chavarría, his voice barely above a whisper. 'Don't you?'

As their eyes locked across the table, Ryan was determined not to be the first to give way. He would win this one. He had to. It would tell the greasy sod something or two if he thought he was just going to roll over. Chavarría felt the vibration of the phone in his pocket and was content to give ground to Ryan Dinsdale in order to answer it. If it gave the young man any satisfaction, so be it. He knew he had him. The short and satisfying text message from Luís Banda told him that.

Living in a foreign country didn't mean changing your whole way of life. It was just about achieving the right balance between the past and the present, the familiar and the fresh. You didn't have to give up HP Sauce or Branston Pickle, or wanting to keep abreast of the latest developments from the Oval or Albert Square. Not if you didn't want to. That wasn't what mattered. It was about embracing the opportunities to grow and develop as a person that a new environment and culture brought. The same applied to tourism. At least those who spent their time entirely within the walls of all-inclusive resort hotels like the Solanis were escaping life back home for a while. Why some people came to the Costa just to sit in British-style cafés and bars all day, wolfing down bacon and eggs or pie and chips, watching SKY Sports and wondering what the weather was like back in England was mystifying to Tony. 'Brilliant in there!' one such holiday-maker, a middle-aged scaffolder from Romford, had said to Tony as they chatted outside a bar called The Kings Head. 'You wouldn't even know we were in Spain!' It was all Tony could do to offer a simple smile in response, hardly daring to let his true thoughts on the matter get a public airing.

He had also met a couple from Hastings who had cooked themselves a week's worth of evening meals – mainly casseroles – and brought them out in their suitcase in individually labelled Tupperware dishes. 'You never know where you are with foreign food,' they had said to Tony. Fools.

Then again, he knew the reason why. Of course he did. Most people didn't come to Spain because they wanted to visit Spain. They came for the sun and the beaches. And why not? Today was another beautiful day, and Tony wondered whether he would ever tire of it. The heat could be draining, he knew that. Dangerous too. A two-minute walk along Cieloventura's main beach was enough to spot dozens failing to heed the warning signs. It only made Tony despair when it was children, playing in the sand with little protection as their parents dozed off on nearby loungers. The heat certainly needed to be adapted to, but to tire of it? He hoped not.

Sat at a terrace table in a small restaurant overlooking the quayside, Tony gazed out onto the calm blue waters of the Mediterranean. A couple of trawlers bobbed gently on the horizon. The fish he'd enjoyed for his lunch, lightly grilled in a *romesco* sauce, had only come in with that morning's catch. From sea to plate in little over an hour. The few tourists that made the effort to visit El Marquesa were well rewarded for their trouble. The village was not served by the costal railway line – the scenic Costa Blanca

Express – that linked many of the towns and resorts from Alicante to Benidorm, including Cieloventura. With its narrow streets, lined with quaint houses ornamented with fine stonework and wrought-iron balconies, El Marquesa was a welcome contrast to the glitz and bustle of life in the major resort towns. Orange and almond groves nestled among small vineyards on the sloping hills behind the village and, as the vegetation changed slowly changed with increasing height, crops of olive and palm trees began to dot the land.

El Marquesa had not been totally spared from development, however. Tony could see several villas being constructed in the hillsides, but their design was sympathetic to the surroundings and they were not the blight on the landscape that could be said for some of the buildings along the coast in Cieloventura.

His phone rang. It was Consuela.

'I thought I would call you with the news, Tony. The Policia Nacional have made an arrest.'

'Has she been found? What's happened?'

'Found?'

'Natalie Brooks.'

'No, no, sorry. I'm talking about Leanne Piggott.'

Tony didn't chastise himself for the misunderstanding. It wasn't as though he'd abandoned all thoughts of poor Leanne. It was simply because there was nothing he was able to do. The police effort to find her killer was, as far as Tony could see, thorough and her family were no doubt being supported through this difficult time by the British

Consulate. And they needed all the help they could get.

Tony had glanced through a copy of a British Sunday tabloid in a shop he'd passed on his way to the bus station. Although a number of UK newspapers had Spanish print runs, there weren't too many places outside the larger hotels that went to the trouble and cost of having daily deliveries. And there weren't too many people who were willing to pay out the four or five Euros each one cost. Certainly not Tony.

A photograph of Leanne, apparently taken at a friend's BBQ several weeks before, adorned an inside page. It showed the girl swigging from a two-litre bottle of cheap cider while a similar-aged boy, his face concealed, groped under her T-shirt. The muck-raking had started. Even a fourteen year-old child was not immune to such treatment, it seemed. It would have been standard procedure for the Spanish police to request some assistance from the local force in Warrington, Leanne's home town, to obtain some background information from her peers. It seemed they'd been beaten to it by the press.

The article that accompanied the photo was short on facts but high on salacious gossip. Naming a 'close friend of Leanne' as the source, the story told of the girl's apparent fondness for getting drunk, an incident the summer before where she'd been cautioned for shop-lifting, and how a teacher at her school had been suspended pending an enquiry for sending her an 'inappropriate' text message. The article compared their photo of Leanne with the one shown to the assembled media at the press conference, with a salutary warning to parents about how well they thought they knew their children. Another source, one 'close to the investigation', also revealed that cannabis and alcohol had been found in Leanne's system.

Tony hoped the Piggott family were being protected from such distasteful reporting. The town of Cieloventura had not fared much better. The newspaper highlighted incidents of young tourists taking drugs openly in nightclubs, brawling with gangs of local youths, and shaming the reputation of Britain abroad with their drunken antics. There was also a pointless regurgitation of the story from two years before about sexual activity, encouraged by baying holiday reps, on an organised boat trip, though no mention was made of *Holiday18*. A photograph taken, according to the caption, late Friday night along the Avenue showed three inebriated young women baring their breasts for the camera. While the newspaper attributed the blame for such behaviour to failings in British society, rather than anything to do with Cieloventura itself, the Mayor's Office would not be pleased with such press. The charm offensive had already began. and it would now surely move into overdrive.

The town had its problems with a small percentage of tourists — Tony knew he wouldn't be here otherwise — but the image portrayed by such irresponsible reporting still made him fume. Isolated and rare incidents were being blown out of proportion. Since the election of the new Mayor, the town had taken significant steps to curb excessive behaviour and, though he said it himself, Tony's own presence in Cieloventura was beginning to have a positive effect. He had already been told by an official at the courthouse than the morning sessions were running a little smoother and quicker than in previous holiday seasons, and Tony hoped to build on these early successes.

Progress in the case would be an important step forward for all concerned, not least Leanne's family.

'They have someone?'

'Yes. It is another British tourist. The Mayor will be on television shortly to announce the charges.'

'Thank you for calling me, Consuela'

'You are welcome. Are you having a nice day?'

'Yes, thank you. Lunch in El Marquesa.'

'Ah, *bueno*.'

Tony could see a small television from where he sat, high on a shelf behind the restaurant bar. It showed a rolling news programme, rather than wall-to-wall sports like most bars and cafés, but it didn't matter. He wasn't going to stay and watch.

An arrest in itself didn't mean much, but if charges were being brought then the Policia Nacional must be confident they had their man. Tony was pleased. The sooner it was all over, the better. Cieloventura could return to normality, or as near to normality as it had been. The television news crews and journalists would decamp to the scene of the next tragedy to be dished up for public consumption, and those damaged by the awful events could begin the process of rebuilding their lives.

Tony settled his bill and headed for the quayside. The walk back to town would take a couple of hours, but he was in no hurry.

CHAPTER EIGHT

TONY made his way out of the town hall not knowing whether to celebrate or cry. His meeting with Mária Ocasio Cruz had gone well, and his plans for an information sheet about local policing had been approved. There were one or two amendments to the design that needed to be made, such as replacing the photos he had downloaded from the internet of various representatives of the Spanish police forces with official images supplied by the press office at the town hall, but that would take little extra effort. Tony had gone into the meeting armed with the agreement of three of the largest British tour operators in Cieloventura to place the sheet in their official welcome packs for holiday-makers, as well as displaying larger poster versions on notice boards in their hotels in the town.

Sra. Ocasio had also informed Tony that the Mayor himself had expressed an interest in publicly launching the campaign the following week. Although Tony felt this gesture was linked to the bad press the town had recently received, he considered it by no means a bad thing. It would give the campaign extra publicity and possibly result in more tour operators, hotels and apartment complexes joining in with the scheme. Tony had been quite buoyant in the meeting until Sra. Ocasio sought to prick his bubble. Arrangements had been made with the Solanis Resort to host the first of his planned talks on Spanish law enforcement, and he was told he needed to call in at the hotel by midday tomorrow with details of talk in order for it to be advertised around the complex.

Tony was dreading it. It wasn't simply a question of putting across the facts, it needed to be done in an interesting and, he hoped, entertaining way. Sra. Ocasio had told him that representatives from the Mayor's Office were to be there, as well as the local press. Maybe it wouldn't be such a good idea if it flopped after all.

It was important the event should be inclusive of all ages, reflecting the wide range of people who stayed at the Solanis, so Tony planned to ask Consuela and Rafá if they could attend in their official capacity, and maybe allow some of the children staying at the complex to have a short ride in their police car. He felt sure they would enjoy an hour or so away from patrolling the Paseo de la Solana. Tony was due to visit Rafá's for dinner that evening, and so would talk to him about it then. José had already told Tony that, somewhere in the bowels of the Policia Municipal offices, were remnants from a stall a couple of the Agentes had ran during a festival in the town a couple of years before; a box of badges, stickers and balloons. He promised to try and dig them out when a free moment presented itself.

As Tony made his way across the town square, he noted the television news crews gathered outside the entrance to the small courthouse. It was the first time he had seen such a large media gathering in the town since Sunday. It was Spanish law that a person accused of a crime must appear before the *Juez de Instrucción* — the examining magistrate in charge of the investigation — within seventy-two hours of their arrest. The officers in charge of the Leanne Piggott enquiry had clearly used every hour at their disposal to put their case together.

The accused was a nineteen year-old from Leechmere, near Sunderland, called Ryan Dinsdale, Tony knew. He had been arrested at Alicante's El Altat airport trying to board a flight home, and had refused to make any official statement to the investigating officers. At the hearing, Juez Pedro Sandoval Esparza — a distinguished-looking gentleman in his fifties — questioned Dinsdale about the evidence the Policia Nacional had presented to the court and invited him once more to make a statement. Again, the young man — through a translator — refused. The British reporters present had apparently roared with laughter as Dinsdale's rebuff, which had been stated in fruitful language of one syllable, was expressed by the embarrassed translator as 'I do not wish to make a statement at this time.'

The purpose of the hearing was not to look into the merits of the case, Tony knew, but an opportunity for the judge to examine the accused based on the evidence put before the court. Juez Sandoval concluded, to no-one's surprise, there was a case to answer and had instructed Dinsdale to be committed to prison pending further investigation.

As well as the translator, an official from the British Consulate was also present, along with a duty lawyer from the *Colegio de Abogado*, the Spanish Bar Association, as Dinsdale did not have sufficient funds to hire his own lawyer. It didn't matter at this stage. The lawyer was not there to defend him of the charges, but rather to ensure his rights were being protected.

Tony had not been present at the hearing. His business at the courthouse, sorting out the mess from the night before, had been concluded by eleven, and he needed to spend the time before the meeting at the town hall going over his proposals. There had only been four British tourists facing the force of the law that morning, all of whom had been arrested for public order offences along the Avenue. Their fines varied from €100 to €250, and all but one were paid. The remaining tourist — a twenty-five year old man — claimed he had no means to pay the fine, either cash or in the bank, and as he was due to fly home later that evening, the magistrates ordered he be accompanied back to his hotel by officers of the Policia Municipal to collect his belongings and passport, and then driven directly to the airport. The man protested, claiming he could spend the afternoon by the pool and not sat in the stifling departure lounge at El Altat for several extra hours, but his pleas fell on deaf ears.

Tony decided to make for The Green Dragon and, over a pot of tea, attempted to make some notes for the forthcoming talk. Public speaking had never been his strong point. He had done it before, addressing resident and tenant associations, neighbour watch groups, and paying occasional visits into schools. Community policing had never been on his list of career choices, his ambitions had lain firmly elsewhere, but he seemed to have a certain aptitude for it. The atmosphere at resident meetings could often be tense. It was usually when a local estate had been plagued with crime or anti-social behaviour that he found himself called upon to address such a gathering, and Tony would often find himself at the brunt of peoples' anger. Still, he had developed skills of diplomacy and mediation that had proven useful, and would no doubt do so again.

'What's happening to the lad that's up for that murder?' Karen asked as she passed by, carrying a tray of drinks destined for a young family sat at a table outside on the pavement. 'He was in court this morning, wasn't he?'

'Remanded until the trial, I was told,' replied Tony. 'I don't know how long that'll take. Months, probably.'

'It must be hell for the poor lass's family.'

Tony scribbled down some initial thoughts, keeping an eye on the large clock behind the café counter. He had telephoned the comisaría that morning to arrange a time to go in and receive an update on the Natalie Brooks case. He had heard nothing officially from the Policia Nacional since his last visit on Sunday morning, though he knew steps had been taken. Tony had spoken with Marie Reynolds on Monday evening, and she had told him that a Sergeant had visited the *Holiday18* apartments earlier that day to take a statement from each of the reps. Marie also reported seeing a small number of officers searching the immediate vicinity around the apartment block, rooting through bins and skips, and looking down drains. Of Natalie herself, though, there had been no news. There was still no trace of her.

Tony made as much progress as he could in the time – though most of his notes were scribbled out or written over – before heading off for the comisaría. He was shown in to see the same Agente as before, this time without waiting, and, through a translator, the officer explained the progress of the investigation so far. He started by telling Tony what he already knew, that statements had been taken from each of the *Holiday18* reps, and that a search had taken place of the surrounding streets for the stolen items. Nothing had been turned up, however, and the Agente was unconvinced that the burglary of the apartment was linked to Natalie's disappearance. There had been several other thefts from holiday rep accommodation reported to the comisaría that morning alone, and apparently it was not exactly an irregular occurrence.

There were several new points of interest. Firstly, Natalie's cashpoint card had been used in Benidorm. €20 had been withdrawn from her savings account on Monday morning. While the Agente said he wasn't at liberty to discuss Natalie's financial status with Tony, he did indicate she didn't appear to be in debt. Secondly, a visit had been made to *Breeze* and Donnie Lane had been spoken to. The nightclub manager repeated what he had told Tony, that he had not seen

Natalie on the previous Thursday night, and this was apparently supported by those who had worked the door. Tony challenged the Agente with what he had been told by Stuart Miller, that he had bought tickets for the *Holiday18* boat trip from Natalie at *Breeze* in the early hours of Friday. The Agente acknowledged this but, since Stuart Miller and his girlfriend had returned to the UK, the Policia Nacional had been unable, as yet, to confirm this statement.

Tony thanked the Agente for the work that had been carried out so far, and, mulling everything over in his head, left the comisaría. The withdrawal of the money from Natalie's account was interesting. It hardly seemed the sum of money a thief would take, assuming they knew her PIN, but, then again, there might not have been much more in there. The fact that her card was used at all was more relevant than the amount taken. Did Natalie herself use the card? If not, when could it have been taken? Did she have it on her when she disappeared or could it have been taken in the burglary? Marie had previously told Tony that Natalie carried a small white handbag on her nights out, which was barely big enough to hold her compact, a lipstick, and her door key. The handbag wasn't anywhere to be found in Natalie's apartment, as were none of the clothes the young woman had gone out in on the Thursday evening. Marie had told Tony during their conversation on Monday that a replacement rep had been sent down from Benidorm to cover Natalie's duties. The new arrival had moved into the apartment with Ross, and Natalie's possessions, in a suitcase and a couple of cardboard boxes, were now being stored in Marie's bedroom.

Another phone call Tony had made on Monday evening was to Geena Brooks back in England. Natalie hadn't been in touch with her since they last spoke, and she still remained in blissful indifference to her daughter's disappearance, but Tony did manage to get an agreement from her to ask Natalie's friends back home if they had heard from her.

Tony was certain the burglary was linked to Natalie's disappearance and couldn't hide his disappointment that the search of the area around the apartment block, something he had pushed for, had drawn a blank. While it didn't disprove his theory, the items could have been disposed of anywhere, it was a spanner in the works.

And what about Donnie Lane? He was lying, Tony was sure of it. Another visit to *Breeze* was certainly in order, although he knew he would receive the same response yet again if he went in asking the same questions. A different approach was needed. Tony doubted whether the Agente who had questioned Lane would have mentioned the statement, unconfirmed as it may be, made by Stuart Miller, so that was at least one card he could play.

Tony knew he should spend his time working on the talk at the Solanis, but he couldn't rid himself of a sense of responsibility for Natalie Brooks. Who else was there to care for her? Her mother seemed a dead loss, the alcohol which slurred her speech during their conversation could almost be smelt down the line, and there was little more Marie could do. The rep had also told Tony that Phil, the regional manager of *Holiday18*, had formally sacked Natalie when she hadn't reappeared by Monday. The company went through reps like a dose of salts – most were college leavers wanting a summer in the sun and responsibility wasn't exactly their forte – and there were duties to be met, but it was a crass gesture nonetheless. Tony knew who his first call would be to if he needed resources to mount a poster campaign to help locate Natalie, and woe betide them if they were reticent.

It was ironic how Geena seemed so disinterested in her daughter's life, regardless of her actions in the past, while Tony was doing all he could to remain an important part of his. He had sent an e-mail to Helen first thing Monday morning about Lucy coming out for a week, but she hadn't replied as yet and Tony was starting to feel the awkwardness of the situation. True, it had only been a couple of days, but with the newspapers at home full of the death of Leanne Piggott and lurid tales of life in Cieloventura, he would hardly feel in a position to complain if she said no.

Tony made up his mind not to press the point by sending further messages. He would let Helen reply in her own time and he wouldn't mention it to Lucy when he next spoke to her, which he hoped would be sometime this coming weekend.

'Mr. Lane?'

As Donnie Lane looked up, Tony could've sworn there was the faintest look of amusement on his face. It was gone in an instant, but Tony had learned to trust his first impressions over the years. And his impressions of Donnie Lane were currently sending alarm bells off in his head.

'What can I do for you, Mr....sorry, I can't remember your name.'

'Heather.'

With no sign of life at the front entrance of the club, Tony had decided to try his luck around the back. There he found the manager, clad in shorts and flip-flops, unloading boxes of mixers from the back of a small van. The driver sat at the wheel, his feet up on the dashboard, smoking a joint and listening to what Tony guessed would, to the young man's ears, pass for music. To Tony, though, it was just one loud thump after another. There wasn't even a discernible tune to it.

'That's it, yeah. What can I do for you?'

Picking up a couple of the boxes from the ground, Donnie headed into the building. Tony followed, glancing into the small office as they made their way along the corridor towards the interior of the club.

'I understand you've spoken with the police?'

'I speak with the police most days,' he replied. 'Goes with the job. I'm expecting someone today to come an' take a picture of that.'

As Donnie made for the bar, he gestured towards a seating area in the corner of the club. One of the large mirrors that adorned the wall behind the sofas was shattered.

'Someone chucked a bottle at it. An' if it ain't

reported, the insurance won't cough up.'

'You spoke to the Policia Nacional about Natalie Brooks.'

Donnie heaved the boxes onto the counter and, turning back to Tony, hesitated slightly before responding. It was just for effect, Tony knew, but was determined not to let it irritate him.

'Of course, yeah.'

'What did you tell them?'

'What I told you. That I didn't see Nat on Thursday night. Oh, and neither did either of the doormen. I managed to speak to 'em about it. I meant to phone you, sorry about that, but I've been up to my eyes in it the past few days. Short-staffed, you see.'

It was a perverse thought to have at that point, but Tony actually admired Donnie Lane's ability to lie so convincingly. There was no hesitation in his voice, and he looked Tony squarely in the eye as he spoke. If Tony hadn't already formed his opinion about the man, an opinion that was unshakable, he knew he would be taken in completely.

'It's just that new information has come to light that suggests Natalie was, in fact, in here late on Thursday night.'

'What kind of information?'

'A statement from someone who was in the club.'

'Well, I wonder why she never popped into the office to say hello? Strange. Still, good news, isn't it? I mean, any information that helps find her can only be a good thing. Tell the police I'm more than happy to have another word with my doorman about it. You never know, they may remember something when they've had a chance to think about it.'

Tony knew Donnie would easily fend off the blow he was trying to land, though he was a little taken aback by the gall he displayed in doing so, but he considered it still worth throwing. A seed had been sown. Who knew how it may take root and grow?

After a further ten minutes of conversation, where everything from the price of a pint in Cieloventura to the proposals for further development in the town were discussed, Tony took his leave. As he walked into the Avenue, he reached for the small slip of paper in his back pocket. It pained him, but there was nothing for it. It hadn't taken him more than a couple of minutes, en route to *Breeze* half an hour earlier, to find out what he needed to know.

Tony took out his phone and dialled the number scrawled on the paper. It was answered on its first ring.

The Solanis Resort was the jewel in the crown of *SunTravel Premier*, one of the largest tour operators in Cieloventura. The complex was only five years old but had already had a facelift prior to the new holiday season, and a small presentation in the reception area detailed plans by the owners to expand. Land adjacent to the rear of the property had already been secured and proposals for a new apartment block and entertainment complex were being finalised.

Sat in the small office with the head rep from the company, Tony outlined his programme for the planned event; a short talk, followed by some fun activities for the kids – run by the *SunTravel Premier* reps – while Tony circulated among the adults to answer any questions and give general advice about staying safe while on holiday. Rafá had called him that morning to say his superiors had given the okay for both he and Consuela to attend the talk. It was good PR for the Policia Municipal after all, especially with the local press in attendance, although the plan to give children a ride in the patrol car had been vetoed. They could sit in the driver's seat and have their photo taken, but Rafá's superiors had said no to any rides. The officers were still on official duty and may be called to an emergency at any moment.

The meal at Rafá's the previous evening had gone very well. The young officer's wife had prepared tapas, followed by *lacharzo* – a lamb dish from the Castilla y León region of Spain, where she originally hailed from – and honeyed rice. It was exceptional, and as Tony had offered to return the compliment by inviting them to dinner at his apartment the following week, along with Consuela and her family, the pressure of living up to such a spread was daunting.

'Leave this all to me,' said Emily Johnson, gathering up the notes she had made during the meeting, 'and I'll get some posters put up around the complex this afternoon.'

The young woman waited for Tony to drain the remaining coffee from his mug before leading him out into the reception area.

'Actually, this has come at a good time,' she said, as

they made their way towards the main doors. 'It's important the guests feel reassured, and there's only so much I can tell them.'

'People are still worried by the Leanne Piggott case, then?'

'I had hoped it would all have died down. I mean, give it a few days and most of the people who were here at the same time as Leanne would've left. We'll have a whole new lot in. But now we've got this. Have you seen it?'

As they passed a wire rack of daily newspapers on the wall at the side of the reception desk, Emily stopped and took down one of the tabloids. She opened it to show Tony an article on an inside page. Beneath a photograph of a smiling Natalie Brooks was the headline 'FEARS FOR MISSING REP.'

Tony nodded. 'Yes, I'm aware of that.'

'Not that it's anything to do with the Solanis,' replied Emily, 'but it'll worry our guests nonetheless.'

'You've never had any dealings with Holiday18?'

'God, no! I sometimes see their reps out on the town, flashing their tits and arses everywhere and getting plastered. I don't know how they can behave like that.'

'Do you remember seeing her at all?'

'No, can't say I do.'

'Well, nobody's heard from her for nearly a week now, and people are getting very concerned for her wellbeing. Hopefully, now more people are aware of what's happened, she'll be found soon.'

Tony's journey to the Solanis that day had been via

the Irish bar, where over a breakfast of a cup of coffee and a plate of biscuits, he had sat and watched three patrol cars of the Policia Nacional arrive outside *Breeze*. Donnie Lane, looking quite relaxed by the turn of events, had been escorted from the club by two Agentes and was driven off in one of the cars. A van had also arrived, and several people in white overalls, carrying a number of bags of equipment, had gone into the building. The cleaning staff, arriving for duty, found their entry blocked and they busied themselves with hushed, almost conspiratorial, chats further along the pavement.

'Well, let's hope there's a happy ending,' the rep said.

'Amen to that.'

After Tony said goodbye to Emily Johnson, he was at last able to respond to his mobile phone, which had been vibrating in his back pocket at regular intervals during his chat with the rep. The messages all amounted to one thing, and Tony knew a taxi would get him to the town hall quicker.

'The last thing Cieloventura needs is more stories like this,' said Sra. Ocasio, gesturing to the tabloid newspaper open upon her desk. 'The Mayor is most unhappy with this article.'

'Yes, I did see it,' replied Tony.

'I understand from the Policia Nacional that you have been involved in the search for this missing woman?'

'Well, a little. It was one of her colleagues from

Holiday18 who came to me about it last Friday. I made a few enquiries, and recommended she put the matter before the police. They seem to be handling things quite well.'

'Have you spoken to the press?'

'They wouldn't get anything out of me even if they tried,' Tony said, hoping he was as convincing a liar as Donnie Lane. 'I assume it was one of her fellow reps that went to the newspaper with it. Normally, they probably wouldn't bother with such a story, people go missing all the time, but what with the Leanne Piggott case...'

Shaking her head in frustration, the woman got to her feet and paced across to the window, which overlooked the town square. Maria Ocasio Cruz was the Head of Tourism at the town hall, and was the person who had officially hired Tony. Though the idea behind his appointment had been the Mayor's, it had fallen to Sra. Ocasio to find and recruit the right man for the job. She spoke excellent English, having spent five years working in London, firstly as a translator after leaving university and then in a position at the Spanish Embassy. It was during her time in England that she made the contacts that would ultimately lead to Tony heading for a new life in Cieloventura.

'There is no connection between the two cases,' said Sra. Ocasio. 'The Policia Nacional tell me they have looked into the possibility and discounted it. The man imprisoned on the murder charge has no links to this woman or the tour company she worked for.'

Common sense suggested that a man arrested in

connection with the murder of a young female would be interviewed about another than had disappeared on the same night, but Tony had never felt there was anything to connect Leanne Piggott, or Ryan Dinsdale, with Natalie Brooks.

'It is the hypocrisy of these people that is frustrating for us all,' added Sra. Ocasio, gesturing to the newspaper. 'I would willingly wager any sum that things are no better in any British city.'

'If it's any consolation, Sra. Ocasio, it's probably a lot worse.'

Tony knew the behaviour seen in Cieloventura, especially late at night when people had had too much to drink, was no different to that in any major town or city centre in the UK come Friday or Saturday nights. He had attended all manner of late-night brawls and disturbances in his time as a policeman, and taken more statements from bloodied young men and women in over-stretched A&E departments than he cared to remember. His move into community policing, and then the family's relocation to Aylesbury, was a welcome change. It was ironic that the violent incident that would signal the end of his career in the police force would happen in a leafy suburban avenue and not an inner-city back street.

'Then I hope you will tell others that,' Sra. Ocasio replied. 'In the meantime, we need to do something about this publicity the town is receiving. Redress the balance. We cannot have a situation where people believe it is unsafe for young women to walk the streets of Cieloventura. The Mayor is giving an interview to this newspaper this afternoon, and he would appreciate it if you attended also.'

'I would be delighted.'

Tony winced on the inside. His only previous meeting with the Mayor had been a brief exchange of conversational pleasantries and a handshake on his first day in the town, and, while he had been looking forward to the Mayor launching his information campaign for British hotels and apartments, he wasn't so keen on doing a interview alongside him.

Not only that but he and the journalist in question would need to pretend they'd never met before. Jerry Field was in Cieloventura covering the Leanne Piggott case and, while it hadn't been his newspaper that had printed the article that had so irked Tony on Sunday, the corresponding reports in his paper hadn't been a great deal more sensitive.

Tony loathed resorting to such a tactic, but felt it was necessary to bring attention to Natalie's disappearance. He had told Jerry over an afternoon pint in a small bar along the Paseo de la Solana enough for him to write an accurate article, but without revealing too much that would identify himself as the main source. Information he'd received directly from the Policia Nacional, such as the cashpoint card being used in Benidorm, was not among the details he had provided, though the burglary of Natalie's apartment, had been.

Jerry had used his contacts back home to find out a little more about Donnie Lane, though he wasn't named personally in the article. It mentioned the manager of a nightclub had been visited by the police in the process of their enquiries – true enough – and that the man in question had served a term of imprisonment in the UK for tax evasion and theft. He had also filed for bankruptcy in 2001, Tony had been told, and had been barred from running a company. While that didn't surprise Tony, it wasn't anything that seemed to have any bearing on the case. Violence, especially against women, would be a different matter, but there seemed no stains of that sort on Donnie Lane's character.

'What do you think may have happened to her?' asked Sra. Ocasio, picking up the newspaper and taking a close look at the photograph of Natalie Brooks.

'Well, I'm hoping it's as people think it is. That she's met some chap here on holiday and is staying with him.'

'What about her job?'

'Perhaps she cared little for that. It seems she may have been looking to earn extra money, she was doing some work for the Breeze nightclub in her spare time.'

'And you believe that's what has happened?'

Tony took a moment before replying. 'No,' he admitted, 'no, I don't. Many reps, especially those with companies like Holiday18, just chuck in the towel if the work proves too hard and go home or find summer work elsewhere. But Natalie just vanished. Her clothes, personal belongings and, more importantly, her passport were all left behind. No, I'm worried this could be something a lot more serious.'

'The Policia Nacional showed admirable zeal and effort in finding the killer of Leanne Piggott,' said Sra. Ocasio. 'They assure me they are working on this case with the same endeavour. In the meantime, the British public need to know that Cieloventura is a safe and happy place to come on their holidays, and it is your job to help do that.'

'Of course. I'll be happy to be of any help I can.'

Although there was nothing in Field's article that directly slighted the town's reputation, it wasn't much of a leap to assume people planning a holiday may have second thoughts about coming to Cieloventura. British tourists made up the largest percentage of visitors, and the income they generated was crucial to the town's economy. Tony felt terribly guilty about the bad feeling he may have caused by turning to the media but was comforted by the fact that he himself would be helping to repair the damage. It wasn't that he felt the police weren't doing enough. On the contrary, he had been pleased with their efforts but time was of the essence and the publicity was crucial.

When he had seen the article for the first time that morning, Tony smiled wryly at the quote from a *Holiday18* spokesman that concluded the story. 'We are all deeply concerned to hear about Natalie', it had read, 'and will do all we can to assist the police in order to ensure she is returned to us safely.' No mention of them sacking her then, Tony thought.

'Well, that went quite well, all things considered,' said Jerry Field, as he and Tony headed out into the late afternoon sunshine.

'What will you do now? Go home?'

Jerry shook his head. 'No, I'll give it a few more days. If there's no developments, I'll get pulled off the story anyway, but I might as well stick around for a while and see what happens. Come on, you can treat me to a pint.'

Chatting over a drink with a tabloid hack like Jerry Field wasn't the best way Tony thought of spending an hour, but as the journalist had been working on the story most of the day, there may be more information he had managed to dig up. They repaired to the nearest bar and, while Jerry typed out his story on his small laptop computer, drank a couple of beers.

'She had a bit of a reputation, you know?'

'She was just a typical nineteen year-old, Jerry.'

'Did you know she's got a kid?'

'No, I didn't.' Tony was stunned by the bombshell. It hadn't occurred to him that Natalie would have a child of her own. It hadn't been mentioned by Marie, who may not have known, or Geena, who most certainly would have done.

'Lives with its Dad,' nodded Jerry. 'Exeter way. Eighteen months old. She ain't seen it for a year.'

'Let's not turn this into a hatchet job, Jerry. Please.'

'Look, the story worked, didn't it? They brought Lane in for questioning, like you wanted. They've even been searching the club.'

And not just the club. Tony had left a message on Marie's voicemail that morning, as he walked from the

Irish bar to the Solanis Resort, telling her about the story in the newspaper and of the increased police activity in the case. She had called him back within minutes, telling him all the *Holiday18* apartments were also being searched and that the reps had been shepherded into a single kitchen, all except for the new girl, who had already left for the morning to meet an incoming flight from Leeds-Bradford. The power of the media.

'Besides, it might work in our favour. Nice picture of the baby in tomorrow's paper might give the cops an ever bigger kick up the arse.'

Tony managed to conceal his frown from the shameless journalist by raising the beer glass to his mouth. Jerry flicked through the small notebook he had used during the interview with the Mayor.

'What do you make about her bank card being used on Sunday?'

The Mayor had been thoroughly debriefed on the findings of the investigation by the Policia Nacional before the interview, and used as many of them as he could to counter points in Jerry's original article.

'That doesn't prove anything,' Tony responded.

'Of course it don't,' said Jerry, 'but it's interesting. Needs following up.'

Sra. Ocasio was right about one thing. The police had worked with speed and efficiency on the Leanne Piggott case, and now, with the eyes of the British press and the Mayor's Office on them, they would be doing the same with Natalie Brooks. Tony felt justified in his actions. The revelation that Natalie was a mother only reinforced this belief. Her personal life was more complex than he had thought. Abandoning her responsibilities to her employers paled in comparison to abandoning those as a mother. He didn't know the circumstances of that, however, and so reined in his thoughts before they galloped out of control.

Tony left the bar with an agreement to meet Jerry the following day once the journalist had delved deeper into the story. For all his faults, a man like Jerry, and his contacts back home, could be invaluable.

Tony headed back to Calle Neuva. He would spend the evening in tonight, preparing his talk and eating something of his own creation. There were a few things in the cupboard and fridge that he knew he could rustle up into a quick meal. While he had developed a taste for Spanish cuisine, he wasn't yet up to the task of preparing it. He planned to cook a traditional British roast with all the trimmings for Consuela, Rafá and their families. Space would be at a premium, so the sofa would need to be cleared from the lounge for the evening. Dave and Pat had told him he could use a couple of the tables and a set of chairs from *Bar Loco*.

'We'll manage for the night,' Pat had laughed. 'If it gets packed, we can always get people to sit on each other's laps. You never know, it might catch on!'

The previous night had been a sleepless one for Tony. He was worried what the newspaper's take on Natalie's disappearance would be, and what the reaction of the Mayor's Office would be to it. His night of fitful rest was finally put out of its misery with a phone call at around four 'o' clock to help officers of the Policia Municipal deal with a drunk and distressed British woman who had had a row with her boyfriend and found herself stranded in the town square with her suitcase, with no money and no idea where she was going to go.

In the end, events had turned out better than Tony could have expected, and, as his head hit the pillow, he hoped he would be rewarded with a good night's sleep. He closed his eyes tightly and prayed there would be a happy ending, but his heart was telling him otherwise. Natalie Brooks would be found, he knew that. But she would be found dead. He just hoped and hoped he would be wrong.

CHAPTER NINE

IT gave Tony an eerie feeling to see Natalie Brooks walking through the busy Avenue without a care in the world. She stopped briefly to adjust one of the straps on her high-heeled shoes before continuing on his way, her head moving slightly to the beat of the music permeating all around.

She suddenly stopped and, momentarily looking a little self-conscious in her environment, stood silently in the middle of the bustling thoroughfare as activity exploded all around her. She gazed across at Tony, standing on the pavement outside a nearby bar, and, their eyes meeting, seemed to wait for his reassurance. He smiled and nodded. Everything was going well.

Tony, Marie and an English-speaking uniformed Subinspector of the Policia Nacional had spent several hours that morning along the Paseo de la Solana and the main beach, trying to identify a woman with a close resemblance to the missing holiday rep. Eventually, when Tony was close to giving up hope, Marie had pointed out someone who seemed to tick most of the necessary boxes. Justine Bernard was a Belgian tourist, three years older than Natalie at twenty-two, who had only been in Cieloventura for one day. Fortunately, her desire not to appear pasty on her first day on holiday had meant she resorted to several sessions of spray-tanning at home before setting off, ensuring her skin was bronzed.

Justine was alarmed to be asked by the police officer if they could speak to her in private, but when the matter was explained to her, and what they would be asking her to do, she was quick to offer her help. The young woman was less pleased with the request for her hair to be dyed – it was a shade too light to match Natalie's exactly – and restyled, but she was more than happy with Tony's offer for her to visit one of Cieloventura's leading salons the following day at his own cost. Changing her hair back again afterwards, or to whichever new style she fancied, would also ensure no-one would mistake her for Natalie after the reconstruction and waste valuable police time making false reports.

Marie had taken Justine shopping that afternoon to select clothing as close to what Natalie was wearing on the night she disappeared. It was clear the Belgian girl was uncomfortable wearing such a revealing outfit – the skirt, she said, was barely enough to conceal her underwear – but she persevered without complaint.

The reconstruction of Natalie's last known movements needed to work. It had to. If it drew a blank, Tony didn't know where he, or the Policia Nacional, could go from here. In the two days since the story had hit the news-stands, there had been no shortage of activity, but Tony could sense the investigation was starting to slow down. Energy and commitment levels were beginning to flag, and the manpower provided by the Policia Nacional, though slight compared to that in the Leanne Piggott enquiry, couldn't be sustained for long.

Jerry had followed up his original story with articles in both Thursday and Friday's newspaper but, without any new developments, the journalist knew time was running out.

'I've booked a flight home for tomorrow night,' he had told Tony earlier that day, 'and, unless something breaks, I'm gonna be on it.'

Donnie Lane had spent less than an hour on Thursday morning being interviewed by officers of the Policia Nacional. He had remained resolute throughout – he had not seen Natalie Brooks at anytime the previous Thursday night. The two doormen, Jimi and Max, had also been brought in and had said much the same, though the latter added, on reflection, he may have seen her in the crowd at some point but couldn't be sure. As for the club manager's movements, there were witnesses that could place him in or around the club from mid-afternoon on the Thursday to late Friday evening.

Since he had left the comisaría, Donnie had been keeping a low profile. Tony had ventured into *Breeze* the previous night – a week to the day since Natalie had last been seen – with posters about her disappearance. He had asked to speak to the manager, but the barman said he was taking a few days off.

Detective work in a holiday resort like Cieloventura was a frustrating business for Tony. The transient nature of its population, great numbers of people being in the town one week and gone the next, was akin to a crime being committed in one place and attempting to solve it in another. Trying to find people who were even in Cieloventura at the time of Natalie's disappearance was hard enough, let alone whether they had seen her. That had been another reason why Tony had felt it necessary to turn to the British press. It wasn't just the publicity would encourage the local authorities to do more, it was also to reach out to those holiday-makers who had since returned home. Indeed, the story had had a bigger impact in the UK than in Cieloventura. A number of people had come forward to say they remembered Natalie from their holiday, one of which was able to provide several photographs of the woman taken a day or two before her disappearance, leading a crowd of *Holiday18* guests on a bar crawl.

Stuart Miller, the tourist who had told Tony he had bought the boat-trip tickets from Natalie in *Breeze*, had made an official statement to the police back home in England. In it, the young man said he was 'seventy-five to eighty per cent' certain the tickets had been bought at around half one in the morning. The couple he and his girlfriend had gone out with that evening had also been traced, but they remembered few details of the night in question, not even recalling how they had got back to their hotel in their paralytic state.

As Justine stood still, trying to look impassive as the barrage of flash-bulbs from a dozen photographers went off around her, police officers and volunteers radiated out to speak to the clubbers and bar-goers along the Avenue. Their route had already taken in the Paseo de la Solana and Carrer de Trato and, after the Avenue, it would move onto Calle Veijo, where *Breeze* was located.

The reconstruction was due to take place twice, once at the time Natalie herself had headed out for the evening, and again two hours later. The time between the two processions was spent at an open-air 'incident room' along the Avenue, manned by officers of the Policia Nacional, Tony, and two off-duty *Holiday18* reps. Most people, however, were out to enjoy themselves and, while there was a lot of curiosity as to what was going on, there was little forthcoming in terms of positive feedback.

As the event came to an end, Tony thanked a relieved Justine for her help. She had given up a night of her precious holiday with her friends — fellow workers at a textile factory just outside Kortrijk - to assist the case, and he was grateful. He had bought her a voucher to spend at the Hermosa Boutique, though the money, in the end, had come from *Holiday18* rather than his own pocket. The company had also agreed to fund a poster campaign in the town, which the reps had taken on the responsibility to organise the day before. He had seen one that morning in the window of the small supermarket on the corner of Calle Neuva when he had picked up some groceries.

Someone, somewhere, must have seen her.

Saturday morning was a busy time at the town's courthouse. A brawl the night before between a group of lads from Manchester and another from London, for which seven had been arrested, had flared up again during the court session. Punches had been thrown, and the police, along with the courthouse's security staff, had been called to restore order. Some had been removed to the courthouse's own holding cells, while others had been taken to those of the Policia Municipal next door. Tony worked hard to ensure there would be no further trouble between the two groups, which had apparently started when an unflattering comment had been made about a girl who was with the other group, and the matter was eventually resolved. The fines had been heavy – very heavy – and one had been remanded pending an investigation of assault on a police officer.

It was mid-afternoon when Tony was free from all his other commitments to have the time to meet up with Jerry Field.

'Few more blokes have put their name up for givin' her one at some point in the past couple of weeks,' he reported, flicking through the e-mails he had received from his newspaper's offices back home, 'but nothin' from that Thursday night, except what we already know.'

'No-one can put her anywhere after ten-to-one?'

'Not at my end. Yours?'

Tony shook his head. One thing that had come out of the case was that he no longer needed to go through the formalities of phoning the comisaría to arrange a visit in order to be kept up-to-date. The work he had carried out on the case, and his insight into the ways and customs of the British, had been appreciated by the Policia Nacional and, in return, they were keeping him in the loop.

The majority of people along the Avenue that had been spoken to simply hadn't been in Cieloventura the Thursday before last, and those that were did not recognise Natalie. It was bar staff and doorman that the Policia Nacional had been particularly interested in hearing from, but while a fair number could identify Natalie from her photograph, mostly in her role as a *Holiday18* rep, no-one could place her anywhere in the town after the time she been seen by Marie Reynolds.

One development the police had informed Tony about was a report that had come in from a bar owner in Denia, nearly fifty miles along the coast from Cieloventura, that morning. He had seen a copy of a day-old British newspaper, which had been left on a table by a customer. The man claimed Natalie, for he was convinced it was she, had come into his bar for a drink late on the previous Saturday night. She had ordered a white wine and sat in the corner, where she appeared to be waiting for someone. After the woman had been there for nearly half an hour, a man duly appeared and the two, seemingly having cross words with one another, went off into the night. The man who had met with Natalie was described as North African – Moroccan, the bar owner guessed – and about six feet in height. The police in Denia were trying to find other witnesses to corroborate the bar owner's account, and where she may have gone after leaving the establishment.

'So where do we go from here?'

'You, you mean. I'm off 'ome.'

'Is the newspaper pulling the story?'

'I can't write a story if there's nothing more to write about, Tone. We had a decent half-page on the reconstruction this morning, and three other papers carried it an' all. I think it's played out. If there ain't anything by the end of the day, there won't be. It'll be tomorrow's fish and chip paper.'

Tony knew the media would need regular developments to maintain their coverage, but was disappointed nonetheless. On his way to meet Jerry, he had noticed one of the posters of Natalie, which had been pinned to a tree just two days before by one of her fellow reps, lying dirtied and torn in the gutter. He had stood looking down at it for quite some time, the image having an awful parallel in his mind, before forcing himself to move along.

'She's been here an hour,' Pat said, gesturing to the middle-aged woman sitting in the corner of the bar. 'I said I didn't know how long you were going to be, but she insisted on waiting.'

Tony glanced over at the woman, staring into an untouched cup of coffee. It wasn't someone he had seen before, and from her fair complexion and unusual clothing for such hot weather — jeans and a sweater — she didn't look like a conventional tourist. Tony smiled his thanks at Pat and walked over to the table. The woman didn't seem to notice him approach, and it was only when he practically loomed over her, casting a shadow across her, that she seemed to come out of her trance.

'I understand you wished to see me?'

'You must be Mr. Heather?' The woman jumped to her feet, knocking the table as she did so and spilling a little coffee.

'And you are?'

'My name is Maureen. Maureen Carr.'

'What can I do for you? Please...'

Tony gestured for her to sit back down and took the chair opposite.

'I didn't know where else I could turn. I've been all over this soddin' town but nobody seems to know anything or want to do anything.'

'Well, maybe I can be of some help. What is it concerning?'

Maureen looked as though she hadn't slept or eaten properly in days. Though her face was made up, it failed to conceal the dark rings under the eyes.

'It's my son. He's been arrested for murder.'

Tony was taken aback. 'Your son?'

'Ryan Dinsdale.'

With all the activity of the past few days, the Leanne Piggott case had slipped clean from Tony's mind. Not that there was a reason for it to have remained there. The police investigation had gone well and a man was in custody. Nevertheless, he was a little shocked at having the case brought so dramatically back to his attention.

'I see.'

'He's in a terrible state, so he is. He didn't do it,

Mr. Heather, he swears he didn't.'

Maureen was clearly struggling to keep her emotions in check. To Tony, she seemed on the edge of a breakdown and, while he didn't know what the woman required from him, the most important service he knew he could offer at this stage was comfort and reassurance.

'I only arrived yesterday,' she said, a faint trace of a Wearside accent perceptible in her speech. 'It took me a few days to get enough money together to get a flight. I had to borrow, beg and all but steal in order to get it.'

'And you've been to see your son?'

'This morning.'

'I don't know if there's anything I can really do, Mrs. Carr.'

'Just go an' see the lad, Mr. Heather, please. Talk to him. You'll see.'

Maureen took a small sip of coffee from the cup. Though it was clearly cold, she swallowed it all the same. Tony looked over to Pat, chatting jovially to a customer at the counter, and signalled for two fresh coffees.

'Whereabouts are you staying?'

'I've got a room at a place called the Belle Vue. I didn't know whether I should stay in Alicante or come here, but I thought here would be better. After all, this is where the whole thing happened,' explained Maureen. 'I can only afford to stay there a week or so at the most. Then I'll have to go home or find somewhere cheaper. Assuming Ron can send me some more money.'

'Is Ron your husband?'

'Aye. He's Ryan's stepdad, but they don't see eye-to-eye much. Ryan's always lived with his real dad. I moved out when he was just a lad.'

Tony doubted whether there was anywhere cheaper, in any sense of the word, in Cieloventura than the Belle Vue. It was one of the first high-rise hotel blocks built in the resort and, in proposals for the next stage of development in the town, was earmarked for demolition.

'Someone at the town hall mentioned your name and where I could find you. Said you might help me. What are you? Some kind of private detective?'

Tony shook his head. He didn't know *what* he was supposed to be anymore. Delving into the Leanne Piggott case at the stage wasn't something that would go down well at the town hall, and the British Consulate in Alicante would be ensuring Ryan Dinsdale's rights, under Spanish law, were not being violated.

While Tony knew there was little he could do, he was aware of Ryan's lack of cooperation with the investigation. If, by visiting him in Fontcalent Prison, the young man could be prevailed upon to start talking, then it would be worthwhile.

'You'll need to speak to your son and tell him to request authorisation for me to visit him. I'll do likewise. That's the way things need to be done out here.'

Maureen nodded. 'Aye, I know. Thank you.'

'Do you have a number I can contact you on?'

Maureen reached down to the floor for her handbag and brought it up onto the table. She rooted through its contents, eventually producing a small mobile phone.

'I bought this thing in Alicante yesterday,' she said, 'an' then the prison go an' tell me Ryan's not allowed to call me on it.'

'Pay-as-you-go?'

'Aye.'

Tony nodded. 'Prisoners are only allowed to ring authorised numbers. A bill or a contract, something with a name and address, has to be submitted to the prison to prove who the phone is registered to.'

'Stupid. It'd be easier for me to keep in touch with him from home than it is from out here.'

The two exchanged numbers.

'Does he have a lawyer?'

'I got this from the British Consulate,' Maureen replied, retrieving several sheets of folded paper from her bag. 'It's a list of English-speaking lawyers in Alicante. For all the good it'll bleedin' do me!'

'I take it from that you won't be able to afford it?'

'I'm on benefits, Mr. Heather, an' they're not likely to last if the social find out I'm out here. An', believe me, there's plenty along our street that would take delight in tellin' em! Ron's only been workin' part-time this last year or so.'

'If a prisoner doesn't have the means, the courts will appoint an *ex officio* lawyer. Legal aid to you and me. Don't worry about that, he won't go without proper representation.'

'Ryan doesn't trust 'em. He reckons everyone's out to get him. That's why I want you to speak to him, Mr. Heather. He might tell you things.'

Tony could understand how someone, particularly a young person, held in a foreign prison, and part of a justice system they didn't understand, could feel frightened and vulnerable.

'There are people who may be able to provide you with more practical help, people with more specialised knowledge' he told Maureen.

Tony excused himself and went up to his apartment. He sorted through a box file he had been slowly building up since his arrival in Spain; information he had gathered about the policing and judicial systems, local by-laws and regulations, and helpful tips for tourists to avoid becoming victims of crime. A new plan Tony had in mind was to collate all of the information on a website, but that was something for another day. One thing at a time. He found what he was looking for and returned to the bar.

'I'm sure the Consulate will give you a lot of support,' Tony said, handing over the paperwork, 'but hopefully you'll find this of some use. There's details there of a charity that helps Britons, and their families, imprisoned in foreign countries. They'll be able to give you advice.'

In his absence, Pat had brought the coffees and a plate of biscuits to the table. Tony watched as Maureen nibbled nervously at a piece of shortbread.

'Has Ryan told you anything the case?'

'Only that he didn't kill the girl and that he's being fitted up. He just wants me to get him out, Mr. Heather. Look, is there no chance they could release him 'til the trial? I could find a job out here, he could live with me.'

'No,' Tony shook his head. 'There's no chance of bail, I'm afraid. Not in something like this.'

'He reckons it's hell in that prison. There's three in his cell and they're both foreigners.'

Tony thought it best not to comment on that. While they finished their coffees, he explained his role in the town, and though he went to some pains to emphasise what limited use he felt he could be in this case, Maureen seemed to take little of it in.

'I just need somebody to do something,' she said. 'I know that poor lass got killed an' everything, but my Ryan didn't do it. You have to believe that.'

Tony knew he didn't have to do anything of the sort. He had seen too many parents bury their heads in the sand when it came to their children. Ryan Dinsdale was innocent until proven guilty, however, and he was willing to keep an open mind. If the young man was prepared to talk to him about what happened that night, he owed it to everyone, including Leanne Piggott and her family, to listen.

Tony and Maureen parted company, with a promise to get in touch once Fontcalent prison had authorised a visit. Tony returned to his apartment and made straight for the bedroom. Having a short nap was less about joining in with the Spanish way of life and more about preparing himself for whatever awaited him that night. While he was going to spend most of the evening working on his talk for the Solanis Resort, Tony planned on heading out at some point to talk to the clubbers and workers along the Avenue. There would come a point when the search for Natalie would need to draw to a close, and he knew it would be soon, but until that point came, Tony was determined to press on. And Saturday night being Saturday night, he expected to be summoned at some point to come to the aid of a fellow countryman or woman.

After a light brunch, Tony made for the offices of the Policia Municipal. While he attended the courthouse each morning during the week as a matter of course, Tony made it his policy not to go to any session arranged on a Sunday unless his presence was requested. Not having set working hours for his job gave him flexibility but it also imposed a sense of being permanently 'on duty' that would prove suffocating unless he had the strength to resist.

José told Tony the night before was 'a little quiet' and happily acceded to his request to use the computer in the small office. Tony settled down at the desk and opened his e-mail account. A message from Jerry Field awaited him. 'Received these. She sent them to a friend a few weeks back. Helpful???' There were five attachments with the e-mail, all *jpeg* files. Tony clicked on each in turn and waited patiently for them to download. When they did, he examined each one with interest. They were photographs of Natalie Brooks, taken – it looked to Tony – high in the hills behind the town. Dressed in summer shorts and a T-shirt, she smiled at the camera and seemed to be taking delight in showing off her surroundings. One particular image showed Natalie looking down at Cieloventura, a good few miles in the distance, her arms spread like a compére welcoming an act on stage.

Tony was intrigued by the photographs and asked José for permission to print the images off. It was granted. Tony was close to logging off the computer when, at that moment, an e-mail came through from Helen. It was brief and to the point. They were having a few days away, and Lucy wouldn't be able to speak to him that evening. She would send him another message when they returned and they could make new arrangements then. That was it. No details about where they were going, and nothing about Tony's request for Lucy to come out to spend a week with him. Tony cursed under his breath and went to collect the photographs from the printer. They had come out larger than on screen, but in black and white and of lower quality. Still, they would suffice.

Since he had first looked into Natalie's disappearance, he had visited every location in the town that the rep was known to have been to – every café and bar, every hotel and apartment block – either in her duties for *Holiday18* or in her personal time. However, he had never been out of Cieloventura itself and, save for her regular journeys to and from the airport, neither, to his knowledge, had Natalie. The photographs were a fresh lead, however vague, and the enquiry had precious few of those. The corner of a building could be seen in the background of one of the photos. It was thirty or forty feet away, Tony guessed, and he didn't think it an impossible task to locate where the shots had been taken. Tony thanked José for his assistance and left the building. If he was going to travel up into the hills, transport would be needed.

When Tony first arrived in Spain, he hired a car for the drive to Cieloventura, and also so he could spend a few days exploring the town and the surrounding area. For the most part, however, the vehicle had remained parked in the narrow alley behind Calle Neuva. Most places tended to be within reasonable walking distance, and the narrow town roads combined with the left-hand drive, which he struggled to adapt to, made driving a hairy pursuit.

Tony visited a hire shop and, within twenty minutes, was heading out of town on a yellow and silver 125cc scooter. It had cost him €45 for the day, something he had slightly baulked at paying, but it was necessary. While taxis were plentiful in Cieloventura, he didn't know exactly where he was going, and the scooter would turn out to be more convenient and probably cheaper.

He hadn't ridden such a thing in years, way back once in the mid-eighties, if he remembered correctly, and the instructions he'd been given by the proprietor of the shop had been basic in the extreme. Several local youths overtook Tony as he carefully traversed the busy intersection leading out of Cieloventura, laughing and tooting their horns. Gradually, though, as he got used to the handling of the scooter and his confidence increased, Tony was able to pick up speed.

There were only several roads leading up into the hills and, while progress up some of the steeper inclines was slow, the miles began to tick by. The hills gradually gave way to the mountains, though precisely where one stopped and the other began, he wouldn't like to say. The terrain, which looked quite bare when viewed from the town, was home to a variety of colourful flora and wildlife. Cieloventura had, for many years, been pushed as a tourist resort solely to the cheap package holiday crowd, but the town council wanted to expand its appeal by promoting the town as an ideal base to explore the vast mountain range, the most mountainous region in the whole of Spain, that stretched from Alicante to Valencia. Attracting hill-walkers, climbers, bird-watchers and nature lovers was something Tony was all for. He couldn't imagine people with pursuits such as those drinking themselves into a stupor or frolicking naked in the town fountain. He hoped not, anyway.

Every so often, Tony brought the scooter to a stop and gazed back at the bustling town he had left behind. It seemed to him it wasn't getting much smaller than the last time he had looked, and he knew his original guess that the photos had been taken just a few miles out of Cieloventura was a serious underestimation. Heading up into the hills wasn't exactly leaving all civilisation behind. There were a number of properties along the road, mainly private villas or farmhouses, but, with their white-washed walls, none served as a likely candidate for the building visible in the photo, which had walls of natural stonework.

After driving on for another half an hour, Tony parked the scooter and, refreshing himself with a bottle of juice taken from the compartment under the seat, wandered towards the low guard barrier at the side of the road. The land began to fall sharply away less than a few yards from the single galvanised rail, and the high vantage point offered an unobstructed view of Cieloventura in the distance. Tony allowed himself a few moments to take it all in. It was magnificent. He had gazed up into the mountains many times from along the Paseo de la Solana, but this was the first time he had seen the view from the opposite direction. Why had it taken this to bring him up into the hills?

Using the relationship between two high-rise hotels in the distance, one towards the back of Cieloventura and the other closer to the coast, Tony tried to orientate his current position to that in the photograph of Natalie looking down at the town. From where he looked, the high-rise blocks were some way apart, whereas in the photo, only a thin slither of daylight could be seen between them. Tony needed to move some distance to the right, but the road, as it snaked its way up the ever steepening hillside, was curving back to the left. Nevertheless, he had little alternative but to continue onwards, hoping that, eventually, the road would bring him further to the right than his current position.

Tony boarded the scooter and continued on for some time until he reached a sign pointing towards an old Moorish fortress, five kilometres further on. He could see the structure in the distance, recalling it from the guidebook to the region that had been his first purchase when news of the job reached his ears back in Britain. Continuing on the road would be taking Tony well out of his way, and he didn't want to run the risk of being stranded on the mountain roads with no petrol. The scooter had come with a full tank and, judging by the gauge, it had been reduced by over a third already. As the crow flies, the distance from Cieloventura to the fortress was a little less than ten miles, Tony knew, but with the road winding its way back and forth, it could well be at least double that.

Tony had no choice but to return the way he had came. He slowly drove back down the road, taking great care whenever a distant rumble foretold of an approaching coach of tourists. While the road was generally wide enough to accommodate traffic heading in both directions, some of the tighter corners required larger vehicles to take up the lion's share of both lanes, and the thunder of a large coach as it passed close by made him feel decidedly vulnerable.

Tony suddenly pulled the scooter off the road and came to a shuddering halt, sending a cloud of dust into the air. He had not noticed a lane forking off from the main road on his journey up the hillside but, approaching from the opposite direction, it was more visible. The lane was nothing more than a dirt track, its entrance partially concealed with overhanging trees, but it would take Tony in the direction he knew he needed to go. He wasn't going to leave the scooter at the roadside, and riding it along the dried mud track looked dangerous, so Tony wheeled it into the trees and, making sure it couldn't be seen from the road, started along the lane.

After about ten yards, a wooden gate barred his path. Despite the apparent newness of the padlock and chain, there seemed no sign of life and Tony didn't hesitate to climb over it. The lane, which curved slowly to the left, continued on for some time before opening out into the grounds of a *finca*, a small farm. Tony paused only briefly, to see if he could see anyone on the property, before making for the large terrace at the front of the main farmhouse building. From there, he was able to gaze down at Cieloventura in the distance.

Tony took the photo from his shirt pocket and, using the camera on his phone, tried to reproduce it. It couldn't be done using his eyesight, as the perspective was different, but the camera gave him a better image for comparison. It was, for all intents and purposes, identical. There was the faintest of gaps between the two high-rise hotels in the town, and several other landmarks seemed to be in similar positions. The photo was taken here, he was sure of it. Why on earth had Natalie Brooks come here?

Tony turned and looked at the farmhouse. The stone walls matched that of the building in the background of one of the photos, confirming his belief he was in the right place, and, even in spite of its general state of disrepair, it was an attractive property. He suddenly had the curious feeling he had seen the building before, but where and when he could not begin to think. Despite looking uninhabited, Tony was aware he was trespassing and so made for the front door. He rapped on the ornate knocker several times and waited a good minute or two for a response. As expected, there was none.

When returning to Cieloventura, Tony decided he would go straight to the comisaría. If the police were intrigued as he by Natalie's connection to the finca, whatever it may be, they would have no qualms about forcing entry into any of the buildings on the land and investigating its ownership. In the meantime, however, Tony saw no harm in having a brief scout around. He walked around the farmhouse and attempted to peer through any gap that presented itself between the locked wooden shutters on each window. Only one gave him a view of the room beyond the glass, but it was bare of any furniture.

The land at the rear of the property stretched for a hundred or so yards up the hillside, and had once – Tony assumed – been home to an orchard or small vineyard. It seemed, to his limited knowledge of the subject, ideal for the purpose, but it had lain uncultivated for some time. There were a couple of small storage buildings on the land, which all proved empty except one. It contained a number of items of old-fashioned, rusting items of farm equipment, whose only use would be ornamental, he thought – a nostalgic throwback to the finca's glory days.

Tony returned to the terrace and followed a pathway leading through a narrow, overgrown garden into a small area of trees. At the end of the pathway stood a small outbuilding that had long fallen into ruin. One wall had collapsed, and the roof was delicately perched on just two corner posts. As Tony neared the outbuilding, he was suddenly frightened. The knots in his stomach came on with little warning, his body reacting to the sight in front of him almost before he was consciously aware of it. The pile of bricks from the collapsed wall seemed too ordered, too arranged. There was something about its shape that scared him. And then there were the flies.

Some of the broken bricks had fallen from the pile, or been pulled back by scavenging animals, and, even from his distance, Tony could see the bare arm exposed beneath. He dropped slowly to his knees and began to sob. It was several minutes before, with trembling hands that he fought to control, Tony took the mobile phone from his pocket and speed-dialled the number he had been given by the investigating officers on the case. Nothing. Confused, Tony cancelled the call and began to re-dial before realising there was no signal. He would need to ride down the mountain until the phone kicked into life but, first, there was something he needed to do.

Tony inched slowly towards the side of the outbuilding and began to lift the bricks from the top end of the pile, placing them with unnecessary neatness by his side. As a policeman, he may have got used to the smell of vomit, but the pungent odour that began to attack his nostrils as he removed the bricks was one he had hoped never to experience again. His mind briefly revisited the moment when, as a young constable, he had broken down the front door of a house belonging to an elderly lady who had not been seen for two weeks by her neighbours. It was the smell, not the sight, of her decaying remains that stayed with him for a long time.

Once enough of the bricks had been removed, Tony gently scraped back the layer of dust and dirt that covered the face. He didn't react when it was finally exposed. He simply took a few moments to gather his thoughts before getting to his feet and slowly, and without looking back, returning along the path towards the terrace. The face was bloated and discoloured, and almost unrecognisable. Almost, but not quite. It was not Natalie Brooks. The face beneath the bricks belonged to Donnie Lane.

CHAPTER TEN

INSPECTOR Jefe Roman Lopéz Chavarría carried the tray of fresh coffee, toast and pastries into the bedroom and set it down gently on the bedside table. Loosening the damp towel from around his waist and letting it drop to the floor, he climbed back beneath the sheet and gazed up at the gently-rotating fan above. The detective had always been the reflective sort, his mind lingering on his work no matter where he was or what he was doing. Sometimes he wasn't even aware his attention had drifted off onto a current case until an exasperated shout from Isabel, or a well-aimed cushion, brought it back into line.

He was satisfied with the investigation into the murder of Leanne Piggott. Save for a few procedural matters, his day-to-day involvement in the case would be reduced. They had their man, and it was now simply a question of ensuring the case against him was as tight and effective as possible. Chavarría still wanted a confession, however. And he was confident of getting one. True, the arrogant young Briton had not seen fit to co-operate so far, but he must soon realise the futility of his position. A week or two in Fontcalent would soften him up. Chavarría's relationship with Juez Sandoval had also thawed a little, and that could only be a good thing. The meeting they'd had before Ryan Dinsdale's first court appearance had been strained, with the judge analysing every move the investigating team had made and going over each piece of evidence with a frustrating eye for detail. Still, the final comment he had made before leaving to chair the hearing was complimentary and, from a man like Sandoval, that was something.

The week ahead would be a stark contrast to the one just gone. A number of meetings, including one with Comisario Principal García, head of the *Grupo de Homicidios de Alicante*, awaited him, as did his annual medical, and with him being less tied-up on the Piggott case, he doubted he could find much of a reason to postpone it. But all of that would be fine. It would be a welcome release from the pressures of the past ten days. Chavarría coated a slice of toast with a liberal application of jam and took a large bite out of it.

The sound of the shower from the bathroom almost drowned out the gentle vibration of his mobile phone and, if it wasn't for the screen lighting up, he probably would have missed the call. Chavarría stretched across to the small table on the other side of the bed, remembering he had switched the ringer off the evening before, and scooped up the phone. He looked at the name on the screen and cursed. The detective debated for a few seconds over whether to answer it or just let it run into voice-mail, but duty got the better of him. They just better have a damn good reason for calling him on a Sunday, that was all.

Sitting on the small wall at the front of the terrace,

Tony was transfixed with the sight of the blue Mediterranean in the distance. He hardly dared to blink. Blinking would bring him back to the present, the here and now, and he didn't want that. Not just yet. Staring at the sea took him away from the horror of it all. He could swear he could hear the gentle crash of the waves against the rocks and the feel of the fine spray against his face.

'Excuse me, señor?'

Tony was aware the question had been asked at least twice, but it was only when it was repeated with a touch of frustration underlining it that he was able to respond. He glanced around to see a tall Spanish gentleman standing on the terrace.

'You are?'

'Tony Heather.'

'Ah, the Englishman,' the man smiled warmly, approaching him. 'I am Inspector Jefe Roman Lopéz Chavarría.'

Inspector Jefe. The equivalent of a Chief Inspector back home, Tony knew. And he knew of Chavarría. He was the detective who had been in charge of the investigation into Leanne Piggott's death. Tony swung his legs back over the small wall and stood up. Chavarría offered his hand, which Tony gladly accepted.

'It was you who found the body?'

'Yes. Yes, I did.'

Chavarría looked around the finca. Even with the noise and activity of half-a-dozen uniformed officers of the Policia Nacional, the desolation of the surroundings could not be lost on him. 'And what led you to come here, Sr. Heather? It is a little out of town, yes?'

Tony produced the copies of the photographs from his pocket and handed them to the detective. He explained how, via Natalie's friend and Jerry Field, they had come into his possession. Chavarría looked through each image in turn.

'You did well to find the place from these.'

'There's not many other candidates along this stretch of road,' said Tony. 'I was able to match the view from the terrace, and the stonework of the main building.'

Chavarría folded the sheets of paper and, after looking to Tony for approval, put them in his pocket. 'I understand you disturbed the grave?'

The question was asked almost as an aside, a casual remark with little, if any, importance attached to it, and the Inspector Jefe's disarming smile reinforced that impression. Tony knew, though, that it was a serious matter. He couldn't really explain to himself why he had felt the need to see the body, let alone to anyone else.

'I apologise. I just wanted to make sure before calling in the police. It could just have been a pile of old bricks for all I knew.'

'And yet you suspected something?'

'I felt uneasy, certainly.'

Chavarría nodded. He wasn't too happy, but there was nothing that could be done now. He just hoped no evidence had been tainted or destroyed. He knew who Tony Heather was. A former policeman from the UK who was now employed by the town hall to work with British tourists in Cieloventura who had gotten themselves in, or more likely were the cause of, trouble. And he looked every inch an Englishman. The floppy sun hat he wore to shield himself from the sun was clearly an afterthought going by the burned, flaky skin on his face.

'And you expected it to be the missing woman Natalie Brooks, am I right?'

'It seemed logical.'

'I am aware of some of the details of the case,' the policeman said, 'although I have not been working on it myself. Did you know the victim personally?'

'His name was Donnie Lane. He was the manager of the Breeze nightclub on Calle Veijo. I've spoken to him a couple of times.'

'English?'

'Yes.'

Chavarría groaned inside. Coming so soon after the murder of Leanne Piggott, the death of another foreign national, and another Briton as well, was the last thing he needed.

'And it is thought he may have been connected in some way with the holiday rep's disappearance?'

'Natalie Brooks was in Breeze the night she vanished.'

Chavarría ran over the few details of the case he was able to recollect in his mind. He had glanced through the file in the course of the Leanne Piggott enquiry but there seemed nothing to connect the two investigations. When interviewing Ryan Dinsdale for the second time, Chavarría allowed an officer working on the Natalie Brooks enquiry to sit in and ask him a few questions. The young Briton had shown no greater willingness to answer their questions than his own, but the blank look on Dinsdale's face when shown a photo of the missing rep seemed genuine enough.

'But Sr. Lane denied seeing her, is that right?'

'Yes.'

'And you didn't believe him?'

'No.'

Chavarría took a few moments to consider all that Tony had told him and, with a brief nod and a smile, signalled an end, for the moment, to their conversation.

'We have your contact details, I trust?'

'Yes.'

'Then I do not think we need detain you here any longer. We may need to speak again another time.'

Tony didn't need a second invitation. The police had their job to do, and so did he. The two men shook hands once more and Tony made his way back along the lane towards the main road. It was there he had waited for the police to arrive after making the call. By the time Tony had ridden back up the hillside from the point where he was able to get a signal on his mobile phone, it had only been a matter of minutes before the first patrol car arrived. He had accompanied the officers as far as the terrace and pointed them in the direction of the outbuilding, preferring to remain behind.

Tony boarded the scooter and set off once again

down the hillside. Having recovered from the initial shock, where he seemed incapable of any rational thought, his mind was now racing. Donnie Lane was dead. Murdered.

Inspector Jefe Chavarría approached the outbuilding and watched from a respectful distance as the police doctor diligently carried out his initial inspection of the body. The minutes ticked by and, after an exchange of frustrated glances with Official Luís Banda Molina, standing patiently by the doctor's side, he could wait no longer.

'What can you tell me?'

The doctor glanced around and, looking more than a little inconvenienced by the interruption, peered at Chavarría through half-moon spectacles. 'Dead for around three days, I would say. Possibly less.'

Flicking through his notebook, Banda walked over to Chavarría. 'He was questioned at the comisaría on Thursday morning. Released at around ten 'o' clock. He must have been killed the same day.'

Chavarría looked back to the doctor. 'Cause of death?'

'With the body in this condition, I would not like to hazard a guess.'

'Try.'

The doctor frowned at Chavarría — his Sunday had been ruined as well, you know — and turned his attention back to the body. He moved the head of the victim, first to one side and then the other, and spent several minutes conducting a close examination.

'There appears to be trauma to the back of the skull,' the doctor said. 'I cannot say more at this stage. You will need to wait for the report.'

Although the Leanne Piggott case was now just a matter of dotting the i's and crossing the t's, Chavarría knew he could well do without another large-scale enquiry to head. The victim was English, but at least he was a resident and not a tourist. That made things different. Better. Hopefully he wouldn't have to contend with the added pressures placed on his by the Mayor's Office and the media, and the frequent none-too-subtle reminders about the consequences of such crimes on the town's reputation and economy. Chavarría gestured to Banda, and the two men walked back along the pathway together.

'I want everything on the Natalie Brooks enquiry on my desk by the time I return,' the Inspector Jefe said. 'And I want to know all you can find out about the victim.'

'Right.'

Banda strode off across the terrace towards the lane. He passed Official Elisa Valle Huerta heading in the opposite direction.

'You took your time,' commented Chavarría.

'Some of us don't like to leave the house with wet hair.'

'You are familiar with the case of the missing British holiday rep?' the Inspector Jefe said, deciding it best to restrict their conversation to business matters.

'I know of it. She has been gone for over a week, yes?'

'That's correct. According to the investigation into her disappearance, there is a witness that can put her in the Breeze nightclub in the early hours of Friday morning. But, according to Sr. Lane, who was the manager of the club, he did not see her there. He was brought in for questioning on Thursday morning. Now, he turns up dead.'

'What would you like me to do?'

Chavarría looked up at the main farmhouse building. 'I want to know who owns the finca,' he said. 'And why Natalie Brooks and Donnie Lane may have had cause to come here.'

Valle nodded and turned her interest to the house. One of the first officers on the scene had forced an entry through a window, but an initial search had revealed nothing but empty rooms. Chavarría returned to the front of the terrace and, lighting a cheroot, looked down at Cieloventura in the distance. Life was getting complicated. He had only had one communication with Isabel since she stormed out, and that was just a message left on his voice-mail, telling him that she needed some space and would be back within a week. That was five days ago. When she returned, he would need to spend some time with her. Serious time. Not just a snatched hour here or there. Another murder enquiry was the last thing he needed.

With Isabel away, he had gone against his better judgement and allowed Terésa to remain in Catalonia with Conchita and her family. Although her daily text messages told him she was having a nice time, he still felt they were failing her in some way.

'Inspector Jefe? The search team has arrived.'

Chavarría turned to see Agente Narváez standing at the end of the lane.

'I want a full search of the property,' the detective said. 'Everything.'

The uniformed policeman nodded and, with a few barked instructions and hand gestures, began to allocate areas of the finca to the dozen or so officers that were appearing along the lane. Chavarría gazed up at the hillside. The land had not been worked for some time and the earth was baked as hard as concrete. He could understand why the body had been concealed where it was.

There was only one other property further up the hillside that overlooked the finca, but it was some distance away and Chavarría doubted whether anything of use could have been seen. Still, it needed checking out all the same and he duly despatched Narváez to make enquiries.

Chavarría took out the photographs he had been given by the Englishman, and looked at the one of the young woman posing in front of the farmhouse. It was hardly a typical tourist photo. There had to be a reason why she came here, but what could the connection between a British holiday rep and an abandoned finca miles out of town possibly be?

'Donnie Lane?'

'The manager of Breeze.'

'Yes, I know. Oh, my god! This is getting more horrible by the day!'

Marie started to pour boiling water into two mugs but, her hand shaking, was forced to put the kettle back down for a moment until she was able to regain her composure.

After returning to Cieloventura, Tony had paid his first visit to the Iglesia de Santa Matilde. He had no idea why he had been drawn there, it wasn't something he seemed consciously aware of until he was in the process of parking the scooter outside, but sitting inside gave him the opportunity to reflect on the day's events. His heart pounded in his chest and there seemed nothing he could do to slow it down. He was alone except for an elderly lady clad in black, whose chesty cough echoed around the interior of the church. Tony lit a candle, placing some loose change in the collection box, and said a prayer. He didn't know who it was for, or who it was to, but it seemed an appropriate gesture.

From the Iglesia de Santa Matilde, Tony went to the *Holiday18* apartments. It was Marie's afternoon off, and he explained to her all that had happened. The rep finished making the tea and carried the two steaming mugs to the sofa. 'So what does all this mean?'

'I just don't know,' said Tony, taking one of the mugs by its rim and quickly transferring it to the small table in front of him before the skin on his fingertips burnt completely through, 'but don't worry. We'll get to the bottom of it.'

'How did he die?'

'I don't know that either.'

Marie returned to the kitchen for a packet of

biscuits.

'Did Natalie ever mention a farmhouse in the hills? A place she'd been to or that someone had told her about?'

'Not as far I know,' the young woman said, slowly shaking her head. 'Of course, she was always saying how she'd like to live in one of those mountain villas. Catch herself a millionaire or something.'

'So talk to me about Natalie. What did she do in her spare time?'

'She never really said. Of course, she used to hand out leaflets for Breeze, but you were the one who told us that.'

'Natalie e-mailed the photos to a friend of hers back home,' said Tony. 'Did she have a camera of her own?'

'Only the one on her mobile,' Marie said.

'Her own mobile?'

The price of using a mobile phone to call back home could be prohibitive, Tony knew, and it worked out cheaper to use a pre-paid card to call from a public booth. The *Holiday18* reps, however, had all been issued with mobile phones so they could be contacted at any time by hotels or guests, as well as keeping in touch with each other. Marie had already told Tony that Natalie carried both her phones with her at all times, but they had been switched off since the night of her disappearance.

'Yeah, the company ones are just shit basic.'

'What about access to a computer?'

'She didn't have her own, but I know she often

popped into one of the internet cafés in town. An' sometimes she would cadge a go of mine or Ross's. We've got mobile broadband, but the signal's not all that great.'

Natalie had not gone to the finca on her own. Somebody must have been with her to take the photos and, if it wasn't her camera that had been used, they must have been sent to her by the person who took them. The police would obviously have the same idea and be able to access her e-mail account, if they hadn't done so already, something Tony would not be able to do.

'How's the new girl?' asked Tony, reaching for a biscuit.

'She prefers Benidorm,' Marie chuckled, 'but, other than that, she's fine, yeah. Far too pretty for her own good, though. Now we're going to need to find someone to replace Ross. He's handed in his notice. Reckons he doesn't feel safe living here anymore after the burglary.'

Tony nodded at two cardboard boxes and a small suitcase in the corner of the room. 'Those are Natalie's things?'

'Yeah. I was pushed for space in my room, so I made room for them there.'

Popping the biscuit in his mouth, Tony got to his feet and went over to the boxes.

'I don't mind hanging on to them for a while,' said Marie, following him. 'I mean, she'll be wanting all her stuff back, won't she?'

Tony glanced around to see Marie looking at him

with a hopeful smile. 'Yes,' he nodded. 'Yes, she will.'

He opened the first of the boxes and looked inside. It was full of neatly-folded summer clothing, mainly T-shirts, shorts, and skirts.

'I doubt she'd mind if I borrowed some of 'em, but I don't think I could squeeze in most of these anyway,' Marie grinned, producing a silver mini-skirt from the box that, to Tony, could more aptly be described as a belt than a skirt. 'My thighs have already run up the white flag! Too many fry-ups of a morning.'

'Are most of these clothes new?' asked Tony, lifting the small suitcase and noting its fullness.

'Well, she brought 'em out here, if that's what you mean,' said Marie. 'No point luggin' too much from home when you can pick up nice cheap stuff around town. An' there's the indoor market too. That's always good for a bargain. I only bought out a small case myself, just a few nice things for my evenings off.'

Marie dug into the bottom of the box and pulled out a neatly folded skirt suit.

'Mind you, this is nice,' she said. 'Don't know when I'd get a chance to wear it, though.'

The young woman unfolded the jacket, made of a dark grey cotton with a delicate silver pinstripe, and held it up against her chest.

'Very posh,' Tony smiled, striking her the merest of glances as he opened the second box. It contained the missing rep's personal belongings, including a plastic bag full of cosmetics, a trashy 'chick-lit' novel with a garish pink cover, and more equipment to style her hair than Tony cared to know. He owned one comb, plain and simple. And that had half-a-dozen teeth missing.

'What about all those condoms?' Tony asked casually, those being the only items he could recall from his first visit that were not apparent to him in the box. He looked up to see Marie turn a slight shade of red and attempt to cover her nervousness with a smile. He decided not to press the matter and quickly sought to save the head rep from any embarrassment by taking a couple of second-hand CD's from the box, each with a sticker advertising a stall at the indoor market, and asking Marie about her favourite music. Life for a *Holiday18* rep must go on, after all.

'What will you do now?' asked Marie, as they sat back down.

'Keep on digging,' Tony replied. 'I know the police will be on it, but I can't just sit back and do nothing.

As Tony drank his tea, he tried to work out what his next move would be. He didn't know whether to contact Jerry Field with the news but, after some deliberation, decided not to. He would learn of the development soon enough and would no doubt be contacting him. Although Tony was free to admit he had used the journalist for his own ends, and he certainly owed him one for passing on Natalie's photographs, he had no desire to become an 'insider' for a British tabloid. Not only that, but he was feeling guilty. It was the newspaper article, and the increased police activity that resulted from it, that had led to Donnie Lane being brought in for questioning. Was his death connected to that? If Tony hadn't turned to the media, would Donnie still be alive? He knew he needed to banish such thoughts from his mind. If Donnie was involved in Natalie's disappearance, as Tony suspected, then he wasn't going to feel in any way responsible for anything that had happened to him as a result.

Tony thanked Marie for the tea and biscuits and left the apartment block. He was halfway back to Calle Neuva when he realised he had driven there on the scooter and, cursing his absent-mindedness, walked back to collect it. He was angry at his inability to stay focused. Maybe his lack of progression in the police force had not been down to the combination of bad luck and missed opportunities that he'd always put it down too. Maybe they hadn't seen the right stuff in him? Perhaps he wasn't cut out for working on major criminal investigations? Tony felt embarrassed at how easy the tears came when he was confronted with the make-shift grave at the finca, and how the ice that seemed to run through his veins had all but paralysed him on the spot.

The disappearance of Natalie Brooks had given him a chance to do some real detective work, but what use had he really been? His discovery of Natalie's visit to *Breeze* had been the result of donkey work, the laborious combination of foot leather and door knocking that were the staple part of any investigation. His oversized sun hat, summer shirt and shorts may be a stark contrast to the his old blue serge uniform, but he was still a plod. Then, of course, there was the finca. How long would it have been before Donnie Lane's body was discovered if it wasn't for him? No, he was doing well, Tony told himself. He didn't have the resources open to the Inspector Jefe but he needed to keep going. Keep asking questions. Keep plugging away.

Tony parked the scooter in the alley behind *Bar Loco* and went up to his apartment. He took a shower to refresh himself before popping downstairs for a quick snack. Tony tried to get his head around his talk at the Solanis on Wednesday morning, flicking through the notes he had made so far. While he didn't want to prepare a script as such — reading from written sheets was a guaranteed way of losing the attention of the audience — he needed to have a fair idea of what he would be saying. Progress was slow, however. He just couldn't concentrate.

'Didn't you fancy that?'

Tony had only picked at his food. 'Sorry, Dave. It's been one of those days, know what I mean?'

'Oh, I know too well, my friend. Too well.'

Dave cleared the table and returned to the bar. 'How's the planning going for big meal?'

Tony had forgotten all about it. Somewhere in his notepad was a shopping list he'd started to make. He found it and looked through the list of ingredients. Tony hoped the local supermarkets would stock all that he needed, and decided to take some time for himself to find out. He felt tired, the events of the day had been draining, and yet sitting still made him restless. A walk around the town would serve him well. Tony visited three local supermarkets in turn, gradually ticking off most of the items on his list and totting up the value of it all as he went along. He had been able to locate most of what he needed, and felt he would be able to improvise the rest.

Tony then returned to his apartment and spent an hour watching a game show on the small TV set in the lounge. While the language had the better of him, he didn't find it difficult to follow what was going on. The host was as cheesy as any he'd seen at home, and the artificial tension created with blue lighting and atmospheric music seemed the same the world over. Tony laughed as the tubby middle-aged woman won the jackpot, throwing her arms around the host in glee and, just for a moment, knocking the look of smug aloofness from his face.

At eight 'o' clock, Tony rode the scooter to Calle Veijo. Although *Breeze* did not open for business until nine, the staff were starting to arrive and set up for the evening. The music was pumping out from the DJ deck, a raised platform at the opposite end to the bar, and a banner being attached to one of the walls announced that tonight was 'Old Skool Nite.' Tony approached a man at the bar, giving instructions to a couple of fresh-faced girls in their late teens. It was the same barman he'd spoken to before; a young Irish man called Keith. He broke off from his conversation as he saw Tony approach.

'When I spoke to you on Thursday night, you said Donnie had gone away for a few days?' Tony asked him, as they moved into the corridor to try and make themselves heard over the music.

'That's right. I dunno when he'll back, like.'

'Was it actually him that told you he'd be away?'

'Yeah, he phoned me Wednesday afternoon. Said he would be gone for a bit an' could I hold the fort 'til he got back. Said he'd see me alright.'

'And you were okay with that?'

'It's hardly rocket-science, is it? Just re-stockin' the bar, supervising the staff, bankin' the takings. I've done it before.'

'Do you know where Donnie lives?'

Keith shook his head. 'Look, what's all this about, mate? I've got work to do.'

Tony wasn't going to let it fall to him to break the news. The police would have that joy. 'Who runs the club? I mean, I know Donnie's the manager but he's not the owner, is he?'

'Some company,' said Keith, with a dismissive shrug. 'Look, you really need to talk to Donnie if you wanna know stuff like that. I'm sure he'll be back tomorrow or the next day.'

Tony left the young barman to his duties and hurried back across the deserted dance floor to the exit before the assault on his ear-drums became terminal. It wouldn't be long before the police arrived at the club, he was surprised they weren't here already, and there would need to be another 'nite' for 'old skool'.

After attending the Monday morning session at the courthouse, Tony called in at the offices of the Policia Municipal and collected his e-mails. The first was from

Jerry Field, asking for more details on the death of Donnie Lane. Tony checked the newspaper's online edition and read an abridged version of the article that had appeared that day. It was scant on details, simply stating that he had been found dead and that police were treating it as suspicious. According to a spokesman, 'no connection was currently being made between the death and the disappearance of the missing British holiday rep, Natalie Brooks.' An expected police response at this stage.

The second was from an officer of the Policia Nacional, asking for the original *jpeg* images of Natalie at the finca and the e-mail address of the journalist who had sent them to him. With just a couple of clicks of the mouse, Jerry's original message was forwarded on.

Finally, there was a message from Fontcalent Prison, giving Tony a time and date to visit Ryan Dinsdale. Eleven 'o' clock the next morning. Sooner than he'd expected. As Tony left the building, he called Maureen Carr and they arranged to meet for dinner the following evening. He had been tempted to tell her he was unable to visit Ryan after all, that he was too busy with work, but the sound of her voice on the phone stopped him from doing so. The desperation was clear.

Tony took the scooter back to the hire shop – his twenty-four hours all but up – and collected his deposit. He'd enjoyed the freedom the vehicle had given him, and the time it had saved, but he could little afford to keep it any longer. He would get either the bus or the Costa Blanca Express to Alicante the next morning. Walking back to Calle Neuva, Tony called the comisaría for an update. He was told the Natalie Brooks enquiry was now being handled by *homicidios y desaparecidos* — the department responsible for investigating murders and disturbed missing person cases that had not been resolved by the regular branch — and that he would need to go through official channels, requesting a meeting with an officer as he had previously needed to do. So much for being kept in the loop.

'The finca is owned by a man named Hector Romo de Anda. He lives in a nursing home in Villajoyosa,' Valle told the small gathering. 'The place has been empty nearly two years. There is a dispute amongst his children about who will get it. As far as I can tell, they're practically waiting for the old man to drop off his perch before World War Three commences.'

'So what is the connection with Donnie Lane and Natalie Brooks?' asked Chavarría, perched on the corner of the nearest desk.

'I do not know, neither does Sr. Romo. He still has most of his faculties, thank god, and he didn't recognise either of them from their photographs.'

'Okay. Luís?'

'Our victim is Donald Alan Lane, known as Donnie,' Banda said, getting to his feet and exchanging places with Valle. He pinned an enlarged copy of the photograph taken from the man's passport to the wall. 'An Englishman. He has been living in Spain for five years, and has been the manager of the Breeze nightclub for two.'

Banda turned to look at the group, which consisted of Chavarría, Valle, representatives from the Policia Nacional's technical support and forensic teams, and a small number of uniformed officers who had been allocated to him for the investigation, many of whom had barely returned to their normal duties after the Leanne Piggott case.

'According to the British police, he has three previous convictions. One for theft, two for fraud. He served a three-year prison sentence in the late-nineties. Twice divorced.'

Banda pointed to a photograph already up on the wall. It was the one that had featured in the 'missing' posters of Natalie Brooks that had been distributed around the town by the *Holiday18* reps.

'Natalie Brooks used to do some work for Lane, this we know, handing out leaflets along the beach. On the night she disappeared, a witness claims to have seen her in Breeze, selling tickets for a boat-trip the next day. Sr. Lane claims not to have seen her there. He says he and Natalie were friends and that they got on well together. There had been no falling out between them, there was no sexual relationship of any kind, and he does not know anything about her private life or the company she kept.'

'Is it just the one witness who puts Natalie at Breeze?' asked Valle.

'Yes. One of the door staff says he *may* have seen her there but cannot be definite. The interviewing officer thinks he was just covering his ass.'

'Bring him in again,' ordered Chavarría. 'No kid gloves treatment this time. Get the truth out of him one way or the other.'

Banda smiled and nodded. That was the kind of task he knew he could be relied on to perform. The official's career had been dogged with accusations of heavy-handedness, and while many of the senior officers he had worked for had been willing to turn a blind eye, it tended to be on the understanding that, should the proverbial shit hit the fan, they would claim no knowledge of his activities, nor be prepared to take any responsibility for them. Chavarría was cut from a different cloth. While he was more than happy to allow his team to work on their own initiative, he was also prepared to take personal responsibility for whatever may result. It was the Inspector Jefe's refusal to throw Banda to the wolves when he had meted out instant justice to a suspect involved in a drug ring the previous summer that had blighted Chavarría's working relationship with Juez Sandoval.

'These photographs were taken at the finca,' said the Inspector Jefe, pointing the attention of the team to the enlarged colour photographs that had been pinned up on the board only minutes before, interrupting Chavarría's initial talk to the gathering. The young Agente had apologised, telling him he had only just received the original files, despite an e-mail requesting them being sent the evening before.

'They had been sent by Natalie to a friend of hers in the UK,' Chavarría explained. 'When the story of her disappearance featured in the British media, the friend sent them to a newspaper, no doubt hoping to earn something for her trouble, who then sent them to Tony Heather. It was he who was able to locate where they had been taken, and subsequently found the body of Sr. Lane.'

The Inspector Jefe looked to Valle. 'I want to know the e-mail account from which these were sent. So get onto this friend of hers. Go through the journalist. His details are in the file.'

'Right.'

Chavarría set about allocating tasks to the remaining officers in the room. Every member of staff at *Breeze* was to be questioned about Donnie Lane, his movements, habits and circle of friends. Officers had visited the club that morning and seized documents and a computer, despite the protestations of a staff member who, after being informed of Donnie's death the night before, had taken it upon himself to assume managerial responsibility until he was contacted by the club's owners.

'I want the club's business records gone through,' Chavarría said. 'Suppliers, staff, licences, everything. And I need a list of all incidents involving the club in the past, say, two weeks. Whether they were reported to the police or not. Brawls, drugs, underage drinkers…'

The Inspector Jefe was aware how fierce competition between nightclubs in Cieloventura could be. A new ruling made by the town council at the beginning of the holiday season that clubs were only allowed to tout for business outside their own premises had helped to resolve many of the smaller incidents the rivalry often caused. Previous to that, it had been common for young people employed by the clubs to hang around certain areas of the town, each trying to attract customers to their establishment by offering a variety of drinks promotions and free gifts. While it was rare for matters to spill over into aggression, there had been complaints from some tourists that they felt harassed and pressured, as well as reports from local residents and business owners that the behaviour of the touts, often taunting and swearing at each other, was disturbing them. While the Mayor's initiative had not ridden the town of the club touts completely, the Policia Municipal arresting two or three people on average each night for illegal promoting, it had proven a successful and popular measure.

Linking the death of Donnie Lane to the competition for business among the nightclubs of Cieloventura, or even to an incident at the club itself, such as someone being thrown out or an employee sacked from their job, was plausible. The Inspector Jefe knew he would be unwise to throw all of his resources trying to connect the murder to the disappearance of Natalie Brooks, even though his gut was telling him the two were linked.

'Who is this Tony Heather?' Valle asked, flicking through the case notes on the Natalie Brook's disappearance.

'Our Mayor's wonderful idea to curb the behaviour of the British,' said Chavarría. 'Have some ex-cop from their homeland patrol the town waggling his finger at them like naughty schoolchildren.'

'He seems to have done a lot of work on the missing girl,' said Valle, noting the Englishman's name appearing several times in the notes.

'Yes, I know, but this is a murder enquiry. I don't want any outsiders blundering about.'

The Inspector Jefe had spent the first hour of the morning searching Donnie Lane's place of residence, a small ground-floor apartment on the outskirts of town, but there was little he could report. He had left a team of officers behind to take the place apart but he wasn't hopeful. The kitchen seemed rarely used, the fridge containing nothing but beer and ready-meals, and the bedroom and lounge were basically furnished. There was little by way of personal possessions that Chavarría wouldn't have expected to find in an apartment lived in by a single middle-aged man. There were a number of unmarked DVDs among a pile of Hollywood action movies and what appeared to be British comedy shows at the side of the television set. The Inspector Jefe had made a note to have their contents checked.

'Check with the force at Denia,' said Chavarría to the only officer remaining who he hadn't given a job to, a young Agente who, to the detective, barely seemed old enough to be out of school let alone in uniform. 'See if they've been able to corroborate this sighting of Natalie last Saturday. And also check to see if her bank card has been used again.'

Chavarría's phone rang and, noting the name on the display, he excused himself from the group. Sandoval. He had half-a-mind to ignore the call but, if it was about what he expected to be about, he knew he shouldn't. The call was brief. Sandoval confirmed he was the examining magistrate on the case, and asked Chavarría to report to him at three that afternoon to discuss the priorities for the investigation.

The Inspector Jefe confirmed the orders he had given his team and clapped his hands, scattering them in all directions. He then scooped the car keys from the corner of his desk and made for the door. The worst task he had left for himself. He had another visit to the pathology lab to make.

CHAPTER ELEVEN

IN all his years as a serving police officer, Tony had only once set foot inside a prison. He had been asked to take a statement from an inmate in connection with an ongoing fraud enquiry, and while the journey, as he had expected, was largely a waste of time, it was an experience he hadn't forgotten. Fontcalent was a very different beast. It was over an hour's bus ride from the city, and the Alicante mountains made for a startling, and intimidating, backdrop. The stark buildings that made up the penitentiary were dominated by a single tall guard tower and, to Tony, it was like something he'd only over seen in an American prison movie. Looking through the scratched, reinforced glass, telephone receiver to his ear, Tony felt like he was *in* a prison movie. He didn't know which one but they all seemed the same to him; a man usually incarcerated for something he didn't do, pressing a desperate hand against the glass to match that of his loved one opposite, their tear-filled eyes locked in mutual despair. Only, in reality, Tony was on the better side of the glass. And the person opposite was no beauty.

Ryan Dinsdale was all Tony thought he would be. An angry young man who thought the world owed him. An angry young man for whom respect was a one-way street; something he insisted upon from others but offered rarely in return. Ryan sat slumped in his chair, barely acknowledging Tony's presence.

'What's it like in here?'

'Shit! Two fuckin' Moroccans in wi' me. Don't speak a word of English, the pair of 'em!'

'Are you eating okay?'

'If the muck they serve up can be called food, then yeah, I s'pose.'

Tony knew that Fontcalent had its problems. Overcrowding was one of them. Built to hold just under five hundred prisoners, it was currently said to house more than double that. Only half the population were Spaniards, with thirty different nationalities estimated to make up the remaining half. Gang rivalry and turf wars were common, and the overcrowding, poor conditions, and rumours of rough treatment at the hands of guards had created a tinder-box atmosphere that could be, and often was, set off with the slightest spark.

Tony had spent the best part of the evening before trying to find out as much as he could about the circumstances of the young man's arrest and detention. While the contacts he'd made at the courthouse didn't prove as useful as he had hoped, a conversation with Rafá over a coffee in the *cantina* proved enlightening, especially the suggestion that Ryan Dinsdale may not even be of this earth.

'A ghost?'

Rafá smiled. 'It is what we call someone who stays at a hotel without the staff's knowledge.'

'How is that possible?'

'Well, it usually happens like this. A couple of people book a package holiday; flights, accommodation, the 'works' as you would say. Then some of their *amigos* book a cheap flight with a low-cost-airline, maybe arriving a day or two later, and they all stay in the same room. They split the cost of everything between them and it can work out a lot cheaper.'

'Doesn't the hotel realise?'

'Tony, my friend, you have seen some of them!' said Rafá. 'They are big places. They have many hundreds of guests, with new ones arriving each day. It is impossible to keep track of who is meant to be there and who isn't.'

Tony recalled at that moment his failure to locate some of the guests on the *Holiday18* boat-trip that had bought their tickets from Natalie Brooks. Despite taking the names and their hotels from the list Marie had showed him, he had found some of the hotels in question had no records of anyone matching those names staying there. Perhaps they were also members of Cieloventura's very own spirit world?

'I remember an incident some time back,' the officer smiled. 'A family room for four at the Belle Vue was found to be sleeping eleven! They even used the bath as a bed. And the sun lounger on the balcony. When the management went into the room one morning, there had been a tip-off from the people next door, there wasn't a centimetre of floor space to be seen! We were called to assist in their eviction.'

Sitting opposite Ryan in the sweltering interview

room, trying to concentrate over the wailing of the middle-aged women in the next booth, Tony had no doubts the young man was the type to pull off such a scam. But that didn't make him a killer.

'Why haven't you been co-operating with the police?'

'They reckon I killed her,' Ryan barked. 'I ain't gonna speak to 'em, ain't I?'

'Maybe if you spoke to them, they might have cause to stop thinking that.'

The stubbornness carved onto the young man's face would need more than a verbal equivalent of a shake of his shoulders, Tony knew. He needed Ryan to trust him, to believe he would do his best for him.

'You were staying at the Hotel Mar Azul?'

'Yeah.'

'But you weren't actually booked in there, am I right?'

'Jus' kipped on a lilo I bought from one of the shops.'

'How long have you been in Spain? Your mum wasn't sure.'

'Got 'ere Tuesday before last,' Ryan sniffed. 'Was only s'pose'd to be 'ere a week.'

'Why do the police think you killed Leanne Piggott?'

'I was with her that night, weren't I?'

'But there must be more to it than that?'

Ryan shrugged. What was it with the younger generation and shrugging? Tony thought it seemed to be their response to everything.

'You have no ideas?'

'There was the band, I s'pose.'

'The what?'

'Her wristband. They found it at the 'otel.'

'What wristband was this?'

Ryan sighed with impatience. For the first time, he sat up in his chair and leaned forward to look at Tony through the glass.

'The Solanis is all-inclusive, ain't it? Everything's free. Entertainment, food, the lot.'

'Hardly free, Ryan. The guests are paying for it.'

'You know what I mean. Everyone has to wear a wristband. Saves people who ain't really guests there from usin' the facilities.'

Tony didn't need to say 'People like you?' as Ryan had already read his expression.

'Look, it was Leanne's idea. She said they don't really check the bands all that often. The staff get to know who's who. An' she said her family all ate their meals together, an' the others would all have their bands showing, so no-one was likely to notice hers missing, 'specially as her mum always made her wear a long-sleeved top 'cause of the sun.'

'So you visited the Solanis using Leanne's wristband?'

'First time was Friday mornin', 'bout half-eleven. Jus' queued up with everyone else. Had bacon an' sausages. Nobody battered an eyelid. I left straight after, didn't wanna push me luck, like. But I went back later to use the pool.'

'When was this?'

'In the afternoon. I 'eard people talkin' 'bout a child being killed, some girl, but I didn't make the connection. Leanne never said she was that young.'

'You didn't suspect?'

'I met her in a bar along the Avenue,' protested Ryan, the indignant look on his face telling Tony exactly what he felt about the suggestion that he should have known Leanne's age.

'Carry on...'

'Well, she said I could use the band so I could get meself somethin' to eat. She knew I didn't have much money to spare, like. I was gonna give it back to her the next night, that's what we agreed.'

'But she didn't show?'

'No,' Ryan shook his head. 'So I jus' went on to a few bars wi' me mates. Then a bit later on, we got stopped by a copper. He was showing people her photo. She looked different. Younger. But it was her alright.'

Tony frantically tried to scribble verbatim what Ryan was saying into his small notebook, the only item he was allowed to bring into the interview room, despite the glass preventing anything from being passed across. He didn't want to tell Ryan to stop or slow down, not now the young man was finally talking.

'Why didn't you say anything?'

'She was just a kid, weren't she? I knew what people would say.'

'And so what did you do then?'

'Jus' went straight back to the hotel. Didn't sleep a wink all night. Anyway, I thought it best not to stick around, so I got a bus to the airport. Told 'em there was a family emergency an' I needed to get 'ome.'

'And what did you do with the wristband from the Solanis?'

'Jus' chucked it away. I weren't gonna try an' use it again, no way!'

As Tony was writing, he tried to make some sort of sense of the information Ryan had given him. He knew the young man had been caught on CCTV along the Avenue with Leanne in the hours before her death, images from that had been in all the newspapers and on the television, and his attempt to flee the country didn't look good. The significance of the identity band from the Solanis Resort wasn't immediately clear to him. Surely the police didn't think Ryan killed for that?

'Did you have sex with her?' Tony asked, watching the young man's reaction very carefully.

'No!' Ryan spat. 'We kissed, felt each other up a bit, but that was all.'

'Did you want to have sex with her?'

A shrug. 'S'pose so. But it never happened.'

'Did you take any drugs?'

'No.'

'You didn't smoke anything?'

'No! Look, the cops asked me all this. I ain't lyin', mate, I'm in enough shit to worry about a poxy spliff!'

Tony nodded and allowed Ryan a few moments to compose himself. The young man was a hot-head, he could see that. Tony took the time to stretch and bend his left arm, trying to get some blood flowing back into it. He wanted to swap ears, the phone receiver was heavy and his arm was starting to ache, but he wasn't able to write with his left hand.

'Okay. Let's go back to the beginning. Tell me how you met Leanne?'

'It was Thursday night, 'bout midnight. Me an' me mates were havin' a drink in a bar along the Avenue when she came in. I'd had a couple by then, an' me mates dared me to go an' chat her up.'

'And you did?'

Ryan nodded. 'I bought her a drink an' we talked. Had a laugh. I asked her if she'd come out with me the next night. She said she would but it'd have to be late 'cause she was with her family an' she had to wait 'til they went to bed. Didn't bother me.'

'And you took her to Platinum, yes?'

'That was her idea. Fuckin' well dear that place is. She wanted to see Streax. I said I didn't know if I could afford it, an' that was when she offered me the band to use.'

'Streax?'

'He was mixin' there.'

Tony nodded, even though he didn't have a clue what Ryan was talking about. 'So you met as planned and went to Platinum. What happened there?'

'Not much,' said Ryan, with another shrug. 'Had a few drinks, few dances. Had a right laugh. She even got to meet Streax. Decent night.'

'And what happened when you left?'

'She said to had to go, wanted to be back by three so she could get a few hours kip, like. I was gonna stay on for a bit but, jus' after she left, I realised she didn't gimme the wristband like she said she was gonna, so I went out after her.'

'Did you catch up with her?'

'Further along the Avenue,' Ryan nodded. 'She was goin' a diff'rent way, mind. Towards the beach. I almost missed her.'

'Did she say why she was going a different way?'

'Jus' that she fancied a walk back along the seafront. Clear her 'ead, I s'pose.'

'And what did you do then?'

'Well, I couldn't get back into Platinum, never got me 'and stamped as I left, see,' replied Ryan. 'So I found another bar to drink in.'

'Where?'

The young man shook his head. 'Dunno.'

'You don't know it's name?'

'I said I dunno!'

Tony tried to not let his frustration show. He only had a thirty minute visit and he could sense the guards, sitting some twenty feet behind him, starting to rouse themselves in readiness to see all of the visitors back out into the stifling Alicante heat.

'Look, you really need to start co-operating with the police,' said Tony. 'If you didn't do it, you need to work with them, not against them.'

'What good will it do me, man? They'd've 'ung me already if it was up to that lot.'

'Are the Consulate keeping in touch?'

'I've spoke to 'em on the phone,' Ryan said. 'An' someone's visited me.'

It was standard procedure, Tony knew, for a Consular official to visit any British subject remanded in a Spanish prison. They weren't able to provide legal advice or make a case for a prisoner's release, but they would ensure Ryan was being treated according to Spanish law and suffering no harm or mistreatment. They would also aid him in communicating with family and friends.

'And you have a lawyer?'

'Jus' the one appointed by the court. Me Mam said she'll sort me out a decent one.'

If Maureen's financial status was indeed as bleak as she had indicated, Tony doubted she would be able to do much. He took down the contact details of the lawyer and, after thanking Ryan for allowing him to visit, said his goodbyes. Ryan just nodded in response, and it wasn't until Tony had almost placed the phone back into its cradle that the young man spoke. He wasn't able to hear what was said, but it wasn't hard to lip-read.

'Please, Mr. Heather?'

Tony put the receiver back to his ear. As he looked through the glass, the defiant and stubborn young man morphed into a frightened and vulnerable boy in front of his eyes.

'Get me out of 'ere.'

'I'll see what I can do.'

It was all Tony could say. He wasn't going to make promises he couldn't keep. Ryan replaced his phone first and left the booth. Tony watched him go, swaggering unintimidated under the close gaze of a prison officer, towards a barred doorway at the back of the large interview room. He had been in custody for over a week and, all things considered, seemed to be holding up well. But how long would that last?

Tony left the penitentiary and joined many of the other visitors at the side of the road for the next bus back to Alicante. He wanted to help, and while there were a few things he thought he could follow up on, he knew he had precious little time to spare. Tony had a full-time job after all, and if that didn't have enough of a claim on his time, there were also his enquiries into the disappearance of Natalie Brooks and the subsequent murder of Donnie Lane.

As he boarded the bus, helping a tearful woman on with a pushchair and two small children, Tony decided he would find an hour or two from somewhere to look into the matter, and then, for his own sanity, would need to draw a line under it. While he felt for the young man imprisoned in Fontcalent, possibly for many months ahead, and even more so for his mother, Tony knew he was taking on more than one person could be expected to handle. Working so hard wasn't why he came to Cieloventura.

Max Okeke didn't exactly come quietly but, if he was honest, Banda wouldn't have had it any other way. The punch that caused him to sink to his knees, gasping for breath, was probably unnecessary but he surely had it coming after leading the Official on an exhausting, though ultimately futile, chase through the backstreets of Cieloventura's northern district. The address given in *Breeze*'s employment records had proved false, and it had taken Banda over a day to track Max down. With the doorman recovering in a cell, the Official headed up to the offices of *homicidios y desaparecidos*.

'He's talk, don't worry,' Banda replied to Inspector Jefe Chavarría's enquiry. 'He's an illegal. He'll tell us anything to avoid being sent back to whatever shithole he came from.'

'We don't do deals.'

'No,' agreed the official, sitting down at his desk, 'but he won't know that until he's halfway to the airport.'

Banda nodded at the written report that Chavarría held in his hands. 'Anything of interest?'

'It confirmed what I was told yesterday,' the Inspector Jefe replied. 'Death was due to blunt force trauma to the back of the skull, causing an acute subdural bleed in the brain. There were three separate blows, though the first alone would have probably killed him.'

'The killer wanted to make sure. Any clues as to who it may have been?'

'Right-handed going by the angle of the blows, but they apparently could have been delivered by anyone of average strength,' Chavarría said, flicking through the pathologist's report. 'He hadn't eaten that day, but there was a small amount of alcohol in his system. Toxicology came back negative. Estimated time of death was around midday Thursday.'

'So Sr. Lane is brought into the comisaría for questioning,' considered Banda, 'and then walks out of this building to his death?'

'It would seem so, yes. I've had the security tapes from the lobby and the main entrance checked. Lane was timed out at ten-zero-six. This is interesting…'

Chavarría took a print-out from his desk and held it up for Banda to see. The picture, lifted from the CCTV footage, showed Donnie Lane walking down the steps outside the front of the comisaría, mobile phone in hand.

'It looks like he's calling someone,' said Banda.

'His phone wasn't at his apartment,' Chavarría replied. 'Nor was it at the scene. But that is no surprise, there was nothing to identify him on his body.'

Chavarría turned his attention to Elisa Valle Huerta as she strode past towards the coffee machine in the corner. Having the desk nearest the machine was the sole perk the Inspector Jefe had since the office, to 'maximise space and efficiency and enhance teamwork', according to the memo, had gone open plan. It was either that or the fire escape. The need for a ready, and reachable, source of caffeine came before health and safety.

'Have you had a chance to check those DVDs?'

'I have had a look through them, thank you,' responded Valle, cursing at the barest inch of coffee that remained in the machine. The office rule was that whoever drained the jug prepared a fresh lot but, after the morning she'd just had, let anyone dare point that out to her.

'And?'

'What do you think they were?'

The Inspector Jefe, if he guessed correctly, knew Valle wouldn't have relished such a task, but with the ownership of the finca proving to be a dead-end as far as a lead to the Englishman's murder was concerned, that was the next thing that needed doing.

'Anything out of the ordinary?'

Valle wondered what constituted 'ordinary' pornography and what didn't. It wasn't her type of sex, she knew that, but it wasn't anything that shocked her either. Each of the DVDs found in Donnie Lane's apartment had to be watched from beginning to end, albeit in fast-forward mode, as Valle was well aware that prohibited material could often appear halfway through legal films. It was only the last two DVDs that had made the official reach for the video controls and pay closer attention.

'There were a couple of homemade ones.'

'Homemade?'

'Sr. Lane and various women young enough to be his daughter.'

'What do you mean by homemade?'

'Well, I don't think his partners knew they were movie stars, if that's what you are getting at.'

'Was Natalie Brooks one of them?'

'I don't think so,' said Valle, shaking her head. 'I'll get some stills printed off and see if they can be identified.'

The middle-aged greasy Englishman was hardly a gift to the opposite sex, the Inspector Jefe thought, but, as manager of a nightclub, he was in a position where he came into contact with, and probably exploit, plenty of young people. Most of the staff at *Breeze* were temporary workers; youngsters wanting some money to extend their holidays, budding dancers and DJ's looking for a break, and, like Max Okeke, the odd cash-in-hand illegal immigrant.

Questioning of the few staff that had been at the club long enough to have anything useful to say had thrown up several points of interest. There was a disparity between the number of people said to be paying at the door on an average night and the figures reported in the accounts. *Breeze* wasn't considered one of Cieloventura's leading nightspots, anything but, yet the figures suggested it was close to capacity on an almost nightly basis. Possible irregularities had also been uncovered with suppliers and duty. Chavarría had decided a more thorough enquiry into the club's affairs was needed and had passed the information onto the Policia Nacional department tasked with investigating fraud and monetary crime. *Breeze*, though, did not appear on a list of nightclubs and bars considered 'known' trouble spots. Police officers only rarely had cause to visit the establishment, and there was a well-enforced zero tolerance policy on drug use. Donnie Lane would clearly not have wished too much attention from the authorities.

Chavarría's mobile phone rang and, after the quickest of glances at the screen, he rejected the call.

'Breeze is owned by a holding company with registered offices in Madrid and Gibraltar,' the Inspector Jefe said, looking back to Valle. 'Messages have been left but nobody has so far got back to us. See if you can get something out of them. If you can't, get the city boys to go and interrupt their siestas. This is a murder case. We don't wait for when it is convenient for people to talk to us.'

Chavarría took the fax he had received from the local Tax Office, with details of the club's ownership, and handed it to Valle. He waited until she had returned to her desk and was speaking on the phone before returning his missed call.

'Sorry about that,' he said. 'I was in a meeting.'

'Will you be home sometime today? I was going to make dinner.'

'Of course.'

'It'll be on the table at seven.'

Isabel had returned home earlier in the day, a simple text message had told him that, and, murder investigation or not, Chavarría knew he needed to be home on time this evening or he could kiss his marriage goodbye.

The Inspector Jefe took in the array of information presented on the large wall opposite his desk and considered his next move. The fingertip search of the finca and the surrounding land had thrown up little of interest. The nature of the injury sustained by Donnie Lane meant there was no external blood loss, and so finding the exact spot where the murder had been committed was going to prove difficult. Lane's car, a ten year-old Seat Arosa, had been found parked less than a hundred yards from his apartment and it was currently being examined. The club manager could have been killed at the finca, or met his end elsewhere and been transported there. The autopsy had revealed a pattern of lividity that was consistent with the position in which the body had been found, but that didn't conclusively prove Lane was attacked where he was buried.

The children of the finca's owner, Sr. Romo, had all been spoken to by Valle and none had visited the property in the previous three months. Though entry into the finca had been forced, and the door subsequently repaired with a new lock, Valle had borrowed the key for the building from its elderly owner and tried it in the original lock. It did not fit.

The bar owner from Denia who claimed to have seen Natalie Brooks on the previous Saturday evening had been spoken to by the local force, and shown more photos of the missing rep. He confirmed his original statement, and seemed even more certain that it was Natalie who had visited his bar. There was also no record of her bank card having been used since. The friend of Natalie Brooks who had received the photos of her at the finca had forwarded the original e-mail to the Police Nacional. It had come from a *2linx* account, a free web-based service, and Chavarría had already set the necessary wheels in motion to gain access to the account. There was also Donnie Lane's mobile phone records, although if he was involved in any illegality, Chavarría doubted he would be so stupid as to use a phone registered in his name to conduct such business.

The officer looked to the large map of Cieloventura next to the case information. His eyes scanned the most likely routes Donnie Lane could have taken after leaving the comisaría, mentally noting any of the CCTV cameras in the town that he may have passed by. It was probable, though by no means certain, that the Englishman would have returned either to *Breeze*, where he had been arrested earlier that morning, or to his apartment. Once Banda had finished with the errant doorman, he would get him onto it.

'I know who she is,' Max said, ignoring the photographs of Natalie Brooks that Luís Molina Banda was arranging on the table between them. The African man wondered if he had a broken rib, as each intake of breath he took caused a sharp pain in his side, but he resolved not to let it show in front of the policeman.

'Where did you last see her?'

'I have told you people this already. She may have been in the club Thursday before last, but I cannot remember.'

'You cannot remember?'

Max stared at his interrogator. 'No. I cannot remember.'

Banda placed the next photograph in front of Max. This one did not show the bright and smiling Natalie Brooks, but the cold and lifeless Donnie Lane. The official knew the doorman would need to look down at that one. It would be suspicious if he didn't. And he was right.

'Why did you run when I came to talk to you?'

Max looked back up. 'What do you want from me? Looking for a convenient fall guy?'

'I just want the truth.'

The doorman leaned back in his chair, masking the sudden stabbing twinge in his side by turning the expression of pain that appeared on his face into a smile.

'That, you will find, comes at a price.'

Tony picked up the cigarette stub that still smouldered in the ashtray and held it up to his nose. It wasn't the strongest he'd ever smelt, but he recognised the familiar odour as soon as he had climbed up onto the top deck of the boat.

'Sorry to keep you waitin', mate.'

Tony replaced the stub and turned to see a man in his thirties, clad only in shorts, flip-flops and an array of tattoos that barely left an inch of his torso on show, scaling the steps. He approached Tony with a welcoming smile.

'The name's Streax.'

The moniker was well chosen, for the man's long black hair was highlighted with several lines of bright colours. Before heading for *Platinum*, Tony had called in at the offices of the Policia Municipal and spent a quarter of an hour on the net reading up on the career of their star DJ. His real name was Duncan Cox, a former radio presenter and sound engineer from Manchester who, under the 'Streax' guise, had achieved some fame in the early years of the millennia for his innovative remixes of classic songs. While he hadn't troubled the charts in a while, Streax remained a popular DJ across the party resorts of the

Mediterranean.

Tony shook hands with the DJ and, aware that the man had no doubt been forewarned of who he was and why he was there, introduced himself before producing from his pocket a photograph of Leanne Piggott he had taken from the offices of the Policia Nacional. It was a copy of the image that had appeared in the first press conference given by Inspector Jefe Chavarría, the one taken by Leanne's father in the gardens of the Solanis Resort. He handed it to Streax.

'Do you recognise this girl?'

'Yeah, course I do.'

The DJ quickly sought to extinguish the spark of hope that he duly noted on his visitor's face. 'Mind, I wouldn't have done if she hadn't been plastered all over the papers,' he added. 'That's the girl they found on the beach, right?'

'Yes,' nodded Tony, taking the photo back. 'She was at Platinum the night she died.'

'So I read, yeah.'

'I was told she met you.'

Streax blew out his cheeks and sat down in the helmsman's chair. 'If you expect me to remember, you're outta luck,' he said. 'The place was heavin', man. Holds nearly two thousand.'

'How often do you play at Platinum?'

'Twice a week throughout the season. Wednesdays an' Thursdays. I'm in Ibiza or Majorca at weekends.'

'Do you sail there?' smiled Tony, looking around the top deck of the motor yacht in admiration. The vessel, some fifty feet in length, was the jewel in the crown of the various boats that lined the private marina.

Streax laughed. 'Naa, this baby's purely for pleasure! We're heading up the coast this evening. A sundown cruise.'

'Some life.'

'Can't beat it, my friend.'

Tony gestured to a pair of small binoculars that hung from a hook to the side of the yacht's steering wheel.

'May I?'

'Sure, be my guest.'

Tony took the binoculars and gazed out across the expanse of blue sea that stretched invitingly out in front of the private marina. A speedboat roared past, some hundred yards or more into the distance, and Tony followed the line that came up from the boat's stern. A somewhat overweight young man, chubby arms and legs waving in glee, was hanging precariously from a parasail at the opposite end. Tony had not yet dared to take a ride in such a contraption, one of the many types of water activities offered along this stretch of the Cieloventura coast, and doubted he ever would. Thrill-seeking was best left to the young and the foolish.

The sound of several pairs of high-heeled shoes on the wooden jetty below brought Tony's attention back. He glanced down to see three young woman tottering towards the short gangplank that led onto the yacht, accompanied by a couple of members of Streax's entourage that he'd already run the gauntlet of in his attempt to gain an audience with the man himself.

'Have the police been to speak to you?' Tony asked, handing the binoculars back.

'Nope,' replied the DJ, shaking his head. 'I mean, I was told they came to the club but I've never spoke to anyone. Their best bet would've been the door staff. An' then there's the CCTV footage, of course.'

Tony gave Streax his card and finished the brief meeting with a request for him to get in touch if he should learn anything that may have a bearing on the case. The DJ readily agreed and they parted. Tony made his way off the boat and walked across the small marina towards the gates. As he negotiated the chicane of iron railings that made up the pedestrian gate, Tony glanced back at the motor-yacht. The triumvirate of excitable young women were now on the top deck, looking on with awe as the star DJ proudly showed off his craft.

Tony glanced at his watch. It was now just after five 'o' clock, and he had arranged to meet Maureen in a small restaurant along the Carrer de Trato at seven. That would give him enough time to return to his apartment for a shower, a fresh change of clothes, and a chance to go over what he was going to say to her. When he had spoken to her on the phone earlier in the afternoon, there seemed so much hope in her voice that Tony knew it would, for her own sake, need to be dampened. Ryan was in serious trouble and would likely be held on remand for many months ahead. Tony narrowed his eyes slightly as he took one final look back to the berth that housed the yacht. It appeared to him that, just a moment, Streax had turned the binoculars in his direction, but he couldn't be sure.

'Tell me you don't think he did it, Tony?'

Tony winced inside. It was the question he'd hoped Maureen wouldn't ask him. Not only that but he came at the moment he placed a forkful of pasta into his mouth and it was after some awkward seconds of chewing before he was able to offer a reply.

'It doesn't really matter what I think...'

'Of course it does. To me.'

'You don't even know me.'

'I need someone to believe in him,' Maureen pleaded, reaching out and placing her hand on Tony's. 'Look, I can't stay out here for much longer, I know that now, but I'd feel better if I knew there was someone here who was looking out for him.'

It had been many a long year since Tony had spent an evening in a restaurant with a woman other than Helen. Not that his meeting with Maureen Carr was anything other than professional, of course, but it had still given him a strange feeling. While she had not exactly transformed herself into a beauty, Maureen's efforts to make herself more presentable than at their first meeting had clearly paid dividends. She had even laughed at his awful jokes.

'I'll pass the information Ryan told me onto the lawyer the court appointed,' answered Tony, 'and I'll also give it to the officers in charge of the case. How about you? What are your plans?'

'I gave that number a call, the one in that leaflet you gave me,' Maureen said. 'They got back to me with a lawyer in Benidorm to try. Apparently, he specialises in working for overseas prisoners, mainly British. I've made an appointment for tomorrow afternoon. Will you come with me?'

'I'm afraid I'll be busy with work,' said Tony. If it hadn't been perfectly true, he would have felt the need to claim so anyway. 'But I'll give you a call at some point and you can let me know what happened.'

Tony reached for the wine bottle and topped up both his and Maureen's glasses.

'Does Ryan have a history of violence?'

'Nothing serious,' Maureen said, 'just a few scraps.'

It was an old and familiar story for Tony. He had heard parents on far too many occasions dismissing the crimes of their offspring as just horseplay or something 'all kids of their age do.' That or how it was always someone else's fault. It was a rare event indeed when a parent, summoned to the police station by a call telling them their child was in custody, did not turn up ready to do battle with the local constabulary. Tony could recall on the fingers of one hand the number of times a parent arrived and, after the situation had been explained to them, supported any and all police action being taken. The parents who would hear no wrong against their child were the ones Tony used to see at the station time and time again.

'When I walked out on them, Ryan has just turned eleven,' Maureen told Tony. 'I didn't leave his father for another man. I just had to get out of that marriage.

I moved into a bedsit above a takeaway, got myself a job in Tesco's an' started all over again. Ryan an' his dad were thick as thieves, the pair of them. I couldn't have taken him with me even if I wanted to.'

'And did you want to?'

'Truthfully? No, I don't think I did. Course, I tried to make myself feel better about it. Told myself it was for the best for him to stay where he was. That things'd worse for him if I forced him to come an' live with me. It was well over a year before I met Ron an' moved in with him.'

'Did you keep in touch with Ryan?'

'I tried. He didn't want much to do with me for a long time, an' his father did his best to poison his mind against me. He started getting into trouble at school, got picked up by the police a few times...'

'And these scraps?'

'Just fights when he's had too much to drink or someone says something to him he doesn't take kindly to,' Maureen said, shaking her head. 'Nothing worse than that, honest. He hasn't got it in him to harm a young lass.'

'What was it about your marriage that made you have to leave?' asked Tony. 'Was it violent?'

'Terry was never violent to me,' Maureen replied. 'He was a gambler an' a womaniser, but he never laid a finger on me. Ryan didn't grow up in that kind of household. He was always a good lad. I blame myself for not being there for him when he was growing up.'

Even though Maureen continued to talk, her words no longer seemed to register with Tony. His mind had drifted on to Lucy. Would he end up blaming himself for not being there for her? Would she end up going off the rails like Ryan Dinsdale?

Tony settled the bill, waving away Maureen's offer to contribute some towards it, and they began the walk back to her hotel. It was a balmy night and Tony knew he would probably have trouble sleeping.

'I'll leave you here if that's okay,' he said, coming to a stop outside a small bar on the corner of the road leading to the Belle Vue. Tony knew, if he accompanied Maureen any further, he may be stepping close to a line that could prove difficult to move back from.

'Do you not want to come up? I have some coffee.'

'I have a busy day tomorrow,' he said, his face pleading forgiveness, 'and I still have some paperwork to catch up with this evening.'

It would be wrong to accompany the woman to her room. Maureen's life had been turned upside down and, over a thousand miles from her home and friends, she was desperate for solace and understanding. Reading between the lines of their conversation over dinner, Tony took it her marriage was on shaky grounds. She didn't even appear sure whether she had a marriage to go back to. They stayed and chatted idly outside the bar for a few more minutes before Tony took the initiative and brought an end to their evening together. He waited until he had seen Maureen go into the entrance hall of the Belle Vue before taking a slow walk back to Calle Neuva.

It wasn't until he climbed into bed nearly an hour

later, time spent going over his notes for the next day's event at the Solanis and making endless, and probably needless, last-minute revisions, that a half-asleep Tony found the object deep beneath the sheet. He half-jumped half-fell from the bed and, with the pounding in his chest almost loud enough to hear, stood in the dark for what seemed an eternity before the calmness slowly began to return to his body. Tony stepped back towards the bed and switched on the lamp. After a moment to gather his thoughts, he slowly pulled back the crumpled sheet.

CHAPTER TWELVE

MAX Okeke knew what people saw when they looked at him, and he rarely bothered to go to any effort to change their minds. If nobody saw past the thick jaw or the muscled arms, then so be it. It made his job a whole lot easier. But there was something between his ears as well. More, he felt, than anybody in his life had ever given him credit for, and he was determined to use it. There was a word that summed up why he had become such a trusted employee at *Breeze*. Why instructions were obeyed without qualm or question, why a blind eye could be dependably turned. And the word wasn't loyalty. It was insurance. Now it was time to cash it in. Sleeping on the situation he now found himself in had told Max Okeke how best to play his cards; drip-feed what he knew, slowly but steadily. Become valuable. And he knew a lot. The contacts for the illegal alcohol supplies, the businesses that laundered money through the club, the backroom used for illegal poker games. But those matters could wait.

'She was there.'

'You mean Natalie Brooks? She was at Breeze the night she disappeared?'

'Yes.'

Luís Banda opened his notebook and took a pen from his shirt pocket. Now the big lug was talking, he was going to keep him talking. Make him feel important. That was the key.

'What time did she arrive, señor?'

'Around quarter past one. She wanted to see Donnie, but he was busy at the bar. So she went around selling tickets for a boat trip while she waited. Some people will buy anything when they're pissed. Those that have any money left!'

'Did she get to see Sr. Lane?'

'They went into the back together.'

'For how long?'

'Twenty minutes,' Max replied after a moment's thought. 'Maybe a little more.'

'Do you know why she wanted to see him?'

'No.'

The doorman leaned forward and placed his forearms on the table.

'But I'll tell you what I do know…'

Max registered the interest in the official's eyes. It was like a dog hoping for a bone. He was playing his hand well. He wasn't going to be sent back.

'This is terrible!'

Sitting together in the coffee bar at the Solanis Resort, Tony had told Rafá and Consuela of the discovery in his apartment the night before. They were as shocked as he and, just by being able to speak about it to someone, he felt a weight being lifted from his shoulders.

'Was the knife one of yours?' Rafá added.

'From the kitchen, yes,' nodded Tony. 'I wouldn't

have known it was missing. Not until today, at least.'

'Was there any sign of forced entry?'

'Not that I could tell. And I spoke to Dave and Pat. They didn't see or hear anything suspicious, but I wouldn't expect them to. The bar can get busy. It's possible, of course, that whoever was responsible didn't come in through the back door, but slipped into the back from the bar.'

Tony reached for his black coffee, his third of the day.

'You should have called the police, Tony,' Consuela said, reaching out and placing a hand on his shoulder. 'It must have been a frightening experience.'

'Did you touch the handle?' asked Rafá. 'We could have it checked for prints.'

Tony dismissed the idea with a small shake of the head. He knew it would be futile. If the idea was to rattle him, then it had worked. He had spent a fitful night trying to work out who could have put the carving knife in his bed and why before only complete exhaustion had sent him to sleep. It was a warning, but for what? Tony had gotten himself involved in two major enquiries, as well as countless smaller affairs, but had never considered his investigations could be putting his own safety at risk. And who knew where he lived? He was careful to give no-one his home address, something he had learned very early in his career, and his business card gave only his mobile phone number, e-mail, and the address of the town hall for any correspondence. Maureen Carr knew, of course, and while he did not consider her a likely suspect, he recalled how she had been told where she could find him by a helpful employee at the town hall. He would need to make sure that would not happen again, as well as checking if anybody else had made a similar enquiry. When walking back to his apartment at anytime, Tony had never taken any measures to conceal or vary his route, nor had he ever felt the need to.

Since arriving at the Solanis, Tony had spent a busy two hours preparing the function room for the event that afternoon, assisted by one of the *SunTravel Premier* reps. José had come up trumps, providing a box of stickers and balloons, even managing to find a couple of small teddy bears dressed in the uniform of the Policia Municipal, and Tony had prepared a number of information sheets that the reprographics department at the town hall had blown up to poster size. With the room suitably decorated, Tony took advantage of the time remaining before the planned start of the event to have a quick bite to eat in the coffee bar. He hadn't felt like breakfast when he woke, hadn't felt like doing anything, but a shower and the anxiety surrounding the afternoon's event was enough to fuel him through the morning's activities.

'You'll have to take extra precautions, Tony,' Rafá said, 'and you need to call us should anything like this happen again.'

'I will.'

'And we can rearrange the meal for another time, do not worry about it.'

'No, no,' Tony said. 'I've been looking forward to

tonight.'

In truth, it had passed completely from his mind, but keeping busy was something Tony knew he needed to do. The talk at the hotel would, with luck, be over by three and, after calling in on the courthouse and making sure no matters awaited his urgent attention, he could turn his attention to preparing the evening's meal for Rafá, Consuela and their families.

Upon arriving at the Solanis, Tony had met with Emily Johnson and found, to his surprise, that the event had attracted quite a lot of interest from guests at the resort. The holiday company had agreed to lay on refreshments, and two of the reps had been drafted in to host an event for young children at the adventure playground so their parents would be free to attend.

Tony glanced at his watch. The event was due to begin in half an hour, and people may begin drifting into the function room at anytime. He decided against draining his coffee cup, suddenly having a premonition of being caught short halfway through his speech, and smiled at his two friends.

'Right, here's what I'd like you to do...'

'Natalie Brooks came out of the office after around twenty minutes,' said Banda, 'and, according to Okeke, she was not in the best of moods. Stormed right past him. Mind you, he reckons she was pretty drunk.'

'Did he say which way she went when she left the club?' asked Chavarría.

'Turned right, away from the Avenida Del Puente.

That would be the route back to her apartment. Now, at around half past two, there was a dispute at the bar. A customer claimed he had paid with a €20 note but had only been given change for a ten. Both he and the barman started accusing each other of a scam. Another of the staff went to find Sr. Lane, but he was not in his office.'

Chavarría raised an eyebrow. 'Is that so?'

'Okeke said he didn't leave the club by the main door, but he could have gone out through the rear without being seen by anyone. When Breeze closed at four, he was back in his office.'

The Inspector Jefe spun slowly in his chair, trying to fit the new information in with what they already knew. He knew Natalie had been in *Breeze* the night she disappeared, his instinct had told him that, but now Max Okeke had confirmed it. The doorman knew much more, he would bet his last euro on that, and they would need to get it out of him. Time was crucial and perhaps something would need to be offered in return. He galled at the prospect but it may be the only way. If Natalie arrived unannounced at such a time to see Donnie, and was prepared to wait instead of coming back the following day, that suggested a sense of urgency. And it seems their meeting had not gone well.

Chavarría turned his attention to Official Valle, who he had given the task of sorting through Natalie Brooks' e-mails. Access to her *2linx* account had been granted by the service provider with the minimum of hassle.

'Anything?'

'This is interesting. It is a message to a friend of hers in the UK, dated one month ago. She says she has found a great job and, if things go well, she wouldn't be working as a holiday rep much longer.'

'Does she give any more details?'

'No, but she cannot be referring to handing out leaflets on the beach, surely? That would just be for some extra cash in her pocket, hardly a career move.'

'Carry on looking,' said Chavarría. 'See if there's anything else.'

There were over a hundred messages in Natalie's inbox, a large number from men she had met during the summer who were hoping to stay in touch with her, though only a small number had been read, let alone replied to. There were general messages back and forth between friends, usually exchanging gossip or comments about celebrities, and the odd reply to free offer promotions, usually for cosmetics, the rep had found on the internet. However, there wasn't a message that contained the photos Natalie had sent to one of her friends, so they were no nearer in identifying the person who took them.

Valle reached for her sandwich as she continued to flick through the e-mails. She had had a busy morning and was making the most of the time at her desk to have lunch, even if she didn't have the luxury of stopping work while she ate it. The official had spent the best part of the morning at *Breeze* with the printed stills taken from Donnie Lane's homemade pornographic films. Two of the young women in the films were identified as current members of the club's bar staff, while another was a former employee who had since moved on to pastures new. Valle spoke to the two women, both English, neither of whom seemed particularly bothered at having to sleep with the boss in order to get a job. While it confirmed her opinion that Donnie Lane was a repellent piece of work, Valle didn't judge the women too harshly. She had been accused several times of using her looks to gain advantages in her career and it was usually an unjustified charge. Not always, but usually.

'None of the stills are of Natalie Brooks,' Valle had told Chavarría on her return to the comisaría, 'and there's three women the staff at the club were unable to identify.'

'Well, we may need to try and trace them at some point,' the Inspector Jefe had told her, 'but I do not believe Lane's death is connected to those tapes.'

Chavarría tried to make sense of all the new developments. He had a meeting with Juez Sandoval later that afternoon and needed to get things in order in his mind. The e-mail was the first indication they had of Natalie having another job. Thanks to the work of the Englishman Heather and her fellow holiday reps, there had been posters of Natalie Brooks around Cieloventura for nearly a week, as well as a well-staged and publicised reconstruction of her last known movements, and no-one had come forward with any relevant information. Certainly no-one who claimed to have hired or worked with her. The team had also heard back from officers in Madrid. They had been to the address of the company that owned *Breeze*, only to find it was a business centre providing a virtual office and telephone answering service. The registration address for the account holder was the Gibraltar address already known to the investigators. Chavarría knew that dealing with the Royal Gibraltar Police would involve extra red-tape as the request for assistance would need to be done through official channels but, as it involved the death of one British subject and the disappearance of another, he trusted there would be little delay.

Calls from a mobile phone registered to Donnie Lane had been checked. There had been nothing in or out on the day he died, and those logged in the previous weeks had all been legitimate business calls, confirming to Chavarría that Donnie had separate phones for business and personal use. The CCTV had also failed to offer any important leads. Donnie had been captured on three cameras in the town after leaving the comisaría, but he appeared to be heading neither to his apartment or to *Breeze*, not by any direct route. His last appearance on CCTV showed him making in the direction of the Paseo de la Solana.

'So where do we go from here?' asked Banda.

'You just keep working on the doorman,' Inspector Jefe Chavarría replied, helping himself to the jalapeño pepper Valle had picked out of her sandwich and left on a piece of scrap paper on the corner of her desk. 'See if he knows anything about this other job Natalie Brooks may have had. And I want everyone who knew her questioned again.'

Chavarría walked up to the information board and

stared at a triangle he had drawn in the centre. The words 'Lane, 'Natalie' and 'Finca' were written at each of the three points. The line that joined the two names had the word 'Breeze' written along it, but the remaining two simply had question marks.

'The finca is the key, I am sure of it,' he commented. 'We need to know what the connection is between that, Sr. Lane and the missing girl.'

Chavarría hoped he had enough to put before Sandoval to convince him the case was proceeding as well as could be hoped. If the examining magistrate felt otherwise, he could decide to take a more hands-on approach and guide the investigation himself. Chavarría was far too used to being the puppet-master to feel comfortable with suddenly being at the other end of the strings. He contented himself with the thought that Sandoval could surely have done no more. The team were working hard on every lead that presented itself and, sooner or later, something would break. Thinking about the help Tony Heather had given the investigation suddenly set the Inspector Jefe's mind off on an entirely separate matter. He had received an e-mail the evening before that had given him cause for concern. The Englishman had visited Ryan Dinsdale at Fontcalent.

The round of applause that brought an end to the event at the Solanis give Tony the signal to breathe easily once more. The question and answer session at the end of his talk had been more complex than he had imagined, and he was grateful for Consuela stepping in and clarifying the more finer detail on points of Spanish law. Only one guest had brought up the subject of the deaths of Leanne Piggott and Donnie Lane, and Tony sought to reassure her that Cieloventura remained a very safe place and only sensible precautions, the kind that would be advised anywhere, were required when venturing outside of the complex, especially at night. With the refreshment table all but cleared and the guests gradually filtering back to the pool or their rooms, Tony only had a brief moment to thank Rafá and Consuela for taking part in the event, and to say he would see them later for dinner, before they had to leave to resume their duties. Maria Ocasio Cruz had attended on behalf of the Mayor's Office, the Mayor himself finding a committee meeting on sanitation a more appealing option. Tony didn't blame him. With two recent killings in the town, and the local media present, the Mayor's presence may have turned the event into an unintentional press conference on the cases and that was something all involved were keen to avoid. Several of the journalists had not even stayed after discovering the Mayor was not going to be present, and only one, who doubled as interviewer and photographer for a local free newspaper, remained behind afterwards to conduct a short interview with Sra. Ocasio and Tony, and to take their photo in front of the poster display.

'A successful event, Tony,' Sra. Ocasio beamed, 'and the first of many.'

Tony managed to hold his smile until Maria Ocasio Cruz said her goodbyes and turned away. Still, maybe it wouldn't be so bad. He wouldn't need to do any more preparation at least. His speech and the information leaflet he had provided each of the audience with had seemed to go down well, and Sra. Ocasio was positive about the long-term effects of promoting local police policies to visitors to the area.

One interested visitor to the talk was Paul Schier, the new German Liaison and Communications Officer in Cieloventura. He had been in the town for just a few days and, like Tony had done in his first week, was busily trying to find his feet and develop a better understanding of the job at hand. The two men exchanged phone numbers and promised to meet up for lunch at some point the following week.

Tony gathered together his paperwork, said thank you to the holiday reps and staff, and made his way out of the hotel. As he passed through the lobby, his eye caught a display showcasing the Solanis Resort's plans for the new wave of development in Cieloventura. The resort hoped to expand their operation by creating a number of small villas on a piece of land further along the coast, a development that sought to provide guests with the facilities of an 'all-in' holiday complex coupled with the seclusion and exclusivity of a private villa. While the images of the new properties were computer-generated and not actual photographs, Tony wondered whether they were really an improvement on the buildings they were replacing. Something suddenly seemed to fall into place in Tony's mind. He could almost have sworn there was an audible click, as though a piece of jigsaw had slotted satisfyingly into place. Tony recalled how, when he had located the finca high in the hills overlooking Cieloventura, he felt he had seen it before. Although there was no way he could have done, it had nagged away at him for a while until being relegated in his mind by more pressing matters. Now, looking at the display showcasing the planned new development, he remembered where. Tony took his mobile phone from his pocket and, hurrying out through the main doors, dialled a number.

It could almost be described as fate that, at the moment Inspector Jefe Chavarría decided he would look into Tony Heather's visit to Ryan Dinsdale that the office received a call from downstairs, informing them that the man himself was in reception and wanted to speak to an officer involved in the investigation. Chavarría would normally leave such an interview to Banda or Valle but, regardless that they were busy, this was something he wanted to do himself. He made his way down to the ground floor, where he was told the Englishman awaited him in one of the interview rooms that led from the large reception area.

'Sr. Heather? We meet again.'

Tony stood up and smiled as the senior detective entered the small room

'Inspector Jefe. How is the investigation going?'

'It is progressing nicely, thank you.' Chavarría gestured for Tony to sit back down and took the seat opposite. 'Now, how can I be of assistance to you?'

'I don't know how it's related but I'm convinced of

its importance,' explained Tony. 'When I went to Natalie Brooks' apartment for the first time, there was some paperwork in one of her drawers. I didn't pay much attention, but they were advertisements for a new holiday villa development.'

Chavarría took a small pad and pencil from his pocket and, after making a few notes, looked at Tony to continue.

'I've just been back to the apartment and the paperwork is no longer there. You may be aware there was a burglary at the apartment sometime on Saturday.'

'Yes, I have read the report. How do you think this may be connected to the case?'

'The photograph on the advertisement was the finca where I found Donnie Lane's body.'

'Are you sure about that?'

'As sure as I can be,' said Tony. 'I knew as soon as I saw the finca that it was familiar to me, there was just something about it, but I couldn't place it before now.'

'Do you recall any other details of these advertisements? A company name or address, perhaps? Even a logo?'

'No, nothing,' Tony replied, shaking his head. 'As I said, I didn't pay much attention. Was the finca being developed into a holiday villa?'

'We are currently awaiting further information concerning the finca from the owner,' smiled the Inspector Jefe.

'Everyone who knew Natalie told me she could charm the bees from the trees. If the finca was being redeveloped, could she somehow have been involved in that? On the sales or promotional side?'

'We do have information that leads us to believe Natalie had employment other than her work for Holiday18 and Breeze,' said Chavarría. 'Thank you for bringing this to our attention, Sr. Heather, it is certainly something my team will look into.'

For all the detective's charm, and that was something he clearly had in abundance, Tony knew when he was being fobbed off. Chavarría hadn't given him much in return for his information, but the revelation that Natalie possibly had another job was an interesting development. Working for a property development company in Cieloventura would certainly explain the smart suit in her apartment. Selling boat trips to night clubbers might benefit from a short skirt and plenty of cleavage but selling villas or holiday developments would require a more classy and professional approach.

'Is there anything else I can help you with today?' asked Chavarría. The Inspector Jefe was keen to talk to the Englishman about his visit to Ryan Dinsdale at Fontcalent but preferred his visitor to be the first to bring the subject up. Chavarría wondered whether he could make better use of Tony Heather. Both murder investigations he was working on involved British victims, and at least one had a British perpetrator, for he was convinced of Ryan Dinsdale's guilt. Taking the Englishman into his confidence could be like having an extra officer on the case, one with the advantage of having knowledge of the British in Cieloventura. And also one that was outside the chain of responsibility.

'I visited Ryan Dinsdale.'

'Ah, is that so?' Chavarría replied. 'Tell me, did you learn anything that may be of use to us?'

'He says he last saw Leanne Piggott along the Avenida del Puente at around three a.m. on Friday morning. Apparently, she had promised he could borrow her wristband from the Solanis so he could get some free food. He went there at half past eleven later that morning for something to eat, and then again in the afternoon to use the pool.'

'I see.'

'According to Ryan, Leanne left Platinum without giving him the band, so he ran after her. The last he saw of her, she was heading towards the beach.'

'And what did Dinsdale do then?'

'Spent the rest of the night in a bar, apparently. He doesn't recall which one.'

'And did you, by any chance, convince him to start co-operating with the investigation? I cannot do much to help him if he remains silent.'

'I did what I could,' Tony replied.

'In that case, I will send an officer to Fontcalent to see if he is more willing to talk to us,' said Chavarría.

'Ryan also mentioned that it was Leanne who wanted to go to Platinum. She was a fan of the celebrity DJ that was performing there, a man called Streax. She got to meet him, according to Ryan, but I spoke to Streax and he doesn't remember it.'

'I appreciate this new information, Sr. Heather, but I would be grateful if, in future, you allowed my officers to conduct interviews with possible witnesses.'

'Yes, of course,' Tony nodded. 'I understand.'

Tony felt suitably chastised. He realised speaking to Streax before passing the information on to the police had perhaps exceeded his remit, but he couldn't help feeling more than a hint of resentment that he wasn't being trusted more, especially in the Natalie Brooks enquiry. Tony gave Chavarría details of where the DJ could be contacted and reported as accurately as possible the conversation he'd had with him.

'Leanne Piggott had cannabis in her system. Ryan denies smoking anything with her, but when I visited Streax on his boat, there was the butt of a joint in one of the ashtrays.'

Which won't be there when one of my officers call on him, thought Chavarría. He wrote down everything Tony had told him and made a note to mention this new information at the next team briefing.

'What motive do you think Ryan would have had for killing her? They had arranged to meet the next night, according to him, when he was going to return the wristband.'

'We are looking into all possibilities regarding motive, Sr. Heather, I can give you my assurance on that. All leads will be followed up.'

The two men passed a further five minutes in trivial conversation, Tony telling Chavarría of his experiences since arriving in Cieloventura and, in turn, the Inspector Jefe recommending a quiet family-run restaurant a few minutes' walk from Calle Neuva, before parting company.

Tony left the comisaría and took the list of ingredients for the evening's meal from his pocket, most of which had been crossed off. Preparing the dinner would give him a chance to forget, even for just a few hours, everything else that was going on. As Tony walked to the first of the local shops he needed to visit to get the few remaining items, his mobile phone rang. It was Maureen and, while he was tempted to let it go to voicemail, courtesy swiftly won the day.

'What happened at the lawyers?' Tony asked after a brief exchange of pleasantries.

'He wants too much money, Tony. I can't even afford the deposit he's asking for. I don't know what I'm going to do.'

'You'll need to leave it in the hands of the court-appointed lawyer, at least for the time being. Don't worry, they'll do their best for him.'

'Can we meet up this evening?'

'I'm afraid I have plans. Business.'

'Just a drink? Anything?'

'I can call you when I'm free,' Tony conceded, noting the plea in the woman's voice, 'but it might be late.'

'Anytime. Thank you.'

Tony hung up at the phone and sighed in despair. There was really little more he could do for Maureen, and he wondered what further use he could now be in either of the investigations he had gotten himself entangled with. Everything he had managed to learn was now in the hands of the police and he had been warned off twice; politely by the Inspector Jefe, and rather less subtly by whoever left the knife in his bed.

'Go back and talk to Sr. Romo,' Chavarría told Valle. 'I'm thinking he maybe he got a little fed up with his children hovering above him like vultures, waiting for him to drop dead before swooping, and decided to cash in on a life of hard work.'

'Right.'

Chavarría watched Valle leave the office. Dinner with Isabel the night before had been a slightly awkward affair, their love-making afterwards even more so, and he did not honestly know what the future held. It was the first time he and his wife had had sex in over three months, and it was as predictable as it ever was. They knew what each other liked in bed and there was no reason to try anything new. If truth be told, it would probably have freaked him out if she had done something different to him, or asked him to do something differently to her, and his mind would have imagined all sort of things.

The Inspector Jefe say down at his desk and, leaning back in his chair, stared up at the gently-rotating ceiling fan. He wondered why he still felt unable to trust Tony Heather with too much information. The man seemed more a lucky blunderer than an adept investigator, but how information was found was irrelevant. He was certainly providing important leads, and while his co-operation in the Natalie Brooks case was something Chavarría felt he should nurture and encourage, it wasn't something he was prepared to permit in that of Leanne Piggott. The detective knew his case against Ryan Dinsdale was largely circumstantial at present, but there was sufficient time to build a strong case. He didn't believe the young man had killed over the wristband, but it was a vital piece of evidence nevertheless. The CCTV footage from the entrance to *Platinum* had shown the band to be on Leanne Piggott's left wrist as she left the nightclub, the opposite wrist to that which held her new blue coral bangle, but was missing in the crime scene photographs of her body on the beach. The subject of the band, and its subsequent discovery in a waste bin at the rear of the Hotel Mar Azul, had been put to Ryan Dinsdale during questioning, but the young man had long since lapsed into a defiant silence. It seemed Fontcalent was starting to soften him up, however, and Chavarría made a note to despatch Banda, once he had finished with the African, to Alicante to interview him once more. If he was still displaying reticence, perhaps they could ask Tony Heather to sit in. Although the Englishman would not be allowed to conduct the interview, his presence may have a softening effect on the young man.

The events after Leanne left *Platinum* and began her journey back to the Solanis Resort were starting to come together in Chavarría's mind. Dinsdale had set off in pursuit of her in order to collect the wristband that she had promised him earlier in the evening. Once down on the beach together, out of sight and with alcohol inflating his sense of self-worth and confidence, he had made his move. Leanne may have willingly shared her wristband but had clearly baulked at whatever else Dinsdale may have been after. Perhaps he had got aggressive with her, unwilling to take no for an answer. Leanne had a trump card, of course, guaranteed to make any potential suitor step back and throw their hands up in defeat. Her real age. Instead of forcing him to retreat, her revelation had had the opposite effect on Dinsdale. He had got angry. He accused the girl of using him to get into *Platinum*, leading him on, and luring him to the beach with the implicit suggestion of a quick fuck in the sand, only to then spurn his advances. She attempted to leave, threatening to tell her parents or, even worse, the police if he didn't leave her alone. Either that or, as Valle suggested, Dinsdale may have failed to rise to the occasion and was cruelly mocked for his incompetence. While Chavarría considered this scenario less likely, the consequence may have been the same. He needed to shut her up.

It was a logical pattern of events, the detective felt. Disposing of the wristband behind his own hotel was foolish, but was the action of someone who felt there was nothing that could connect them to the events being investigated. Chavarría had seen many such a thing in his career. It wasn't until his photograph, courtesy of the CCTV images from *Platinum*, started appearing on the streets that Dinsdale sought to remove himself from Cieloventura and catch the first available flight home. He had also disposed of the clothing he had worn that night, even his prized football shirt. That action alone suggested to the detective that something more serious had happened between the two of them that Dinsdale had so far indicated. But the young man's claim, via Tony Heather, that he visited the Solanis to get some food and use the swimming pool, mere hours after Leanne's death, was a spanner in the works. Was that the behaviour of a killer?

The Inspector Jefe mentally closed the door on the Leanne Piggott enquiry, for the time being, and opened the one belonging to Natalie Brooks. His attention needed to be focused on the missing British holiday rep. Two dead bodies on his patch were pushing his resolve and resources almost to breaking point. Three would not, he considered, be a good thing. Not good at all.

Tony knew going to the Belle Vue to meet Maureen for a late-night drink would be a recipe for disaster, and so invited her instead to a small sports bar he had noticed on the corner of the Carrer de Trato. The lack of romantic ambience would dampen any inclination either of them may have had to that end and, from what he had seen of the establishment, it attracted a more family crowd, even at eleven 'o' clock at night. The dinner had gone as well as he'd hoped and both Rafá and Consuela, and their respective families, had seemed to enjoy themselves. Consuela's youngest, a delightful boy of three, had turned his nose up at Yorkshire Pudding, but everyone else had cleared their plates, and Rafá had even helped himself to a second helping of roast potatoes. The added bonus of having children present was that there was no talk of crime and murder over the dinner table; the preferred topics of conversation being parenting, sport, and life in Cieloventura.

With his fitful sleep the night before, the event at the Solanis Resort, and the busy evening cooking and entertaining his guests, Tony doubted he had the energy for more than a single drink with Maureen.

'I've spoken to the Chief Inspector leading the investigation,' Tony told her. 'He's going to send an officer to talk to Ryan again. Co-operation is the only way forward, he must understand that.'

'Don't worry, I'll make sure he does.'

While Tony didn't doubt Maureen's sincerity, he held serious misgivings as to whether Ryan would start being full and frank with the police. If the wheels of justice turned as slowly in Spain as they did in the UK, however, the lad wouldn't be going anywhere in a hurry. The long months ahead in Fontcalent Prison would play its part.

'You look done in,' chuckled Maureen.

Tony's eyes snapped open and he realised, to his embarrassment, that he had momentarily drifted off. He knew his workload, mostly of his own doing, was starting to take its toll and if ever he needed an uninterrupted night's sleep, it was tonight. Tony downed the remainder of his lager and regretfully expressed to Maureen that, unless he soon made his bed, he was likely to collapse where he sat.

After a brief argument over who was going to settle the bill, which Tony gave in to after only token resistance, they headed out into the night and began the walk to the Belle Vue.

'I'll have to return home,' said Maureen. 'I know there's nothing more I can do out here. I'll have to do what I can to raise some money.'

'It would be for the best,' agreed Tony. 'And, if it's any consolation, you know I'm here in Cieloventura if you ever need anything done at this end.'

Maureen stopped and, to Tony's surprise, threw her arms around him. The scent of her perfume and the feeling of her breasts pushing into his chest gave Tony a moment of uncertainty, but the thought that passed briefly across his mind was soon banished.

'Let me know when you can arrange a flight home,' said Tony, peeling away from Maureen as casually as possible. 'We'll meet up before then and work out the best thing to do.'

Tony saw Maureen to the entrance to the Belle Vue and took a slow and tired walk back to Calle Neuva, doubling back on himself several times as a precaution. Once settled in his apartment, he took the further safeguard of making sure all the windows were shut and secured. Although it would make the small apartment stifling, Tony didn't want to take any chances. Not for a while at least.

He barely looked twice at the women that flocked around him. They were easy and he didn't much like that. It killed the thrill of the chase. The conquest. On occasions, he even needed to resort to chemical stimulants to be able to perform. Hard to get. Now *that* was attractive. There was no need for pills then. From now on, though, he would need to rein in his desires. If the visit by the British bloke from the town hall had spooked him a little, then the police detective that called on him before he went on stage had given him greater cause for concern. Still, he had stuck to the same story and the cop seemed more than satisfied when he left.

It was awkward being back at *Platinum*. He had considered crying off, blaming some random sickness, but that would mean having to miss Ibiza as well and he didn't want to do that. No, he would see out the two days this week and then get out of the rest of his contract somehow. There were many other resorts than wanted him. He didn't need Cieloventura.

The knock on the door signalled it was time for his second, and last, set of the night. He took a final drag and flushed the remains of the joint down the toilet. Showtime. He looked in the small mirror above the sink and ran his fingers through his long hair. Time for Streax to entertain.

CHAPTER THIRTEEN

'THE owner of Breeze is an Englishman called Peter Harris,' announced Luís Banda, walking into the offices of *homicidios y desaparecidos*. Inspector Jefe Chavarría and Officíal Valle broke off their hushed and, to Banda's eyes, rather tetchy conversation and both looked in his direction.

'The name is familiar to me.'

'The Piggott family,' injected Valle, removing herself from the corner of Chavarría's desk where she had been perched and walking across to her own work space. 'When they left the Solanis, they moved into a villa just outside town. It was loaned to them by a Peter Harris. His name is in the report.'

'Ah, yes.'

It was the first item on the Inspector Jefe's to-do list to call in on the Piggott family sometime this morning to inform them that Leanne's body could be released into their care. Numerous messages had been left for him, each with increasing desperation, by the British Consular official staying with the family, telling him how Shelley Piggott's mental state was deteriorating by the day, and their enforced stay in Cieloventura was causing them all considerable anguish. They just wanted to take their daughter home, he was told.

'And did he tell you where we can find this Peter

Harris?' asked Chavarría.

'He did, yes.'

'Good work, Luís! I'll call on him today after I have been to see the Piggott's. Anything else from the doorman?'

'He knows more, I'm sure of that, but he wants legal representation from now on. He wants everything on the record, including any assurances we make to him about his immigration status.'

'If he keeps talking, I don't care what we have to promise him. Arrange it, will you?'

'Sure.'

'And then you need to go to Fontcalent and talk to Dinsdale.'

Banda frowned. He had seen the note from the Inspector Jefe stuck to his computer monitor when he arrived for work this morning. Driving all the way to Alicante to try to prise open that particular shell did not appeal. Just because he'd talked to the Englishman didn't mean he would start co-operating with the police. If anything, he would've preferred Ryan Dinsdale to keep his mouth shut. It always made a case stronger, in his eyes, when a suspect refused to talk.

'And me?' asked Valle.

'Go to the Solanis. I want to know if anyone reports seeing Dinsdale there sometime last Friday.'

'And if someone does? It would take a pretty cool customer to go there and use the wristband of someone they had just murdered? How could he be sure he wasn't going to be challenged by a member of staff?'

'Just find out,' snapped Chavarría. 'If we learn

anything of use to us, then we'll take things from there.'

Valle decided to hold her tongue. She had already driven to Villajoyosa and back before breakfast to talk once more with the octogenarian owner of the finca who, for a reason that was a mystery to her, distrusted telephones.

'Sr. Romo denies any dealings with property developers', Valle had reported to the Inspector Jefe when he arrived at the office. 'He's been approached several times in recent years but has no interest in selling. The old man is hoping the finca will one day be restored to its past glories, instead of becoming yet another tourist pad. No doubt his offspring think otherwise.'

While it couldn't exactly be described as good news, Chavarría was pleased he was now free to tell the Piggotts they could return home to the UK, taking their daughter with them. His last meeting with the family, where he had briefed them on the progress of the investigation, as well as answering candidly their questions, had been difficult for all involved. He could only imagine their pain. If anything ever happened to Terésa, he didn't know how he would ever begin to deal with it. Over a pleasant meal the evening before in a small restaurant in Relleu, Chavarría and Isabel had agreed not to ruin Terésa's holiday by asking her to come home early. They also agreed on the need for Chavarría to focus all his energies on his work, leaving the long talk they both knew was needed about their marriage on hold. For a short time at least. The fact that Terésa was the same age as Leanne Piggott had not been lost on Isabel, and she also confessed to feeling a sense of anxiety about their daughter when reading the circumstances of Leanne's death, and life, in the newspapers. Isabel also appreciated the pressure her husband was under with the murder of Donnie Lane and the disappearance of Natalie Brooks.

Chavarría didn't mind the pressure. It gave him focus. With Banda and Valle busily, if not entirely happily, occupied, and the forensics team promising their report on Donnie Lane's car by this afternoon at the latest, he was satisfied with progress. Tracing the owner of *Breeze* was an important breakthrough. While he hadn't yet met him, the Inspector Jefe already disliked Peter Harris. No completely legitimate business owner made himself so difficult to find. Chavarría was rather looking forward to meeting him.

Tony had a spring in his step walking to the courthouse, courtesy of an unbroken night's sleep, and an even bigger one as he left after finding no British tourists had been arrested in Cieloventura the night before. While it was more likely due to luck than any seismic shift in attitude and behaviour, he was grateful for the small mercy. After a visit to the offices of the Policia Municipal to check his e-mails, of which there were none, Tony made for The Green Dragon and treated himself to a brunch of eggs and bacon and a pot of tea. From there, he took a walk to the Solanis Resort to see if any feedback forms had been left for him. The forms were normally used by *SunTravel*

Premier to obtain comments about the welcome lectures and excursion talks given by their reps, and copies had been available to those who attended Tony's talk. In spite of Maria Ocasio Cruz's praise for how it went, he felt it important to get some audience feedback, especially if he was going to be repeating the presentation.

Half-a-dozen forms were waiting at the reception desk for Tony to collect. As he wandered back across the lobby, casually glancing through the remarks that had been made, not all entirely complimentary, his ear picked up something of interest. He stopped and looked over to where a slim, smartly dressed woman was talking with a member of the Solanis staff. She was showing him some photos and pointing out through the window towards the main cafeteria area of the complex. Tony edged a little closer so he could observe the photos for himself. They were of Ryan Dinsdale – one a copy of the CCTV image from *Platinum*, the other a police mug shot. Tony looked on with interest as the two spoke. The staff member then shook his head apologetically and, after a nod of appreciation from the woman, headed back out towards the pool.

'Excuse me?'

The woman turned in Tony's direction and smiled warmly. She was certainly very striking, he thought.

'I couldn't help overhearing what you were talking about. My name is Tony Heather. I work for the Mayor's Office.'

'Yes, I know the name. It's very nice to meet you.

I'm Official Elisa Valle Huerta of the Policia Nacional. Actually, I'm here following up information you gave to us yesterday.'

'Any luck?'

Valle wondered whether she should confide in the Englishman. She was aware of Inspector Jefe Chavarría's reticence in the matter but was unsure whether it was to do with confidentiality or a desire to remain the alpha male. They never really left the playground, did they? Valle had no such issues.

'Perhaps you have time for coffee?' she asked.

Within minutes, Tony and Valle were sat at a table overlooking the main pool where they were served, with the management's compliments, with two large coffees and a selection of pastries.

'Not for me,' laughed Valle as Tony offered her first choice from the plate. 'It goes right here!'

Sitting cross legged at the table, she rubbed her fingers along the top of her thighs. Tony chuckled and, realising his eyes had lingered on the woman's legs for half-a-second more than they should have done, quickly switched his attention to his cup of coffee. He added only a touch of cream. The stronger the better, he felt.

'No member of staff has confirmed seeing Ryan Dinsdale the Friday before last,' Valle told him. 'There are no cameras located either around the pool or in the restaurants, and most of the guests who were here on that day have returned home.'

'That doesn't mean he wasn't here.'

'True. But, of course, he could just be saying he

came here and used the wristband. That way, it would look less likely that he were the killer.'

'I don't think he's that clever,' Tony replied, shaking his head. 'He more likely would've just asked his friends to cover for him. Tell me, how did you track Ryan down in the first place? He wasn't a registered guest at the Hotel Mar Azul.'

'A British tourist staying there recognised his photo. It's true he wasn't registered but his friends were. We questioned them and they admitted he was staying in their room. They also told us he had left for the airport. The Inspector Jefe was fortunate to get there in time.'

At that moment, a young family hurried past their table on their way to claim the only two sun beds around the pool that remained unoccupied. Tony's eyes were caught by the wristbands they all wore. He had always assumed the bands, colour coded depending on the package deal the guests had, were non-transferable and, once secured around the wrist by the staff upon arrival, could only be removed by cutting through the plastic.

'They're not usually fitted too tight,' said Valle, responding to Tony's question on the matter, 'so they're able to move about and avoid tan lines. It also means, if you have quite thin wrists, you should be able to remove it quite easily.'

Tony recalled one of his first impressions of Ryan Dinsdale upon meeting him at Fontcalent was how skinny the lad was. He guessed it wouldn't be impossible, with some effort, for Leanne's wristband to slip over his hand.

'We originally thought the band may have been taken to delay identification of the body,' added Valle, 'but we are working on the theory that Leanne gave it to Ryan in the Avenida del Puente before they walked down to the beach together. It's possible that Ryan did not realise he still had it in his possession until he was back at his hotel and so disposed of it at the earliest opportunity.'

'He could just have panicked when he heard she was dead.'

'He also threw away the clothing he wore that night, before running for El Altat, and refuses to tell us where.'

This was new information for Tony. He realised how bad that looked, but also understood the panic Ryan must have felt when he found he was being hunted.

'One of my colleagues is going to speak to him later today,' said Valle. 'Hopefully he will tell us much more.'

Tony was pleased the information he had provided to the Policia Nacional was being acted upon, and even more pleased that Official Valle was being straight with him. There was, however, an even more pressing subject he wanted to discuss.

'How are things with the Natalie Brooks case?'

Valle spent a few minutes telling Tony of the progress they had made, revealing only what she thought would help the investigation and not disclosing any sensitive information. She asked Tony whether he had heard of Peter Harris, the owner of *Breeze*, but it wasn't a name he had come across before.

'I'm positive the photo on the advertisements in Natalie's apartment was of the farmhouse where I found Donnie's body,' said Tony. 'And you say it's not subject to development or up for sale?'

'No,' replied Valle, gently blowing cool air across the surface of her coffee.

'The Inspector Jefe mentioned that Natalie had found another job?'

'She mentioned it to a friend of hers in an e-mail, but gave no other details. We've been in touch with all of her friends and family in England but no-one knows anything more about it.'

'You've spoken to her mother, then?'

'A little.' From the face the official pulled, Tony sensed her feelings about Geena Brooks were much the same as his. 'She seems to think Natalie will reappear soon enough.'

'Is there anything more I can do?'

'You don't need any guidance from me, Sr. Heather,' smiled Valle. 'You have done very good work. Your help in this case has been much appreciated.'

'Tony, please', he replied, passing off the compliment with a nonchalant shrug. Inside, however, he was beaming.

'So, Tony, how are you enjoying Cieloventura?'

'Very much, thank you. Well, until the dead bodies started appearing, that is...'

Despite the seriousness, Tony and Valle allowed

themselves to share a slight smile.

'Do you live in the centre of town?'

'Yes, I've got an apartment in Calle Neuva. Above Bar Loco.'

An expression – part quizzical and part amusement – appeared on the woman's face.

'Isn't that a ga…'

'Yes,' interrupted Tony with a smile. 'It's just for the season. If the Mayor's Office decides to extend my contract, I may look at getting a small place on the outskirts of town. The apartment's convenient but it can get a little noisy. How about you?'

'Oh, I'm new here also. Recently transferred from Córboda. I was expecting a quieter life after the big city.'

'Why did you decide to move?'

'That's a very long story.'

Sensing a slight unease in her reply, Tony decided not to pursue it. After all, he rarely answered so openly when asked a similar question himself.

'If you ever need to speak to someone about the case, you can call me.' Valle took a pen from her pocket and scribbled her mobile phone number on a San Miguel beer mat. 'Anytime,' she smiled, handing the mat across the table. 'Now, my apologies but I need to run. There are things I have to do.'

'Yes, of course. Don't let me hold you up,' replied Tony, 'and thank you.'

'You're welcome. Adios.'

Helping himself to two of the complimentary pastries, Tony reflected on the new information Valle had given him. The start of his fitness kick would need to be put back another day. It was always a long shot that anyone at the Solanis would have remembered Ryan Dinsdale. If he didn't attract anyone's attention at the time of his visit, then he would hardly stick in the mind almost two weeks later. Tony glanced around the pool area and saw at least a dozen young men of a similar age and appearance.

The news that the finca was not a holiday development project was puzzling. He was certain he wasn't mistaken about the paperwork he'd seen in Natalie's apartment, and the fact that they were no longer to be found there was all the confirmation he needed. Tony had been convinced all along that the items taken in the burglary were just a diversion. The finca remained the key to the case, he was sure, and a theory was slowly beginning to take shape in Tony's mind. It had been a week since his journey into the mountains and the discovery of Donnie Lane's body, and almost two since the last confirmed sighting of Natalie Brooks. The trail was running cold. The way he saw it, from Valle's words, he had tacit permission to continue his investigations his own way, and there was no time to delay. Tony drained his coffee cup and, passing on a further pastry, decided to return to the offices of the Policia Municipal. He had an e-mail to send.

'How long have you been involved with the Breeze nightclub?'

'We took a controlling interest about two summers

back,' Peter Harris replied. 'It's doing pretty well, considering the competition. We thought of changing it into a gym but, if things continue as they are, it may as well stay as a nightclub. It could do with some investment in the off-season, though. The place needs a bit of a make-over.'

Inspector Jefe Chavarría glanced down at the notepad in his hand and read through the brief reminders he had made before leaving the office. He didn't need the prompt but liked the few seconds silence it brought. And the extra discomfort he hoped it gave the interviewee. Not that the man sitting on the other side of the ornate wooden desk was showing any signs of being under pressure. Chavarría put Peter Harris somewhere in his late thirties and with a carefully nurtured tan that gave him a look of health and confidence.

'Synergist Holdings? That is your company, yes?'

'A junior partner only,' Harris replied, holding his hands up in modesty. 'I keep an eye on our Spanish interests, but most of what we do is UK based. Health clubs, gyms, bars. We've been involved along the Costa Blanca now for over ten years.'

'How did you meet Donnie Lane?'

'He was already at Breeze when we took it over,' Harris told him, 'running the bar. He had a pretty decent head for figures and good ideas for promoting the place so I made him manager. I don't take much of a hands-on role with the day-to-day stuff as you can imagine.'

'You, or your company, I should say, have some

interests in local properties, I understand?'

'We own a few villas and apartments in Cieloventura, yes.'

'Including the one that you have loaned to the family of Leanne Piggott?'

'That's right, yes. A shocking business, Inspector Jefe. The renovation isn't quite complete, so it's not yet available for let, but I felt I ought to do something. It wasn't right for them to stay at the Solanis after what happened.'

Chavarría took a photograph of the finca from his pocket and handed it across the desk to Harris.

'Do you own this property?'

'No, where is it?'

'It's a small finca in the hills, about ten miles out of town. I am wondering whether your company is involved in its development?'

'No, it's nothing to do with us.' Harris shook his head. 'Mind you, I'm sorry we've let this one slip through our fingers. It's a prime location and finding suitable properties can be a challenge. Are the owners willing to sell?'

'Not as far as I know,' replied Chavarría. 'Tell me, Sr. Harris, in your experience, how much would a property like this sell for?'

'Well, it would need a lot of work if it was going to be used as a holiday villa. It looks a little run down. But, as I said, it's a great location. It wouldn't surprise me if it went for somewhere around the half-a-million mark. Maybe more.'

Valle had already had the finca valued by one of the

town's real estate agents and Harris's estimate wasn't far off the mark. With the right renovation, including landscaped gardens and a pool, the agent told them there was a healthy profit to be made.

'Do you recognise this woman?' asked the detective, passing across a second photograph.

'Ah, that's the holiday rep, isn't it?' said Harris. 'Natalie Brooks. I saw the reconstruction on the news.'

'Donnie Lane employed her on occasions at Breeze,' Chavarría told him, 'handing out leaflets on the beach.'

'That's news to me. Mind you, Donnie would often use youngsters to do spot promoting around the town. Though it's not as easy as it used to be since the Mayor's clampdown.'

'Tell me, Sr. Harris, how did you learn of Sr. Lane's death?'

'My business associate told me the news.'

Harris gestured over Chavarría's shoulder to the door. The detective assumed he was referring to the man who had greeted him when he arrived and who, after being kept waiting in the hall for over ten minutes, had shown him into the small study at the back of the villa. Some business associate. Chavarría knew hired muscle when he saw it.

'He typically calls on the place several times a week at least to make sure everything is going ok. The police were there when he went on Monday. It came as a hell of a shock, I can tell you. I knew I should expect a visit at some point.'

'We would have spoken to you earlier but you were not easy to trace, Sr. Harris. The tax records for Breeze have sent my officers on something of a goose hunt.'

'My apologies, if that's been the case, Inspector Jefe. We don't actually have a permanent office in Cieloventura. This villa is my own residence, it's not owned by the company. It makes sense for me to work from here and save the cost of renting office space in town.'

Sensible, yes, thought Chavarría. Truthful, no. No honest businessman made his trail so slippery. The Tax Office in Cieloventura were usually very efficient in making sure their records were precise but if Synergist Holdings paid their dues in full and on time, which Chavarría didn't doubt would not be the case, they were probably able to avoid any close attention.

'Where were you last Thursday, Sr. Harris? Between the hours of ten a.m. and, say, four in the afternoon?'

'Last Thursday? Was that when Donnie was killed?'

'Please answer the question, señor.'

'Sorry, of course.'

Harris opened his desk diary and flicked back several pages. He ran his finger down several rows of small, spindly writing.

'I spent most of the morning here catching up on correspondence, and then I had a telephone conference with our company accountants back in England at about one.'

'His name and contact details?' Chavarría wrote

down the information as Harris gave it to him. 'Did you call from your office phone?'

'Yes, I did,' nodded Harris, tapping the receiver of the telephone on his desk. 'This one right here. Then I took a walk into town. Had lunch in a burger bar along the Paseo de la Solana.'

'And after that?'

'I went sailing. Headed along the coast to Altea. Came back some time on Friday afternoon.'

'Your own vessel?'

'Yes,' smiled Harris, pointing to a framed photograph of a motor boat on the wall. 'My pride and joy. Well, one of them.'

'Were you alone?'

'No, Mitch was with me.'

'Your associate?'

'Yes, Darren Mitchell. Have a word with him when you leave, if you like.'

'Thank you,' Chavarría replied. But no thank you, he added to himself. He wasn't in the mood to play those kind of games. Darren Mitchell would no doubt be spoken to, but it would be where and when the detective chose to.

'When was the last time you saw Donnie Lane?'

'Oh, must be at least three weeks, I'd say,' replied Harris after a moment's thought. 'We discussed modernising the club. He had a few ideas on the subject.'

'Do you have any idea why anyone would wish to harm him?'

'Heavens, no. Look, I know Donnie wasn't an

angel, but the nightclub business can be dog-eat-dog, especially in a holiday town like this, and you need someone who's been around a bit, if you know what I mean.'

'He had no business enemies?'

'Rivals by the dozen, but enemies? Not that I know of.'

Chavarría leaned forward and picked up the photograph of the finca from the middle of the desk where Harris had placed it. He held it out for the club owner to look at once more.

'This was where we found Sr. Lane's body. Are you certain you have no knowledge of this place at all?'

'I've never seen it or been there,' Harris replied, looking unflinchingly into the Inspector Jefe's eyes. 'I assure you.'

Chavarría considered challenging him on the discrepancies uncovered in the club's accounts but knew Harris could, and probably would, pass responsibility for such matters onto its conveniently dead manager. The Inspector Jefe also chose to make no mention of Max Okeke being in custody. It was doubtful that would be unknown to Harris, especially if Darren Mitchell was his eyes and ears on the streets of Cieloventura. Chavarría also assumed that Harris must have wondered how the police traced him to his own private villa, an address which did not appear on Synergist Holdings records at the town hall. It wouldn't take a genius to work out that Okeke had started to talk.

'I think that will be all, Sr. Harris.' Chavarría took

back the photo of Natalie Brooks and got to his feet. 'I thank you for sparing the time to see me.'

'Not at all, Inspector Jefe. Feel free to call on me at anytime if you think I can be of any more assistance.'

Harris stood and proffered his hand, which Chavarría took, before leading the officer out of the study and asking his associate to show him out.

Chavarría made his way out of the villa grounds and, once out of sight of Darren Mitchell, who remained in the open front doorway for some time, called the office on his phone. He instructed a full background check of both Harris and Mitchell to be made, which meant more co-operation from the British police. Chavarría could almost predict the responses they were going to get. Mitchell probably had a track record of general thuggery while Harris would have an unblemished character. Still, he would wait and see. He'd been surprised before. One piece of welcome news was the arrival of the preliminary report from the forensics team about Donnie Lane's Seat Arosa, which had been placed on his desk literally the minute before his call.

'Read it to me,' Chavarría instructed the Agente on the other end of the phone. The detective ducked into a small tobacconists on the corner of the street to escape the traffic noise and, as an afterthought, to replenish his stock of cheroots, and listened to the response. His interest began to grow by the second.

For the first time since Tony had been in Cieloventura, he needed to dig out his waterproof jacket. Accompanied by a succession of loud cracks of thunder, the heavens opened and rain lashed down in heavy sheets, driving thousands of tourists from the beach and the streets into the cafes, bars and shops.

Tony waited until the last possible moment before braving the conditions. He'd received a call from Maureen Carr, telling him she'd managed to get a cheap flight back to the UK later that evening, and would need to leave for El Altat Airport by mid-afternoon at the latest. Tony planned to invite her for a drink somewhere in the town square but, owing to the conditions, offered instead to meet her at the Belle Vue.

In a small British bar next to the hotel, Tony spent most of the hour they were together reassuring her that all that could be done for Ryan would be done. He reiterated the support several charitable organisations would be able to provide her, offering to contact them on her behalf, and the need to keep in regular touch with Ryan's duty lawyer. Tony decided not to tell Maureen of anything he'd learned from Offic*í*al Valle, electing instead to wait until they both received word of what had happened with Ryan's new interview with the police.

With the rain finally easing off, Tony and Maureen walked to the bus station. Buses left for El Altat airport every half an hour and were a cheaper option than hiring a taxi. Though Maureen objected to Tony paying her fare, he settled the matter by ignoring her protestations and buying a ticket direct from the morose driver, which he placed into her hand. Maureen hugged him and tearfully thanked him for all his help. Tony resisted the temptation to reassure her that everything was going to be all right as he just didn't know whether that would be the case.

After waiting patiently for the bus to leave, and waving Maureen goodbye, Tony began the walk back to Calle Neuva. As he turned into the street, his mobile phone rang. Tony glanced briefly at the screen before answering it. The display didn't register a number but he hoped it was the call he'd been expecting.

'It was a hard sell, but you're lucky it's a slow news day,' said the voice of Jerry Field. 'You've got a deal.'

'The cadaver dog went mad when she had a good sniff around the trunk,' Inspector Jefe Chavarría told the gathering of officers. All of those working on the investigation were present except Official Luís Banda, who had called en route from Fontcalent to say he was delayed. 'But the forensics team could find no blood or hair. They said the trunk was the tidiest part of the car, which says a lot in itself.'

'So she's dead, then,' a uniformed Agente piped up, a little louder than he had originally planned, from the back of the room. The young man smiled nervously at the ten pairs of eyes that looked in his direction.

Chavarría took a moment before responding. He had attended a conference organised by Europol the previous autumn in Hamburg where, among others, a presentation had been given on the use of cadaver dogs. He was amazed to see how the dogs could, with almost unwavering accuracy, pick out small pieces of fabric that had been in contact with a recently-deceased body for just a matter of minutes. The lecturer was unable to explain how the dogs were able to detect the organic compounds released by the process of decomposition, what he colourfully referred to as the *bouquet of death*, but their value in an investigation was clear to see.

While the findings in the forensic report were persuasive, Chavarría always ignored the rule that a detective's head should rule his heart. He preferred, on occasions, for it to be the other way round. He got better results that way. And it kept him human.

'Natalie is alive and missing,' he said, 'and will remain so until we find her. Nobody should forget that.' He turned to Valle. 'Peter Harris has a boat, an old style Monterey 276. It's called Misty Blue. Find out where it's moored and whether he took it out last Thursday afternoon. I also want to know if he took it out in the days following Natalie's disappearance.'

'I'll get on to it.'

Chavarría gestured to the nearest of the uniformed officers, an experienced Subinspector, and listened to the summary he gave. Door-to-door enquiries in the area of Donnie Lane's apartment had thrown up little of interest. A neighbour, a retired fisherman, had reported only seeing a handful of visitors to the apartment in all the time Lane had been living there, mainly young women. He had been shown a photograph of Natalie Brooks but the way they dressed these days, the neighbour claimed, they all looked the same to him. The Inspector Jefe decided there was little more to be achieved from continuing with that line of enquiry and stood all but two of the uniformed officers down from the investigation, allowing them to return to their own units, for the time being. Chavarría had only just brought the meeting to an end when Banda strode into the office.

'Anything, Luís?'

'The boy's an idiot,' the official said, heading straight for the coffee machine. 'He picked a fight with one of his cellmates last night and they both turned on him.'

'Did he talk?'

'Only to tell me to fuck off,' replied Banda. 'He wouldn't confirm anything he told the Englishman.'

'Elisa found no-one at the Solanis who remembers seeing him there.'

'He's as guilty as hell. And that's where he's going to end up.'

Chavarría sat down at his desk and tried to collate the scribbled notes he'd made during the meeting into some kind of order. He had two reports to make; one in person to Juez Sandoval at four 'o' clock, two hours from now, and one by phone to Comisario Principal García in Alicante. While his scheduled routine meeting with the latter had been postponed, due to the murder of Donnie Lane, García required regular updating on the progress of the investigation. There were little extra resources, in terms of detective manpower, García had said he could offer him. The city of Alicante had its own large-scale murder hunt to contend with – a mother and her young child had been found slain, a crime that was being linked to a major drugs trial that was currently taking place – but the Inspector Jefe was happy with the team at his disposal. Banda was as dependable as ever and Valle was proving herself to be an efficient detective. The number of uniformed officers allocated to the investigation, while never enough for his liking, had been passable and their job, which was mainly legwork and door-knocking, was largely complete. The Mayor's Office, keen to protect the good name of the town, could also be relied on for cooperation but officers of the Policia Municipal, the Inspector Jefe found, lacked the necessary skills to conduct important enquiries in a major investigation. Let them stick to parking violations and booking in the drunks, he thought. There had been talk of merging the Policia Municipal, Policia Nacional and Guardia Civil into a single unified force, but such talk had been going on forever, it seemed to Chavarría, and nothing ever came of it.

The Inspector Jefe's confidence of getting a result had grown after meeting Peter Harris. Despite the businessman's coolness under questioning, he'd have to be made of stone not to feel the pressure he would now be under. The net was closing in.

There were several private marinas in Cieloventura, mostly attached to apartment or villa complexes, and a larger municipal marina where, as well as providing permanent berths for boat owners, a variety of vessels could be hired for anything from an hour to the entire season. It didn't take long for Official Valle to discover that Misty Blue had a permanent mooring at the municipal marina just south of the main beach. The records couldn't be emailed to her, she was told on the telephone, as it was a hand-written log but she was welcome to come and look at it.

Valle took a walk from the comisaría, taking a slight detour to buy a sandwich from a charming delicatessen she had recently discovered, to the Paseo de la Solana and followed the main promenade to the marina. Now the rain had stopped, the hordes of tourists were slowly returning to the beaches and many outdoor activities Cieloventura had to offer. The official followed the sign at the marina entrance that took her to the office, a small whitewashed wooden building on the quayside.

'As long as the mooring fees are paid, the privately-owned vessels come and go as they please,' Fernando Prado, the marina duty manager, said. 'We only log their time of departure and return due to coastguard regulations. We take more details of the hire boats, of course.'

Valle looked through the large log book she'd been handed and tried to orientate herself to the columns and rows of times, amounts, engine sizes and various other entries that made little sense to her.

'And were Misty Blue's fees paid?'

'Yes, in full until September,' replied Prado, leaning across and pointing Valle to the entry in the far column of the log. 'You'll have to ask at the town hall if you want the financial details, that's nothing to do with us. We take the money for boat hire but not for the permanent moorings.'

'It says here Misty Blue was taken out last Thursday,' Valle said. She run her painted fingernail across the page to the relevant column. 'It left at fourteen hundred hours.'

'I remember. It's moored at peg A18, just along there,' said Prado, pointing out of the large panoramic window at the front of the building, 'so I always notice when it leaves.'

Valle gazed out at the first of many rows of moored vessels. They all looked much the same to her. Chavarría may be able to spot a Monterey 276 from just a single glance at a photograph on a wall but, to a city girl, a boat was just a boat. She turned over the page to check the following day's records.

'It returned on Friday at fifteen thirty,' she noted. 'Do you keep track of where the boats go?'

The marina manager shook his head. 'We don't have the technology for that. As long as they stick to the rules and don't go into the zones marked for swimming, diving and water sports, the entire Mediterranean is their playground.'

'What about the names of any passengers?'

'Only for the hire vehicles for insurance purposes,' replied Prado. 'Not for the private boats. The owners take out who they please.'

'Do you recall if Sr. Harris had anyone with him with he took his boat out last Thursday?'

'Yes, he did,' said Prado after a moment's though. 'A big guy, short grey hair. Tattoos.'

That was good enough for Valle. It was almost word-for-word the description Chavarría gave the team of Darren Mitchell. The official opened her attaché file and produced a photograph of Donnie Lane. It showed him, cocktail in hand, posing behind the bar at *Breeze*. Found during the search of his apartment, it was easier on the eye for potential witnesses than the other photo of Lane in her possession, which came courtesy of the morgue.

'Do you recognise this man?'

'I've seen him a couple of times with Sr. Harris,' nodded Prado.

Valle exchanged the photograph with one of Natalie Brooks.

'How about her?'

'I couldn't swear to it,' the man said after some careful deliberation, 'but she looks familiar. Maybe if you had other photos…'

Valle turned her attention back to the log, making a mental note to return with some further images, and flicked back a week to the days following Natalie's disappearance. After a few minutes searching, she found what she was looking for. Misty Blue had been taken out early on the previous Saturday morning, around twenty-six hours after the holiday rep had last been seen by Max Okeke, leaving *Breeze* in the early hours of Friday. The boat returned later that afternoon.

'I need to take copies of this,' Valle said to the marina manager.

The tear fell from the old man's cheek and landed on

the newsprint, smudging the ink and causing several of the words to run into each other. It had been his dream to spend his last few years in the sun but now it had all crumbled to dust. The two hours he had spent on the telephone to Spain, being passed from person to person, given various other numbers to try, and generally messed about, had sapped him of any hope there would be a way out. And he didn't have the energy or the health for the long fight ahead to try and rescue the situation.

The news that he wasn't the only person to have called that morning with a similar story wasn't reassuring. It was confirmation of his worst nightmare. He had also had a phone conversation with the bank but soon realised that nothing he did would be of any use. It was all too late.

The old man got up from the table and hobbled slowly out of the kitchen into the small back yard. Damn this bloody arthritis! The climate was going to be so good for him. He shut himself in the shed and found the coil of rope among a pile of odds and ends at the bottom of a cupboard. There! He knew he had some. The joints of his fingers may have been stiff and painful, but he could just about force them to work for a short while. And he hadn't forgotten how to tie an effective knot.

CHAPTER FOURTEEN

IT wouldn't be long now. The flight had been booked and all he needed to do was see out the last day in Cieloventura without attracting any undue attention. He was actually going to get away with it. There had been a few moments when he didn't think he would but, this time tomorrow, he'd be on a plane. And it would all be behind him.

'The finca was being used in a property scam,' announced Inspector Jefe Roman Lopéz Chavarría, 'and it appears Lane and Natalie were both involved.'

The detective went on to explain to his team how the town hall had received a number of calls that morning from the UK. Each of the callers had claimed to have read a story in an English newspaper about holiday development fraud, and how the photograph featured in the article appeared to be a property just outside Cieloventura they had either recently visited or, in at least four cases, actually purchased. Their concern, especially the latter group, was understandable and the town hall had passed the details to the Policia Nacional. The officer who received the information had been part of the Donnie Lane and Natalie Brooks investigation and it was he who had made the connection.

'One of the victims of this apparent deception has sent us an e-mail detailing exactly how he became involved in the purchase,' the detective continued. 'He, and another who has been affected, are flying back out to Spain this afternoon. I've left a message at the town hall for them both to be sent here without delay. I want them interviewed as soon as they arrive.'

Chavarría gave his team a few moments to absorb the new information, using the time to glance through once again the e-mail that, only minutes before, had been forwarded to him from the town hall. While his written English wasn't as proficient as his spoken, he could understand the gist of it.

'The buyer paid fifty thousand Euros into a Banco de Valencia account held in the name of Anglo-España Dream Properties. I want the account traced as a matter of urgency. Don't stand for any fudging from the bank. Go straight to Sandoval if they try and piss you about.'

'Leave it to me,' said Luís Banda, writing down the details in his notebook.

Chavarría looked to Valle. 'Anything?'

It had taken Official Valle only minutes to locate a website for Anglo-España Dream Properties and, more importantly, to suspect it wasn't quite what it seemed.

'They are all genuine properties on here,' she told Chavarría, turning her computer monitor around so the Inspector Jefe could see it from his desk, 'but when you click on any of them for further information, it just links to the site of the actual agents dealing with the property.'

'Get the computer people onto it anyway,' Chavarría said. 'See if they can trace who it is registered to.'

From the moment he had learned that Sr. Romo hadn't been interested in selling the finca, the detective had suspected the vacant property was being used in some kind of illegal enterprise. The information he had received from Tony Heather concerning the promotional adverts he'd seen in Natalie's apartment, which were then apparently taken in the burglary, reinforced his belief. There were always plenty of people who came to the Costa, usually foreign retirees, looking to find their little bit of paradise in the sun. And such people could easily become targets. There had been a problem, Chavarría was told by a veteran police officer who had spent his entire career in the town, with timeshare scam artists a number of years before but several high-profile prosecutions, as well as changes in both national and regional legislation, had driven them out and Cieloventura had a virtually unblemished record since then.

The finca had clearly been very carefully chosen by those behind the scheme. Its location, with picturesque views of the mountains and the town below, was perfect for a holiday villa, and its seclusion from any neighbouring properties not only ensured privacy for the potential new owners, but also meant any suspicious activity by those involved could go unnoticed. It couldn't have been more ideal for their purposes. Banda had been instructed to press Max Okeke on what, if anything, he knew of the property scam but the doorman plead ignorance and the official believed him.

Chavarría suddenly slammed his fist down on the desk, sending a small pot of paper clips and staples flying, and attracting brief glances from everyone else in the office. The Inspector Jefe had wanted to play this closer to his chest. For a few more days, at least. He was certain Peter Harris was involved and the story in the British press would only serve to put him on his guard. The background check he'd requested had also come in that morning. Chavarría almost felt like congratulating himself on his foresight. Darren Mitchell had a long criminal record and numerous stays in prison, mainly for offences involving small scale violence and theft. Peter Harris, on the other hand, was clean. As was Synergist Holdings. Comparing Mitchell's record with that of Donnie Lane had revealed they had been in the same prison together in the late nineties. Chavarría wasn't surprised.

The Inspector Jefe left the comisaría and drove the three miles to Peter Harris' villa. While he hadn't planned on visiting him again so soon, circumstances had changed. And he wanted to annoy him. To be a fly that wouldn't be swotted away. Chavarría parked a few minutes' walk from the villa and walked the rest of the distance. He arrived to see Peter Harris loading a large holdall into the boot of a silver saloon on the road outside.

'Good morning.'

'Inspector Jefe,' smiled Harris, closing the boot.

'Sorry to call on you unannounced, but there have

been developments in the investigation.'

'Anything I can assist you with?'

'Perhaps you are aware of a newspaper story that appeared this morning back in England?'

'Don't bother with British papers out here,' Harris snorted. 'They're only full of celebrities and gossip. I moved out here to leave all that crap behind.'

The businessman strolled back to the open gate leading to his villa and pulled it shut, rattling it several times in its casing to ensure it had locked.

'So what's happened, then?'

'From information we now have in our possession,' explained Chavarría, 'it appears the finca we spoke about was being used in a property development fraud. It was offered for sale by people with no ownership or rights to the land.'

'That's awful,' Harris replied, shaking his head in dismay.

'We know of at least four people who have paid deposits to secure the property, each paying anything from fifty to one hundred thousand Euros. No doubt there will be more.'

'Surely you'll be able to trace the money and find out who's behind it?'

Chavarría smiled disarmingly. He knew it was no use talking to Peter Harris like this. He would have an answer to everything, and it would always be the answer of an innocent man.

'We will do our best.'

'So why do you think the girl was killed?'

'We don't know she has been, Sr. Harris.'

'Of course. Sorry, I just assumed.'

Chavarría nodded towards the boot of the car. 'Are you going anywhere, señor?'

'The Piggott family are flying back to England this evening,' Harris said. 'I'm going to say my goodbyes, collect the keys, and arrange for the contractors to go back in and finish the decoration. Then I'm off out on the boat.'

'Will you be away for long?'

'No, I'll be back tonight.'

For the first time since they had met, Chavarría knew Harris was answering a question truthfully. Of course he wouldn't run. Why would he? That would make him look guilty. If Harris was confident there was nothing to connect him with any criminal activity, then he would front it out. He would stay in Cieloventura, very visible, right under the Inspector Jefe's nose. Maybe it would be Harris that would turn out to be the fly.

'It appears Sr. Lane was involved in the fraud.'

Harris held Chavarría's gaze for a few moments before responding. 'Look, Inspector, let me make my position clear. Synergist Holdings is a respected and long-established company. We don't get involved in anything illegal. If it turns out Donnie was somehow mixed up in all this then, believe me, I knew nothing about it. I wouldn't have stood for any employee of mine doing anything like that. He'd have been out!'

'That's good to hear, señor. Please, don't let me keep you any longer.'

Harris climbed into the driver's seat and started the

engine. As he attached his seat belt, Chavarría moved forward and leaned on the top of the open door.

'By the way, where is your associate?'

'Doing his job,' Harris said. 'He'll be back some time later if you need to talk to him.'

The businessman went to pull the door closed, hesitating awkwardly as the Inspector Jefe's grip on it prevented him from doing so. Chavarría waited a second or two before stepping back from the door. Harris pulled it shut and drove off along the street. Taking a cheroot from his pocket, the detective walked back to his own vehicle. Chavarría knew people wouldn't be parted from their money so easily. For the scam to work, it had to be convincing. Harris was a legitimate property developer and would have the expertise and know-how to pull it off. It did, also, throw up other possibilities. Everyone involved with the fraud would be a legitimate suspect in both Donnie Lane's death and Natalie Brooks' disappearance, including those who had been conned. If someone found out that they had been ripped off, that would certainly be a motive. Had the discovery of the finca scam helped to focus their investigation? Or had it blown it wide open?

Tony shielded his eyes from the dust thrown up by the tyres of the taxi as it accelerated away and walked towards the wooden gates. He was surprised, and a little daunted, to receive the assignment from the Mayor's Office but was glad of the opportunity at last to meet the family of Leanne Piggott. The British

Consular official looking after them had informed the town hall that flights had been booked to return the family to the UK later that evening. Tony had been asked to call on the Piggotts before they left Cieloventura to express once again the condolences of the Mayor for their tragic loss, and to reaffirm the support that would be available to them in the difficult months ahead.

While Tony was at the town hall, he'd learned of a number of calls that had been received that morning from the UK. His theory had borne fruit. The newspaper article by Jerry Field, which was largely an update on Natalie Brooks, had contained a carefully worded story of alleged holiday property fraud along the Costa Blanca. The accompanying photo had showed Natalie posing outside the finca. While there was nothing in the article that actually claimed the finca was being used in any such fraud, Field was the type of journalist that could make a story say one thing while cynically implying something else. With his new assignment a clear priority, Tony had no time to stay and find out any more details of the calls from the UK but, with all information being passed onto the Policia Nacional, he was confident an important new lead in the holiday rep's disappearance had been uncovered. A job well done, he thought.

Tony walked up the pathway towards the small villa. The single-storey stone building was bordered on either side with narrow gardens and, though the climate prevented the lush green grass that he would forever associate with England, it being more a yellow-brown, it made for an attractive welcome. There was even an old stone well, but he couldn't tell whether it was original or a decorative folly. This was where Tony, if his job became long-term and secure, saw himself a few years down the line. Not this kind of property – his wallet would never stretch to that – but a place on the outskirts of the town, away from the hustle and bustle.

As he approached the front door, Tony took note of the large car parked in the driveway and a number of suitcases and bags on the terrace. He paused on the threshold and ran a finger under his collar. A long-sleeved shirt and tie wasn't ideal in this weather but the occasion called for something more formal than his usual attire. Tony's knock was answered by a small man in his early fifties who introduced himself as the official from the British Consulate. Stepping to one side to allow Tony to enter the villa, the official turned his attention to the collection of luggage and began loading it into the car.

Tony walked through the hall into the lounge, where a middle-aged couple were sitting. So this was John and Shelley Piggott. The man stood up to greet him and, though his hand shake was strong, he clearly had the weight of the world on his shoulders. The strain of events had left him looking drawn and older than his years. Tony was shocked at Shelley's condition. She looked frail and with a vacant look in her eyes that told of her growing dependence on sleeping pills at night and anti-depressants during the day.

Despite his visit being expected, Tony formally introduced himself and several minutes of polite small talk were exchanged. Though he didn't want a hot cup of tea, Tony readily accepted Shelley's offer, more to give her something to occupy herself than anything else. He was already sweating profusely and hoped the shirt he'd chosen wouldn't show the dampness that was accumulating under his arms and the back of his neck.

'How is your son coping?'

'He has good days and bad,' John said, his voice barely rising above a whisper. 'Sometimes he acts like nothing has happened, splashing in the pool and having fun. Other days, he won't come out of room. Won't even eat.'

Shelley walked back in from the kitchen with a mug of tea, which she placed down on the small table in front of where Tony was sitting. He smiled graciously.

'Things will start to get better when we get him home.' John added.

Tony took a card from his pocket.

'If you need any assistance over the coming months, the Mayor's Office will do all it can to help,' he said, handing it to John. 'The investigation is still proceeding, of course, and then there'll be the trial.'

'How long will that take?'

'Difficult to say,' Tony said truthfully. 'It could be anything from six months to a year or more'

John shook his head in disgust. 'Just put me in the same room as that evil bastard. Just five minutes, that's all. Spare us all a bloody trial!'

Tony was lost for a reply and allowed John a few

moments to gather himself.

'There's no way of hurrying it along, I'm afraid,' he continued. 'The legal process needs to take its course. Ryan Dinsdale will stay in prison until the trial.'

'Don't say his name!' Shelley suddenly screamed, taking both Tony and John by surprise. 'I don't want his name mentioned!'

'I'm sorry,' Tony said, 'I didn't mean to upset you. I know it's no consolation, but Fontcalent Prison is by no means an easy place to be.'

'Have you visited him?'

It was more of an accusation than a question, and Tony felt the full force of Shelley's eyes boring into him. He sought to diffuse the situation, considering it best not to mention the circumstances of his visit to Ryan in Fontcalent or any opinions of his own of the young man's guilt or innocence.

'I'm a liaison point for British visitors to Cieloventura who, for whatever reason, have dealings with the Spanish police,' he explained. 'I just needed to call on him to assess the situation. As a British citizen, he has certain rights which need to…'

'Rights?!'

Tony realised instantly he had committed a terrible faux pas and leaned back defensively as a furious Shelley leapt to her feet.

'He's not a person, he doesn't have rights! He's a monster!'

'I'm sorry, I didn't mean to…'

'What about my daughter's rights?! What about her right to a life?! What about her right not to be murdered?!'

John stood up and attempted to put a consoling arm around her wife's shoulders but she pushed him roughly away and stormed out of the lounge. John looked awkwardly at Tony and winced slightly as a door slammed, shaking the walls of the villa.

'Sorry about that.'

'No, not at all,' said Tony, apologetically. 'That was my fault. I can't begin to imagine how this has affected you all.'

'It's being stuck in this place. It's been driving us all up the wall. We've hardly set foot outside since we came here.'

Tony felt for the family. It had been such an awful situation for them and he couldn't help thinking about his own family back in Aylesbury. He still hadn't heard anything from Helen and resolved to send her a further e-mail at the earliest opportunity. If he couldn't persuade her to let Lucy come out for a week, he would book a flight and return home for a couple of days instead. Maybe next weekend.

After a brief conversation about the arrangements that had been made to repatriate the family, John excused himself and went after Shelley. Taking his mug of tea with him, Tony stood up and wandered over to the patio doors at the far end of the lounge. They opened out onto a large sun terrace and pool area. A young boy was sitting on a low wall at the side of the terrace, idly tossing small leaves he was picking from a nearby bush into the pool. Tony stepped out onto the terrace and approached the wall. The boy stiffened slightly but didn't look up or acknowledge the man's presence.

'Hello. You must be Todd?'

Staring down at his feet, the boy nodded. Tony sat down beside him.

'My name's Tony.'

'Are you another policeman?'

'Sort of. How are you getting on?'

'Alright. We're going home today.'

'Yes, that's right,' nodded Tony. 'You parents were just telling me.'

The sound of Shelley quietly sobbing could be heard from a nearby window. Tony looked back to the boy to see him struggling to hold back his own tears.

'Mam and Dad blame me.'

'Oh, I'm sure they don't, Todd.'

'I knew Leanne was going out when everyone was asleep and didn't say anything.'

'You were just being a good brother,' Tony smiled warmly, playfully patting the boy on the arm. 'I would've done exactly the same.'

Todd wiped his eyes on the back of his hand and looked around at Tony for the first time.

'Do you have a sister?'

'A couple, yes. Did Leanne tell you where she was going when she went out?'

'Just clubbing.'

'Did she mention a place called Platinum?'

'Streax was playing there,' Todd nodded.

'She told you about him?'

'She saw a poster along the Avenue. Reckoned all

her mates would be well jealous if she actually got to meet him.'

'Todd. It's time for us to go now.'

Tony and Todd looked around to see John standing by the open patio doors. The boy got to his feet and walked back to the villa. Tony took the opportunity to dispose of the rest of his tea in the dirt beneath the nearest bush before returning inside. After a quick detour to the kitchen to rinse and dry out his mug, Tony walked though the villa and out into the driveway where the family were gathered. A second car, a silver saloon, was now parked there and Shelley and John were in conversation with a man Tony had not seen before.

'Thanks once again for letting us stay here again, Mr. Harris. We couldn't have coped with the Solanis,' John said.

'Not at all. Please, it's been my privilege.'

Shelley clutched a pink holdall to her chest, shaking her head at John's request to put it into the boot with the rest of the luggage. Tony, watching on from the shade of the front porch, assumed it belonged to Leanne. Todd suddenly dashed back into the villa to collect a miniature red sports coupe from beneath the coffee table. He then ran back out to the car and climbed into the back.

'See you, Todd.'

'Bye, Pete.'

So this was Peter Harris, the owner of *Breeze*. And also, Tony now realised, the owner of the villa that had been loaned to the Piggott family. He suddenly recalled seeing the silver saloon before. It was the car that had dropped Donnie Lane outside *Breeze* two days after Natalie's disappearance, with Tony looking on from the Irish bar opposite.

Harris stood at the edge of the drive, idly playing with his touch-screen mobile phone, as John and Shelley climbed into the vehicle and made their final preparations to leave. Eventually, with Shelley once more in floods of tears, the car set off along the driveway and out onto the dusty road beyond.

'Good morning. My name's Tony Heather. I'm with the Mayor's Office.'

Harris looked around as Tony approached him. 'British?'

'Yes.'

'Nice to meet you. Pete Harris.'

The two men shook hands.

'You must be the owner of the villa?'

'That's right.'

'Well, it's a very nice place. Very nice indeed.'

'It will be when it's finished,' Harris agreed, standing back to take in a view of the front of the property. 'Just a few touches here and there and it can go on the market.'

'What are you asking?'

'Interested?' Harris smiled, taking off his sunglasses.

'Well, it's probably out of my price range,' admitted Tony, 'and it's a little too soon, to be honest. I'm not sure whether my contract here will be extended. If it is, I'm keen on getting something just outside of town.'

'Well, when you're in a position to start looking around for a place, give me a call,' said Harris, taking a business card from his pocket. 'There's a number of reputable agents in Cieloventura but a few dodgy ones as well. You've gotta be a bit careful.'

'Thank you, yes. I'll do that.'

'At least if you're dealing with a fellow Brit, you know you can't be conned by some dodgy local and it all being blamed on the language barrier when it goes pear-shaped. All our contracts are written in English and Spanish and, although it's the Spanish one that's the legal one here, I always insist any potential clients have them both checked out independently to ensure nothing is lost or added in translation.'

It was convincing salesmanship, and would have been even more so if Tony had not already held suspicions about the man. He recalled Valle, when asking if he had heard of Harris, mentioning the difficulties the police had had in tracing the owner of *Breeze*. What involvement, if any, could he have had with the fraud at the finca, the death of Donnie Lane, or the disappearance of Natalie Brooks? Harris seemed, for all appearances, a successful businessman.

'I'm actually in the process of selling my house in the UK,' Tony lied. 'If I hear about my contract soon, which may possibly any day now, I may be able to do something sooner rather than later.'

'Well, look, give me a call when you're free and I'll take you on a tour of my current properties. If this place is outside your budget, there's a few others that might catch your eye. You can meet some of my previous clients as well. Nothing like getting a personal recommendation.'

At that moment, Tony's mobile phone rang. He took it from his pocket and looked at the display. It was Official Valle. He and Harris bade each other a hurried farewell and, striding back towards the road, Tony answered the call.

'Tony, can you possibly do me a favour?'

'Of course,' he replied, glancing over his shoulder to make sure he was out of Harris' ear-shot. 'Something to do with the investigation?'

Valle informed Tony of her visit to the marina the previous day. 'If we can place Natalie in the company of Peter Harris, that could be a vital connection in our case. I understand you have a number of photographs of her?'

'I do, yes.'

'Could you go along to the marina at some point today and show them to the manager? His name is Fernando Prado. He was unable to give a positive identification on the only one I had on me. I should go myself but things are like a madhouse here at present.'

'Of course, I'm happy to help. How are things going? There's been developments, I gather?'

'We are getting somewhere. Fortunately, leads seem to be popping up at the right time. Perhaps the investigation has a fairy godmother looking over us. Or, as the Inspector Jefe would say if he ever found out, an interfering British ex-police officer with too much time on his hands.'

Tony winced. 'Leave it to me,' he said, after

waiting a few seconds to see if any more comments on the matter were going to be made. 'As soon as I'm finished for the day, I'll collect my folder and head straight to the marina.'

'Thank you. Let me know what he says. Adios.'

Too much time on his hands? He wished. There weren't enough hours in the day for all the tasks he needed to do but, with the investigation moving fast, he remained grateful to Valle for allowing him to play a role in it. Tony glanced at his watch. He would need to skip lunch today if he was going to fit everything in. Still, what with that and the few pounds he must have sweated off in the past hour, maybe there was no need for that gym membership after all?

It was early evening when, instead of letting his team leave for the day, Inspector Jefe Chavarría decided to call a briefing so everyone could be kept up-to-date with everything that had happened. As expected, two of the people caught up in the finca scam had arrived in Cieloventura and, via a brief visit to the town hall, had arrived at the comisaría to be formally interviewed. One of them, to his great relief, had been able to stop the money transfer going through as it had been post-dated to coincide with a salary cheque that was being paid into his account that week. The other, however, was not so lucky and was down to the tune of €50,000, a figure that represented a significant bulk of he and his wife's life savings. The stories they had given had been remarkably similar in their detail. Official Valle had also been busy on the telephone talking to those people back in the UK who had contacted the town hall or, in several cases, made calls direct to the Policia Nacional.

'We've spoken briefly to everyone whose details we currently have,' she informed the meeting, 'all except one. A retired engineer from the north of England. He's not answering his telephone, but I'll keep trying. Luís and I have compared notes and a common thread has started to appear.'

'All those who visited the finca have one thing in common,' said Banda, taking over after a nod from Valle in his direction. 'They had all previously seen properties in and around Cieloventura owned by Synergist Holdings.'

The official allowed a second or two for the news to sink in before continuing. 'All of these people visited a variety of agents along the Costa Blanca, some went as far as Alicante, others stayed in and around Cieloventura and El Marquesa, in search of a holiday or retirement property. They each inspected a number of villas and apartments but, for whatever reason, none were suitable for their needs or purse.'

'They were then contacted by Anglo-España Dream Properties and told about a place that had just come on the market,' continued Valle, 'an old finca in the hills overlooking the town. Priced high enough to look legitimate but low enough to make people feel they were getting a bargain.'

'Did any of them know anything about this company before?' asked Chavarría.

'Some had seen their website,' Valle answered, 'but the properties tended to be far more expensive than they could possibly afford. If you look on the site, you won't find one priced under a million. But, as I said before, the properties weren't even theirs to begin with.'

'And no-one queried why they had been contacted by this company out of the blue or how they had got hold of their information?'

'They've all told us they left their contact details, either an e-mail address or a phone number, with all sorts of people from agents to developers to fellow property hunters. It wasn't unusual for them to receive cold calls regarding places for sale along the Costa.'

'Anyway, those attracted by the prospect and keen to arrange a viewing were picked up in the centre of Cieloventura by a man and a young woman from Anglo-España they knew as Donald and Natalie' said Banda. 'The man had keys for the finca, as well as copies of the property deeds and architect blueprints, as well as some computer-generated images, showing the proposed plans for the development.'

'We know some showed little interest in the place, either because of its isolation or it didn't fit what they were looking for, and only contacted us in case they could be of assistance,' said Valle. 'Others, though, clearly saw its potential and felt compelled to push a deal through as soon as possible before someone else came along and took it out of their hands.'

'Apparently, the owner wanted a quick sale,' Banda commented. 'So that added to the pressure for any interested buyer.'

'Did none of them recognise this woman as the missing holiday rep?' the Inspector Jefe asked. 'The story has been all over the British press.'

'They didn't make the connection,' Valle replied. 'The photos of Natalie in the newspapers showed a young woman in short skirts and make-up, partying in clubs with people her own age. In most of them, she was either drunk or flashing her underwear. The Natalie they knew was a smartly dressed and polite young businesswoman, not a holiday rep.'

'Anyway, four interested parties, as we so far know, committed to purchasing the property and paid deposits into Anglo-España's bank account,' said Banda. 'All of them had the contract checked before paying anything and, apparently, all seemed above board. Juez Sandoval is arranging the necessary warrants for the account details to be released.'

'Good,' said Chavarría, nodding in satisfaction. He knew any money wouldn't have stayed in the account for long. It would've been transferred as soon as it had cleared into another bank, no doubt overseas, and, from there, to yet another and so on. The trail would no doubt be littered along its course with fake companies, false names and more than a fair share of innocent dupes. It would be cumbersome and time-consuming to follow. The people behind this scam were no amateurs. But neither, Chavarría knew, were the Policia Nacional.

The Inspector Jefe stood and wandered over to the information board. The question marks that linked the names of Donnie Lane and Natalie Brooks to that of the finca had been wiped off.

'With his hair styled and a sharp suit, he could look every inch the successful property agent,' said Chavarría, looking at the photograph of Lane that adorned the board, 'and he even had an attractive young assistant in tow.'

'And Natalie was no mean saleswoman herself by all accounts,' Valle added.

'They made quite a team,' nodded Chavarría. He switched his gaze to the photo of the young woman. As Valle had indicated, it showed her in her role as a *Holiday18* rep, guiding her young charges through a week of drunkenness and casual sex, rather than the smart businesswoman she apparently became.

'One of them was murdered and buried at the finca, and the other is missing,' the detective said, his eyes moving back and forth between the two photos. 'Something went wrong.'

Tony's visit to the marina didn't prove as productive as he had hoped. Fernando Prado wasn't on duty and his replacement was unable to offer any information of use. Tony left several of his photographs in an envelope, with a small note asking Prado to look at them when he arrived for duty later that evening, and to contact him as soon as possible. As he began the walk back to Calle Neuva, Tony took out his phone and called Officíal Valle. It went direct to her voicemail so he left a brief message, explaining what had happened and, if he hadn't heard anything from Sr. Prado by the morning, he would chase it up first thing. While Valle had chastised him over the phone for his 'interference', it was said almost amusingly and was certainly not meant, he felt, to dissuade him from any further investigations. He considered his next move. If Peter Harris had any involvement in the affair, he would shut up like a clam on questioning by a police officer. He wouldn't know anything of Tony's involvement in the case, however, and that gave him an advantage over someone like Inspector Jefe Chavarría. Perhaps he should take up Harris' offer of a further meeting after all. He wanted to get to know the man a little better.

The loud blast on the car horn almost gave Tony a heart attack. He span around and saw Marie Reynolds behind the wheel of her battered Fiat Uno. At that distance, surely she could have just spoke his name out of the window? Marie waved and pulled the car into the side of the road. Tony walked over to greet her as she got out.

'How's it all going?'

Tony gave Marie a quick summary of the investigation so far, skirting over matters he felt should remain confidential, quickly getting to the point concerning the illegal sale of the finca. She listened without interruption, showing genuine shock at Natalie's involvement with such a deception.

'That explains the posh suit, then,' she said.

'Seems she had a whole other life no-one knew about.'

'Is she dead, Tony?'

Tony thought for a second or two before answering.

There was no point giving Marie any more false hope. 'It's looking likely,' he nodded.

'So do the police know who did it?'

'Well, the investigation is going well. I've played quite a part in it. I'm confident it won't be long before the police make an arrest.'

'I'll tell the others that the great detective Sherlock Heather is closing in on his man,' she said, attempting to lighten her mood with a nervous laugh. 'I know how worried they've all been about it.'

'So how are things with you? Still busy?'

'God, yes,' Marie sighed. 'I think I'm getting old, you know. All I wanna seem to do these days is put my feet up with a cup of cocoa.'

Tony grinned. 'Well, when you've finished for the day, you should do exactly that! Treat yourself.'

'No chance. It'll be another hectic night tonight.'

'What's happening tonight?'

'It's Friday,' Marie said, looking at him as though he was an idiot. 'Carnival night. It won't be much of a late one for me, at least,' said Marie. 'I'm meeting some extra flights tomorrow until Ross's replacement turns up. He was meant to start in the morning but there's been some fuck up somewhere. How about you? Any plans for the evening?'

Tony knew that, despite all the work he'd been putting in on both the Natalie Brooks and Leanne Piggott cases, he couldn't forget why he was in Cieloventura, and what he was being paid for, in the first place.

'I'll need to pop out for a bit,' he said. 'There's a

few places I want to visit. I'll have a chat with any groups of young British tourists I see before they get too hammered to listen.'

'Well, don't worry about our lot,' Marie said. 'The crew'll make sure they all get back safely and don't cause any major problems.'

'That would be appreciated,' smiled Tony, 'and take care of yourself. If you finish before the others, make sure you don't walk back alone.'

'I'm sure I can find a knight in shining armour somewhere to see me home,' winked Marie. She climbed back into the old Fiat and, after another unnecessary blast on the horn, drove away. While Tony had never been a fan of *Holiday18*, and others of their ilk, and the kind of hedonistic holidays they promoted, he realised he'd only met a handful of tourists in his dealings with the Policia Municipal and the local court system who were travelling with the company. For all their faults, and there were many of those, at least the events were organised and the reps, who usually drank almost as much as the guests they were meant to be looking after, were on hand to try and prevent any excessive or illegal behaviour. Tony turned his mind back to what he had been considering before Marie's car horn had so violently interrupted him. He took out the business card he'd been given by Peter Harris. Apart from a stylish company logo, it just gave his name and position – *Partner* – and a telephone number. No address. Tony reached for his phone.

'These are our current properties in and around Cieloventura,' said Peter Harris, handing Tony a folder containing around twenty colourful advertisements, as well as various information and photographs of the company's interests back in the UK. 'We've several further out, including a number of apartments in a new development just outside Benidorm.'

While promotional adverts like this would all tend to follow the same format, Tony was struck by their similarity to those he'd seen in Natalie's apartment. Synergist was not a company he recognised but they seemed, from the details supplied in the folder, a reasonably big player in the leisure and property businesses.

'I don't think I could go that far,' Tony said. 'It needs to be convenient for work.'

'So what is it you do at the Mayor's Office, may I ask?'

'Tourism basically. I help to promote Cieloventura as a destination for British holiday-makers.'

'And so what brought you to visit the Piggott family? I hardly feel they'd be in the mood to return here on their holidays.'

'I was just picked on because I'm British, I think,' Tony said, which did, in his mind, have an element of truth to it. 'The town hall wanted to express their sorrow for what had happened and thought it would sound better coming from me than yet another Spanish official.'

'So what did you used to do back in Blighty?'

'Public relations.'

Tony had thought of what he considered a reasonable cover story for his presence in the town and, like the best cover stories, it contained enough of the actual truth to be credible. Harris didn't press him any further, though.

Sitting together in the comfort of an upmarket tapas bar in the centre of the town, Peter Harris was more laid back than during their first meeting at the villa. After receiving Tony's call, he had invited him to get together for a drink that evening where he could, in his words, build up a personal property plan that would fit Tony's budget and requirements. Harris had began by giving him a tour of the apartment above the bar, both of which were owned by Synergist, and explaining the potential that was to be had by investing in property along the Costa Blanca. Tony had also had the fortune of meeting Darren Mitchell. Casting his mind back to the evening he'd spent observing *Breeze* from the Irish bar, Mitchell certainly fitted with what he could recall of the driver of the silver saloon.

After nearly an hour discussing the various merits of each of the properties that Tony said were within his price range, they parted with an agreement to visit together a two-bedroom apartment in a private complex in the northern district of the town the following Monday morning. Tony planned to call and postpone at some point over the weekend, blaming pressure of work, but the meeting had been helpful to him and he felt he knew Peter Harris a little better. He was certainly an ambitious man and, while he gave little away of his life in England before relocating to the

Costa Blanca, he had commented several times on how far he had come from a humble background.

Tony went back to Calle Neuva for a shower, a change of clothes and a round of tea and toast, before it was time to head out again. After making his rounds of the bars he'd previously highlighted, talking to the several groups of British tourists that were gathered there about the need for responsible behaviour, Tony decided to take in a moonlight stroll along the beach and then to return home via the Avenue. He fancied a cool beer in a quiet bar where he could, just for half an hour, try to relax. *Bar Loco* was fine for a coffee or bite to eat during the day but, come nightfall, he knew he didn't fit in with the clientele it attracted. They usually made excellent company, he thought, but some of the antics he'd witnessed in the only full evening spent in the bar since he moved in left him feeling slightly uncomfortable. In spite of all the equality and diversity workshops he'd been on while in the force, indeed he'd even run a few, no-one ever taught him where to look when two men started kissing in front of him.

Tony sat down on a bench overlooking the beach and took in a breath of the cool night air. He tried to make sense of the day's developments. The finca had been used to con a number of people, all British it had seemed, out of tens, if not hundreds, of thousands of Pounds. And Donnie and Natalie were responsible. It was while he sat there, looking across the darkness of the Mediterranean stretched out in front of him, that he finally accepted Natalie was dead. Despite her apparent involvement in such a large crime, he couldn't help but feel pain for the loss. He'd done so much to find her, got to know her so well, it seemed, and he knew he needed to fight on to get justice for her.

With Donnie Lane also dead, someone else must have been involved. Peter Harris, with Darren Mitchell, were the likely suspects. The hour he'd spent in Harris' company earlier that evening had been pleasant enough, but Tony felt it was one long sales pitch. Harris had once again brought up the subject of exercising caution when dealing with local property agents but he'd made no mention of the finca fraud. Wouldn't that have been a prime example of the kind of thing he was warning Tony against? Then again, was Harris' silence on the matter actually surprising? The story had featured in a sole British newspaper that morning and, with the exception of the odd copy floating around the town, it wouldn't be something known to many inhabitants of Cieloventura.

Tony's chain of thought was suddenly broken by a scream to his side. A man in his early twenties was running down the beach to the water's edge, carrying a shrieking young woman in his arms. Despite her loud and desperate pleas, he hurtled headlong into the water and they both soon disappeared beneath the wash. Surfacing within seconds, the woman was the first to stagger back to the sand and, cursing at the state of her ruined dress, waited to berate the man. She began to slap him on the arms and chest, while he playfully attempted to restrain her, before the two suddenly began to passionately embrace. Tony chuckled to himself and decided it was time to take his leave. Tomorrow would no doubt throw up even more developments and chances are he wouldn't be getting an undisturbed nights' sleep. Besides, he was looking forward to that cool beer. He'd earned it.

The request from despatch, asking them to respond to a call from a concerned local resident regarding a drunk in the street outside, was so similar to the last one, and the one before that, that Consuela wondered whether it was actually a real voice or just a recording played on an infinite loop. While dealing with drunks were preferable to breaking up fights, they'd already had two of those to deal with tonight, they weren't always without problems. While protocol required them to sling the offending member of the public, no doubt a tourist, into the back of the car and take them to the lock-up for processing, she and Rafá saw that as a last resort and would elect, if possible, to see these people safely back to their place of residence. Policing, for her, wasn't always about catching wrongdoers and earning a few more cents for the town coffers. It was about helping people. Despite that, however, she didn't relish dealing with another drunk so soon after the last and resolved that, this time, it would be scissors. No last minute changing of mind. Scissors!

Rafá acknowledged the call and, after laboriously turning the patrol car around in a very narrow side street, ignoring Consuela's claims that it would be quicker to just drive the long way around, they made for the location given in the report. Consuela was the first to see the drunk, staggering along some twenty yards in the distance on the opposite side of the street, trying to keep himself up by leaning against the wall. Rafá pulled the car to a halt and smiled at his partner.

'Ready?'

One game of Rock Paper Scissors later, Consuela grabbed her cap from the dashboard and opened the door. Cursing her luck, that was five times in a row now, she made her way across the road. Damn those scissors! If she had a real pair on her, she'd make Rafá get off his lazy backside for once and no mistake.

The drunk suddenly crashed to the ground and, from where she was, it looked a pretty nasty fall. As she approached him, Consuela's initial caution – she knew her first duty was to assess any risk to her own safety – was overtaken by urgency and she broke into a run. This may not be a simple case of someone having too much to drink after all. The large amount of blood that trailed behind the man on the pavement told a different story. And there was something else that worried her too.

'Rafá!!'

Consuela arrived at the stricken man's side and dropped to her knees to assess his condition. In the light of a nearby street lamp, she could see the blood running from a deep wound on the crown of his head. The police officer reached down and placed the tips of her first two fingers beneath his jaw bone. The pulse was still strong, that was something. She heard the sound of the patrol car pulling level on the opposite side of the road.

'What's the matter?'

'Call an ambulance! Quickly!' Consuela screamed back across the street. 'It's Tony!'

CHAPTER FIFTEEN

HE had only been aware for a split second that someone was approaching him from behind but it was enough to trigger a rapid release of chemicals in his brain that sent his body into a state of panic. As the blow sent him reeling, scrambling his senses, his mind suddenly transported him elsewhere. For a short moment, he was no longer in Cieloventura but in Aylesbury. And he was back in his uniform.

Responding to a call that a youth had been seen breaking into a house, Tony, who had just finished attending a meeting of local shopkeepers and businesses nearby, had quickly arrived on the scene and managed to corner and apprehend the suspect. He hadn't noticed the young man's accomplices until it was too late and, while he was able to fend off the initial blows and draw his baton, they had continued to rain down on him with such ferocity that he soon succumbed. Even when he had slumped to the pavement, the brutality showed no sign of abating. It was reported during the trial that between twenty and thirty kicks and stamps had been delivered to Tony's head as he lay defenceless on the ground. While he couldn't recall the precise number himself, they seemed to go on forever and he just prayed he would survive.

Three youths were charged and convicted for the

assault, the youngest was only fourteen, and each received a lengthy custodial sentence. Tony had sat in the courtroom and listened to the boy's families and social workers making their representations to the judge. Their pleas for leniency thankfully fell on deaf ears, the judge regarding the impact of the assault on Tony's life was far more deserving of his consideration than anything said by the defence. A number of all-too-familiar expressions had been used, such as 'broken home', 'lack of a male role model', 'getting in with the wrong crowd' and 'poor job prospects,' but it cut no ice with the judge. Some enterprising officers in Tony's station had made a bingo card that included many such phrases and, whilst sitting in a variety of courtrooms in the course of their duties, they would tick off each expression as it was rolled out by a well-meaning but, in their eyes, misguided do-gooder. Tony had been told afterwards that one of his fellow officers, a large chap by the name of Little who had been second-on-scene, arriving minutes after Tony's attackers had fled, had come the nearest to a full house during the sentencing hearing, and was now a bottle of whisky to the good. The banter of station life was something he had missed but, after returning to work three months after the assault, it just didn't seem the same anymore. He knew his days in the job were numbered.

The last thing Tony remembered of that incident was somehow finding the strength to radio for assistance before his body shut down on him. When he eventually woke, Helen was sitting in a chair by his side, her head resting on the edge of the bed. She was sleeping and, by the look of the circles under her eyes, she'd had precious little of that in recent days. He was barely able to move his hand enough to stroke her hair. This time, though, there was no-one sat in the chair beside the bed.

As he lay there, the early morning sun just beginning to make an appearance through the blinds, he forced himself to try and recall any details of what had happened to him. Everything seemed so frustratingly vague. He couldn't remember feeling the blow itself but he recalled everything suddenly spinning, his hands reaching out wildly to try and find something solid to hold on to. The sound of footsteps running into the distance mingled with the muffled din from nearby bars and clubs. Though he didn't check his wallet was still in his back pocket, he instinctively knew this was no mugging or a random assault.

Tony recalled reaching round to the back of his head and feeling the warm fluid flowing freely through his fingers. He knew he needed help. He gulped in large mouthfuls of night air, desperately trying to clear his head and think straight. His apartment must only have been a few minutes away but Tony couldn't understand why he decided to try and make for home instead of using his mobile phone to call for an ambulance. Maybe it was the concussion and the resulting disorientation. He just wasn't able to think clearly.

Tony couldn't remember how long he'd staggered for, or in which direction. He remembered several people passing by him, one was a young woman who screeched in alarm and backed away as he reached out to her, but no-one came to his assistance. Then it all become hazy. The next thing he was aware of was the ambulance journey that brought him to the hospital in Villajoyosa and the swift and professional work of the emergency medical team that greeted them.

Eventually, when he'd answered all their questions and allowed them to perform whatever investigations they told him were needed, he was taken into a quiet side room off a busy ward where he soon fell asleep. When he opened his eyes several hours later, it took him a moment to remember what had happened and where he was. He'd called out and a young nurse had come into his room. When she took his hand in hers and reassured him that everything was going to be okay, he didn't want her to ever let go. Eventually, she peeled his fingers away from her hand and slipped quietly out of the room. Left alone, Tony pulled the sheet up over his head and began to cry.

Elisa Valle Huerta had made yet another early morning journey to Sr. Romo in Villajoyosa. Her fuel allowance for the month was fast disappearing and, with the amount of overtime they were all putting in, she doubted whether a request for more money would be entertained. The old man had indicated to her on her previous visit that he'd declined to sell the finca to property developers and Chavarría had impressed on her the need to visit him once more and get him to expand on that. As expected, Sr. Romo had never heard of Anglo-España Dream Properties. He did, however, recall one particular developer that caught her interest.

'He was visited by Peter Harris from Synergist earlier this year,' the official told the Inspector Jefe. 'He was offered just above the market value for the property – a tempting deal – but, as we know, he wasn't interested in selling. Three other developers have also called on Sr. Romo in the past eighteen months with legitimate propositions but they too were sent away.'

'Harris lied,' said Chavarría. 'He told me he had no knowledge of the finca.'

'Shall we bring him in for questioning?'

'I know the line he'll give us,' he replied, dismissing the idea. 'How could we expect a busy man like him to recall a property he'd made an enquiry about months back? No, not yet. We need more on him.'

'There's something else too,' said Valle, unable to prevent the edge of her mouth curling into a slight smile. 'Harris mentioned to you in your first interview with him that Synergist was involved in health clubs, bars and gyms back in the UK. So I decided to take a closer look at all their business interests along the Costa Blanca.'

The Inspector Jefe looked at Valle and tried to work out what she could have uncovered. If Peter Harris was involved in the fraud, it would be something outside of his legitimate work with Synergist who, the reports had shown, were a reputable company.

'Turns out they own a bar in Denia,' Valle announced.

Chavarría frowned. 'Don't tell me. It's the same bar where a sighting of Natalie was made less than two days after she was last seen alive here in Cieloventura.'

Valle nodded. Chavarría chortled loudly and slapped the side of his leg. It was another link in the chain but, inside, he cursed at failing to spot the possible connection himself. The witness statement had been made by a man passing himself off as the owner of the bar. In reality, he was just a hired manager and, if that had been known, the matter may have been flagged up earlier. The Inspector Jefe knew he'd have to watch Valle closely. Not that he wasn't doing that already for another reason but if she carried on like this, he thought with a smile, she'd soon have his job.

'Get the force at Denia to bring him in,' Chavarría ordered, 'and, this time, he's not to be treated as a witness but as a possible collaborator in a serious crime. I want the truth out of him. Did he actually see the woman or was he told to say that?'

Valle picked up her phone and made the necessary call to officers in Denia. Chavarría poured himself a coffee and, seeing Banda enter the office, decided to was time to pool their thoughts. Sending out for sandwiches and pastries, he instructed the two officials to bring their chairs to his desk and, over their food, they went over all of the known facts before he invited opinions.

'Donnie Lane and Natalie Brooks were the front for the scam,' the Inspector Jefe began, 'with Peter Harris working behind the scenes. With his experience,

Harris would ensure the deal would seem legitimate. He had no contact with the victims of the scam himself, only in his genuine guise for Synergist where he had first met them. He chose carefully those he felt would be more easily fooled, people with no prior experience or knowledge of the Spanish property market or regulations.'

'The fraud had been running for a few months at least,' said Banda, 'and it was now time to call it in. They had a total of over four hundred thousand Euros going through their account in that time.'

'Which is now empty,' interjected Valle. The report from Agente Narváez, who had been charged with liaising with officials from the Banco de Valencia, that awaited them that morning had provided a considerable amount of information. The account details had shown eight separate payments, ranging from €35,000 to €120,000, had been credited within the last eight weeks. Most of the payments had remained in the account only long enough to clear before being transferred elsewhere, in smaller amounts and to a number of different banks. It was clear that there had been more victims of the scam than the Policia Nacional currently knew of. The bank's fraud department had committed their full cooperation to assisting the police in following the money trail, and the account details of everyone who had paid any money in were being traced as a matter of urgency.

'One of the couples who have been conned were planning to move into the property later this month and do the renovation work themselves as a retirement project,' said Chavarría, 'and the others were expecting the developers to begin shortly. It was time for the con to be wrapped up. So what went wrong?'

'An argument over division of the spoils?' Banda suggested.

Valle shook her head. 'No. I'm thinking about the message Natalie sent to her friend back in England. She told her she had a great new job. It seems a strange way to describe taking part in a grand scam. Apart from that, why would she risk telling anyone anything?'

'You think she knew nothing of the true nature of the deal?' Chavarría asked.

'It would make more sense. Donnie Lane would have seen her sales skills first hand at Breeze. She was a pretty and confident young woman.'

'A flirt too, no doubt,' scoffed Banda.

'If it helps people part with their money,' Valle shrugged, 'then why not? She would've made a great asset. Maybe even added more credibility to the whole thing. Anyway, what if she believed all along that this was a legitimate property deal?'

'And it was only when they reached a point when they were going to call it all in that she discovered the truth?' Chavarría finished.

'Exactly. She called into Breeze the night she disappeared, remember? And she wasn't in the best of moods when she left.'

'And Lane went after her.'

Chavarría stood up and wandered over to the window. He gazed out into the busy street below and gave himself a few moments to arrange his thoughts. Natalie had disappeared and Peter Harris, thanks to the records from the marina, was known to have taken his boat out early the following day. He wasn't liking where this was going but it all seemed so terrifyingly plausible. The forensic report of Donnie Lane's Seat Arosa suggested a body had been in the trunk at some point. Getting the body from the vehicle to the boat without arousing suspicion wouldn't be the obstacle it may have seemed to some. Chavarría himself had been out sea fishing on a similar sized boat to Misty Blue and had little doubt that a slim young woman could be made to fit inside one of the large canvas bags that was often used to carry a selection of rods and tackle. It wouldn't pose a problem for a man like Darren Mitchell, with his obvious strength, to carry it either.

'If she was silenced to stop her talking,' asked Banda, 'why was Donnie Lane killed?'

'Simple,' replied Chavarría, turning back away from the window. 'He was the only remaining link between Peter Harris, the scam and Natalie's murder. Harris would be staying in Cieloventura, of course, he has legitimate business interests here. But Lane would have needed to leave. It would have been taking too much of a chance for him to stay in the town.'

'He told the Irish kid at the club that he was going away for a while the evening before we brought him in for questioning,' said Banda.

The Inspector Jefe nodded. 'He was going to start up somewhere else with his share of the money. Natalie's death threw a spanner in the works. Maybe

Harris thought it was too big a risk to let him walk away.'

'The question is how do we prove it?'

'We can start by getting the truth from the bar manager in Denia,' he said after a moment's thought, 'and I want those phone records chased up.'

During the interviews with the known victims of the scam, a phone number for Anglo-España Dream Properties, belonging to the man they had known as Donald, had emerged. The number was now, to no-one's surprise, unobtainable. The team knew Donnie Lane had a second mobile phone, he'd even been caught on CCTV outside the comisaría using it, but this was the first occasion where they had a potential number to go with it. The phone company had been contacted by Banda and he was waiting to hear back from them.

'In the meantime, I'll contact Alicante,' said Chavarría. He had a job in mind for their cadaver dog. If Natalie had indeed been kept in some kind of canvas bag on Misty Blue and then deposited, bag and all, into the depths of the Mediterranean, it was highly doubtful there would be any trace on the boat but it was worth a try.

'My apologies for not calling yesterday,' Fernando Prado said, a little slowly due to a lack of confidence in his English. 'My assistant failed to tell me of the envelope you had left for me.'

'That's okay, no problem,' Tony said. The phone ringing in the bedside cabinet had woken him from a snooze and, while he wasn't sure whether he was allowed to receive a call in the hospital, the corridor outside the open door to his room seemed empty. 'Thanks for calling me back. Were you able to recognise the girl in the photos?'

'I'm sorry, no. As I told the lady officer, she looks familiar but I cannot recall seeing her with Sr. Harris. I have also showed them to my maintenance staff and they too do not remember her.'

Tony closed his eyes, trying to ignore the pounding in his head, and hoped the investigation wasn't relying too much on making the connection between the missing rep and Peter Harris.

'Was it just the girl you wanted to know about?'

'I'm sorry?'

'I recognise someone else from one of your photos. He has been one of my best customers so far this summer. It's sad to see him leave.'

'Sorry, Sr. Prado, you'll need to start from the beginning.'

Tony tried to sit up in bed, hoping it would help him to concentrate on the call and clear the confusion that seemed to exist along the line somewhere between the marina in Cieloventura and his hospital bed in Villajoyosa. He listened to what Fernando Prado had to tell him, stopping him several times to ask him to repeat what he had just said. It wasn't that the marina manager's English was difficult to follow, he just wanted to make sure he had understood the chain of events correctly as this was throwing a whole new light on to the disappearance of Natalie Brooks.

Thanking Sr. Prado once again for his call, Tony threw back the bed sheets and swung his legs out to the side. Moving so suddenly from a supine position to an upright one gave him a sudden lightness in the head and he had to sit on the edge of the bed for a good thirty seconds before he felt ready to stand.

'No, no, Sr. Heather,' objected the young nurse that entered the room at that moment, 'you must rest for a while.'

Tony dismissed the idea and sent her scurrying off for whatever paperwork he needed to sign to check himself out of the hospital. It was only a flesh wound after all, plus some minor abrasions due to his eventual collapse. He'd already been giving the all-clear and knew the only reason for remaining in hospital was for a short period of observation. Lying in that scanner was like being in a tumble dryer, he thought, but it had at least told the doctors there was no serious damage. The wound had bled profusely and he had sustained a concussion but there would be no lasting effects.

He grabbed the few clothes of his that were stored in the bedside cupboard – where the hell was his shirt? – and, getting dressed, dialled a number on his phone.

'Official Valle? It's Tony Heather.'

'Tony, how are you?'

'Not good.'

'Oh?'

'That's for another time. Look, I've just had a call from Sr. Prado.'

'Can he place Natalie with Peter Harris?'

'No, I'm afraid not. But he told me something else

that's very interesting. And he mentioned you took a copy of the records about the comings and goings of the marina in the days after Natalie's disappearance, is that right?'

'Yes, I have them here with me. Harris has a boat called the Misty Blue. It was taken out...'

'I need you to check something else for me,' interrupted Tony.

Inspector Jefe Chavarría and Agente Narváez looked on from the quayside as the dog, its handler following a short distance behind, approached the Monterey 276 moored at A7. It was a well-maintained vessel and the detective could understand why Harris had described it as his pride and joy. Or one at them at least.

'What if it smells dead fish instead? The boats must be reeking of them.'

'No,' Chavarría replied, shaking his head. 'The cadaver dogs detect the odour given off by human decomposition only. They can sometimes mistake pig remains — they use them for training, I believe — but I don't think any of these vessels would have been involved in pig fishing.'

As Chavarría and Narváez watched, the dog boarded the boat and began to sniff around. Technically, this was a search of private property but Chavarría wanted to be sure before he made it official. If there were any comebacks for his actions, he'd have to take them on the chin. From the corner of his eye, he noticed a taxi pulling up outside the marina and was surprised at who alighted from the back. The man handed the fare to the driver and then headed directly towards where he and Narváez were standing.

'Sr. Heather.'

'Good morning, Inspector Jefe.'

Chavarría was about to berate the Englishman for his presence at the quayside during an important investigation, and that whatever it was would need to wait, when he was suddenly struck by Tony Heather's appearance. His T-shirt was old and shabby, and at least two sizes too big for him, and there appeared to be dried blood stains on the leg of his trousers. When the Englishman turned to look along the row of boats, he also noticed the large dressing on the back of his head.

'What's happened to you?'

'Never mind that for a moment,' Tony answered, staring at the activity aboard Misty Blue. 'Any luck with the cadaver dog?'

Chavarría frowned. Whoever it was at the comisaría that was providing the Englishman with information would be made to suffer. He had suspected Tony Heather was behind the newspaper report concerning property development fraud along the Costa Blanca and, if he'd been less busy, he would have found out for sure. This interference had to stop! Before he had a chance to reply, a noise caused him to look back along the quay. The dog had jumped off the boat and was ambling slowly back to the feet of his handler.

'Nothing,' Chavarría said with disappointment. 'It was always a long shot.'

'That's because I think you could be looking at the wrong boat.'

'I'm sorry?'

'There's another boat here, a small yacht moored at E6,' Tony said, pointing to a row of vessels at the furthest end of the marina. 'Could you ask the handler to check it out?'

'What's this about?'

'I'll explain afterwards. Please.'

The Inspector Jefe took a moment to consider the request. The look on Tony Heather's face appeared earnest enough but he could think of nothing that linked any other boat at the marina with Natalie's disappearance. Without a word, he turned and strode along the wooden jetty to speak to the dog handler. The conversation lasted some time, to Tony's frustration, before they finally made their way across the quayside to row E.

'Apparently, this will constitute two jobs and not one,' the Inspector Jefe said as he passed Tony. 'I told him if he doesn't find anything, he can send the second bill to you. Wait here.'

Tony felt himself swoon and slowly approached a short mooring post to sit down on. He held his head in his hands and prayed for the throbbing to stop. He reached into his pocket for the pills the nurse had issued him with and popped two of them from their blister-pack. They weren't meant to be taken for another two hours but he didn't care, and swallowed them whole without any water. It wasn't just the injury though. The information he'd learned that morning were surely just as responsible for making his head spin. He struggled to make sense of it all, to put everything he had discovered over the course of the investigation into its proper place.

Tony looked round at the flurry of activity at the yacht moored at peg E6. It was smaller than that belonging to Peter Harris, which was purely a motor boat, and was typical of the small sailing craft that would use engine power to take them out to sea before the sails would be unfurled and an engagement, or occasionally a battle, with the elements would commence. The dog was wagging its tail and being patted warmly by its handler. Inspector Jefe Chavarría turned to look at Tony across the marina with a face that registered both amazement and annoyance. It was at that moment, when the theory that had began to form in his mind only half an hour before seemed to be confirmed, when Tony was suddenly struck by a more pressing thought. He realised that it may actually be too late. He took out his phone and quickly dialled a number, angrily waving a hand at Chavarría, who marched up to him demanding an explanation, to shut the hell up.

'Hello?'

The conversation was short and to the point. The Inspector Jefe listened on and, though he didn't have a clue what was going on, he quickly realised its implication.

'My car is parked on the road!' he said, running back along the quay with Tony in quick pursuit. 'You can explain on the way!'

Within a minute, Chavarría had pulled his car out into the busy mid-morning traffic. He knew the most direct route was straight along the Paseo de Solana but realised it would be futile at this time of day and so began to manoeuvre the vehicle at speed through a succession of narrow alleys and backstreets. The Inspector Jefe glanced at the rosary beads that hung from his rear-view mirror and prayed they wouldn't meet anybody coming the other way.

'How long until the flight leaves?'

'Forty minutes.'

Chavarría thumped the steering wheel, accidently sounding the horn in the process. Forty minutes was pushing it. It had taken him almost an hour to reach El Altat Airport a week previously when he was in pursuit of Ryan Dinsdale, the British tourist that had murdered Leanne Piggott, and he had got there with literally minutes to spare. He couldn't believe he was making the same journey again, this time to catch the murderer of Natalie Brooks, but as Tony Heather had begun to explain, that was indeed where their prey was. He couldn't be allowed to leave Spain. It could take months of legal wrangling for the man, whose name he vaguely remembered from one of the reports he'd read on the work done on Natalie's disappearance before the case had been passed to his team, to be extradited back to face questioning. The Inspector Jefe's theory about the young woman's death had gone completely out of the window but, right now, he didn't care. He just needed to concentrate on the road ahead. The car tore out of a side street and joined the main thoroughfare heading out of the town. He couldn't remember the last time he'd driven so fast, weaving in and out of traffic like a man possessed. His horn didn't seem to be having much of an effect. A few drivers edged their vehicles to the side of the road, giving him space to overtake, but others just gave a loud blast back or resorted to offensive hand gestures in their mirror.

'Call the airport police! Tell them who we're after and what time the flight leaves.'

'Will they listen to me?'

'Then call Narváez and tell him to do it! Here!'

Chavarría took one hand off the wheel for just long enough to take his phone from his inside jacket pocket and toss it onto Tony's lap. Seeing a gap in the traffic, and a welcome clear stretch of road ahead, the Inspector Jefe pressed his foot down harder on the gas.

The flight was just beginning to board. Rows 1 to 18 first. He looked down at the pass in his hand. 29B. A few more minutes then. Then he'd be setting off for home. The final bar crawl with the *Holiday18* lot had been fun. It was a shame he would never see any of them again. He didn't feel able to let his hair down as much as he would've liked, he'd only had three pints all night, but he didn't want to risk sleeping through his alarm and missing his flight. Another day or two in Cieloventura would have been too much. And the first two pints were enough to give him the Dutch courage for what he found he needed to do. The third was a toast to a job well done. Now he could look forward to home.

He watched the passengers filing past him towards the desk. Their holidays at an end, they were all now on their way back to the daily drudge of work or school. He wondered what he going to do with the rest of his life. Repping had been fun, and he'd been good at it, but he doubted whether he could do anything like that again. And he would never return to Spain. No, it would be a completely fresh start.

It was then, through the large plate glass window at the back of the departure gate, then he saw the two men, closely followed by a uniformed officer of the airport police, running down the escalator, pushing past the few stragglers that were still casually making their way to the gate. Fuck! No! Please, no!

It was Tony Heather that first spotted where the young man was sitting and led his two companions through the busy seating area towards him.

'Hello, Ross,' said Tony, trying hard not to appear too breathless. He gestured to the man standing to his right. 'This is Inspector Jefe Chavarría of the national police. He'd like to ask you a few questions about the disappearance of Natalie Brooks.'

Ross's arms were like those of a rag doll as the Inspector Jefe reached down and cuffed his wrists together. The life had gone out of him. Chavarría told him to stand and, when he showed no sign of doing so, dragged him to his feet by the handcuffs. Tony took a step closer to the young man and looked him directly in the eyes.

'Maybe you should've hit me a bit harder.'

CHAPTER SIXTEEN

TONY gazed out through the window and saw the sun beginning to set over Cieloventura. For life in a holiday resort, nightfall didn't signal the end of another day. It was a new beginning. Throughout the town, thousands of people were getting ready to go out, and the buzz of excitement in the air would be palpable. Within an hour or two, the bars, restaurants and clubs would be heaving with people having a good time. When the meeting was finished, Tony was determined to get back out there. He needed to force himself to feel safe. He wouldn't allow himself to feel afraid of Cieloventura.

Tony looked around as the door to the small conference room opened. The initial reluctance of the first few officers to enter the room to be the first to sit down, as though their choice of position at the table would somehow reflect their status, or what they thought their status should be, was soon settled when Inspector Jefe Chavarría marched in and just sat in the nearest chair that came to hand. Tony, Officíals Elisa Valle Huerta and Luís Banda Molina, Agente Narváez and, the last to arrive, Juez Pedro Sandoval Esparza made up the rest of the group.

For Tony's benefit, the meeting was being conducted in English. Banda wasn't as fluent as everyone else in the room, but he was damned if he was going to miss this debrief. With the exception of Sandoval, he knew least of anyone at what had transpired that day and that frustrated the hell out of him. Valle began by explaining the background to the day's events, including her request for Tony to call upon Fernando Prado at the marina. She could see Chavarría visibly bristle at that point, he would never have countenanced such a move, and so sought to explain to Juez Sandoval how, due to the amount of work there had been following up the development that the finca was being used in a property fraud, and owing to the work Tony had already out in on the case, she felt it was the best way to ensure no police time or manpower was wasted. Sandoval dismissed it with a casual flick of the hand, reminding himself to have a word with his Inspector Jefe on correct operational procedure when the right moment presented itself. Valle then looked at Tony to continue. He coughed to clear his throat, more nervous than he'd been when giving his talk at the Solanis Resort, and took a moment to collect his thoughts.

'One of the photographs I'd left at the marina showed Natalie with the other Holiday18 reps. Ross Webster was among them. He was recognised by Sr. Prado as a good customer of his and, his recollections of the days following Natalie's disappearance, together with the records from the marina, tell us a lot.'

Tony stopped to catch his breath and to give any of the gathering a chance to ask him to repeat anything if they were having trouble with his English. No-one spoke up, indeed he seemed to have their full attention, so he continued.

'I remember Marie Reynolds telling me that Ross practically spent all his spare time sailing and, of course, he would need to hire a boat from the municipal marina. The private marinas, and the kind of vessels that would be moored there, would've been well out of reach for someone on his income. Anyway, the records from Sr. Prado show that Ross had booked a boat for the Friday — it was his day off that week — but Marie forced him to work instead, covering for Natalie. According to Prado, Ross called the marina and, instead of cancelling the boat and getting a refund, he asked for it to remain reserved, saying he hoped to finish work early and still get in maybe an hour or two sailing. Prado was a little surprised, hiring a boat for just an hour is far cheaper than the day rate, but Ross told him it didn't matter. The truth was, of course, that he couldn't let anyone else use the boat. It already had a passenger on board.'

'How did he get Natalie to the marina in the first place?' asked Banda. The official had been busily sorting through the records of calls made to and from Donnie Lane's second mobile phone when the Inspector Jefe had walked in and announced, to everyone's surprise, that their investigation was now focused solely on the murder of Lane. He had made an arrest in the Natalie Brooks case, he had told them, a crime which he now knew to be unconnected to either Lane's death or the fraud at the finca. Chavarría had then turned and left the room, gesturing for Official

Valle to follow him, leaving everyone else in the office to cast bemused glances at each other.

Chavarría had chosen Valle, with Agente Narváez accompanying her, to conduct the initial interview with Ross Webster. From the state of him when he was booked in, he looked like he was ready to get something off his chest. He also gave Tony Heather permission to watch the interview via CCTV in the next room, and to have notes passed to Valle if necessary. Chavarría, meanwhile, had seen to arranging the collection of Marie's car and the impounding of the small yacht at the marina for a detailed forensic examination.

'He used the car belonging to Marie,' Tony clarified. 'It was her perk as senior rep, the others had to make do with a couple of scooters between them, but Ross, as she told me, had the spare keys.'

'The cadaver dog did indeed pick up a positive trace in the Fiat belonging to Marie Reynolds,' Chavarría confirmed to the gathering, having received the written report from the forensic dog unit minutes before the meeting began.

Tony shuddered. He thought back to when Marie had first stopped him to ask for his help, and the conversation they'd had the previous afternoon. The thought that Natalie had actually been killed in the vehicle sent a shiver down his spine. When he had called on Marie that afternoon to request paperwork that dealt with Natalie and Ross's schedules, he had quickly told her of everything that had transpired since that last meeting, including the arrest of her fellow

Holiday18 rep. She had burst into tears and almost collapsed. Tony told her that, while the car would need to be seized and examined by the police, Ross's confession had told them what had occurred inside.

'I don't want the fucking thing back!' she had screamed at him. 'Tell the police to fucking burn it!'

Tony's attention was brought back to the meeting as Valle, sat to his left, began to speak.

'The boats moored along row E are the smallest and cheapest in the marina's fleet. They've all seen better days to be honest. But they are also the nearest to the marina's car park. People can literally back their vehicles up almost to the boats themselves. Ross would only have needed to carry Natalie maybe five yards to put her aboard and, in the early hours of the morning, there was no one to see him anyway. The marina has a security guard but, apart from half-hourly patrols, he just sits in the hut and keeps an eye on the private vessels.'

'So Ross put Natalie's body on the boat, concealing it beneath the canvas sheeting that protects the sails when it's at shore,' continued Tony. 'That's where the cadaver dog indicated the scent was at its strongest. He planned to return first thing in the morning and take the boat out but, and you can appreciate the irony of this, it was Natalie's failure to return that forced him to miss his day off.'

Tony looked down at the *Holiday18* schedules he'd collected from Marie. Valle had kindly run off photocopies for everyone else around the table and he distributed them like a pack of oversized playing cards.

'Ross was busy all day meeting Natalie's flights and ferrying guests all around the town. I've checked the records from Holiday18 of the day in question – the flights, the hotel drop-offs and collections, the welcome meetings – and it's clear he wouldn't have been free until after half past six. By then, it was too late. The hire boats are only available from ten in the morning to eight in the evening, and he wouldn't have been able to get to the marina in time to take it out.'

Tony allowed everyone a moment to run their eyes down their copy of the documents. 'He called Sr. Prado and arranged to extend his hire into the next day. After finishing all his duties, he was free by around three 'o' clock. He returned to his apartment to discover it had been ransacked, which I'll come back to in a moment. After making his statement to the police about what had been taken, he headed to the marina. Sr. Prado remarked to him that he'd paid for two whole days use of the boat and was only going to get a couple of hours at sea for his money. He offered Ross a much better boat at no extra charge, by way of making up for the disappointment, but he told the manager he was happy with the one he'd booked.'

It was now Valle's turn to pass photocopies around the table. They were of the pages from the marina's log book that detailed the movements of all the boats on the day in question. She had marked the relevant entries with a yellow highlighter pen.

'The boat left the marina at 5:05pm and returned a few minutes before eight 'o' clock. I've sent the information we have to the coastguard and, with their knowledge of the tides and weather conditions in those hours, and the distance Ross could've covered in that time, they may be able to come up with a reasonable estimate for where he disposed of the body.'

'Reasonable probably being something like twenty square miles,' sighed Banda. 'We'll never find her. She's fish food.'

There was a short silence as everyone reflected on the situation that had been laid out in front of them, and at Banda's rather blunt, if honest, assessment.

'So what about motive?'

It was the first time that Juez Sandoval has spoken since the meeting had begun. The examining magistrate had sat quietly as Tony and Valle explained the results of the interview with Ross, and of the confirmatory documentation that had been collected, making the occasional note in an expensive-looking leather-bound journal.

Sandoval had been expecting a visit from Chavarría, updating him on the progress on the investigation, when he received a message from the comisaría informing him that, due to a major breakthrough in the case, the Inspector Jefe was unavailable and would fill him in as soon as he was free. With his wife attending a charity function, and only a cold salad in the fridge to look forward to at home, Sandoval had elected to walk to the comisaría from his office at the courthouse to find out for himself what was happening. Chavarría didn't mind the examining magistrate's presence in the room as it spared him a long phone conversation or face-to-face meeting afterwards.

'It seems, that night, Natalie humiliated Ross once too many,' said Tony. 'Not only did she beat him in a drinking competition, but she also bragged about the commission she'd already earned that evening by selling spare boat trip tickets. But that was just the last straw. It had been going on since the beginning of the season. Natalie would often get Ross to fill in for her when she went off places. It had been getting more frequent in the past couple of weeks and he was starting to get a bit pissed off about it, but she always managed to sweet talk him around.'

'He didn't know where she was going or what she was doing, but we can assume she was with Donnie Lane, meeting potential buyers for the finca,' commented Valle.

'When she left Ross that night, she told him she was off to Breeze to get rid of the last of the remaining tickets for the Holiday18 boat trip.'

'But we know she actually went there to talk to Lane,' interjected Banda.

Tony glanced briefly at the official. That was news to him. Still, it could wait.

'Ross returned to their apartment and, humiliated and fuelled with alcohol, he began to brood over it all. She'd pushed him too far and he was going to make her pay. Taking Marie's car, he drove to Calle Veijo and parked where he could see the entrance to Breeze. When she finally appeared, a little worse for wear after all the drink she'd had, he followed. He offered her a lift home and, in her condition, she was only too pleased to accept it. He didn't head back to the apartment though. He drove to a quiet lay-by just out by the N-322 instead. Anyway, sat in the car together, everything came pouring out. He screamed at her for humiliating him, for using him to cover for her, for parading around the flat half-naked all the time and teasing him. Up until that moment, he claims he was only going to, as he put it, teach her a lesson. To show her that flirts sometimes had to make good on their promises.'

'He was going to rape her?' Sandoval asked.

'Who knows what was going on in his mind? But she wasn't scared of him, it seems. On the contrary, she just laughed in his face. She hitched her skirt up to show him she wasn't wearing any underwear, apparently she'd given them to some guy she'd met in a bar that night in return for buying a ticket for the boat trip, and told him to just get on with it if he had the balls. He did try but couldn't maintain an erection. She just mocked him and told him to drive her home. She laughed, said she couldn't wait to tell the others what a pathetic little worm he was. Even when it was offered on a plate, he couldn't get it up.'

Juez Sandoval looked to Valle and spoke to her in Spanish, asking, Tony assumed, for clarification of his last account. The official repeated it in their own language and Sandoval, his eyebrows raised, made a further note in his journal.

'The man just cracked,' Valle continued, back in English. 'He began to punch and slap her. She screamed and started to fight back and then, in his words, he found his hands were suddenly around her throat. He says he doesn't remember squeezing very hard. But she just went quiet.'

The gathering took a few minutes to absorb all of the information and to send out for refreshments. It was Sandoval who took out his wallet to pay for the coffees and biscuits that were collected by an Agente from a nearby cafe, the cafeteria in the comisaría having closed for the day. Chavarría exchanged a look with Banda across the table. He would've just told the Agente to take it out of petty cash.

When everyone had sat back down at the table, grateful for the short break to dash to the toilet or, in Banda's case, a quick cigarette, Tony began once again.

'When their apartment was burgled some time on the Saturday, Ross couldn't believe his luck. He had a cast-iron alibi for that, he was taking a group of holiday-makers back to the airport, and with everyone linking Natalie's disappearance to the burglary, it was looking all the better for him. The next day, when he was tidying up the apartment, he discovered Natalie's cashpoint card. It was tucked inside a book and the PIN was written on the back in the corner of the signature strip. Numbers were not her thing, apparently.'

'Except when it came to money,' Banda commented to no-one in particular.

'Ross thought if he could make it seem Natalie was still alive, the police would be less likely to focus on anything that had happened to her on that final night. He caught the bus to Benidorm and, finding an ATM that didn't seem to be covered by CCTV, he used her card to withdraw twenty Euros. He then threw it away.'

'And, as we know, a week later someone came forward with a reported sighting of Natalie in Denia,' Valle said, giving Tony a break to drink some of his coffee and to wash down another two painkillers. When they had met up at the comisaría that afternoon, she began by expressing her remorse for the role she had inadvertently played in his assault. Tony, however, dismissed any such notion that she should apologise. None of the police photographs of Natalie featured her fellow holiday reps, and that asking Tony to visit Fernando Prado was the break the investigation needed. The bump on his head was a small price to pay, he reassured her.

'Ross just assumed it must have been a woman who looked like Natalie but, still, he couldn't believe the good fortune,' the official continued. 'How would he be suspected of murder when all the evidence suggested the victim was still alive and well?'

'It looked like he was going to get away with it,' Chavarría said.

'Acting like nothing has happened is one thing. It is another to have such a terrible crime on your conscience. Staying in Cieloventura and trying to live life as normal, staying in the apartment with the new girl who was sent to replace Natalie, who also paraded around with next-to-nothing on without a care in the world, was starting to get too much for him. He was feeling the pressure.'

'Marie told me this afternoon she'd had a complaint

about him from a couple of the guests,' said Tony. 'He'd snapped at them when they complained about an excursion they'd bought, but she just put it down to his worry over Natalie. I was still on the scene as well, poking around and asking questions, and that was making him nervous. I had organised a reconstruction of her movements the night she disappeared, as well as a poster campaign, and he was worried I would stumble on something that would give him away.'

'So he decided to quit his job and return home?'

'Yes,' Tony nodded at Sandoval. 'Last night, Marie told all the reps that I was close to working out who had killed Natalie.'

Tony smiled awkwardly, a little embarrassed at Marie's embellishment, but no-one around the table seemed to take umbrage at it.

'Ross panicked,' he continued. 'His flight was the next morning. During the bar crawl last night, he saw me along the Avenue. He thought if he could just put me out of action for a day or two, he would feel safe. It wasn't a problem to slip away from the crowd, he knew he could just skip one of the bars along the way, and no-one would miss him. He followed me and, when I was taking a short cut back to Calle Neuva, took his opportunity.'

As the group finished their coffee, Sandoval asked a series of short questions in Spanish, to which either Official Valle or Inspector Jefe Chavarría answered. Tony, unable to follow their conversation, simply sat in silence and reflected on the events of the day. He couldn't believe that it was over. His quest to find

Natalie Brooks, which had, in turn, become a hunt for her killer, was at an end. Ross's tearful and frank confession had been difficult for him to watch. He couldn't help but feel some pity for the young man. He didn't mean to kill her, he said – something he repeated over a dozen times during the interview – and the release of emotion he'd displayed told Tony of the difficulty the young man had experienced in trying to live with what he had done. Ross seemed glad to be able to talk to someone at last.

Tony had no proof that Ross had been behind the assault on him the previous night. Indeed, as he lay in his hospital bed, he had been convinced that it must have been something to do with his visit to Peter Harris. But there was something in the young man's eyes when he and Chavarría had confronted him at the airport. Something he couldn't have described to anyone else but it felt very real to him. Valle had questioned Ross about the incident and he acknowledged what he had done and why. Tony sent one final note into the interview room, via an obliging young Agente, with one more question for Valle to ask. He realised she wouldn't have known what it meant but, to her credit, she didn't seem fazed.

'And what about the knife? Did you put it in Tony Heather's bed?'

The blank expression on Ross's face was all the answer Tony needed.

With all his questions answered to his satisfaction, Juez Sandoval congratulated the team on a job well done and excused himself from the meeting. Chavarría followed him out of the room.

'The case will need to be presented to me in court,' said Sandoval, 'but the evidence speaks for itself. And there is the confession also. Murder or manslaughter? That will be for others to decide.'

Chavarría glanced at his watch and made the quick arithmetic in his head. 'Juez, we do still have over sixty hours left on the clock.'

Sandoval stopped and looked at the Inspector Jefe. 'Why wait, Roman? Why not tomorrow morning?'

'Natalie's death may not have had anything to do with the fraud at the finca, but the timing of her disappearance certainly sent the cat among the pigeons with those who were behind it. Outside of this building, no-one knows we have someone in custody. Let's keep it that way.'

With two murders cleared up, Juez Sandoval knew things were looking pretty good for him. He had aspirations for higher office and, under his leadership, the local success rate in solving major crimes was looking impressive. The fact that it was Tony Heather that had finally cracked the Natalie Brooks case was immaterial. Chavarría and his team had earned a little slack. And if that could help to make it three out of three, a hat-trick, he was prepared to give him as much as he needed.

'Ross Webster will need to be my court by Tuesday morning at the latest,' Sandoval said, heading along the corridor. 'Don't miss the deadline.'

Chavarría returned to the conference room to have

a few final words, in Spanish, with his team regarding where they currently stood in the ongoing investigation into the finca fraud before ushering them out of the room and telling them to get themselves home. Agente Narváez also happily took his leave. His shift had officially ended more than two hours before but, having been involved since the beginning, he had wanted to see the day's events through to the end.

Tony waited by the window until just he and the Inspector Jefe remained in the room. Chavarría, gathering together his paperwork, looked up at him.

'Was there something?'

'I wanted to ask you about Ryan Dinsdale.'

'What about him?' asked Chavarría, a touch bemused at the unexpected change of topic.

'Do you think he killed Leanne Piggott?'

'Of course I do. I am not in the business of trying to convict people I believe to be innocent.'

'No, of course not. I wasn't suggesting that, it's just…'

Tony stopped. Explaining the results of the day's events, where the facts were clear and in order, was one thing. Putting a series of hunches and gut feelings into words was less easy. Chavarría looked at him for a while before making a snap decision and turning to the door.

'Come with me.'

'Where to?'

'I know a bar not five minutes' walk from here that serves a wonderful single malt,' he said, heading out into the corridor. 'I'm going to let you buy me one.'

El Laberinto was certainly the kind of place where Tony felt able to relax. And it felt like the real Spain. Places were the locals drank didn't need to advertise themselves with garish neon signs and boards advertising cheap drink promotions. They knew to stay discreet if they wanted to avoid groups of tourists necking back bottles of Stella and cackling loudly at each other. Tony would never have stumbled on the bar by accident. The entrance, an unassuming door between two shops along a side street off Carrer de Trato, lead to a downward flight of stairs, from which a narrow warren of a corridor finally opened out into the main bar area. It was certainly well named. The Maze. Sat together at the end of the counter, Chavarría signalled to the barman for two whiskies.

'So, Tony, tell me what concerns you have?'

'Did you send someone to speak to Streax?'

'The DJ? Yes, I sent Narváez to talk to him. He was unable to shed any further light on the case.'

'There's still the matter of the cannabis. Ryan Dinsdale didn't smoke any with her and yet it was found in her system.'

'If everyone in Cieloventura who has smoked a joint is on your suspect list, Tony, then it would be very long. She may have smoked it in the club. Platinum are pretty good at keeping drugs out but they're not invincible.'

'Ryan would've mentioned it to me if she had.'

'Only if he saw her do it,' Chavarría pointed out. 'From the few witness statements we managed to get from fellow clubbers who remember Leanne and Ryan, the two of them weren't exactly joined at the hip all night. Leanne spent over half-an-hour waiting at the side of the stage in the hope of meeting Streax, and Ryan made at least two trips to the bar.'

Yes, that was possible, Tony conceded.

'We also ran a background check on him,' added Chavarría. 'Apart from a conviction for breaching the peace fifteen years ago, some anti-capitalism march through London that got out of hand, he is clean. Also, there is nothing to corroborate Dinsdale's account of his actions. He cannot recall the bar he supposedly drank in after leaving Leanne, and there are no witnesses who can put him at the Solanis the following day. The only actions we know he committed in the time between leaving Platinum and trying to fly back to England are those of a guilty man.'

'There's just something about this DJ character that sends off alarm bells,' Tony said, acknowledging the points the detective had made.

'What possible motive would he have?'

'He could've arranged to meet Leanne on the beach. She was star-struck by him. Maybe he tried to have sex with her and, when he realised she wasn't going to play along, things began to get out of hand. He could've feared she was going to tell someone about it and that may have ruined his career.'

'The man is a celebrity DJ,' said Chavarría. 'There are plenty of young woman here on holiday who will happily open their legs for him. Why would be bother with Leanne Piggott?'

Tony had no answer to that. But there was another matter that troubled him more than the question of the cannabis or the man's sex appeal to female tourists. He had seen a row of posters outside *Platinum* when he had walked along the Avenue the previous night in search of the right kind of bar for that cool drink he'd promised himself. They advertised forthcoming attractions at the club and Streax no longer appeared. In his place, as 'special guest DJ', was a former 80's pop star that Tony vaguely remembered from Top of The Pops.

'Streax is no longer in Cieloventura.'

Tony was disturbed by the DJ's absence. During his interview with him on board his motor boat, the man gave no indication that it was his last week working in the town. If anything, Streax was revelling in the lifestyle he had made for himself. Why had he decided to leave? It wasn't even halfway through the main tourist season.

'I assume it is the nature of his work,' Chavarría said. 'He will go where the biggest money is to be made. Cieloventura is a nice town but it is hardly Ibiza.'

The Inspector Jefe went on to explain to Tony that Official Banda had been to Fontcalent to interview Ryan once more, and that he didn't prove any more forthcoming, and also how the young man had been beaten up by his Moroccan cellmates. Tony knew he'd be hearing from Maureen Carr again.

'Are you glad you came here?' Chavarría suddenly asked. 'Is Cieloventura the place you wanted it to be?'

The question surprised Tony and an answer didn't come to mind straight away. 'I'm not exactly sure what I wanted,' he confessed. 'I don't think it was just the idea of a new life in the sun.'

'Ah, the sun. For many people, it suggests happiness, fun, freedom,' Chavarría said, 'but there is a dark side to life in the sun. People come to places like this to run away from their problems, but they tend to follow them here. The brighter the sun, the darker the shadows.'

Tony wondered whether that applied to him. Had taking the job in Cieloventura been running away from what had happened to him at home? When the opportunity had first been suggested to him by Jim Garside, that was the first thought that entered his mind. He knew he had problems, but Spain? Garside, an old friend from Tony's since their early days together as probationers, had spent most of his career in the close protection field in one form or another, including a five-year stint working the rounds of the foreign embassies in the Diplomatic Protection Squad. It was there that he had met, and become friends with, Maria Ocasio Cruz. The election of a new Mayor in Cieloventura had brought with it a whole new raft of measures to combat the excesses of visitors in the town and, when it had fallen to Sra. Ocasio to find a suitable candidate for someone to work with the British tourists, she had, in turn, sought the advice of Jim Garside.

'Spain?'

'It's only for a season, a trial period. To see if it

works.'

'But I can't speak Spanish.'

'You can learn as you go along,' Jim had said. 'Besides, they're not looking for a Spanish speaker. How many British people know a second language anyway?'

As Jim explained, the job mainly involved liaising between the Mayor's Office, the Policia Municipal and British visitors to Cieloventura. All of the officers of the Policia Municipal who patrolled the town spoke English, it was a requirement of the job due to the large number of British tourists they came into contact with, and so speaking Spanish was not a prerequisite. The position, he was told, would suit a retired or former police officer with experience in organising community projects and working on his or her own initiative. Garside knew it could almost have been written for Tony Heather, and he also knew his friend needing something in his life to focus on. His career in the force had been brought to a sudden and violent end, and his marriage was in tatters.

'You're a bloody good copper, Tony! I know you feel you can't stay in the job anymore, and I understand that, but you can't let all that know-how go to waste. And just think of it! The Costa Blanca! Blimey, if I was a year or two off retirement, I'd be tempted to take the fucking job myself!'

Jim Garside had soon set the wheels in motion and, within a week, Tony was flying out to Spain to meet with Sra. Ocasio. It also gave him the opportunity to take a look around the town. While it wasn't yet peak season, Cieloventura was already a hive of activity. The letter that arrived on his doormat within a few days of his arrival back in the UK had officially offered him the position. The salary was basic and a six-month contract was hardly the kind of security he'd been looking for but there was just something about it that appealed to him. England was just be a three-hour plane journey away, after all.

Tony pondered over the question that had been put to him. Yes, he was glad he came here. But he wasn't sure he wanted to stay, not after all that happened. He told Chavarría so.

'Anyone who comes to live in a place like this is searching for something,' the Inspector Jefe said, 'the sad thing is they don't always find it.'

Chavarría asked Tony why he had chosen to leave the police force and, for the first time he'd been asked that question since his arrival in Cieloventura, he decided to be open about his reasons, and the event that had precipitated it all. Chavarría just gave a slight nod in response but that was enough to tell Tony he understood.

'So how about you? What made you decide to join the Policia Nacional?'

'My mother. She was, and remains, an inspiration to me. I always wanted to be a murder squad detective.'

'She was one as well?'

'No,' said Chavarría, taking a large gulp from his glass. 'She was a victim.'

Tony was stunned. 'Oh, I'm sorry to hear that.'

'Orphaned at fifteen but with a focus in life that drove me harder and faster than any of my peers, either at school or at police college. Nothing would have stopped me getting what I wanted.'

Tony had seen the steely determination in Chavarría's eyes as the detective propelled his car along the roads to El Altat earlier that day, expertly navigating through the busy traffic in pursuit of their quarry.

'Did the police catch who was responsible?'

'Yes, indeed,' the Inspector Jefe replied. 'I said I was orphaned, didn't I?'

It took Tony a moment to realise the full meaning of the statement. He felt he could do nothing but just smile in sympathy. What do you say to something like that?

Tony wondered whether Cieloventura was just a stopping off point for the Inspector Jefe. There couldn't be much call for a dedicated murder squad based in Cieloventura, he thought, as he knew crimes of that nature were thankfully rare. There had been three in recent weeks, of course, and that would no doubt skew the statistics, but it was a safe town. Missing people were a different matter. Reports were common and the majority turned up safe and well. The holiday resorts along the Costa Blanca weren't just a magnet for foreign tourists, but also for runaway kids, illegal workers, and anyone who saw romance in the idea of throwing in their dull lives at home and heading for the sun. The large transient population of Cieloventura was a considerable complication for the small team charged with investigating reports of vulnerable missing people.

'I appreciate all you have done, Tony. But there is nothing more you can do in the Leanne Piggott case. I am happy to consider any new information you may uncover, of course, but the matter, I fear, is closed.'

Chavarría no longer felt it was necessary to hold a grudge against the Englishman. Not after all that had happened. Racing through the traffic together to El Altat Airport to catch a killer had formed something of a bond between the two men. Maybe bond was too strong, Chavarría thought. An understanding maybe. He had also ticked Valle off for getting the Englishman involved in the investigation. If a playful slap on the wrist could be considered a ticking off, that is. Sandoval hadn't yet said anything to him on that score, but knew it would come eventually. While results were the most important thing, the examining magistrate was a stickler for procedure and took pride in the fact that he'd never had a case of his fall through yet on a legal technicality.

'Thank you for the drink,' said Chavarría, downing the remainder of his whisky and getting to his feet. 'It is time I returned home. Tomorrow will be another busy day. There's still another murderer walking the streets of my town. And I intend to catch him.'

The Inspector Jefe smiled his farewell and made for the exit. Tony decided to stay for a while and enjoy the atmosphere of the bar. Another whisky would be too much so he ordered a light beer instead.

Walking back to the comisaría from collecting the

paperwork he needed from Marie Reynolds, Tony had called in briefly on the offices of the Policia Municipal to explained what had happened, and why he had been unable to fulfil his duties in the town that day. He discovered José knew all about the assault, showing such concern for his well-being when he walked into the building that Tony was almost overcome with emotion. Knowing that Tony was indisposed, the Policia Municipal had not called him during the night with any requests for his assistance, and a message had been sent to the courthouse to excuse his absence for that morning's proceedings. It was speaking to José that Tony discovered it was Consuela and Rafá who, responding to a report of a drunk, had found him and called an ambulance. He called Consuela as he walked back to the comisaría and couldn't stop the tears from welling up in his eyes as he thanked her for what she and Rafá had done. He also summarised briefly the events of the day so far.

'Call me the moment you have some free time,' she had told him, agreeing to pass his gratitude to Rafá who at that moment, she said, was queuing up for doughnuts and orange juice. 'I want to hear everything that has happened.'

Tony glanced at his watch. It was nearly nine 'o' clock and, while he was probably fit to resume his duties, he decided a good sleep and a long lie-in were in order. He would report to the town hall some time tomorrow and inform them he needed a couple of days before feeling well enough to return to work. There was something he wanted to do.

CHAPTER SEVENTEEN

'WE now know that Natalie Brooks was killed by Ross Webster, her fellow holiday rep, and that it had nothing to do with her involvement in the finca scam. However, the timing of her disappearance clearly threw their plans into chaos.'

Inspector Jefe Chavarría paced across the room, holding the attention of everyone in the office. He turned on his heels and returned back towards his desk. 'Donnie Lane and Peter Harris would have been alarmed. They didn't want the police looking into Natalie's disappearance too closely in case they uncovered her role in the fraud. Someone, probably Darren Mitchell, broke into her apartment and retrieved the phony advertisements. They couldn't risk them being seen by the police if they searched the premises.'

'And we also now know it was Mitchell who went to Denia to arrange for her to be 'seen' there two days after she was last seen as Breeze,' added Official Banda. 'Like Ross Webster, they thought if they made it seem that Natalie was still alive, we wouldn't look into her disappearance too closely.'

The police force in Denia had reported back the previous afternoon. They had paid a visit to the bar manager and formally arrested him. He maintained his story under interrogation for a time, only breaking down and admitting he had lied when it was revealed to him that Natalie had been murdered. He had not seen the young woman in his bar that evening and only came forward to say he had on the orders of Darren Mitchell.

'Apparently, he is not a man you would willingly choose to defy,' said Banda.

'I want both Harris and Mitchell brought in,' Chavarría instructed. 'At the same time, but not together. I don't want either of them to get wind of what's happening. Put a tail on both of them and we can decide when best to make our move.'

Banda nodded. He would need a discussion with the subinspector in charge of the duty roster to get the necessary manpower for the surveillance, but two teams of three for a couple of hours at most wouldn't put much of a hole in his plans.

'Darren Mitchell can be arrested,' continued the Inspector Jefe. 'The statement from the bar manager is enough for us to do that. As for Harris, we'll just invite him in for questioning.'

'And if he doesn't come?' asked Valle.

'He will. He'll be keen to know what developments we've made in the investigation. Though he won't be too anxious to show it.'

As Chavarría had expected, Peter Harris was continuing with his life and business in Cieloventura as normal. After visiting the Piggott family and spending an hour or so with the decorators, Harris had gone out on his boat, returning several hours later. Chavarría had an unmarked police car drive past the villa on several occasions since then to check he hadn't skipped town.

Harris and Mitchell would sing from the same hymn sheet. They'd had plenty of time to work out a solid story and would stick to it. Divide and conquer. That was the only way forward, Chavarría knew.

Inspector Jefe Chavarría entered the interview room to find a clearly irritated Peter Harris slumped in his chair. He sat up straight and locked his fingers together on the table in front of him.

'How long do you expect me to sit here for? We said one 'o' clock.'

'My apologies for keeping you waiting, Sr. Harris,' said Chavarría, sitting down opposite him, 'but we are very busy.'

'Yeah, well, you're not the only one.'

'Perhaps your associate can fill in for you until you return.'

'He's not answering his phone. So what's all this about then?'

Chavarría opened his document folder and spent a good half-minute glancing through its contents before finally looking up at an increasingly irked Peter Harris.

'We have new information regarding the murder of Natalie Brooks,'

'So it is murder, then?' said Harris after a beat, a degree of shock registering on his face.

'Yes, señor. It is murder. We also have a signed statement from the manager of a bar in Denia that I believe is owned by Synergist Holdings.'

'Concerning what, may I ask?'

'Maybe you can recall reading of a sighting that was made of Natalie in Denia two days after she was last seen at Breeze?'

'I didn't realise it was the same bar,' Harris replied, slowly shaking his head. 'The article I read didn't mention its name.'

'The manager has since confessed that he lied to the police. He was told to come forward and make the statement by Darren Mitchell. Some might even say threatened. But Natalie Brooks cannot have been at the bar in Denia that night, Sr. Harris. For we now know she was already dead.'

Harris, looking suitably stunned at the revelation, took a moment to gather his thought. 'Could Donnie have somehow been involved?'

'No, señor,' Chavarría said. 'We have also been able to confirm that Sr. Lane had no involvement in the young woman's death.'

Chavarría saw the flicker in Harris's eye. If Harris was the businessman the Inspector Jefe thought him to be, he would be mentally shuffling his cards in his head, examining all the possible permutations and working out how best to play his hand.

'Well, I just wish I could be more helpful to you, Inspector Jefe,' said Harris, shaking his head in dismay. 'It's awful news about the girl, it really is. I'm just at a loss to understand what Darren's got to do with any of this.'

'As for the fraud case, Sr. Harris, I now know that

you were lying to me when you said you had no knowledge of the property.'

'I didn't lie to you, Inspector Jefe, and I resent the suggestion I did.'

'The owner of the finca tells us you visited him several months ago and made him a generous offer?'

Harris sighed in frustration. 'Look, I visit maybe fifteen or twenty different properties each and every week. I'm sorry if my memory isn't that good but, I can assure you, I didn't intentionally lie to you.'

'But a finca in the hills overlooking the town? There aren't many of those available. It's something that would stick in the mind, would it not?'

'Apparently not.'

Chavarría looked back down at his paperwork and began to read through it. He wouldn't be the next to speak, he knew, even if he reached the final page and had to start all over again. As it turned out, he didn't have to wait long.

'How was the girl killed?' asked Harris.

'Strangled,' Chavarría replied immediately, looking back up. 'Charges are to be brought against her murderer shortly. We have a full confession.'

Chavarría chose, on this occasion, to maintain eye contact with Peter Harris. Interview psychology. It wasn't an aggressive interrogation, so he saw no reason to challenge him with penetrating, non-blinking eyes. The Inspector Jefe simply held his natural gaze and waited for a response. He knew he didn't need to say anything else. He knew a successful interview wasn't always about what you said and when you said it.

Sometimes it was what you didn't say and when you didn't say it.

'Do you know where Darren is, Inspector Jefe?' asked Harris, the slight reduction in the volume and pace of his speech telling Chavarría that he already knew the answer.

'Yes, Sr. Harris. I know why he wasn't answering his phone. He is in the cells here at the comisaría.'

Harris looked down at the table and, after several seconds, buried his face in his hands. His shoulders began to gently quiver. Oh, he is good, Chavarría thought. He is very good. The detective waited patiently for Harris to compose himself and look back up at him.

'I'll try and be as helpful as I can to you. I mean, Darren is a good friend of mine but I know he's no angel. I don't want to talk out of turn, of course, and it may have nothing to do with anything.'

'Any information you can give us, Sr. Harris, would be much appreciated.'

'I really had very little to do with Donnie Lane, you know. I left it to Darren to deal with him. Thick as thieves, the pair of them were. Friends from years back.'

Chavarría smiled inside. The division had been made.

The Inspector Jefe walked along the corridor and entered the CCTV room, where Valle and Banda were waiting for him. He had given them the responsibility of arresting and questioning Darren Mitchell.

Chavarría glanced at the large monitor on the desk, which gave a view of the small interview room next door. Mitchell was sitting upright at the table, his arms folded in front of him.

'Is he talking?'

'Not yet, Jefe. And he's refused a lawyer.'

'Does he know Harris is here?'

'Yes, I mentioned he was giving us an interview,' Valle said. 'Voluntarily, of course. He doesn't seem too worried.'

Darren Mitchell would stay loyal to Peter Harris, that was for sure. But there was never any real loyalty among criminals, not when it came down to it. Not when their own neck was on the line. Self-preservation was always the order of the day. If Mitchell was going down, he would take Harris with him. Chavarría would make sure of that. At the end of the day, it didn't matter who delivered the blows that killed Donnie Lane. It Mitchell struck him down, it was only because Harris told him too. They were both culpable.

Chavarría asked for refreshments to be taken into both men. It would give them time to think and, importantly, to wonder what the other was saying. It didn't matter how many times they had gone over their story together in the comfort and security of their own environment. Sitting in a police interview room was a different story. It would take someone with ice in their veins not to feel at least a little pressure.

A less experienced police detective would have targeted Darren Mitchell as the one to crack first.

Indeed, that had been Banda's original idea when he and Valle had brought the man in for questioning.

'Let's go in hard, Jefe,' he said. 'We can make him talk.'

Chavarría shook his head. He knew different. Mitchell had been a felon all his adult life, and probably long before that, and was clearly used to police stations and interviews. He wouldn't be intimidated. He would remain silent. No, the Inspector Jefe knew it would be Peter Harris that would be the first to talk. The businessman would be calm and composed under questioning, Chavarría realised that, but he was a man used to getting others to do his dirty work for him. A man who wouldn't think twice of tossing someone else to the wolves to save his own skin. It was what kept Harris safe, protected him, but it would also turn out to be his weakness.

After leaving the men for half an hour, Chavarría decided it was time to begin again. Leaving Valle and Banda to talk to Darren Mitchell, he returned to speak with Peter Harris. With the interview now being recorded by an Agente with excellent English skills, and Harris offered the opportunity for legal support, which was declined, they resumed.

'When I spoke to you the first time, Sr. Harris, you told me of your movements on the day Donnie Lane was killed. It is important for us to establish what Darren Mitchell was doing on that day. Are you able to help us in any way with this?'

Harris took a long breath. 'First of all, Inspector

Jefe, let me just say that I can't believe Darren was involved in Donnie's death. They were good mates, and I'm going to be there for him for as long as he needs me.'

Touching, Chavarría thought. Harris was going to distance himself from Mitchell while, at the same time, appearing to be supportive. Ensuring the Agente was taking down the interview word-for-word, he wanted nothing to be lost in translation, the Inspector Jefe smiled at Harris to continue.

Less than thirty minutes later, Chavarría watched from the CCTV room as Official Valle delivered the killer blow to Darren Mitchell.

'You have no alibi for the time when Sr. Lane was killed and buried at the finca. Peter Harris says you left the house at around ten in the morning and he didn't see you again until mid-afternoon when you went out on his boat together. Can you account for your whereabouts and actions during that time, Sr. Mitchell?'

Even on camera, Chavarría noticed Darren Mitchell twitch. It didn't take him long to realise that Harris was offering him up on a plate to the police. Like Max Okeke, he would soon appreciate that he had to start looking after number one.

'I want a lawyer now.'

'Harris has contacted his legal representatives on your behalf. They'll be here soon.'

'No,' Mitchell said, shaking his head. 'I want another one.'

'That will be arranged, Sr. Mitchell. And are you

willing to start talking to us?'

'Oh, yeah,' the man replied, the hurt of the betrayal painfully etched onto his face. 'If I get what I want, I'll start talking alright.'

Valle halted the interview to allow for a duty lawyer to be called and, turning to the door, struck the briefest of glances at the CCTV camera high in the corner of the small room. Chavarría couldn't tell whether she had winked or not, but he laughed all the same.

'Ah, at last!'

'Sorry once again for the delay, Sr. Harris.'

'I can go now, yeah?'

'No, I'm afraid that will not be possible.'

'Why the bloody hell not?' Harris fumed. 'I've told you all I know. I came here of my own free choice, you know. You can't just keep me here all day! What's to stop me just walking out?'

'I've just been informed by my colleagues of a statement made by Darren Mitchell,' replied Chavarría. 'He has proven very co-operative.'

He allowed a moment or two for Harris to reflect on the disclosure. Despite the air conditioning that kept the room deliciously cool, Chavarría could see the tiny beads of sweat beginning to form on the businessman's forehead.

'You will be facing charges for fraud and the murder of Donnie Lane, Sr. Harris,' Chavarría announced, 'so the answer is no. You will not be leaving us any time soon. You are under arrest.'

At that point, as the Inspector Jefe fully expected, Harris refused to answer any more questions and claimed he would make no further statement until he had consulted with his lawyers. Leaving Valle and Banda to get a full statement from Darren Mitchell, Chavarría returned to the offices of *homicidios y desaparecidos*. There was still plenty of work to do on the investigation if any charges against the two men were going to hold water in a court of law.

It was another two hours before Valle and Banda returned, and Chavarría called for a meeting of the entire team. It was time for the individual pieces of the puzzle to be finally put together.

'It seems that Donnie Lane was convinced that Harris was responsible for Natalie's disappearance,' Official Valle began, 'and, though he never accused him directly, not before their final meeting anyway, it would certainly have put a wedge of distrust between the two men.'

'What reason did he think Harris could have had?' asked Chavarría.

'Well, it seems Donnie Lane and Natalie Brooks had struck a little deal of their own regarding the finca,' Valle explained. 'Natalie had met a guy in a club and discovered he was interested in buying a property in the area. Apparently, he'd come into an inheritance. She and Donnie saw a way of earning themselves a tidy sum without Peter Harris being any the wiser.'

'Harris would have known nothing about it until the whole finca scam was uncovered,' Banda said. 'By then, Lane and Natalie would have moved on with their share of the money, as well as the extra they'd made on the side.'

'The fraud was well conceived and operated, and it would have worked. There was nothing to connect Harris to it in any way.'

'But then Natalie disappeared,' said Chavarría.

'Donnie Lane was convinced Harris had somehow discovered their secret deal and had got rid of her to teach him a lesson,' replied Banda. 'When Lane was released from the comisaría, he called Harris and arranged a meeting with him. Things were starting to heat up and he wanted out of Cieloventura as soon as possible.'

'Lane would've felt very vulnerable,' Chavarría nodded. 'He was the face of the finca fraud and could be identified by any of those they'd conned. With Natalie's disappearance all over the news, it was always a possibility than someone would come forward who had recognised her as the young woman they had dealt with from Anglo-España Dream Properties. He didn't want to stay in the town any longer than was absolutely necessary.'

'So the three of them — Harris, Lane and Mitchell — met up. It was Harris who suggested the venue, a town house recently acquired by Synergist in the north district. It was empty and out of the way. Donnie Lane demanded his share of the money. He wanted out that very day and wasn't prepared to take no for an answer. But Harris knew the money was still being moved around and it wasn't yet ready. He told Donnie Lane to hold firm for a few more days but Lane wasn't having any of it. He felt Harris was going to cut him out of the deal completely. That's when he finally accused Harris to his face of murdering Natalie.'

'It seems he was quite distraught,' Valle commented. 'Perhaps he had feelings for her after all. I know he always denied they were lovers, but there was clearly something between them.'

'Despite Lane's accusations, Harris knew he didn't have anything to do with Natalie's disappearance,' Banda continued. 'It was then that Lane, probably when challenged by Harris to give a reason why he would have done anything to her, let slip about the deal he and Natalie had struck on the side. He assumed Harris had known about it all along, but it really was news to Harris.'

'The conman discovered he had himself been conned,' chuckled Chavarría.

'The two had a furious row. Lane accused Harris of killing Natalie, and Harris accused Lane of stabbing him in the back. Lane eventually had enough and tried to leave. He threatened to go to the police unless he got his money by the end of the day. He had barely got as far as the door when Mitchell attacked him.'

'What did he use as a weapon?'

'A poker from the fireplace.'

Chavarría winced. The pathologist's report had told of three separate blows to the back of the head. Donnie Lane didn't stand a chance of leaving the house alive.

'So now they had a body to dispose of,' said Valle. 'They put Lane into the trunk of his own car – the house has its own driveway that cannot be seen from any of the other buildings in the street – and Mitchell took him to the finca. Harris, meanwhile, drove back to his villa and spent an hour on the phone with his accountant in London. They chose the finca as it was the only place they knew of that was private and not overlooked, and it may have been some time, at least a couple of weeks, before the body was discovered.'

'And so that was what the cadaver dog detected in Lane's car,' Banda stated. 'It wasn't Natalie after all, but Donnie Lane himself.'

Inspector Jefe Chavarría had contacted the accountant in the UK, who had acknowledged the time and duration of his call with Peter Harris. He had also mentioned how much of what they discussed would have come up anyway at a face-to-face meeting the partners of Synergist Holdings were scheduled to have with their team of accountants the following month.

'The only point of the call was to provide Harris with an alibi,' Chavarría stated, 'in case anyone saw Lane's car driving to or from the finca and he was asked to account for his whereabouts at that time. Darren Mitchell's alibi was Peter Harris himself. No doubt he would claim that Mitchell was with him the whole time.'

'I wonder whether the thought ever crossed their minds of getting rid of Lane at sea, as Ross Webster had done with Natalie?' asked Valle.

'Maybe it did. But getting a big man like Lane aboard the boat wouldn't have as easy as it would've been with Natalie. He must have weighed, what, nearly twice as much? And, of course, Misty Blue was moored at A7. Right in full view of the marina building and quite a distance from the car park.'

Chavarría looked to Agente Narváez and asked him to update the meeting on the reports he'd received back from the banks. He informed them that some of the money had been traced and seized, but the trail had so far run into a series of dead-ends. According to a fraud investigator at the Banco de Valencia, it was a very clever and well-planned operation. As it stood, just under half of those who had been duped were likely to get their money back. For the others, it was looking likely that it would be lost forever. Only Peter Harris knew where the rest of the money had gone and he wasn't about to start co-operating.

'As to why Natalie visited Lane that night in Breeze, and why she was in such a bad mood when she left, it looks like we'll never know,' said Banda. 'Neither of them are in a position to talk.'

'We can speculate, of course,' the Inspector Jefe said. 'Perhaps Natalie wanted to do one more deal of their own at the finca, there was clearly big money to be made, but Lane knew they couldn't risk it. With their share of the money from the other deals, and the one they'd arranged on the side, the two of them already would've had a nice amount to start somewhere new.'

'When Natalie left Breeze, she started to walk back to the Holiday18 apartments and, as we know, was eventually offered a ride by Ross Webster,' said Valle. 'But, according to Max Okeke, Lane left the club as well. We always assumed he had gone after Natalie.'

'Maybe he did, but couldn't find her,' suggested Chavarría. 'It's one of those loose ends that we'll never be able to tie up. By the way, did Mitchell confess to burgling Natalie and Ross's apartment?'

'No, he denies that,' Valle replied. 'I think we may need to chalk that one to Lane. He wouldn't have been able to get hold of Natalie at any time on Friday or Saturday morning and he must have been worried, especially if they argued the last time they saw each other and she wandered off drunk.'

'They were in contact a lot according to Lane's phone records,' said Banda, who had completed the task of sorting through the calls made from Donnie Lane's second mobile phone. 'He would call her at least four or five times a day.'

'So he went to her apartment and, when there was no answer, forced the door.'

'It's possible he did it out of concern for her,' Chavarría conjectured, 'rather than anything to do with the finca scam. But when she wasn't there, he started to panic. He removed the incriminating evidence from her room that linked her to the scam and then quickly ransacked the place to make it look like a random burglary.'

'It's the most likely explanation,' Valle agreed. 'However, Darren Mitchell did admit to placing a knife in Tony Heather's bed to try and warn him off.'

After completing the interview with Ross Webster the previous afternoon, Valle had asked Tony about the final message he had sent in. Tony told her about the carving knife that had been taken from his kitchen and placed in his bed the previous Tuesday night.

'Mitchell and Harris already knew from Lane that Tony had been sniffing around Breeze and asking questions,' she continued. 'After they had killed Lane and buried him at the finca, they didn't want him sticking his nose in any further.'

'So when Tony met Peter Harris at the Piggott's villa, and then again that evening at the tapas bar, Harris already knew who he was?'

'Yes. He was just playing along with Tony's story that he was interested in buying a property from Synergist. If the meetings had continued, perhaps Harris would've tried to find out just how much he knew.'

Chavarría praised Banda and Valle for their work and, leaving them at the comisaría to begin the process of dotting the i's and crossing the t's, walked from Calle de Santa Ana to the courthouse in the town square. He was allowed straight in to Juez Sandoval's office and, after the briefest of formalities, summarised the day's developments.

'Harris was under the impression that Mitchell had been arrested for Natalie's murder, and that he had made a full confession,' the Inspector Jefe said. 'It forced him to re-evaluate everything he thought he knew about the man, and the story the two of them had arranged.'

'But you did not state that directly?' asked Sandoval.
'No.'
'So you made both Harris and Mitchell think the

other had started to talk first.' The examining magistrate nodded his head in approval. 'Harris believed Mitchell had killed Natalie, something that he'd clearly kept from him. The bond of trust between them was broken.'

'The main difference, of course, is that Mitchell has come clean concerning Lane's murder and the finca fraud,' said Chavarría, 'while Harris still maintains his innocence. But, with Mitchell's testimony and forensic evidence, we should be able to build a substantial case.'

'If there is forensic evidence,' noted Sandoval.

'There will be,' Chavarría replied. 'Mitchell returned to the house where Lane was killed and, in his own words, mopped up the blood and gave the tiled floor a polish. It may be clean to the naked eye but the forensics team will find traces.'

Sandoval nodded. 'And what is it that Darren Mitchell has asked for in return for giving evidence against Peter Harris?'

'He wants to serve his sentence in the UK. He is aware of the prisoner exchange programme.'

'It should be possible to arrange. If his testimony clears up a murder and a large-scale property fraud, I don't see anyone in the judiciary will have an objection.'

'A life sentence won't bother Darren Mitchell,' Chavarría commented. 'He's been in prison many times. It's a home away from home for him. But he was damned if he was going to let Harris get away with betraying him to the police.'

'And the records of the interviews were signed?'

'Yes, Harris signed his statement that gave Mitchell no alibi for the time Lane was taken to the finca and buried,' confirmed Chavarría. 'And Mitchell signed the record of his interview, in the presence of the duty lawyer, who also signed it, that detailed everything he told us.'

'Good,' said Sandoval. The written transcripts were the only record of the interviews, with audio or visual recording not permitted, and the fact both men had signed their respective records was an important step. A record of interview could still be presented in court without being signed by a suspect, but any reasons for declining could also be declared, and suspects would often claim they refused to do so as the written report was not an accurate reflection of what was said. As both interviews had been conducted in English, Chavarría knew how vital it for them to be recorded accurately by skilled scribes in that language to avoid any confusion.

'Thank you for all of your hard work on this case, Roman,' Sandoval said. 'Pass my appreciation to all the members of your team.'

Chavarría nodded and, seeing Juez Sandoval switch his attention back to the paperwork he'd been reading on his arrival, took that as his cue to leave. Walking back to Calle de Santa Ana, the detective reflected on the meeting. He wasn't used to such compliments from the magistrate but didn't consider them undeserved. There was still a lot of work to be done over the next couple of days. The clock was ticking for Ross Webster, Darren Mitchell and Peter Harris to be brought before the Juez de Instrucción, but he was confident in the evidence that his team had collected so far, including the confessions made by two of the three. When it was time to present their cases in court, they would be ready.

The Inspector Jefe returned to the comisaría and headed up to the office. In his absence, the large white board that had displayed the information on the ongoing investigation had been wiped clean. He had been looking forward to doing that himself. The past couple of weeks had been the most intense of Chavarría's career. Three murders. But, he reminded himself as he sat down at his desk, three arrests. And there would be no slacking to ensure there were three convictions. He wouldn't let any of the murdering bastards get away with it.

'Will the murder charge against Harris stick, do you think?' asked Valle, as if reading Chavarría's thoughts.

'He was there when it happened. Mitchell wasn't acting on his own volition,' the Inspector Jefe said. 'He was let loose on Donnie Lane like an attack dog. It'll stick all right. Even, if worse came to worse, and we just get him as an accessory, it'll still be a lengthy sentence.'

'And we'll get him on the fraud too,' Banda added.

'While you were at the courthouse, I was called back by one of the other partners at Synergist,' said Valle. 'They've already started to close ranks. They don't want any bad publicity concerning murders and property frauds to be linked to them. When I informed them of Harris's arrest, they said they would be taking legal steps to see if they can suspend his partnership in the company.'

Chavarría chuckled. He wondered whether the other partners were really as in the dark as to Harris's true nature as they had claimed when Valle had first spoke to them that lunchtime. Maybe Harris had been despatched to Spain for a reason?

'They're also going to prevent Synergist's lawyers from acting for him in this matter, which they claim is private and not related to the business, and are getting their accountants to go through all of the company's Spanish interests with a fine tooth-comb. If they discover anything that suggests criminal activity, including any irregularities at Breeze, they'll pass it on to us to use against Harris in court.'

Chavarría leaned back in his chair and gazed up at the fan. He was looking forward to a decent night's sleep at last. He couldn't remember the last one he'd had. Actually, come to think of it, he could. It was the night before the discovery of Donnie Lane's body at the finca. He'd slept like a log that night.

The Inspector Jefe was happy. Juez Sandoval had been satisfied and was one step closer to whatever promotion he had his eye on, or what city he felt was more befitting him. Although his relationship with Sandoval had improved over the course of the past couple of weeks, Chavarría knew he wouldn't feel too sad at seeing the back of him. There was nothing wrong with ambition. He didn't see himself staying in Cieloventura forever, it had to be said, but when advancement was built on the successes of others, it tended to make Chavarría feel a little cynical. No doubt Comisario Principal García would also be delighted with the results of the last two days, as would the Mayor's Office.

But there was something else that made Chavarría happy. In less than two days time, Terésa would be home. Isabel was already making plans for her return. She had been out shopping to buy all her favourite foods, and had even collected an array of wallpaper samples and taster paint pots in a multitude of colours to help decide how best to re-decorate her bedroom. It was the room of a small child, she had told Chavarría, with its cartoon character wallpaper and pink carpet, and they needed to recognise that Terésa was growing up. Chavarría agreed — anything for a quiet life for a while — but, to him, she was still, and would always remain, his little Terésa.

* * *

He had left orders with the door staff that no-one was allowed in to see him. One particularly persistent bloke had already been escorted from the premises and there were a couple of woman still hanging around who were no doubt intent on offering themselves to him. But he only had eyes for one girl. Even with the make-up and fancy outfit, she looked far too young to be in a club. He liked that. It meant she had a naughty streak. And he knew what he was going to do to her.

The occasional one resisted, of course, and needed a slap to force them to be more compliant. None of them ever complained afterwards. What would be the point? It's what they were really after, wasn't it? What else?

Ah, sweet Leanne Piggott. It turned out her idea of sex wasn't exactly what excited him. To snuggle up on the beach and gaze up at the moon together? He didn't have her down as a little romantic at heart. Surely the younger generation didn't go in for all that cobblers? But she was a feisty one! He remembered the look on her face when he pinned her down tightly in the sand and tried to force her legs apart with his knees. When he pulled her hair and whispered his darkest thoughts into her ear. It had turned him on even more. She pushed him off her and tried to run towards the lights in the distance but he soon caught up with her and dragged her back behind the rocky outcrop. He couldn't risk letting this one go. Fourteen! He hadn't bargained on that. He'd put her at sixteen at least. Sixteen was fun and, for a man of his age, bad enough. But fourteen! If she talked, it would finish him.

Killing was so easy. Streax recalled the first time he'd done it. His mother had sent him to the vet with their sickly cat and a £20 note. He only did it so he could keep the money for himself. He tied the cat in a carrier bag and threw it in the canal. He was more annoyed at losing the twenty quid on the slot machines. So much for Tubby Shaw's foolproof method of winning the jackpot. Still, it had been fun while it lasted.

Leanne had been like that. While he didn't exactly tie her in a carrier and toss her in the Mediterranean, it had been almost as simple. He had stripped her of her top and skirt, folding them neatly and placing them by her side. She had worn a bikini under her clothes, a lot of women he did that on a night out, he had noticed, so they could unbutton or take their tops off on the dance floor. Come the morning, it would just look like she was sun-bathing. For all he knew, she would be there all day, surrounded by holiday-makers having picnics and little brats playing beach ball over her. That tickled him. He wondered whether a dead person could get a sun-tan? He hadn't even felt like screwing her in the end. He'd found something he liked more than sex.

Securing extra dates in Ibiza hadn't been difficult. He was five grand down on the deal – the manager of *Platinum* wanted paying off if he was going to let him out of his contract – but he wasn't all that bothered. There was plenty of work out here and he could soon make up the difference. Streax looked at the small pile of notes and messages on the corner of the table. It contained the typical requests from young and talentless wannabes to be allowed to work a guest slot on one of his shows, and the list of hotel rooms and phone numbers that had been left for him by the usual council estate slags on their annual week in Ibiza. One even had a photo attached to it with a paper clip of some chubby bird posing topless on the beach, her massive tits flopping down either side of her chest like a couple of deflating balloons. Thirty if she's a day,

Streax thought, tossing it into the bin. Wasn't his cup of tea.

One of the messages was in its own little envelope. Quaint, Streax chuckled. He opened it and took out the business card inside. For a moment, time seemed to skip a beat. He'd seen a card like this before. The guy had given it to him on his boat when he came to talk to him about Leanne. Mind, he'd just chucked it in the sea as soon as his back was turned. Streax flipped the card over and, barely daring to breathe, saw the hand-written message on the reverse.

I'm watching you.

Daniel Ward was born and raised in Essex, UK. He has been interested in creative writing since childhood, and his previous works include the well-received Sherlock Holmes pastiche *Sherlock Holmes – The Way of All Flesh*. He works as a doctor in a large hospital in the south-east of England.

Readers comments are welcome at
danielwardauthor@outlook.com

Made in the USA
Charleston, SC
24 October 2013